EVELYN HOOD OMNIBUS

The Silken Thread
The Dancing Stone

EVELYN HOOD OMNIBUS

The Silken Thread
The Dancing Stone

EVELYN HOOD

A *Time Warner* Paperback

This omnibus edition first published in Great Britain by
Time Warner Paperbacks in 2002
Evelyn Hood Omnibus Copyright © Evelyn Hood 2002

Previously published separately:
The Silken Thread first published in Great Britain in 1986 by
William Kimber and Company Limited
Published by Warner Books in 1997
Reprinted in 1997, 1998
Copyright © Evelyn Hood 1986

The Dancing Stone first published in Great Britain in 1997 by
Little, Brown and Company
Published by Warner Books in 1998
Reprinted 2001
Copyright © Evelyn Hood 1997

The moral right of the author has been asserted.

A CIP catalogue record for this book is available from the British Library.

ISBN 0 7515 3295 9

Printed and bound in Great Britain by Clays Ltd, St Ives plc

Time Warner Paperbacks
An imprint of
Time Warner Books UK
Brettenham House
Lancaster Place
London WC2E 7EN

www.TimeWarnerBooks.co.uk

The Silken Thread

TO MY MOTHER
MILLIE WEBSTER STEEL

I had a dove and the sweet dove died.
And I have thought it died of grieving,
O, what could it grieve for? Its feet were tied,
With a silken thread of my own hand's weaving.

JOHN KEATS

PART ONE

Chapter One

FOR THE THIRD TIME SINCE they left Beith Meg's stomach began to rebel at the cart's lurching progress. She tried hard to fight down the queasiness, both hands squeezed tightly against her stomach beneath the shelter of her shawl. But finally she had to twitch at Duncan's sleeve until he moved his blue eyes from contemplation of the farmland to her white, apologetic face.

'Duncan, I'm feared I'm—'

'Not again!' her husband said impatiently. 'D'you want us to take two days to this journey?'

'I can't help it—' She pressed her hand over her mouth and made to jump from the moving vehicle in her haste to get out before she disgraced herself, and him, completely.

'You'd best stop.' Duncan tapped the driver on the shoulder and he, without a backward glance at his passengers, drew the horses to a halt and waited, back hunched. The animals immediately began to tear at the dry dusty grass fringing the road, twitching their ears and flicking their tails to ward off flies.

With Duncan's help Meg scrambled down from the cart and stumbled over the springy turf. She reached the shelter of a whin bush just in time and knelt on the grass, vomiting miserably and wishing she was back home in the farm kitchen with her family.

It had seemed such an adventure when they first planned it. Duncan, a weaver to trade, was young and ambitious, and in 1745 the flourishing Renfrewshire town of Paisley, some twenty miles away, was the ideal place for a young man willing to work.

Meg was the envy of her sisters. To be a married woman, with a handsome husky young husband like Duncan – she knew herself how fortunate she was. But now the first sweet shyness of marriage had passed and she had begun to realise that this dark confident man was hers, and she his, for the rest of her life. She was bound to follow him wherever he chose to lead. The thought, which had excited her as she danced with him at her wedding beneath the familiar smoke-grimed beams of home, now made her shiver despite the warm May sun above.

What if they didn't fare well? What if she hated Paisley yet had to go on living there, homesick and wretched?

She stood up and glanced at the cart waiting on the track a short distance away. Duncan had stepped down to stretch his legs. The driver, a man of few words, sat hunched on the cart, a sombre figure against the blue sky beyond.

Another spasm dragged her back to her knees. All at once she wanted her mother – though she had been glad enough to escape her sharp eyes a few hours earlier.

'If you have your wits about you you'll see that there are no babies until you're settled,' her mother had advised as she brushed Meg's hair on her wedding morning. 'You've chosen a wild man – see that he makes enough silver to put food for your belly and a roof over your head before you think further.'

Meg, breathless with loving anticipation, had promised easily enough. She never disobeyed her mother, who was not slow to show her displeasure with a clout on the ear that could send even a full-grown son or daughter flying across the room. But common-sense had no chance when she was safely wedded and bedded and Duncan's youthful passion was sweeping them both headlong on the course they had longed to take since they first set eyes on each other.

When the first signs of nausea and giddiness appeared within a few weeks of their wedding day Meg had done her utmost to hide them from the older woman, and had eagerly agreed to Duncan's proposal that they join the growing army of people lured by Paisley's expanding linen industry. She had succeeded in her deception, for her mother still had no inkling of her condition.

Meg spat to rid her mouth of a bitter after-taste, and walked back to the men.

'You took your time, lady,' Duncan greeted her impatiently. 'Early afternoon, I said we'd be there. D'you think we have a whole day to waste on one short journey?'

'I couldn't help it—' she said faintly, apologetically, as he handed her up to her seat and swung up beside her. His round, handsome face was marred by a scowl. Like his mother-in-law, Duncan felt that their first child should have had the sense to wait a little longer for its conception, and he was inclined to blame Meg for her haste.

The driver had lit his pipe during the wait. Meg's insides quivered as a whiff of strong-smelling tobacco drifted back to her, and panic swept over her. Duncan would never stand for another delay! She squirmed into a position that put her tiptilted nose out of the way of the smoke and sniffed at the grass-scented air with great determination.

Duncan took the slight move away from him as a sign that his wife was annoyed. Compassion flooded his heart as he looked at the soft curve of her cheek and the corner of her kissable mouth. He loved her in his own irresponsible way, and his spirits rose with every turn of the wheels that carried them to their new life. An orphan, raised by an elderly aunt who cared little about anything but her Bible, he had found Meg's large, noisy family oppressive. He wanted to be independent, to look after his wife and make his own decisions. If he couldn't make his way in Paisley – well, he'd go elsewhere. But wherever he went he wanted Meg by his side.

It was almost two o'clock when the driver raised his whip and pointed.

'There's where you're bound.'

They craned their necks to see. Paisley was tucked snugly below the Gleniffer Braes – the Muckle Riggs as they were known locally. The main features to be seen from a distance were the High Church steeple and the ruins of the Abbey, once a great monastic house but now in a state of disrepair.

Smoke from the chimneys smudged the green of the surrounding hills. The River Cart was a shiny ribbon curling through the town, passing beneath the Abbey walls.

Duncan put his arm about Meg.

'There's where we'll find our fortune!'

'You think so?' she asked doubtfully.

'I know so! Paisley's growing, and we'll grow with it. We'll have our own place before long, and our own looms – and sons to carry the trade on after me.' His voice was strong, his optimism catching. 'You'll see, Meg – you'll see!'

The fields and hedges blossomed with great stretches of linen as the cart neared the town. These were the bleachfields, where newly-woven linen was brought to whiten. Then the first cottages, some thatched and some with slate roofs, appeared on either side of the low rutted road.

Duncan fingered his plain jacket as he looked

at the young men strolling along the pathways of raised earth, stylishly clad in blue and green coats, nankeen britches and flowered waistcoats. Meg's eyes widened as she stared at the women's colourful dresses. Obviously, Paisley was the very place for an ambitious young couple like themselves.

The sound of hammering came to them as they passed through the town's fringes, where new houses were being built. Paisley was growing fast and there was plenty of work for builders – hard work, if they were to keep up with the demand from the constant stream of incomers.

At last the cart jolted into the rutted main street, busy with carts and carriages. Housewives hurried along the footpaths or stood gossiping in tight groups. A crowd of young men laughed and joked outside a howff – and judging by the state of one of them, kept on his feet by his companions, they had been inside sampling the landlord's wares. Bewhiskered businessmen paced solemnly, brushing barefoot children aside like flies, too involved in their own fat-bellied importance to notice their surroundings. Dogs, cats and pigs were amiable company for each other as they nosed among the refuse at the sides of the road.

After the pure country air they had just driven through the travellers found the smell of rotting rubbish offensive, but they knew that they would quickly get used to it. It wasn't any worse than the dungheap that sat just outside the farm door in Beith.

'Here 'tis,' the driver announced. With a final squeeze of Meg's hand Duncan jumped briskly down and rapped at the door of the three-storey building. While he waited for an answer he handed his wife down from the cart and she looked timidly at the buildings crowding in on the narrow street. Had she been alone she would have turned round there and then and ordered the driver to take her home again, but being a married woman she could only clutch the bag that held her worldly possessions, and swallow hard.

The door burst open suddenly and a small tornado whirled out of it, almost knocking Meg over with the force of its passing. With a squeak of alarm she clutched at the cart for support while the tornado, which turned out to be a red-headed infant no higher than her knees, recovered its balance and headed in determined fashion down the street, skipping nimbly over holes and hillocks.

'Stop that wean!' a voice shrieked from inside the house, and a plump young woman, her own head topped with glowing red hair, came hurrying along the passageway.

'Get a hold of him, quick!' she shrilled, and Duncan, who had been standing open-mouthed, shot off down the street after the child.

'The wee imp!' The woman leaned on the door frame to catch her breath. 'The times I've told these men to make sure the door's not left on the latch! Do they think I've nothing to do with my time but chase after him?'

9

Then Duncan was back, a screaming kicking bundle of fury held at arm's length before him.

'You rascal, you!' the woman scolded, taking the child and administering an automatic smack on his plump legs. Then she kissed his rosy cheek.

The child stopped screaming at once and settled himself comfortably astride her hip. He rammed a thumb into his mouth and looked at the visitors with round blue eyes. His face was dirty and his head a mass of tangled curls, but even so it was easy to see how beautiful he was.

'You'll be the Montgomerys? I'm Mistress Todd.' The woman transferred her attention to the couple standing before her. 'Come away in – you must be fair worn out after your journey.'

'So am I – am I to stand here all day waiting to get my cart unloaded? I've work to do,' the driver said sourly from behind them.

Mistress Todd's wide green eyes flashed scathingly. 'Poor man, are your arms wasted away, that you can't unload a wee cart by yourself? Well, well, I suppose Mister Montgomery'll help you while we go into the house.' And leaving him at a loss for words she led Meg into the passageway.

'We live above the weaving shop – here it is—' She threw open a door to disclose a large sunlit room noisy with the clack of looms and the hum of deep voices. Peering over her shoulder Meg could see men working at two of the four looms, swaying rhythmically as they threw the shuttles from side to side.

'I'll not tell you again – the next one to leave the door on the latch gets his ears warmed!' Mistress Todd bawled. 'The wean's wild enough without any help from you!'

Then she slammed the door shut on the shouted replies and went on upstairs, remarking over her shoulder, 'They're not a bad lot, but they need an awful strong hand to keep them in order.'

And a strong hand was what Mistress Todd had, Meg thought as she followed her red-haired guide up the narrow dark stairway and into a large spotless kitchen, fragrant with the smell of home-made bread.

'Sit yourself down and I'll make some tea.' Mistress Todd deposited the baby on a rag rug and handed him a wooden spoon. He immediately began to bang it on the floor.

'That's right, my mannie, you give these lazy men below a good fast rhythm to work to. This is our Jamie – a wild ragtail of a boy if ever there was one. He's for a soldier for sure, unless he finds himself beneath a horse's hooves first,' his mother said cheerfully. 'You've got it all unloaded, then?' she added as Duncan came in.

'There wasn't much to unload.'

Her eyes twinkled. 'Best to start married life light. Not that I did, for Peter's first wife died and I came to a ready-made home when I wed him. He had two grown lads too – now he's on his second family.' She nudged the baby with her toe. 'And Peter says this one's more bother than

11

Matt and Colin put together. You'll have some ale, Mister Montgomery?'

'I wouldn't mind,' he said gratefully, and drained half the tankard in one thirsty swallow when she handed it to him.

The tea was being poured out when Peter Todd himself arrived.

'So you're here already? I'd have been home to greet you, but I had some linen to deliver—'

'—and you got talking.' His wife finished the sentence for him, nodding at Meg. 'They say women enjoy a gossip, but you'll find that in Paisley the men know how to do their share of tongue-wagging.'

Peter Todd let the remark run off his broad shoulders as he studied the couple before him. He was a big handsome man with a head of thick white hair and shrewd eyes of the same vivid blue as his son's.

'So – this my new man, is it? Well, we'll get on together if you're prepared to work. We all work hard in this house.'

'You'll find nobody more willing than Duncan,' Meg said sharply. 'Mister Brodie was fair vexed to lose him.' Then she coloured as Duncan shushed her.

Peter nodded calmly. 'I know that, lass, for Mister Brodie himself recommended your man to me. I see a spinning wheel downstairs – is it yours?'

Now it was Duncan's turn to boast. 'Meg's as good a spinster as anyone.'

'I'll be glad of her help, then, for this wee skelf keeps me away from my wheel often now that he's found his feet.' Kirsty disentangled Jamie's groping hands from her hair and handed the child to her husband. The little boy buried his face in his father's shoulder and Meg watched, amazed. Her father would never have allowed anyone, even his wife, to see him making a fuss of a child.

'This one's going to be a weaver,' Peter boasted. 'Matt chose the army and Colin's a grocer now. He had to give up weaving because the fluff bothered his chest. Mebbe I'll be spared long enough to teach Jamie how to work the loom.'

'Of course you'll be spared!' his wife hectored. 'Show Mister Montgomery the weaving shop while we see to the meal. And you can tell these men down there to stop leaving the street door on the latch!' she shouted after him as he led Duncan downstairs.

As she and Meg got the meal ready Kirsty chattered on without waiting for a response. She talked glowingly about Paisley, as proud of the place, Meg thought, as if she had built it with her own capable hands.

'Bragging about the town again, Kirsty?' her husband asked dryly when he and Duncan arrived back upstairs.

'That one comes from Dumbarton—' She jerked her head in his direction, '—and nothing I say'll convince him that this side of the Clyde's better than the other bank.'

'What's wrong with Dumbarton?' Peter wanted to know.

'Nothing – though you were pleased enough to wed a Paisley woman. I'm Paisley born and bred myself,' she confided to her guests.

'I think they realised that,' said her husband, poker-faced.

After supper Jamie was put to bed in the attic room he shared with his parents and the adults were free to sit round the fire, Kirsty's fingers flying nimbly over a pile of mending. Meg offered to help and soon she too was working busily, letting the men's talk flow over her bent head.

Finally, Peter knocked his pipe out against the chimney-head and stretched his arms.

'We rise early and sleep early. And before we go to bed we have a verse or two from the Holy Book.'

His wife put away her mending and rose to fetch the big family Bible from the corner cupboard. Peter took it from her and placed it carefully on the table.

'D'you want to read tonight's passage, lad?'

Duncan's face, flushed by the fire, deepened in colour. He glanced at Meg for encouragement, then burst out, 'To tell the truth, I'm not much of a hand at reading.'

'You can't read?'

'A wee bit – I learned at the school. But I never took to it. Meg sees to that side of things.'

'Learning's a fine thing,' Peter Todd said mildly.

14

'And there's a lot a man can find in books whether he's a scholar or a weaver.' Then he opened the huge tome and began to read in a slow, clear voice. Kirsty folded her hands in her lap and nodded agreement with the words now and then.

The scene reminded Meg so vividly of the final ritual of the day at the farm that she was homesick and comforted at the same time.

When the book was closed and put away again Peter and Kirsty stood up.

'Good night to you,' he said with grave courtesy. 'We rise at five o'clock.' Then the Todds departed up the winding staircase that led to the attic.

In their own bedroom, a tiny apartment that had little space for anything but the bed, Meg snuggled up to Duncan's warm body, but resisted his attempts to make love to her.

'Sssshhh! They'll hear!'

'But we're wed! I'll be quiet as a mouse – come on, lass!'

But she couldn't bring herself to make so free of their new employer's bed on such short acquaintance, and Duncan was finally forced to turn over, grumbling to himself.

Meg lay wide-eyed. The room was very dark, and all at once she was grateful for Duncan's presence, protecting her from the ghosts and bogles of the night. She lifted herself onto one elbow.

'Duncan?' she whispered. 'Duncan – I'll learn you to read, then when we have our own house you can read from the Book every night like Mister Todd. It's easy.'

He heaved himself over onto his back and she felt his fingers tangle themselves in her soft loose hair.

'My wee Meg—' his voice was already thick with drowsiness. 'You're a good lass, Meg. You'll see – we'll have a fine home, and our own looms. I'll look after you, Meg.'

Wrapped in his arms she slept at last, certain of the fine future they had mapped out for themselves.

Chapter Two

M EG AND DUNCAN WERE QUICKLY caught up in the rhythm of Paisley life. There were two other weavers in Peter Todd's shop besides himself and Duncan – one was an irrepressible young man who saw humour in everything, the other a studious man who kept a pile of books by his loom and loved to hold forth on any subject under the sun. The men's tongues worked as swiftly as their looms.

Each morning Meg and Kirsty saw to the housework, baked, visited the market, and looked after red-headed Jamie, a day's work in itself. Any spare time they had was spent spinning coarse thread for the looms. Their wheels were placed close to a trapdoor that allowed communication between the kitchen and the weaving shop below. When the trap was open the women could join in the conversation, and the pirns or reels of spun thread could be passed down to the weavers as they were needed.

When Jamie tired himself out with his continual toddling around and his occasional forays into the street when the door was left open he was lifted into the big wooden cradle, then Kirsty slipped her foot into the rope looped to one rocker, and rocked him as she tended her wheel.

As well as domestic duties, Kirsty and Meg, as the women of the household, were responsible for the upkeep of the long garden at the back of the house. It was stocked with sweet-scented flowers for the benefit of the bees in the two skeps, and there were plenty of bushes where the washing could be spread out to dry.

Meg was happy with the Todds, but she longed for a home of her own, where she and Duncan and their coming child could be a real family. Kirsty was sympathetic.

'I mind when Jamie was on the way – Colin was still living here and I was fair fretting for him to find a place of his own, the soul. Not that I ever let on to him or to his father.' She deftly guided thread onto the spinning wheel as she spoke. 'Then he and Lizzie wed and moved into the rooms behind the wee grocer's shop. I sometimes think he'd have been better staying here with us.'

Then she bit her lip and added swiftly, 'Not that it's any of my business. He chose Lizzie, and if he's content that's all that matters.'

Colin Todd, the grocer, had his father's good looks, but was of slighter build and had none of the older man's vitality. Soft fair hair helped to give him a fragile air, but when he smiled, which happened rarely, his thin face lit up and Meg was charmed.

When she first met his wife Lizzie she found it hard to understand why Kirsty, one of the most generous women she had ever known, disliked the girl. Colin's wife was mouse-like, quiet-voiced, her brown hair tucked beneath a clean white lace cap, her eyes lowered.

It wasn't until Peter and Kirsty held a gathering for their friends that Meg saw the other side of Lizzie's nature; then she knew why Kirsty had her doubts about Colin's choice of a wife.

When she worked in the shop Lizzie wore a grey dress, high in the neck and long-sleeved. But for the social evening she appeared in a white cambric dress sprigged with yellow, red and blue flowers. It was cut low enough to reveal the swell of surprisingly full breasts, and her slim arms were bare. Long brown hair, stylishly curled, fell about her shoulders, and for the first time Meg noticed, and envied, Lizzie's tiny waist. The head that was usually lowered was now held proudly on a long slender neck and her eyes, smoky grey with an Eastern slant to them, were raised boldly to Duncan's handsome face when they met.

'You don't take snuff, Mister Montgomery?' Even Lizzie's voice was different now, self-possessed and attractively husky.

Duncan looked puzzled. 'I don't.'

'That's why we haven't met before. The women and bairns are in and out of the shop for provisions every day, but the men only come in if they want snuff.'

'Mebbe I should think of taking the habit up,' he said with clumsy gallantry and Meg, hovering by his side, felt a flicker of unease run through her.

'You'll do nothing of the kind, Duncan Montgomery – we've enough to do with our money as it is!'

The smoky eyes left Duncan's face and flowed over Meg. It was as though Lizzie was seeing her for the first time, and assessing her.

'I hear you're anxious to find a place of your own before your bairn comes.' Her gaze moved to rest, briefly, on Colin, who hovered by her side. Somehow she managed to make him look insignificant and frail in his brown coat and plain vest. 'We have no family – yet. All Colin's energy goes into caring for his shop.'

There was calculated malice in the remark. Colin flushed and Duncan looked puzzled. Then, mercifully, Kirsty interrupted them and the moment was gone.

As the evening wore on the children were carried to the attic bedroom to sleep, packed tightly together on the Todds' bed, until their parents were ready to go home. The men went downstairs to talk around the fire in the loom shop and the women stayed in the kitchen, most of them with knitting or sewing in their hands.

Meg noticed that Lizzie reverted back to her mouse-like nature once the men had gone. She retired to a seat in a shadowy corner, her face hidden by a curtain of hair, her fingers toying with the looped earrings in her small lobes.

She brightened noticeably when the menfolk came stamping back upstairs for the musical part of the evening. She stood in the centre of the room, eyes bright and cheeks glowing, and sang in a sweet, strong soprano. Meg turned to look for Duncan and caught him watching Lizzie with a frown tucked between his brows, as though he was trying to decide what to make of her.

Suddenly uneasy, Meg made a small movement towards him, and was relieved when he turned his head and slowly smiled at her as though wakening from a dream.

'Are you content with me, Duncan?' she asked later when they were in bed together.

His hands explored her body tenderly. 'What a thing to ask, and us wed these four months past. Of course I'm content with you!'

'I wish I could sing like Lizzie Todd – and look like her.' She waited for his reaction, holding her breath, but he only laughed.

'I'd not have you any other way – my bonny Meg,' he murmured into the valley between her breasts, and Meg was happy.

Two days later Lizzie Todd, busy at the shop counter, looked up from a list of figures as the door opened. She took in the newcomer at a glance then went on totalling prices. Neat as a sparrow in her grey gown and white cap, she completed the list, took money from wee Tommy Burns's hot fist, handed change over, and bundled parcels into his arms.

'Mind that money,' she said automatically as he went out. Then she smoothed her skirt and tilted her chin to survey the customer who stood, hands planted on the counter, awaiting her attention.

A faint smile curved the corners of her mouth and gave added lustre to her smoky eyes. 'And what can I do for you, sir?'

'I was thinking—' said Duncan Montgomery '—that I might buy myself some snuff.'

Matt Todd, Peter's eldest son, came home on leave from the army soon after the Montgomerys arrived in Paisley.

Tall and broad and handsome, he was very like his father, with Peter's boundless energy and extrovert nature. Even Meg, who knew that Duncan was the handsomest man in the town, felt a flutter of excitement when she first set eyes on Matt in the tartan plaid and blue feathered bonnet of the Fusiliers.

His coming was the signal for one gathering after another. Everyone wanted to hear of his adventures, and Matt was more than ready to entertain them. His tales of the life a soldier led had the men roaring with delight and the women blushing. When a story became too embarrassing Kirsty would reach up to slap his curly head and order, 'That's quite enough of that – you'll not be bringing any more of those lies into my house, thank you!'

'Lies? Lies?' Matt's blue eyes opened wide and as often as not he swept Kirsty off her feet as though she was a child. 'Would one of His Majesty's brave soldiers tell his little old mother lies?'

Then Kirsty, struggling in vain, would shrill, 'I am not your little old mother – I'm only six months older than you. And you're still young enough to get a slap on the ear if you don't put me down this instant!'

It was then that Meg was most aware of Colin, sitting quietly in a corner, smiling at the fun, but outside it. Lizzie, too, was quiet when Matt was around, which surprised Meg more than a little.

It was Matt's idea that he and Colin should ride in the annual Silver Bells horse race, due to take place in a few days' time.

'Man, it's a grand event!' he enthused one night when the Todds and Montgomerys were together in the kitchen above the weaving shop. 'Everyone comes to the Silver Bells race – in the old days the three of us used to ride in it.' His eyes blazed blue fire. 'We could all enter for it again—'

'Not your father,' Kirsty said at once. 'He's not as young as he once was.'

'Aye, my day's past for racing,' Peter agreed reluctantly. 'It's a sport for younger men.'

To Meg's relief Duncan declined to take part. He was no horse rider, but she was well aware that although he was now a married man, soon to be a father, there was still a reckless, restless side to his nature and for a moment she had been afraid that he would take up Matt's suggestion.

'Then it's you and me, Colin – just like the old days, eh?'

'No!'

They had almost forgotten Lizzie was there, sitting silently beside Colin. Her chin was up and she was glaring at Matt.

'Risk your own neck if you want to – but leave Colin alone!' she said with startlingly open antagonism.

His face was suddenly stiff. 'I didn't realise you cared so much for your man's safety.'

Lizzie shot him a look of pure venom. 'Colin's got responsibilities. He's not a thoughtless fool!'

'Then he can speak for himself,' Matt said coldly, and turned away from her. 'What d'you say, Colin?'

Meg saw Lizzie's hands clench on her lap. Colin's eyes flicked over his wife's face, then lifted to Matt.

'I'll ride with you,' he said, and Lizzie's hiss of rage was almost drowned by Matt's triumphant, 'Good for you, man – we'll bring the Bells home!'

The town's looms clattered late into the night before the Silver Bells race, so that the weavers could take the next day off. Long after she was in bed Meg could hear the faint thump of the shuttles racing to and fro and she pictured the men, red-eyed and weary, working in the lamplight. When Duncan finally came upstairs he was asleep as soon as he crawled in beside her warm body.

Matt had hired two horses from a local farmer, and had invested enough money in wagers to ensure that if either he or Colin were among the first riders home he would not be out of pocket. Kirsty and Meg scrubbed the spotless house in readiness for the gathering to be held there after the race.

'I hope you've plenty in for our guests,' Peter said anxiously and his wife tossed her red head.

'When have you ever known this house to lack refreshments? Well I know the celebrations you'll have whether your own lads win the Bells or not, and there'll be plenty for everyone, never you worry.'

As she walked with Duncan and the Todds to Love Street, where the race was to begin and end, Meg felt the festival atmosphere stirring her blood. Children ran through the thick crowds, squealing like piglets in their excitement, men congregated in groups to place wagers on the outcome, women wore their best and brightest clothes.

Street vendors had set up stalls at the Cross, strangers flocked into the town from miles around – it was as if the whole of Scotland had congregated in that one small town for the Silver Bells horse race. The Council members massed importantly at the starting point, bearing with them the wooden casket which held the silver bells that gave the race its name.

Duncan held Meg's arm as they picked their way carefully down the street, skirting refuse heaps. Peter was well known and had no difficulty in finding a good spot for his party, where they could see the start and finish of the race.

Many Fusiliers were home on leave like Matt, and their uniforms added an extra splash of colour to the scene. The local gentry were in attendance, gazing loftily over the heads of the crowd from their fine carriages.

Kirsty nudged Meg's arm. 'There's the Laird of Dundonald,' she murmured, indicating a richly dressed young man. 'A wild, wild laddie – they say there's nothing to be done with him at all.'

'Too fond of fighting and womanising,' Peter added bluntly. 'And he's taking a lot of Paisley's lads on the same track as himself.'

Colin and Matt were already at the starting post. Their father eyed their mounts critically.

'Fine animals. You've still got a good eye for a horse, Matt.'

The soldier grinned. 'There'll be no stopping us.' He leaned from the saddle to thump his brother on the shoulder. 'A pound says I'll cross the finishing line afore you.'

Colin's thin face was flushed and handsome, the fragile air gone. Even his voice was stronger, more confident, as he said, 'You'll lose your money!'

'Not me!'

'Pride goes before a fall,' Kirsty reminded Matt, hoisting Jamie more securely on her hip. 'Just you do your best, my bonny soldier, and don't be so sure you're always going to be a winner!'

Colin laughed and nodded agreement, then his eyes moved beyond Meg's shoulder, and she saw a cloud come over his face. She turned and saw that Lizzie had arrived, demure in white linen bonnet and russet gown. The girl's lips were set in a thin line and splashes of colour in her cheeks matched her short scarlet cloak. She looked at her husband unsmilingly, then turned away to scan the crowd. Colin's shoulders slumped for a moment, then he straightened in the saddle, his mouth as firm as Lizzie's.

Nobody else seemed to have noticed the angry, wordless exchange between husband and wife.

'Colin should have found someone better,' Meg thought, and realised that she was sharing Kirsty's misgivings.

The senior Bailie raised his hand and the crowd hushed at once. The riders jostled their mounts into position, the Town Officer bawled, in a surprisingly high thin voice for such a brawny man, 'Mind these bairns! Clear the way, now!' then the signal was given and the horses were off, their riders yelling like savages, the crowd screaming encouragement.

Meg had a brief final glimpse of Colin sweeping past, mouth open in a full-throated roar, eyes glowing. Matt followed, crouching over his horse's neck.

There was a mad flurry of hooves and noise, and the riders were gone, plunging in a tight-packed bunch down the narrow thoroughfare and round the corner into St James' Street. From there they had to go onto the Shambles Road, then circle back to the Love Street starting point.

'My certies, what I wouldn't give to be one of them!' Peter boomed as the last horse swept out of sight and the yells of the crowd in St James's Street drifted back to them.

'No doubt, but it's time you realised that you're too old for such ploys,' Kirsty said mercilessly.

'But not too old for everything, eh, lass?' Her irrepressible husband slid an arm about her shoulders and she fended him off with a scandalised, 'Peter Todd – will you mind where you are?'

He took out a small box and helped himself complacently to a pinch of snuff. 'I'm at the Silver Bells horse race – and the Bells'll belong to the Todd house tonight. It's grand to be the father of sons, Duncan. Before we know it Jamie here'll be riding for the Bells.'

Kirsty rubbed her chin against her son's head. 'Mebbe, for he's as wild as you and Matt ever were. But there's time enough, is there not, my wee mannie? You'll not be in a hurry to grow up.'

'Don't cosset him, Kirsty,' Peter cautioned, but Meg, feeling the child in her womb flutter at that very moment, knew what the other woman meant. She longed to hold her own baby in her arms, and when that day came she would be in no hurry to see him – or her – grow up and away from her.

Small boys as often as not inarticulate with excitement deftly stitched their way through the crowds, carrying the latest news.

'Will Robb in front – Geordie Ogilvie's horse went lame on him – Matt and Colin Todd are well up—' The messages were passed from mouth to mouth and Peter almost danced with anticipation, craning his neck to see the end of the road, where the first riders would soon appear.

The full-throated roar was a dull rumble at first, swelling as it swept nearer. Even Lizzie was caught up in the tension, standing on tiptoe to see the winner come in. Peter scooped Jamie from Kirsty's arms and held him high; Meg gripped Duncan's arm as she heard someone shout, 'Here they come—!' Then the ground shook beneath her feet as the horses pounded back into Love Street, their red-faced riders clinging on for dear life.

Lumps of dried mud sprayed up on either side as they galloped past the line, a huge bay in front with three others fighting for second place behind it.

'Pat McGregor – it's Pat!' a man yelled as the winner, a jovial Paisley cobbler, whooped and threw his bonnet in the air.

Peter Todd stood aghast. 'Would you credit it? They're not there – not a sign of them! What the blazes do they think they're up to, the pair of knuckle-headed, clumsy—'

'Now, now, Peter,' his wife, admonished. 'It's only a race. They did their best, I'm sure.'

'Not a very good best—' he was beginning, when one of the Bailies came hurrying over, an urchin at his heels.

'Peter, this lad says there's been an accident just round the corner. One of your boys – they've sent for a physician—'

But Peter was already shouldering his way through the throng. Kirsty thrust Jamie at Duncan and followed, snatching at Lizzie's wrist as she went and towing the girl along behind her.

'Duncan—?' A chill had taken hold of Meg's limbs.

'Come on, lass, we might be needed.' He put his free arm about her and helped her along, stumbling through the dense crowd, pushing against the flow of people, for everyone else was flocking to the winning line.

They rounded the corner and found a knot of men standing in the middle of the road. Some horses, steaming after their frantic gallop, were being held by wide-eyed gawping boys.

In the middle of the group Matt knelt beside Colin, who lay in a careless, oddly boneless heap as though a giant hand had picked him up then tossed him aside. His eyes were closed and his fair hair was bloody over one temple.

As the Montgomerys arrived Kirsty dropped to

her knees and lifted her step-son's head onto her lap. Peter's hands moved carefully over Colin's limbs. Lizzie stood looking on.

'I'd not move him too much, lass,' Peter said quietly. 'It looks bad.'

Matt rubbed both hands over his paper-white face. 'It – it happened so fast.' He stumbled over the words as though the language was new to him. 'We were out in front and he'd just shouted to me that he'd take the Bells for sure. Then his horse must have put its foot in a hole – the daft gowk, why couldn't he have been watching out for it—?' he added in a burst of anguished fury. 'He went over its head and landed – on his back – on the dyke.'

They all looked at the low wall, at its hard, sharp stones.

'God help us!' Kirsty whispered, stroking Colin's bloodied hair.

Jamie, sensing that something was wrong, began to weep and punch at Duncan's shoulder. Meg took him, clasping the wriggling little body close for comfort.

'It was so quick—' Matt said again, then reeled back as Lizzie broke out of her trance and flew at him, her hands clawing for his eyes.

'It's your fault!' she screamed at him. 'It's always you! Why did you have to come back here and spoil everything, Matt Todd? Why did you have to come back?'

Chapter Three

COLIN TODD SURVIVED THE ACCIDENT that marred that year's Silver Bells Race, but his back was broken and he was paralysed from the waist down. In the space of a few seconds he had become a ruckle of skin and bones lying on a cot in the kitchen behind the grocer's shop.

Peter and Matt were ghosts of themselves, weighed down by guilt.

'Colin's a grown man after all,' Duncan protested miserably to Meg during that bleak time. 'He made up his own mind to race. It's wrong of Lizzie to blame Matt for encouraging him, but the woman's out of her mind with grief.'

But instinct told Meg that Lizzie's claim on Colin was possessive rather than tender. The attack on Matt had been prompted, she felt, by fear of what would become of Lizzie herself if anything happened to her husband. And it went deeper – she was quite sure that Lizzie harboured a bitterness against Matt Todd that went beyond any consideration she might feel for Colin's welfare. But she kept her thoughts

to herself. This was no time to air them, even to
Duncan.

Colin had heard the physician's verdict quietly
– indeed, he scarcely spoke at all. But his eyes
held a look of trapped anguish that tore at Meg's
heart each time she saw him. She and Kirsty did
what they could to help, sitting with Colin to let
Lizzie have a rest, making delicacies to tempt the
invalid's appetite, helping in the shop. But both
Colin and Lizzie seemed to have locked themselves
away behind set, pale faces and tight lips.

When Meg called in at the shop the day before
Matt was due to rejoin the Fusiliers she found
Janet, the girl who had been brought in to attend
the counter, dealing with a handful of customers.

The kitchen beyond was empty apart from Colin,
lying in the box bed. His head was turned away
from the door and he made no move when Meg
went in. Quietly she put her basket down and took
her cloak off. She was reaching up to hang it on
the nail hammered into the door that separated
the kitchen from the 'best room' when she heard
voices from beyond the wooden panels.

There was no mistaking Matt's deep tones –
'You'd expect that of me, you slut?' – or Lizzie's
voice – 'Why not? D'you think I'm going to spend
the rest of my life like this, with a man who's no
use to any woman? You weren't ashamed to touch
me before, Matt Todd!'

The voices came clearly to Meg, but it was a
moment before she glanced at the bed and saw

with sick horror that Colin was awake, his blue eyes fixed on the ceiling, his fists gripping the blanket that lay over his useless legs. She took a step towards him as the door to the inner room was swept open so hard that it crashed off the edge of the dresser.

Matt stood in the doorway, eyes blazing in an angry face, his move into the kitchen checked as he saw Meg. Lizzie's face bobbed round his arm.

Cold anger, the first intense rage that Meg had ever experienced, gripped her.

'Have you no shame?' she asked Matt. 'Have you no feeling for the man at all?'

His eyes immediately went to the bed and she saw the colour drain from his skin.

'Colin! Colin, lad, it was a misunderstanding—' He stumbled over to take his brother's hand in his own. 'I would never—' His voice died away as Colin looked at him, a look that made Meg shiver and sent Matt stumbling from the room.

Lizzie stepped cat-like to the bed and Colin's eyes moved to meet and hold hers. But the gaze that had destroyed Matt held no fears for her. She matched it until his eyes closed against the sight of her and he turned his face back to the wall.

Then she gave Meg her attention. 'You wanted something?' she asked flatly, as though attending to a customer in the shop.

'I came to sit with Colin—'

'I can see to him.' Lizzie's voice was cold, dismissive.

The anger that gripped Meg gave her courage. 'I came to help – I didn't expect to find you and Matt—'

'You never know what you'll find in life,' Lizzie cut through her words. 'I went looking once, and I didn't find what I wanted. You'll learn.'

'Not your way, Lizzie Todd!' said Meg, and walked out before her fingers gave way to an impulse and buried themselves in Lizzie's neat brown hair.

She avoided Matt until he left Paisley; it was a relief to her when she knew that he was away. She couldn't even bring herself to tell Duncan what she had seen and heard, and he began to worry over her pallor and her depression.

'It's been the shock of Colin's accident,' Kirsty told him. 'What she needs is some good country air.'

When he suggested that Meg should go back to Beith for a few days she seized the idea eagerly, longing to escape for a while from Colin's misery and Lizzie's cold, secretive face. Duncan travelled down with her on a cold, drizzly day that gave them an excuse to cuddle together under a plaid rug as the cart carried them away from Paisley.

'I'll miss you,' he whispered, and she hugged him.

'I'll be back soon. You'll keep at your reading while I'm gone?'

He sighed, but nodded. Meg had been a hard task-master since that first night in Paisley, but her bullying was paying dividends and Duncan's reading and writing skills had greatly improved.

Meg fell back into the ways of the farm with surprising ease. It was comforting to be a daughter again, ordered about by her mother, giggling with her sister Mary, treading blankets in the big tub in the farmyard.

In Paisley, Duncan eased his loneliness by spending most of his free time with some of the young married weavers. He hadn't realised before how interested the Paisley men were in world affairs and he learned a lot from listening to them.

He had the sense not to join them in the howffs, for he couldn't afford to spend hard-earned money on drink, but he went with them on their long walks, argued with them, bowled with them, and on more than one occasion fought beside them when they had differences of opinion with men from other districts. Their cheerful rowdiness appealed to that part of him that hadn't yet resigned itself to marriage and its limitations. He enjoyed the life of a bachelor once again; it was only at nights, alone in bed, that he hungered for his wife's soft, warm body, her willingness, her loving.

'It's time for Meg to come home,' Kirsty said shrewdly one evening when Duncan had gone out to meet Davie. 'It's not natural for a young man to be parted from his wife for too long.'

Lizzie, sitting in a corner of the kitchen with her sewing on her lap, looked up from under pale eyelids. The quiet older weaver who worked in

Peter's loom shop, had offered to sit with Colin and free her for a while.

'Meg'll be back soon enough,' Peter said easily. 'I've no doubt she's missing Duncan as much as he's missing her.'

Lizzie's long fingers folded the material she had been working on. 'I'd best get home,' she said.

Duncan, bored and restless, was wandering home when he turned a corner and bumped into Lizzie. The books in her arms would have gone flying if he hadn't caught them deftly.

'I'll carry them for you,' he offered. She said nothing, but let him take the rest of the books from her.

'How's Colin?'

'No different.'

'It must be hard for you.'

She lifted her head for the first time and looked fully at him. 'It's not easy. But folk don't seem to understand what it's like to be young and wondering what's to become of me for the rest of my life!'

Taken aback by the bitterness in her voice he stammered something, but she ignored him.

'Just because I say little they think I don't bother – but I do, I do!' she went on fiercely. 'Night after night I lie there, beside him, and I look into the future, and I'm frightened—'

Her voice broke and she clenched her hands into small, knotted fists. They came to a pothole in the roadway and Duncan took her elbow to steer her safely round it. A strong tremor seemed to run through Lizzie's body and into his hand. He snatched his fingers away as though they had been burned, then slowly, deliberately, took her arm again and guided her along the rough road as though she was made of fine china.

She said no more until they reached her door then she turned and took the books from him, tilting her chin defiantly. 'I've shocked you.'

'No, no—!'

'Aye, Duncan Montgomery, I have.' Her voice had taken on a soft lilt. 'I've shocked you and I'm not sorry for it. You're mebbe the only one who can understand how I feel. I had to speak out to someone. Meg's far away in Beith – you know as well as I do what it's like to lie alone at night, wanting – hurting—' The words hung in the dusk between them. 'I'm not ready to finish with life yet,' she added, low-voiced. 'Not yet! Thank you for listening, I'll not ask you in.'

And with a nod she was gone.

Duncan walked home slowly, thinking over her words. His final thoughts before he fell asleep that night weren't of rounded, loving Meg, but of slender, pale Lizzie with her brilliant eyes and her lilting voice.

He wondered if she was thinking about him at that moment as she lay awake beside her silent, crippled husband.

*   *   *

Lizzie Todd was as intoxicating as strong drink. She haunted Duncan's mind over the next two days. He avoided the shop but on the third day, his work finished and a lonely afternoon before him, he met her in the street.

Her grey eyes held his. 'I'm going to the moors for a breath of air – mebbe you'd like to accompany me,' she said softly.

He hesitated, but only for a moment. 'I was thinking of going there myself,' he said, and allowed his hand to brush hers as he turned to walk by her side.

The grass on the moors at the foot of the Muckle Riggs was short and springy and warmed by the sun. They found a little hollow sheltered by bushes, and Lizzie picked daisies and made a chain while Duncan watched her, drinking in each movement she made. She slit the final stem with sharp finger-nails, tucked a daisy head through it, then put the completed circlet on her hair and smiled up at him.

'What do you think?'

'You look bonnie. Like a queen.'

Her slanted eyes laughed at him. 'I never thought to hear such a compliment again.'

'It's the truth.'

'You're a fine-looking man yourself, Duncan Montgomery.' She reached out to take his hand in hers and again he sensed that tremor flowing between their fingers. It tingled through him, exciting him, and at the same time warning him of danger.

'We should get back.'

Lizzie shrugged, then let herself fall back on the grass, her eyes mocking him. 'It's early yet. Are you scared of me?'

'Mebbe I should be.'

She laughed. Strands of her hair fell across the tiny white flowers that starred the grass beneath her. Her teeth gleamed white and sharp between parted lips. His body burned with his need of her.

'Then why don't you take to your heels and run home, where you'll be safe?' she suggested silkily.

He knew well enough that he should do just that – run over the moors and back to the streets; run all the way to Beith and to Meg. But he was infected by Lizzie. He couldn't rest until he possessed her.

'You know why—' he said hoarsely, and caught at her shoulders, raising her up to where he knelt above her, bringing her mouth to his own hungry lips.

Her kiss excited him, made him want to take her swiftly, fiercely – and yet he must delay the moment of taking as long as possible, because with Lizzie there were so many delights to explore first. She twined her fingers in his hair, then she was writhing like a wild thing against him, her mouth warm and moist, as he bore her down again onto the springy turf.

*   *   *

They had three further meetings before word of Meg's return reached him.

The letter lay in Duncan's hand like a stone. Meg's goodness and love, and her trust in him, shone from those few scrawled words. Like a handful of icy water thrown into his face they brought him back with cruel haste to his real purpose in life – making a home for his wife and his child.

He felt weak, like a man who had just recovered from a consuming fever. His burning lust for Lizzie ebbed away as he read the letter again, and in its place came a longing to hold Meg in his arms once more. The illness had almost been fatal, but now he was cured. Then he remembcred that he still had to face Lizzie, and his limbs trembled anew.

Mercifully, she was alone in the shop when he went in. She looked sharply at him when he stepped through the doorway.

'What's amiss?'

'Meg's coming home – tomorrow.'

Her eyebrows lifted slightly, her eyes mocking him. 'And you'll go back to being the perfect husband, is that it?'

His mouth was dry. 'I must. Lizzie, it was never meant to last – we needed each other for – for comfort, that was all.'

'And after tomorrow you'll have no more need of me?'

He swallowed, and longed for a mug of ale.

'You knew as well as I did that there was no future to it.'

A strange light flared into the grey eyes that surveyed him, and he braced himself to face her rage, then the look was gone, and she shrugged. 'So we'll just have to make the most of this afternoon?'

'No!' His voice was so emphatic that she frowned and put a finger to her lips.

'Ssshhh! The girl's in the kitchen with Colin.'

'I'll not see you this afternoon, Lizzie. It's finished.' He hadn't meant it to sound so blunt but he didn't know what else to say. For a moment her lips parted to speak, then she shrugged again.

'Please yourself. There's other men,' she said deliberately. The contempt in her voice stung, but Duncan welcomed the cleansing, absolving pain of it. He walked out, towards the nearest howff. It was over.

As the time for her baby's birth approached Meg became happier than ever before. Shortly before Christmas she and Duncan were able to move round the corner from the Todds' home into a two-roomed ground-floor house in Lady Lane, scantily furnished, but a palace as far as they were concerned.

Duncan kept well away from the grocer's shop, and didn't see Lizzie at all as the weeks passed. It seemed that their affair had only been a passing dream – then at the very moment when he began to let himself relax he was summoned one night to Peter Todd's house.

'Is there something wrong?' Meg asked anxiously when a boy knocked at their door and delivered the message. 'Should I go with you?'

'No, it's probably to do with the loom-shop.' Duncan shivered as a handful of rain spattered against the window. 'You stay here, by the fire. I'll be back soon.'

But when he walked into the warm kitchen and saw Lizzie, wild-eyed and bitter-mouthed, he knew that his shameful secret was out. His knees dissolved and he had to catch at the back of a chair to keep himself upright.

'No doubt you know what this is about?' Peter asked in a harsh unfamiliar voice.

'Did you have to bring them into it?' Duncan asked Lizzie, indicating the Todds with a jerk of the head. Her eyes narrowed, no longer luminous and inviting.

'I wanted them to know what their fine new weaver's brought to their door!'

'That's enough!' Peter's face was old and drawn, and Duncan was reminded of the day the man had looked down at his son, bloodied and unconscious in the mud. 'What's done can't be cured by harsh words. We have to think of what's best for – the child.'

Duncan cursed himself for a fool. He might have known that their passionate loving would bear fruit. Hadn't Meg fallen pregnant right after their marriage?

'Meg mustn't know—' he said automatically.

'Oh – so Meg mustn't know?' Lizzie mocked shrilly. 'She'll know all right! You've got me with child and now you'll have to acknowledge it! You'll have to set up house with me!'

'Leave Meg for you? But I – I love her!'

'You should have thought of that before you gave Lizzie a child!' Peter made a move forward and Kirsty put a restraining hand on his arm.

'I wish to God I had! But I'm thinking of it now – and I'll not leave Meg! I'll pay for the child's keep, Lizzie, but I'll not leave my wife!'

Lizzie made for the door. 'We'll see what she thinks when she's heard about it—'

Duncan's hands caught her shoulders and spun her round. He shook her until her head flopped on its long neck.

'You dare to go near Meg – you dare to say a word to her, and I'll kill you—!'

'For God's sake, man!' Peter dragged him away and Kirsty pushed Lizzie, spitting defiance and threats, into a chair.

'It's you and me'll have to sort this out,' she told her husband bluntly. 'These two hadn't the sense to leave each other alone, and they've not got the sense now to decide what's best.'

'I'll not leave Meg!' To his horror Duncan heard his own voice thicken with the threat of angry, frightened tears. He had never wanted or needed

Meg's loving arms more than at that moment. 'I'll see you right for money, Lizzie, but that's all. I'll take Meg away, back to Beith – I'll tell her that I can't settle in Paisley—'

'And you'll get out of it that way, will you?' Peter almost snarled at him. 'What about my son? God – this'll be the finish of him!'

'And what about me?' Lizzie screeched. 'A child I don't want, no man to look after me—'

'Wait a minute.' Kirsty's quiet authority cut across the girl's rising hysteria. 'It's too late to start blaming each other. What's done's done, and we're here to decide how to make some sense out of it. Lizzie, how far on are you?'

'Eight weeks,' the girl said sullenly, and as another gust of wind drove rain against the house walls Duncan recalled those sunny afternoons in the little hollow. In the weeks since then he had known more contentment with Meg than ever before. He would have plunged a knife into his heart willingly if he could only obliterate his affair with Lizzie.

'A few weeks here or there wouldn't make much difference,' Kirsty thought aloud, swiftly. 'The child could have been conceived just before Colin's accident. It could be his.'

'It's not!' Lizzie almost screamed at her. 'It's his!' One long finger stabbed at Duncan.

'I'm saying that for all anyone knows – for all Colin knows – you could be further on than you are.'

'You'd let Colin think he'd fathered another man's child?' Peter asked, aghast. 'I'll not have it!'

'Now listen for a minute before you say another word,' his wife ordered. 'Colin's always wanted a family, and the poor soul's never going to father children now. Would it be such an unkindness to let him think it's his?'

She watched her husband's face, and saw understanding dawn in the blue eyes.

'But there's me to consider – what about my wishes?' Lizzie said sourly.

'You might as well face up to it – Duncan's admitted responsibility but he'll not leave Meg for your sake,' Kirsty said flatly. 'You'll either be alone with the child or you'll let Colin think it's his and have a roof over your head. And I daresay Peter would be willing to pay Janet to stay on and see to the shop for you. Eh, Peter?'

'You think I'll be content with that?' Lizzie sneered.

'I don't see that you have much choice, Lizzie. It's that, or manage on your own with a child to birth and raise. Is it worth breaking Colin's heart? Surely the poor man's got enough to contend with.'

'I'll not agree to it!'

Peter caught his daughter-in-law's wrist with strong fingers. 'You'll do what's best for Colin – whatever that might be!'

Kirsty let out her breath in a sigh, eyes bright with relief as she realised that her husband, at least, was beginning to give her his support. 'This is the way I see it—' she began with a new briskness.

Lizzie wrangled for another hour before she accepted that Duncan wasn't going to leave his wife for her sake. Then she sulkily agreed to Kirsty's plan, and slammed out of the door and down the stairs.

For a moment the three left in the room were silent, then Peter said, 'You're mad, woman! It's a daft ploy – the whole town'll see through it!'

'Not unless Lizzie tells them,' Kirsty argued. 'And a crippled husband's better than no man at all to the likes of her. Pay her well and she'll hold her tongue.'

Duncan straightened and felt his joints creak. He was certain that he had aged twenty years since leaving Meg by the fireside.

'I'm sorry, Mister Todd.'

'Well you might be! Colin lying helpless and your own wife carrying her first child, and you—'

Duncan's face drained of colour, then flamed. 'You can't say anything to me I haven't already said to myself.' He picked up his cap, twisted it tightly in both hands. 'And now I've to face Meg.'

'Poor lass – does she have to know about Lizzie? It'll kill her, Duncan,' Kirsty said, her mind already busy with another scheme.

'She'll never know about that, for it's my guilt, not hers. I'll tell her—' he swallowed, thinking of her pride in their first proper home. '—I'll tell her I can't settle here. I'll tell her tomorrow.'

*   *   *

47

'And they'll go back to Beith and you'll lose a good weaver,' Kirsty said as they listened to Duncan's footsteps, slow and heavy, stumbling down the stairs.

'There's other weavers.' Peter's voice was hard.

'But Duncan's better than most, is he not? Admit it, Peter, he's more like a son than an employee already.'

'You see more than your fair share – and talk more than your fair share too!' he said angrily, but she shrugged the reprimand off.

'And there's Meg, too – they both fit well into Paisley. You're angered just as much by the way Duncan's betrayed your trust as by the way he's betrayed Colin.'

'Kirsty, I've never raised my hand to a woman before, but if you don't guard that tongue of yours—' her husband howled, goaded beyond endurance.

'Let them stay, Peter.'

His jaw dropped. 'Let them stay?' he repeated incredulously. 'Let him stay in the same town as Colin after he and Lizzie – after they—'

'Just hear me out before you go jumping around as if you've met up with a flea—' She put a firm hand on his arm. 'It's over between Duncan and Lizzie, you must see that for yourself. The lad's got a good future here. He'll never make a fool of himself again, that's for sure.'

'Keep him on in my employ after—' Peter made

for the door. 'I'm going to my bed.' Then he swung round and snatched his jacket from the back of his chair. 'No, I'm going out for a drink. You're the one that should be going to your bed. It's late, and your mind's addled with all this trouble!'

'Peter, if Duncan suddenly goes it'll cause more talk than if he stays. And you'd not want Colin to wonder at his going, would you? The poor man's crippled, not stupid.'

'D'you think I could go on working with Duncan Montgomery, knowing the truth about him and – and—?'

Kirsty took the jacket from his hands. 'I think you're an honest, just man, Peter Todd. I think you've got a good heart. And if you'd just give yourself a chance to ponder over what I'm saying you'd know I'm right.'

There was a long pause, then Peter said, 'I'm away to my bed.'

'Do as the Book says, Peter—' Kirsty said as he touched the latch. 'Cast your bread on the waters. As far as Duncan Montgomery's concerned, it'll come back to you. You'll see.'

He went out without speaking or looking at her. Kirsty listened until she had satisfied herself that he was going up to the attic and not down to the street, then she went about her duties with hands that shook very slightly, making sure that the room was tidy and putting oatmeal to soak for the morning's porridge.

When she went into the attic bedroom he was sitting on the bed staring into space.

'Mebbe you're right,' he said gruffly. 'Mebbe I'll talk it over in the morning with Duncan.'

Kirsty beamed at him. 'Mebbe you should, Peter.'

'That's not to say he'll stay.'

'I think he will.' She didn't tell him that she, too, would have a word with Duncan.

'But I'm damned if I know why I let you talk me into things against my better judgement, woman,' Peter grumbled.

It was only then that Kirsty allowed herself to believe that her plan was going to work out. Duncan and Meg would stay, Colin would have his child, Lizzie would hold her tongue. Slowly, aware of his eyes on her, she untied her white lacy cap and released her fiery silken hair from the pins that confined it by day. Then she went to sit by her husband, her arms about him, her lips against his face.

'Because I'm always right,' she said demurely.

Chapter Four

MEG'S SON WAS BORN ONE January afternoon just as the last of the grey daylight was ebbing and the weavers were setting tapers by the looms so that they could continue their work. Kirsty, summoned that morning when the pains began, had ordered Duncan off to his loom as usual.

'A first baby can take a while, and you'll just be in the way,' she'd said, pushing him out of his own street door. 'I'll let you know when you can come back.'

All day he blundered through his work, and when word finally came for him to go home he jumped to his feet, almost knocking his taper into the loom.

'Will you watch what you're about!' Peter roared at him, then added, as he looked at the knotted threads Duncan had been trying to unravel for the past half hour, 'Ach, mebbe you'd be as well to burn the lot after all!'

But Duncan was already away, his boots clattering along the passageway then skidding on the hard-packed, ice-rimed earth of the footpath.

The kitchen was warm and peaceful when he burst in; Kirsty was putting on her cloak and Meg lay in the wall bed, her face radiant when she saw him.

'There's food on the table, and I'll look in later,' Kirsty said briskly, and went out as Duncan stared down at the baby, plump and smooth-skinned, with a thatch of dark hair.

'He's like you,' Meg said contentedly. 'Give him to me.'

Duncan lifted the warm, solid bundle from the cradle, balanced it carefully in his two hands, and settled it in the curve of his wife's arm. Then he hid his face in Meg's warm, soft shoulder.

'I promise I'll be a good husband to you for the rest of my life—' he whispered into her hair. 'I'll take such care of the two of you—'

Surprised by the damp touch of his tears on her skin, she reached up to stroke his face.

'But Duncan,' she said, puzzled, 'You've always been good to me.'

Robert Montgomery took to life as a weaver's son without any misgivings at all. Each day Meg scooped him into a shawl and took him out and about with her, and wherever they went people responded to his lop-sided, toothless smile and his large blue eyes.

Everyone, that was, except Lizzie Todd. If Meg was helping Lizzie in the shop or about the house she tucked Robert in at the end of Colin's truckle bed and the invalid, now propped up on cushions, watched over him. But Lizzie ignored the child and Meg wondered uneasily what sort of mother she would be to her own baby when it arrived.

'She's such a cold creature,' she fretted to Duncan. 'A wee one needs love—'

He got to his feet abruptly, pleasure in his own fireside suddenly gone. 'D'you have to talk so much about Lizzie Todd?' he asked sharply.

Hurt, Meg kept her thoughts about Lizzie to herself from then on. But it was hard, especially when Lizzie's baby was born in May. The girl went into labour after a fall from the step-ladder in the shop and had a long and hard labour before William was born, a frail, passive little boy.

'He's dark, like you,' Meg said cheerfully when she went along to visit mother and child. Lizzie, still confined to bed, shrugged, then shook her head and drew back when Meg bent to give the child to her.

'I can't be doing with his crying – put him in the crib.'

'In a minute.' Meg straightened, reluctant to put down the tiny mite that nestled against the curve of her breast. 'A crib's a lonely place for such a wee thing.'

Colin called from the parlour, where he lay on his cot. As she went in he held out her arms. 'Give him to me—'

She handed William over and watched as Colin stroked the small face gently with one finger.

'He'll strengthen fast enough,' Meg assured him. The difference between William and her own chubby, healthy child, now four months old, was frightening.

'I know. I'll keep him by me for a wee while, Meg.'

Going back into the kitchen, looking at the woman who lay like a ramrod in the bed there, Meg was glad that Colin and his son had each other for warmth.

Further north, and almost in another world as far as Paisley was concerned, the Jacobites and the Government troops were locked in a struggle to the death.

On the whole the Paisley folk supported the King and disapproved of the hot-headed clansmen and their loyalty to a young man who, when all was said and done, was 'more a Frenchie than a Scot, and not the man for the crown at all,' in their view. The packmen kept them abreast of the latest news, and where two or more people met there was always some lively argument going on about the situation. Often Kirsty got so caught up in a disagreement with the men in the shop below that her spinning wheel almost whirred right off its mounting, and Peter would be goaded into bellowing up at her, 'Ach, why don't you content yourself with pots and pans and bread making, woman, and leave the opinions to the menfolk?'

To which Kirsty, face crimson, would yell, 'If

you wanted some mealy-mouthed skivvy who'd keep her mouth shut and your belly filled, Peter Todd, you should have stayed in Dumbarton and not come to a place where the women have minds of their own!'

Then she would kick the trap shut and, eyes gleaming and red curls bouncing, say triumphantly, 'That's one argument he's lost, big man that he thinks he is. Never let them have the last word, Meg!'

After a while Peter would bang on the hatch, Kirsty would open it and, with a sweet smile, pass down the old top hat which she kept the loaded pirns in – and the argument would be forgotten, until the next time.

Matt came back home, his old vigorous self again, spilling over with tales of the Battle of Falkirk a few months earlier. Seated in his father's kitchen, a pipe in his hand and Jamie asleep on his knee, he held court to a crowd of wide-eyed listeners, chilling their blood one minute, throwing them into laughter the next with a malicious and hilarious word-picture of poor John Renfrew, who in the noise and confusion had dashed straight into a hedge and stuck fast.

'We'd not have bothered with him, but he was the colour-bearer, and we weren't going to let those Highlanders get their hands on Paisley's standard.' He winked at the ring of faces. 'Man, you should have seen Johnny – head on one side, fat rump on the other, bellowing like a stuck heifer – and his hands clamped round the banner all the time with a grip like death itself. It took three of us to pull him free.'

Meg noticed that Lizzie didn't attend any of those gatherings. The only time she appeared in the Todds' kitchen was when Matt went along to see Colin.

A terrible suspicion began to form in Meg's mind. She could say nothing to Duncan or even to Kirsty, so she had to keep her thoughts to herself until one day when she had to work at home because Robert was teething and too fretful to take out.

Duncan had arranged to call round for the finished pirns, but when the door opened Meg saw Matt's tall figure outlined against the light beyond, his head stooped beneath the lintel.

'I told Duncan I'd fetch the pirns,' he said and she felt warmth rise in her face. She hadn't been alone with him since that day in Colin's kitchen.

'They're in the corner there.'

He closed the door behind him, shutting out the street. 'You've got a fine home since I last was here.'

'Aye,' she said shortly, eyes on her wheel, willing him to go away. Instead, he sat down opposite her.

'Meg—'

Reluctantly, she slowed the wheel and looked up at him – to be stunned by the lost look on his handsome, normally confident face.

'I have to talk with you – about Lizzie.' He put

out a hand as she started to speak. 'Listen to me! I know what you think about her and me, but you're wrong! We walked out together before I went into the Army, but I had no thought in my head then but soldiering, though it turned out that Lizzie had her heart set on marriage.'

His big, capable hands knotted into fists as he spoke. 'God, she had plenty to say when she realised that I was set on going away. She flew at me like a she-devil and near tore my face open with her nails. But I went all the same so she set her cap at Colin instead. When I came back they were wed. And from that day I've never treated her as anything other than my brother's wife.'

'You can say that to me, when I heard with my own ears—'

'What you heard – and, God forgive me, what Colin heard – was Lizzie's doing, not mine!' Matt spoke with a sudden surge of energy. 'I wanted to crush her as if she was a flea on my arm – I still do. It would please me if I was never to set eyes on the bitch again. I've done enough to Colin, making him ride with me that day. D'you think I'd do more?'

'And William?'

'As God's my witness, Meg, he must be Colin's, for he's not mine!'

She studied him for a long moment, then nodded. 'I believe you, Matt.'

Relief lit his handsome face. 'I'm glad that's settled between us. I'll take the pirns to Duncan,' he said, then hesitated at the door.

'Meg, will you keep watch over Colin and the wee one?'

'We'll all look after them—' Meg broke off as the baby started to cough. She went quickly to the cradle, and Matt, whistling, left for the loom shop. Walking up and down with Robert muttering fretfully in her arms, Meg thought of Lizzie and those strange grey eyes of hers, the way they changed when they looked on men such as Matt and Duncan—

She stopped, and Robert squeaked a protest as her arms tightened. Meg kissed his sweat-damp hair and rocked him soothingly, her thoughts in sudden turmoil. As Lizzie and Duncan's names linked in her mind panic caught at her heart, then she forced herself to calm down, to be sensible.

Lizzie looked at all men, other than her husband, in the same way. It meant nothing, particularly to a man as sensible as Duncan. Besides, he never looked the road Lizzie was on, never even encouraged Meg to talk about her.

'You've got a silly mother,' she said shakily to Robert, and made up her mind once and for all, as she laid the baby back in his cradle, that never again would she allow such foolish ideas about Duncan to enter her head.

By the time his son reached his first birthday Duncan had joined the Society of Weavers, and he and Meg had become members of the Baptist Church, attending meetings in the Abbey Close.

To Meg's intense pride Duncan was even invited to speak at a church meeting, an occasion fraught with nerves for them both. Duncan's hands gripped the lectern before him, his face red with effort; Meg sat in the front row, her lips moving in unison with his, leaning forward to prompt audibly if he faltered. When the ordeal was finally over she almost split in two with pride.

A month after Robert's birthday his sister Margaret was born, and six weeks later Kirsty Todd gave birth to a daughter, Kate. In June, when the tiny white flowers were beginning to star the grass on the moors, the whole town was rocked by a piece of scandal.

The gossips were out in force at once, eyes gleaming, tongues wagging. 'Lizzie Todd's run off wi' a farm-worker! Have you heard about it? That poor man – and that poor bairn!'

Meg, who heard the story at the market place, hurried at once to Kirsty's kitchen, Margaret tucked into her shawl, and Robert running alongside as fast as his fat little legs could carry him, complaining breathlessly.

'It's not true!' she said as she burst into the kitchen.

Kirsty, rocking in her chair with Kate in the crook of one arm and William in her lap, was stony-faced.

'It's true. Hell mend the woman, for she's done a terrible thing this day!'

'How's Colin?'

Kirsty shook her head. 'Determined to fend for himself and the boy, though there's no way he can run the shop. There's room here for them both, and food enough, but he's being that thrawn about it – Peter's near out of his mind.'

At that moment an idea came to Meg, such a daring idea that it caught the breath in her throat. She said nothing to Kirsty, or even to Duncan, but the thought stayed with her. When she couldn't stand it any longer she called on Colin, still living in the rooms behind the shop, though Kirsty was looking after William.

The woman waiting to be served eyed her with open curiosity as she went round the counter with a brief nod to Janet. She heard their voices buzzing as she closed the house door behind her.

Already there was an air of neglect about the place, though Kirsty had been in that morning, Meg knew, to see to the housework. But there was something undeniably depressing about a house without its proper housewife.

Colin was propped up on a pile of pillows, staring at the opposite wall. His face, gaunt since his accident, was no more than skin stretched over sharp bones, his eyes, when he glanced up at her, were sunk in their sockets, without any hope in them at all.

'I'm in no mood for visitors – or sympathy!' he said harshly.

'I'm not a visitor. And I've more to do with my

time than pity you.' She sat down on the chair by the bed and stared at him defiantly. He glowered back at her, then turned his face to the wall.

'Go away, Meg – leave me be!'

She steeled herself, recognising his frustration, his despair, his desperate need to be whole in himself.

'We have things to talk about, you and me. Colin, I want the shop,' she said bluntly, and saw his head turn, the grim set of his face slacken with sheer surprise.

'You what?'

'I want the shop. I've worked in it often enough and I managed fine. I could run it with Janet's help. But I'd need this house as well.'

Anger flared in his eyes, and she was glad to see it there.

'And I just take my son and move out to suit your convenience? By God, Meg Montgomery, you know how to take advantage of a man's misfortunes to line your own nest!' He almost spat the words at her. 'I'll chain myself to the grate before I'll move from here!'

Meg tucked her hands beneath her shawl in case Colin saw how they shook. 'Tuts, man, d'you have no sense in your head at all?' She had to speak loudly to quell the tremor that conveyed itself from her fingers to her voice. 'You can't manage the shop by yourself. But I can, if Duncan and me move to these rooms where I can see to the children and the counter at the same time. I'm offering to run the place for you, with financial gain for us both.'

'And what about me and William?'

'You've got brains, Colin. Use them,' she rapped back at him. 'Peter has a storeroom across the passageway from the weaving shop, I'm sure he'd let you turn it into a room for yourself and William. Kirsty can keep an eye on the two of you and you can help Peter to sort out wages and accounts. You could mebbe teach some children their letters too, if you had the time.'

'And what do you get from this daft idea?'

'A home, rent-free, so that we can save up and build our own house one day. And something of my own to do. It's not such a daft idea, Colin, if you'll just think of it.'

She leaned forward, enthusiasm giving weight to her argument. 'I like working in the shop – I like it more than anything else. Ever since I came to Paisley I've wanted to be part of the place in my own way. Now I can be.'

'What does Duncan say?'

'He doesn't know. If you refuse I'd as soon he didn't hear about me making a fool of myself, and if you agree you can help me to persuade him that it's a good idea.'

There was a short silence, then to her surprise Colin laughed, a genuine peal of amusement. 'God, Meg, but you're a breath of fresh air!' he said, and it was settled.

With Colin won over, it was easy to persuade

Duncan to give his approval. Within two weeks Colin and the baby were settled in the Todds' former storeroom, under Kirsty's eye, and the Montgomerys had moved into their new home.

With Janet to help her in the shop Meg was able to combine the roles of shop-keeper and housewife efficiently. The dwelling-house was adequate, and there was a garden where she kept bees and grew vegetables. It was as though Lizzie, with her final act of betrayal, had somehow bestowed the gift of peace on those who had known her.

Meg was too busy to travel to Beith, so her parents came to Paisley to see her new home and her little daughter.

'I don't know how you can live in such a crowded place,' her mother said nervously as she picked her way along a footpath.

Meg laughed and skipped nimbly aside as a passing cart sent water flooding up from the rutted road. 'You get used to it.'

'I never could!' the older woman said with feeling. But she was proud to see the recognition Meg received as they walked along. A gentleman standing at the door of his establishment, resplendent in knee britches, tall hat and tail coat, bowed to them and Meg, pink with pleasure, whispered, 'That's Mister Robertson – one of the biggest cloth manufacturers in the town.'

'Imagine!' gasped her mother and stepped into a

puddle in her excitement. Then she stared. 'Mercy
– who's that?'

A crowd of young men, some dressed in the
height of fashion and others in weavers' working
clothes, stood on the opposite path. In their midst
a good-looking young man held court.

'That's the Earl of Dundonald – a rapscallion,
they say. The Council are always complaining of
the disrepute he brings on the town.'

Her mother tutted disapprovingly. Like most
people of her class she was willing to give the
gentry their place, but only if, like the working
people, they had the sense to keep in it. Rowdies
were rowdies, be they lords or apprentices, and
she had little time for them.

Meg was secretly shocked at the relief she felt as
she watched her parents clamber aboard the cart
for Beith at the end of a week's stay. Despite her
new-found maturity she was still wary of her
mother's sharp tongue, and to her secret annoyance
she had reverted a little during the visit to the
role of submissive daughter. Confidence flowed
back as she watched the cart jolting away, and
she hugged Duncan's arm tightly as they turned
back into the shop.

She had chosen her path, and it was one that
more than pleased her.

Chapter Five

'WILL YOU HOLD STILL, YOU wee scamp? Duncan, get out the back this minute and bring Robert in. He'll be black as the heathens by this time, and us supposed to be at Kirsty's long since! We'll be the last there, and I promised I'd give her a hand before the other guests arrived!' Meg lamented, holding onto Margaret with one hand and wringing out the flannel with the other.

'But I'm—' Duncan stopped, sighed, and made for the back door. Let his shirt be unbuttoned and let his slippers get wet. There was no arguing with Meg when she was in that mood.

His son was at the bottom of the garden, as usual, and climbing the apple tree – as usual.

'Out of it!' Duncan ordered, and grabbed at Robert when he reluctantly slid down the trunk. 'Your mother'll skin you alive!' he fretted, brushing leaves and bark off the boy's jacket with a large but gentle hand. 'Get into the house quick, before she comes out here after the pair of us!'

Robert gave him a gap-toothed conspiratorial grin, and scuttled up the path. Duncan fastened his shirt as he followed. It seemed only yesterday that he had been the wildest boy in Ayrshire, and now his own son was a four-year-old miniature of himself.

Time was moving on, he thought as he stepped into the kitchen. The first dusting of grey could be seen on his dark temples and his waist had that slight thickening that tells of prosperity and contentment.

'I'll have to let out your trousers soon,' Meg said at that moment with uncanny perception.

He patted his stomach defensively. 'A man needs a bit of muscle.'

'There?' She poked him in the midriff, then squealed as he swept her off the floor and kissed her. 'Duncan! The wee ones are watching!'

He let her go, grinning down at her laughing, pretty face. 'Ach, a show of affection'll do them no harm.'

Margaret toddled after him as he went to fetch his jacket, her eyes huge after her afternoon sleep. He held his arms out and she rushed into them.

'Now don't get her into a mess,' Meg cautioned. She scrubbed at Robert's rosy face and he stood uncomplaining, knowing that if he opened his mouth to protest it would be filled with wet flannel.

'And you didn't even see the bonnie flowers, did you?' Duncan was asking Margaret, who had slept in his arms all through their afternoon walk in the Hope Temple Gardens.

Meg smiled to herself as she recalled their promenade round the flower-beds, the pleasant moist warmth within the glass enclosure, the snug fit of her new leather boots, the way the senior magistrate's wife had bowed to them when they met. The memories gave her such pleasure that Robert's features were almost scrubbed off his face.

'There – you'll do.' She released him and he rushed to join his father and sister, who were romping on the box bed.

'Keep tidy, now!' Meg called automatically, and went into the shop to make sure that everything was in order. The outer door was closed and bolted, the floor swept clean, the sacks tied tightly, the scales shining. She stood for a moment, one hand on the counter, and inhaled the rich smell of meal.

She had been in charge of it for two years, and had enjoyed every minute of it. She and Duncan had just put down the first payment on a piece of land on the west fringes of the town. There, in a few years, they would build their own house. She smoothed her skirt, letting her palms linger for a moment over the bulge caused by the coming baby, then called Duncan and the children, and put her cloak on for the walk to the Todds' house.

The place was in a turmoil when the Montgomerys arrived. Kirsty, crimson-faced from the heat, was stirring a huge pot of broth while trying to soothe John, the baby. Kate, Jamie and Willie were chasing each other up and down the stairs, and Peter could be heard from the bedroom, demanding to know where his best shoes were.

'I'm glad you're here!' Kirsty greeted Meg. 'I'm in a right pickle – would you take the wee one for me? Duncan, keep an eye on that broth. And as for you—' she swooped on the older children and deposited them on a settle by the fire '—sit there and hold your tongues for two minutes while I see what that handless man wants. Where are your best shoes always kept?' she yelled as she vanished. 'Seven years, and you still don't know where to look for them!'

By the time she reappeared a minute later, tucking a stray wisp of glowing hair beneath her cap, Meg was setting the table, the baby whimpering fretfully on her shoulder.

'He's not so grand today.' Kirsty took her son and rocked him. 'He's been coughing since morning. I'll try to settle him down before the others arrive.'

She stroked the child's flushed cheek with one finger and John moved his small head against her sturdy arm. By the time he was in his cradle the visitors had begun to arrive, and the kitchen was soon filled.

Duncan and Billy Carmichael, the packman, carried Colin upstairs and put him on a chair by the fire and William, a quiet little boy, immediately climbed onto his father's knee and fell asleep, one thumb jammed into his mouth and his head nestled under Colin's chin.

After supper all the children were taken to the attic where they were packed into bed like sardines to wait for their parents. Billy took his fiddle from his pack, and the evening got off to its proper start.

In an hour or two the house was bouncing with music and the babble of voices, yet the sound of a child in distress broke through the noise easily. First one woman, then another, fell silent, listening to the dry, painful coughing from up in the attic room, fearful in case they recognised their own child. It was the sound of croup, that lung-torturing illness that dogged infants in Paisley's low-lying, damp atmosphere.

Half a dozen anxious women followed Kirsty upstairs. When she came back to the kitchen she carried John, his face crimson, his little lungs crackling and wheezing as he tried to suck in air.

Someone put a kettle on the fire to make steam to ease his labouring lungs, someone else heated a blanket to wrap him in, then they all gathered their children and left. The party was over, and Kirsty would probably be up all night with John, waiting for the attack to pass.

Duncan had scarcely left for the weaving shop the next morning when he was back, white-faced.

'Kirsty needs you. I'll fetch Janet, she can see to the bairns and the shop today.'

Meg didn't stop to ask what was wrong. She didn't need to. In a few minutes she was in the

Todds' kitchen which was no longer the warm, noisy place it had been only a few hours earlier. Instead it was frighteningly silent and Kirsty sat huddled by the fire, oblivious of Peter's arms about her and the bewildered faces of the children who hadn't yet learned to understand the meaning of sudden death.

While Peter went off to make the necessary arrangements for his little son's burial, Meg fed the children and sent them down to Colin's room, then made tea and wrapped Kirsty's cold, stiff fingers about the cup before setting about the housework. The kitchen had to be spotless, and there was a baking to do in preparation for the people who would start arriving as soon as word of John's death spread.

Kirsty sat motionless, scarcely heeding the visitors. She didn't even pay attention to Mistress McKenzie, one of the first callers.

'The Lord giveth and the Lord taketh away,' that lady announced almost as soon as her foot was over the lintel. 'Your bairn's been chosen to reside with his Maker, Mistress Todd, and it's not for poor mortals like us to question or to lament. I'll try one of these scones, Meg.'

'Are you trying to say that Kirsty should rejoice?' Meg heard herself say in a strange, hard voice.

The black ribbons on Mistress McKenzie's bonnet rustled dryly with the force of her nodding.

'Just so. Children belong to the Lord, not to us. It's an honour when one's chosen from among our

70

number. It's not for us to question the ways of the Lord.'

Meg swallowed hard and glared at the woman who sat with her skirts hitched up to let her heavily veined legs soak in the fire's warmth.

'It seems to me that if the Lord knew more about the work that goes into caring for a baby, and the mortal love that goes with it, He'd have a bit more compassion for mothers!'

It was the other woman's turn to gape, and a half-chewed chunk of scone almost escaped past her teeth. She gulped, choked, and muttered something about Baptists knowing no better.

Meg set her lips over an angry retort. This wasn't the time to quarrel.

'But I could have taken her by the hair and dragged her out of the kitchen and down the stairs,' she stormed to Duncan when she was home again. 'The besom! Her with no children of her own – talking about honour and rejoicing!'

And she hugged Margaret so tightly that the little girl's lower lip began to tremble.

A few days later Kirsty and Peter saw John's tiny coffin buried in the churchyard, then they went back home and set about their usual day's routine.

There was little time to spare for mourning in a thriving town like Paisley. Water had to be fetched from wells, bees had to be tended and living children cared for, and thread had to be spun for the ever-hungry looms that beat out a steady rhythm for the townsfolk to live by.

As the time for her own baby's birth drew near Meg found it more and more difficult to cope with all her duties. Janet was a dreamy girl, not to be trusted in the shop alone if there were more than two customers. At times Meg longed to shake the girl hard, just to see if there was any life behind that vacant face. Her temper grew short, and it was as much for his own sake as for hers that Duncan suggested asking her sister Mary to help with the chores until the baby arrived.

Mary arrived within a few days, delighted with the opportunity to leave the farm. With an ease that stunned her older sister she familiarised herself with the shop routine and her happy nature and pretty face, with its sparkling brown eyes and its frame of dark curls, made her a great success with the customers. She even had an impressive effect on Janet, who began to take an interest in her appearance and her work.

'How did you manage to waken that ditherer?' Duncan demanded to know one day after he had found Janet, neat and tidy, chatting animatedly with Mary as they restocked shelves.

His sister-in-law leaned across the table and wiped crumbs from Margaret's chin. 'She just needed a firm hand. Nobody's ever encouraged her to take an interest in the way she looks, that's all.'

Mary was the beauty of the family. Meg was

plump and maternal, but Mary was slender and elegant. They had the same dark hair, but Mary's was glossy. Her manner was confident, her bearing almost regal. Somehow she managed to make even the plainest dress look stylish.

The town's young bachelors flocked to the shop and the snuff jar had to be replenished once every day; but to Meg's astonishment her sister wasn't interested in romance.

'A wee flirtation can be entertaining, I'll grant you,' she said carelessly. 'But I'm not interested in marriage.'

'What else is there?' Meg asked, and Mary threw a scathing glance at her.

'Plenty!'

She was fascinated by fashion, and always willing to take the children to the Hope Temple Gardens where she could study the ladies' clothes. She bought silks and ribbons and made her own bonnets, and on Meg's first outing to the Baptist rooms after her baby, Thomas, was born, she wore a hat made by Mary's nimble fingers.

Duncan's eyes shone when he saw his wife's rosy face framed by the new bonnet. 'You'll be the loveliest woman in the place!'

Meg laughed and blushed. But it was true. Nobody else had such a fine hat.

'Though it's wicked to think such vain thoughts in the Lord's House,' she whispered to Mary, who whispered back, dimpling, 'Mebbe the Lord's too busy admiring my fine bonnet to notice the vain thoughts underneath it.'

If the Lord did admire the hat He wasn't the only one. Within a short time quite a number of the townswomen, including Mistress MacLeod, wife of one of the town's councillors, had asked Mary to make bonnets for them, and the little spare time she had was spent surrounded by ribbons and lace.

One day she came back from delivering a bonnet to Mistress MacLeod with shining eyes and an extra bounce to her light step.

'Meg, it's the grandest place I've ever been in – we sat in the parlour, but she calls it a withdrawing room, and the maid served tea just as if we were two ladies visiting! And I'm to make another bonnet for her!'

She seized Meg's hands and whirled her round. 'And she's going to pay me more money than I would have asked for myself!'

It was fortunate that Meg was back to her former energetic self, for Mary became too busy to give much time to the shop. The kitchen was a riot of colour as she stitched away at her bonnets by day with the children, festooned in ribbons, playing happily beside her. At night, when Duncan and Meg needed the peace of their own fireside, Mary worked in her tiny room.

When the time came for her to return to Beith, she announced that she had decided to settle in Paisley.

'But—' Meg looked helplessly at Duncan. The

house behind the shop was already crowded and Mary's millinery was taking up more room than they could afford.

Mary's sharp eyes saw the look. 'You've nothing to worry about. I'm going to set up a wee shop at the Sneddon and live on the premises. It's all arranged between Mistress MacLeod and me,' she swept on as Meg opened her mouth to protest. 'We talked about it today, when I delivered her new bonnet. I'm to be a milliner!'

'Hold on there, Mary—' Duncan finally made himself heard. 'It's all very well talking of wee shops, but where d'you expect to find the money for all this?'

She gave him a withering look. 'D'you think I haven't thought of all that? Mistress MacLeod's going to pay the rent of the place, and pay me to work for her. And I'll see she gets her money back as soon as I can give it to her. The woman's got more money than she knows what to do with, and it'll pleasure her to help me. At least she'll not be throwing her silver away.'

'What about the farm?' Visions of angry parents swooping down on her and accusing her of tempting Mary away from her proper place in life floated before Meg's eyes.

'I'll see to that – and I'm not going back, whatever they say!' Mary tossed her sleek dark head. 'I was never afraid of hard work, but I'd as soon be doing something I want to do. And I know now that it's got nothing to do with farm work!'

There was no arguing with her. Mary had found her vocation in life, and within the next few weeks she had scrubbed out the Sneddon shop and the rooms behind it, and had settled in. From then on she was often to be seen tripping about the town with a box in each hand, delivering wares to her customers. Almost every time Meg called in at the shop there was a carriage waiting at the door. Mary, like Meg, was a born businesswoman, and her shop thrived.

'That sister of yours has a good head on her shoulders,' Kirsty approved when she and Meg were spinning thread together.

Meg sighed. 'I suppose she's right when she says farm life's not for her. But I wish she would take a husband.'

Kirsty snorted with laughter. 'Why should she? She's managing fine on her own. It was a good day for Paisley when the Montgomerys arrived, Meg. There's you seeing to Colin's shop for him, and Mary doing the same for Mistress MacLeod. And Duncan's the best weaver Peter ever employed. You're all making your mark on the place.'

Meg said nothing, but she smiled at the thread smoothly winding itself onto the pirn. She wouldn't have changed places at that moment with the King himself.

Working silently beside her, Kirsty marvelled at her own words. The ugly wound caused by Duncan's affair with Lizzie had healed. She had been right to persuade Peter to keep Duncan and Meg in Paisley.

Colin was content, and nobody could wish that William, a quiet and lovable little boy, had never been born. For his part, Duncan had learned his lesson and would never stray again, she was sure of that.

'It's an ill wind—' Kirsty thought to herself with a trace of justified smugness as she added another loaded pirn to the old top hat by her side.

PART TWO

Chapter One

T HE GROCER'S SHOP IN NEW Street was Margaret
Montgomery's whole world, and she loved it.
True, there was more world outside its doors –
narrow muddy streets, carriages and horses and
people, rutted footpaths to walk on, houses leaning
above her in friendly curiosity, the weaving shop
where her father worked – but the grocery was the
main part of her existence.

She loved the thick dusty smell of meal, the way
the rough sacks tickled her palms, the exciting
sensation of grain shifting and yet resisting when
she punched the sacks with small knotted fists.
She loved the counter, though at five years old
she was still too small to see over it and all
she knew of it was the feel of its flat surface
beneath her fingers and the sight of raw grained
wood at eye-level. She loved the way her mother's voice changed from loving or irritable to
brisk and efficient when she was waiting on
customers.

Everyone came into the shop, thus proving what
Margaret already knew – that it was the hub of the

town. So she loved the customers too, because the shop gave them a reason to exist.

With the open-hearted trust of one who had never been betrayed she loved the ladies with their rustly clothes, the housewives with their ready laughter, the deep voiced, snuff-buying men, the children struggling with large unwieldy baskets and reciting sing-song lists dinned into their heads by busy mothers. She even loved old Mister Lyle and his dog – and not many people loved them. They both smelled, and she had heard people calling Mister Lyle an old rascal, no better than he should be. Whenever he came in for his groceries Margaret deserted her post by her mother and slipped out to stroke the dog, waiting patiently by the door for its master.

When Mister Lyle came out he smiled at her and patted her on the head with a dirty hand. A lot of people would have found the smile terrifying, a drawing back of cracked lips to reveal gums and a few black teeth, but Margaret saw only its gentleness and its friendship. Then Mister Lyle would go off down the street, his dog at his heels, the two of them old and stiff and unloved by anyone else but Margaret.

Her capacity for affection was vast. It even included her brothers, though Thomas, still a baby, could be a great trial and Robert bullied her if she gave him the chance.

There were times when she could do nothing with Robert. Today was one of those times, she realised wretchedly as he dragged her along the crowded High Street, ignoring her pleas.

'I want to go home!' she repeated again and again, each time raising her voice a little more. But there was such a crush and noise about them that her voice made little impact. She had never known the street to be so busy, and the forest of legs and skirts she was being towed through unnerved her. She dragged back, but Robert merely tightened his grip on her hand and forged ahead, towing her behind him.

Margaret hadn't wanted to go out that day; she had burrowed into her mother's skirts and whined to stay in the shop, but Meg had pushed her at Robert and ordered her in a new, sharp voice to stop being a nuisance and do as she was told.

'You're supposed to be taking me to Aunt Kirsty's house!' Margaret pointed out, but Robert only jerked harder on her hand and she yelped with fright as she almost lost her footing.

William Todd, on her other side, steadied her.

'It's all right, Margaret, I'll look after you,' he whispered, and she squeezed his fingers in gratitude. William wasn't like Robert or Jamie – he was kind, and she felt safe with him. She often wished that grey-eyed, brown-haired William was her brother.

'Come on!' Robert's face glowed with excitement and he plunged into the thick of the crowd, dragging poor Margaret along.

The atmosphere reminded her of the Fair days,

though this wasn't one. Voices clanged in her ear or whizzed past and vanished, leaving half-finished, confusing sentences for her to puzzle over.

'Going to the hanging – the hanging – hanging—' The word was on everyone's lips. She had heard her parents mention it that very morning.

'Today's the hanging,' her father had said and Margaret, supposedly asleep in the truckle bed which by day was pushed beneath her parents' big bed, opened one eye to see him put an arm about her mother.

'Don't cry, Meg – there's nothing you or me can do about it.'

'But, Duncan, he's an old man! And all he did was take some kail from someone's garden—'

'It wasn't his only theft – or his first. You know that, Meg.'

'But he doesn't deserve—' Her mother pressed the back of a hand against her lips to stop the words.

'Why don't you close the shop for once and take the children to the braes for the morning?'

'No!' Her mother's voice was unusually sharp. 'The shop'll be open – though no doubt most of the customers'll be off for some entertainment instead of going about their lawful business!'

Then they had seen that she was awake, and had said no more. She and Robert were hurried through their breakfast and bundled out of the shop with orders to go round to Aunt Kirsty's at once. Instead they had met up with Jamie and William and now, like it or not, Margaret was on her way to the Cross with most of Paisley's population.

Jamie's red head acted like a beacon ahead of them, but they didn't catch up with him until they had reached the site near the river where the stalls were set up on market days. He and Robert burrowed their way to the front of the mob with Margaret and William following.

Margaret felt a little better when she found herself at the edge of a big open space with the bulk of the people behind her. Now the only legs in front belonged to the militia lining the open area. Beyond them stood a queer wooden arrangement of ladders and platforms that she didn't recall ever seeing before. She was trying to puzzle out what it could be when a cart was driven into the empty square, and an expectant sigh rustled through the crowd. The cart drew up before the wooden structure and a group of men clambered out.

Margaret eyed them idly, then her attention was caught by the figure in the middle. She tugged at Robert's sleeve.

'It's old Mister Lyle. What's wrong, Robert? Is he ailing?'

Mister Lyle was being helped along by two of the men. His old legs seemed to have lost their strength, and he lurched against his helpers, almost falling twice. He was escorted to the wooden contraption then the men began to help him up a ladder.

'Robert, why are his hands tied? Is it a game?'

Ignored by the three boys, Margaret ducked down to peer between the legs of the soldier standing directly before her. While the crowd buzzed with anticipation, the old man was heaved onto a small platform. A plump man in a long black coat was hoisted up the steps in his turn, but with his hands free, then he began to talk long and earnestly to Mister Lyle, as though scolding him. The old man stood abjectly before him, a pathetic, defeated figure.

Something grimly purposeful about the rest of the men on the platform, something helpless and shrunken about Mister Lyle's stance, struck an uneasy chord in Margaret's mind. She reached out to William, her only ally.

'I want to get out of this place! I want to go home!'

But the crowd's excitement gripped William fast now. He spoke hurriedly, without taking his eyes from the scene before him. 'Ssshhh, Margaret, we'll go home in a minute—'

Fear began to whisper in her ear. She closed her eyes then opened them again as the rumble of a drum cut across the babble of voices behind her.

The man in the long black coat had stopped talking to Mister Lyle and had stepped back. Then someone else looped a rope about the old man's neck. Completely bewildered, Margaret craned her own neck to see what happened next.

To her horror the platform beneath Mister Lyle's feet broke and he dropped through the hole, to be caught before he touched the ground by the rope about his throat.

His legs kicked and he swung to and fro like a doll. The crowd hushed for a second, then moaned, a sound that reached eerily to the sky. But nobody went to help Mister Lyle. Appalled, Margaret watched him swinging, kicking, choking – while the militia, the crowd, and everyone on the platform just stood and watched. Her hands went up to her own chubby neck in an instinctive effort to relieve the hempen grip on the old man's windpipe. His body swung right round then lost momentum as the legs stopped kicking.

Margaret, too, spun round, gripped by unspeakable horror, searching the faces behind and above her for some sign of compassion. But they all bore a look of rapt fascination, like babies watching a toy dangle before their eyes.

'Robert—' She tugged frantically at her brother's sleeve. 'Robert, what's happening to Mister Lyle?'

He watched the old man's last gyrations on the end of the rope. 'He's hanging, Margaret.' His voice was filled with awe. 'He was a bad man.'

'He wasn't!'

'He was so!' Jamie Todd interrupted her sharply. 'That's why he had to be hanged. He was a bad man – and now he's dead!' There was no mistaking the satisfaction in his voice.

'Dead?' Margaret whirled back to the scene in the middle of the empty square. She suddenly realised that Mister Lyle would never again walk on the ground that lay a tantalisingly short distance below his shabby boots. He would never come into the shop again, never pat her head or walk along a footpath with his old dog again. The enormity of it descended on her like a threatening cloud. She felt a sudden terrible need to get home to her mother—

Her dash for freedom brought her up against one of the soldiers lining the square. The man, almost thrown to the ground by the impact of her sturdy little body against the backs of his knees, caught her shoulder.

'Lassie, what are you doing in a place like this? Someone take the bairn away!' he appealed to the crowd. Margaret, seeing his tall uniformed figure stooping over her, feeling his hand on her arm, took his interest as a sign that she was to be the next victim.

'I'm not bad – I'm not for hanging!' she shrieked with the full power of her lungs, and flailed her arms until she managed to wriggle free. Then she eeled round and dived into the crowd before any of the boys could catch her.

Screaming for her mother she fought her way along, bumping painfully into knees, tripping over feet, half mad with terror and convinced that at any minute a rope would slip about her neck.

When the ground dropped away and left her feet kicking in mid-air as Mister Lyle's had done she shut her eyes tight and redoubled her screams.

'Here, here, lassie, no need to take on like that.'

Billy Carmichael the chapman wrapped his arms about her to still her struggles. 'It's Margaret Montgomery, isn't it?'

Margaret refused to open her eyes. 'They gave Mister Lyle a hanging and I don't want one!' she bawled, kicking and punching at the hands holding her. Then she felt herself carried swiftly along while a deep warm voice rumbled overhead.

'Nobody's going to hurt you, lassie. See, I'm taking you home. You mind me, don't you? Say hello to me like a good wee girl—'

When she finally prised her eyelids open and recognised him she threw her arms about his neck and demanded loudly to be taken to her mother at once.

'We're going, lass, we're going, for this is no place for you. I'd just be grateful if you'd neither smother nor deafen me on the way,' Billy said, and fought his way through the people pressing forward for a glimpse of the still figure swinging on the rope.

Margaret quietened down once she realised that they were leaving the crowd behind and heading for home, but at the sight of her mother and Mary in the shop her terror and outrage returned in a fresh well of tears.

Meg sank down in a chair, clutching her weeping daughter, while Billy explained.

'The hanging? Oh, my poor wee lamb! And I thought they were safe at Kirsty's. Wait till I get a hold of Robert—!'

'And Mister Lyle's hands were t – tied and he fell and no – nobody would help him,' Margaret roared. 'And Robert said he'd been b – bad and it was a hanging, then the soldiers took me for the hanging t – t – too—'

'See now, Margaret, wee lassies don't get hanged.' Mary's practical voice broke through the noise. 'They might get smacked if they need it but they never get hanged. The soldiers wouldn't do a thing like that to anybody.'

Margaret raised her swollen red face from her mother's shoulder.

'They gave Mister Lyle a hanging,' she retorted with as much sharpness as her aunt. 'And he's dead!'

'Aye – well, I'll grant you that, since there's no sense in denying it. Now listen—' Mary lifted her niece from Meg's lap in time to avert a fresh outbreak of sobbing and stood her on the floor, kneeling to wipe Margaret's streaming eyes and nose. 'I'm going to wash your face and then we're going to deliver a new hat to Mistress Black's house. Would you like that?'

Margaret nodded, her body still racked by great tearing sobs.

'But you'll have to stop crying first. Mistress Black'll mebbe have a nice bit cake for you if you're a good girl.'

The sobs were replaced, after a massive effort on Margaret's part, by sniffs and hiccups.

'There's my brave lassie,' Mary said briskly.

'Now come with me and we'll clean your wee face.'

Five minutes later, soothed and washed and brushed, Margaret waited for Mary, one thumb jammed comfortingly into her mouth, the other hand stroking the familiar grain of the shop counter. Billy's voice washed over her as he talked to her mother and helped himself to snuff from the big jar that was always kept on the counter-top.

She felt as though she had had a terrible nightmare and had wakened to find herself safely tucked up in her warm, soft bed. Idly she watched the light catch the thick bottom of the snuff jar as it was lifted up.

Then the jar thudded onto its accustomed place again and Billy's large hand with its square-cut nails rested on the scarred wood, just level with her eyes as she stood on tiptoe, her nose pressed against the edge of the counter.

The significance of what she had just witnessed burst on Margaret in a shower of stars. She stood gaping, open-mouthed, then let out a delighted roar. Meg swung round, startled, and Billy inhaled snuff the wrong way and exploded into a huge sneeze. Mary, emerging from the room behind the shop, stopped short with one hand half in and half out of its glove.

Margaret stood behind the counter, her hands white-knuckled on its edge, her blue eyes wide as they peeped over the top.

'I can see!' she crowed. 'I'm not a wee bairn any longer – I can see over the counter!'

'Did you ever see such a change in a lassie? She's forgotten the hanging already,' Meg said with relief when her daughter had skipped out of the shop with Mary.

'Aye.' Billy had his doubts about that, but he didn't voice them. 'You've got a bonny family.'

'Come early tonight and see them all before they go to their beds.' She knew how much children meant to Billy. A big, easy-going man, he had been a cobbler before his wife and three young children were struck down by fever.

Left alone, he had taken to the roads, joining the band of men who peddled their wares from town to town.

'I'd like that. I hear there's been changes in the town since I was last here.'

'Aye.' She folded her hands over her apron, soothed by the everyday comfort of a wee gossip. 'There's always something going on. The new Grammar School's open now, and the flesh market in Moss Row too.'

'And the Council's put a tax on beer and ale, I hear. Bad news travels,' he said wryly.

'The money's needed to deepen the river and put up more new houses, so Peter says.' Meg spoke with all the earnestness and pride of a true citizen. 'You'll have heard that they've made Peter one of the directors of the new Town Hospital? Kirsty says he's hardly ever at home these days. And Colin's as cheery as ever I've seen him.'

Billy's head came up quickly at mention of Colin. 'I heard news of Lizzie Todd last month, up by Dundee,' he said, and a cold hand clutched at Meg's heart.

'What of her?'

'She was living near there with that man of hers until recently. Things haven't been going well for them.'

'She's only got herself to blame!' After more than five years Meg still couldn't think of Lizzie without deep uneasiness. 'You'll not tell Colin?'

The big man shook his greying head. 'It's best left unsaid.'

'Aye.' Meg took up a cloth and rubbed the spotless counter hard. 'That's all over and done with. Best forgotten.'

The town dismissed old Robert Lyle from its memory almost as soon as Jamie, William and Robert stopped smarting from the punishment they received for going to the public execution. Margaret's pain was buried deep, and everyone thought it, too, had been forgotten, although she had bad dreams for the next six months or so.

Winter closed in and Duncan, now Peter's right-hand man, had extra work to handle when his employer took to his bed with a heavy cold that refused to go, but lay on his chest for weeks.

'You might as well admit it, man – the fluff's

got into your lungs. Either that or it's all these meetings you have to attend,' Kirsty hectored. 'I told you, did I not, that you should have stayed home and looked after that bad cough when it started instead of going out till all hours in the chill air. Remember, you're not as young as you used to be.'

'Away with you, woman!' Peter scoffed. But he couldn't disguise the fact that the illness had left him breathless and unable to climb stairs easily.

The cold weather at the end of 1755 took its toll of young and old alike. One of its most disreputable victims, an inmate of the new Poor's Hospital, went carousing in a bothy with cronies one January night then stumbled homewards in a blizzard. He was found the next morning, frozen to death yards from the hospital door.

Mary's benefactress, Mistress MacLeod, succumbed to a severe chill brought on by a charitable visit to the Hospital on a cold wet day.

'She should never have gone out – and her with a cough that's said to have drowned out half the High Church service two days before,' said Mary sadly to Meg.

'What'll become of your wee shop now?' Meg trailed covetous fingers over a fanciful creation on Mary's counter.

'Nothing, for I've already repaid a fair piece of the money to Mistress MacLeod.' Mary looked about her little shop. 'I called on Mister MacLeod to pay my respects, of course, and while I was there we had a wee talk about the rest of it. He's content to take the payments month by month, just as it was when his wife was alive.' Mary's fingers flew among ribbons as she worked on another hat. 'Poor man, he's bad with the rheumatism, and only a parcel of servants to see to him in that big house. He'll miss his wife sorely. I don't know why it's the best of us that get taken every time.'

Spring came at last, and brought with it the realisation of a dream for Meg and Duncan. By the time May brought warm sunny days to replace April's showers, plans for their new house at Townhead had been drawn up, and the house itself was finished in the early spring of 1756.

After the workmen had downed tools for the last time, toasted a job well done, and departed, Meg ran from room to room gazing out of the small windows, peering up chimneys, opening and shutting doors. The children clattered noisily about and Duncan basked in the glow felt by a man of property.

'I told you we'd do it one day, lass.' He caught Meg's hand and drew her to him when they found themselves alone in the kitchen, across the passageway from the loom-shop.

She beamed up at him through tears. 'I never doubted you.'

The memory of a woman with slanted grey eyes came fleetingly to Duncan but he pushed it away.

'I'll not have my own looms yet, of course. But the shop's here and the looms'll come in good time.'

Meg slipped her hand into his and they stood dreaming for a moment before she shook herself and said briskly, 'Time to get back to the shop.'

'Janet can manage fine without you.'

'I'm not so sure, now that new weaver of yours has put stars in her eyes. Young folk in love can be right stupid at times,' Meg shook her head primly, then blushed like a girl when Duncan laughed.

'You're right there. I mind as if it was yesterday the time you got into trouble with your mother for dropping a basket of new collected eggs – all because you saw me passing by in the road!'

'Mary, you can't!' Meg stopped sweeping the hearth and stared up at her sister, her eyes wide with shock.

'And what's the "can't" for, Meg Montgomery? Just because you didn't have a hand in arranging the match, does it follow that I'm not allowed to get wed?'

'But – Mister MacLeod! Mary, he's an old man! Besides—' she floundered, seeking words to express her dismay, 'his wife's not that long in her grave!'

Mary sighed and began to remove her gloves.

'The man's been widowed for more than eighteen months – and he's crippled with the rheumatism and scarcely able to move out of his house half the time. And here's me, back and forth between my shop and his house this past year and more, trying to see to him – for what good are servants when a man's ailing? It's the wisest thing to marry him, then I can see to him properly and save my legs a lot of running.'

'Have you accepted him, then?'

Mary stared. 'What do you mean, accepted him? There was no accepting about it. I just told him plump and plain – if you've any sense in your head, I said, you'll marry me and save me all this to-ing and fro-ing.'

Meg's apron was thrown over her horrified face. 'Have you no shame in you at all? You mean that you proposed marriage to a gentleman twice your age and as rich as a lord? D'you know what they'll be saying about you in the streets?'

'They can say all they like and it'll not stick in my throat,' her sister said calmly. 'His age doesn't come into it, and neither does his money. If he didn't have it he'd be welcome to come and live in my wee room behind the shop. As it is, I'll move into his house and have more room for my work. And don't start that again,' she added ominously as choking sounds came from beneath the apron. 'I'll keep my shop and my independence. Nobody'll be able to say I married Andra MacLeod so that I could be a lady of leisure. Indeed, it's going to be hard work seeing to it that those lazy servants of his earn their keep for a change.'

Meg's flushed face appeared for a moment round the apron.

'D'you want to shame me entirely in this town?' she squawked. 'Rich men's wives don't keep shops!'

'This one will – for no doubt I'll outlive Andra, poor old soul, and I'll need something to keep me occupied in my own old age.'

'Would you not have a word with Duncan first?' Meg appealed.

'What has it to do with him? No, no, Meg, it's all arranged, and a date set. Not that the minister was entirely happy at first, but I soon pointed out that it was a Christian thing I was doing, and he agreed with me – eventually.'

Mary got to her feet. 'And next week I'm taking Andra down to Beith to tell my mother and father.'

'I forgot about them!' Meg moaned. 'Oh, Mary, what are they going to say?'

'Leave them to me. I don't think they'll make half the fuss you have. Anyone would think I was disgracing you, Meg Montgomery. Take my advice and pay no heed to wagging tongues – or tell them to come and wag at me. I'll soon sort them out.' Mary looked round the cosy kitchen as she drew her gloves on again. 'It seems to me, Meg, that the two of us have come a long way since we used to tread the blankets together down on the farm.'

'Mary, are you sure that you're—'

'You'd best see to Thomas,' Mary said from the window. 'The wee scamp's asking to get himself stung, plunging round the bee-skeps waving a stick.' And she escaped in the ensuing domestic panic.

'You're talking as if Mary's going to bring disgrace on us, instead of marrying with one of the most respected men in Paisley,' Duncan argued when he came home that night to be met by an agitated wife.

'But the scandal—!' Meg almost wept.

'Tuts, woman, we both know well enough that she's not after the man for his money, so what does it matter what anyone else says? Even if she was, she's earned it, the way she's tended him since his wife died. There'll be no more weeping over Mary's plans in my house,' he ended firmly, and Meg had to leave matters at that.

Mary married her elderly husband in the Laigh Church, with a gathering in Andrew MacLeod's house afterwards. Andrew was a tall, lean man, stooped and twisted by rheumatism, but retaining some of the good looks he had once had. Quiet and shy, he obviously doted on his vigorous new wife. His home was a big two-storey building on the hill behind the High Street, looking down on the ruined Abbey with the River Cart slipping beneath its walls.

Mary, taking on the role of mistress of the house as though born to it, sat in the parlour dispensing tea for the ladies and something stronger for the men, and supervising the servants with an ease that made Meg and her mother gasp.

The children were less intimidated by the place than their elders, and explored enthusiastically. Margaret's eyes were round when she returned to her mother.

'It's a castle! How many folk live in it?'

'Just Mister—' Meg stopped, blushed, tried again. 'Your new Uncle Andra and your Aunt Mary and the folk who look after them.'

'But this house is too big for them!' Margaret was outraged. 'Half our street could live in it. Why do they need so many rooms?'

Meg hushed her, glancing guiltily round the room. 'Uncle Andra's got a lot of money, so he can afford a big house. Stop your questions, for any favour!'

'But why should rich folk have houses that are too big for them, when—'

'They just do!' She re-fastened Margaret's jacket and tidied her hair. 'Run and find the boys, there's a good lass.'

Margaret did as she was told, but as she scurried along the big dark hall, hung with paintings, a rebellious inner voice that was to be heard many times during her life continued to ask, 'Why should the rich have so much space when the poor have to crowd together in hovels?'

Chapter Two

MARY TURNED HER PREDECESSOR'S SEWING room into a workshop, took on an assistant, and was a devoted wife to Andrew MacLeod. The fact that she now met most of her wealthier customers on a social basis in the evenings made no difference to her business dealings with them during the day.

'But I'll admit, Meg,' she confessed with a dimpling smile, 'that I have a wee chuckle to myself when I go to one of those grand gatherings and see that most of the bonnets in the room were made by my own fingers.'

She also took on the charitable duties expected of the more well-to-do women in the town, fitting them into an over-crowded day without visible effort. The gossips who had predicted that she would play the fine lady and not bother with anything else soon found themselves proved wrong. Busy as she was, Mary involved herself just as much as ever in other people's lives.

It was she who found a replacement for Janet when the girl married a local stonemason and gave up her work in the shop. Mary promptly produced a capable widow with a family to support and talked Colin and Meg into taking the woman on as a shop assistant and letting her have the empty rooms behind the grocer's shop. Then she organised the task of converting the rooms, now used for storage, back into a home.

She swept into the shop dressed in practical working clothes and festooned with cloths and pails. Robert and Thomas, who were unfortunate enough to be there at the time, were despatched to fetch water.

'And go right to the well, d'you hear me? You needn't think you'll take the lazy way out and climb the wall to get to Mistress Pearson's well.'

She handed them each a stoup to carry the water in. 'That bad-tempered old devil of a man of hers can still run, and he'll keep these if he gets the chance. Now then, Meg, tuck your skirts up out of harm's way, for we've a lot of scrubbing to do.'

'It's a bad deed that benefits nobody,' she added as she set to and scrubbed until drops of water flew from her brush. 'You'll not regret taking the widow-woman on, for she's a hard worker and an honest soul. But I think Janet's made a mistake. That new husband of hers is a shiftless creature that broke his first wife's heart.'

Meg sat back on her heels and nodded, brushing a tendril of hair back from her face with one wet fist. 'For once I agree with you.'

'Just because her sweetheart jilted her,' Mary

puffed, 'If you ask me she's gone out and thrown herself at the first man she saw to prove to us all that she doesn't care. I don't know why women have to be so set on marriage! And if you say one word about me proposing to Andra, Meg, I'll empty this bucket of water about your ears, for that's not the same thing at all!'

As time passed it became clear that Peter's bronchitis had become chronic. Duncan took on most of the responsibility for the loom-shop though Peter kept an eye on everything from his big armchair by the kitchen fire.

Duncan was soon trying to persuade him to let one of the looms go over to the manufacture of silk gauze, a new material that was selling well in London. Some of the town's manufacturers were trying it out on their looms, and Duncan saw it as part of Paisley's future.

'Linen isn't going to keep us going for ever,' he argued. 'The town's growing – we need to try new ideas if we want to grow along with it.'

'He's right.' Colin nodded, fingering the sample Duncan had brought in. 'This is a cloth the gentry'll want to buy, father. The weaving trade can't afford to stand still.'

'Humphrey Fulton's contracting weavers to make it for him.' Duncan was referring to another man from Beith, who had become a successful manufacturer. 'He sees a good market for it –

and he knows what he's about. We have to keep up with the times, Peter!'

'Ach, you're new-fangled, both of you,' Peter grumbled, but his eyes were shrewd as he in turn took the material, rubbing it through his fingers. 'Well, go ahead – but if it doesn't pay its way it comes off my loom, mind!'

'Aye, aye, I hear you,' Duncan agreed cheerfully, and went on to prove that silk gauze was a paying innovation.

The restlessness that had led him into the affair with Lizzie was channelled into his work and his plans for the future. He was a man of property, mellowed and content with his life. He rarely thought of Lizzie now; Duncan was one of those people with a talent for closing their minds against memories that shamed or angered them. Not even the sight of William reminded him of that dark secret in his past. The boy and Colin were devoted to each other, and Duncan always thought of the youngster as Colin's son.

When he was summoned to Mary's shop late one afternoon it didn't occur to him that there might be something wrong. He hovered in the doorway, waiting until her customer had gone, uneasy in this feminine haven. When the woman left, he stepped out into the street to let her by, and re-entered the doorway to see his sister-in-law whisk a cloak about her shoulders.

'I'll not be long,' she told her assistant, and hurried Duncan back onto the footpath.

'What fine new idea have you got in your head now?' he asked indulgently.

'None, as yet – but I wish I had, for it's going to take brains to get us out of this pickle,' Mary said crisply. 'I was at the Poor's Hospital two hours since, and I met a woman there who claims to be Colin Todd's wife.'

'Lizzie?' Duncan stopped short and she almost bumped into him. A hand caught at his heart and began to squeeze it painfully. He felt the colour ebb from his face. 'You're certain?'

Irritation touched her voice. 'I spoke to her. She told me enough to make me believe her, for all that I've never set eyes on the woman myself. In fact, she told me more than I'd like my poor sister to hear, Duncan Montgomery!'

A red mist clouded Duncan's vision and he wondered if he was going to succumb to apoplexy. 'Oh God! Dear God!'

'Well might you call on Him for help – though I doubt if it'll do you a lot of good.' His sister-in-law's eyes raked his face. 'No need to ask if she was telling the truth or just trying to make mischief between you and Meg. The guilt's written on your face for anyone to see. Duncan, Duncan – who'd have ever thought you'd be such a fool!'

'What does she want?' he asked, sick with apprehension, his thoughts filled with Meg and the need to keep this from her.

'She has it in mind to take back her old position as Colin's wife. She arrived late last night, it seems, with nothing but the rags on her back. She's in a sorry state. Lucky for you she went to the Hospital instead of going straight to Peter's house.' Mary wagged her bonneted head. 'A right hornet's nest she'll stir up if she gets her way. But I got her to promise that she'd stay where she was for the moment – if I bring you to see her.'

'The bitch!'

'I told her that Peter's ailing and the shock of seeing her's like to kill him. I said nothing more. Not a word about Colin or the laddie. Not that she asked about them – just about you. I don't care how you do it, Duncan, but you'll have to get that woman away from Paisley before Colin finds out about her.'

The Poor's Hospital was a large building not far from Mary's shop. Homeless and penniless towns-folk found refuge within its walls; the children were schooled, the women set to wash and cook and keep the place clean, and work was found for the men and the older children whenever possible. Duncan shivered as he followed Mary through its big doors and across the hall, past faces blank with misery and despair.

The Mistress greeted them in a small bare room on the ground floor. She raised an eyebrow when Mary asked to see Lizzie, but said nothing. Fortunately, she was a comparative stranger in the town, and it didn't occur to her to connect the new inmate, who gave her name as Lizzie Todd, with the prosperous and respectable Paisley family of that name.

Duncan paced the small room, four steps one way, four steps the other, while he waited. He had thought that Lizzie was out of his life for ever, had never dreamed that after all this time she would return to haunt him like a malignant ghost.

Mary sat motionless on a hard upright chair, watching him but keeping her own council.

'You're thinking of the terrible thing I did, betraying Meg,' he blurted out at last.

'Men can do awful daft things. I take it that she never knew the truth of it?'

He shook his head. 'And she never will, supposing I've to—' He broke off as the door opened, the colour leaving his face then rushing back as he stared at the woman standing before him.

Lizzie came into the room slowly, eyes downcast and hands clasped in the same pose she used to adopt when standing behind the shop counter. Then she looked up and he saw that her once pretty face was gaunt, her hair lifeless and threaded with grey, her slanted eyes set deep in shadowy sockets. She was a cruel parody of the girl who had lain beneath him among the little white flowers on the moors. But her boldness, as she looked him up and down, was unchanged.

'Well, Duncan Montgomery? You're a welcome sight.'

'It's you right enough, Lizzie. I never thought to set eyes on you again.'

'Oh? So it was good riddance to bad rubbish, was it?' Her laugh was harsh, mocking. 'Are you not glad to see me after all those years?'

'I never wished to look on you again, Lizzie – and well you know it!'

'Mebbe – and mebbe not.' She twitched a shoulder in a faintly coquettish gesture he remembered. It was as though some ragged crone was slavishly copying the mannerisms that had belonged to the young, vivid Lizzie. It was grotesque, and Duncan's skin crawled.

'I hear Peter's unwell.' Neither of them paid any attention to Mary, who stayed where she was, silent for once, watching this reunion of former lovers with bright, unblinking eyes.

'He is, and you'll do him no good at all by turning up again. Besides, Kirsty would scratch your eyes out of your head for what you did to Colin and the bairn.'

Her tongue flickered over cracked lips. 'I'm still Colin's wife.'

'Stay away from him, Lizzie! He's happy now – he's more of a man than you ever let him be!'

'Since he's become a man, let him speak for himself!' she flared at him. 'And there's my son. I have a right to see him, have I not?'

A churning, sick feeling stirred in Duncan's belly. 'You cared nothing for him when he was little and helpless. Why should you see him now?'

'Because he's nearing an age when he can go out and work for his own keep.' Mary spoke for the first time, and Lizzie whirled on her with a movement full of grace despite the rags she wore.

'I have the right to take him away with me if I choose!'

'You have no rights!' Duncan's voice was a low hiss. 'Colin raised that boy, not you. He's the one to say what becomes of William.'

Lizzie's teeth, discoloured and broken, showed in a sneer. 'So he thinks. Mebbe it's time he learned that it's you and me that have the say in the lad's future, not him. After all, it was you and me that made William, Duncan!'

Her shoulders were brittle beneath his hands. Even in his anger he was careful not to grip her too tightly, aware that he could so easily crush and snap those fragile bones beneath his fingers. Instead, he shook her hard.

'You ever say that again to a living soul, and by God, Lizzie Todd, I'll spill your blood! If you try to see Peter or Colin or the boy, I'll take you out onto the moors where it all started and wring your neck! Who's to care if you're found lying in a burn one morning?'

She swayed within his grip, her eyes wide and bright, her open mouth uttering little whimpering sounds. But she didn't try to break his hold on her. It was Mary who caught at his wrists and tore him away from the other woman.

'For any favour, Duncan, d'you want to get yourself hanged?'

He let go and Lizzie almost fell. She recovered her balance by catching at the back of a chair, the faint little enigmatic smile he remembered playing round her thin mouth.

At the sight of it, and the gleam in her knowing grey eyes, despair choked Duncan. She had won. Now he must pay for the years of foolish complacency. If the two women hadn't been there he might have sunk down on the floor and given way to tears.

'Why don't you go ahead, Duncan?' Lizzie asked, her voice suddenly young and sensuous, with a provocative lilt to it. 'Why don't you put me out of my misery and get yourself hanged? I'm not the only one who betrayed folk, am I? You're no better than I am, if the truth be known!'

'God damn you, Lizzie Todd!'

'He's done that already.'

'Lizzie, what would you take to keep your mouth shut and leave Paisley?' Mary asked briskly, and the other woman laughed.

'You'll not get me away as easy as that. If it was money I wanted, d'you not think I'd have asked for it long since?' Lizzie mocked. 'It's been a long lonely road for me. I want companionship. I want to be cared for. I want Colin – or the boy – or you, Duncan. It's up to you to decide which it's to be.'

If Mary hadn't stood her ground between them

he would have killed Lizzie there and then and be damned to the consequences. Instead, he stood helplessly by, fists knotting and unknotting, while Mary forced a reluctant promise from Lizzie to keep her mouth shut and stay where she was until the next morning. Then Duncan was hustled out into the street where he gulped the fresh evening air in.

'She's safe until the morning, and we've got time to think about what's to be done. Say nothing and do nothing until you see me again,' Mary ordered. 'There has to be a way out of this without breaking innocent hearts.'

'You heard her – you saw her! The woman's evil! She's hell bent on destroying lives the way hers has been destroyed.' He ran a big hand over his face. 'I'll have to go with her, out of the town, then—'

'Leave her body in a ditch and end up swinging from a rope? You've not got the sense to escape a hanging,' his sister-in-law said scathingly. 'Listen to me – I'll visit the woman again first thing in the morning, and it's my guess that by then she'll be willing to take enough money to keep her for a while and get out of the town. Away home, Duncan Montgomery, and not a word of this to Meg. Come along to the shop first thing tomorrow and we'll see what can be done. Go on, now!'

He went, shambling along the street instead of walking with his usual confident gait. Watching him, Mary sighed and shook her head.

* * *

Duncan couldn't face Meg right away. He wandered into a howff near the Cross and sat alone in a corner with only a jug of ale for company. By the time he was accosted by a well-known voice the level of the jug had lowered considerably and he was finding it hard to focus. He peered blearily up at Matt Todd through the howff's smoky atmosphere.

The soldier lowered his big frame onto a stool at the other side of the table. 'Everyone's round at our house having a grand wee gathering. I told Meg I'd look for you.' He winked. 'She's none too pleased because you never came home from your loom.'

Duncan tried to say something but the words came out as a slurred mumble.

'By God, she'll have something to say when she sees you like this—' Then Matt took a closer look and his expression changed. 'Come to think of it, I've never seen you in such a state myself. What's amiss, man?'

Duncan couldn't keep his misery and worry to himself for a moment longer. His tongue seemed to start wagging of its own accord while one part of his brain, the sober part, stood by, unable to stop the flow of words.

As Matt heard him out one expression after another moved across his face, but Duncan was too steeped in his own misery to notice the other's reaction.

'What in God's name am I to do?' he finished wretchedly. 'How am I to tell Meg?'

'Listen to me—' Matt leaned across the table, his voice low and urgent. 'You're in no fit state to do anything tonight. Go on home and I'll see to Lizzie for you.'

'But I must tell Meg before—'

'You tell Meg and I swear I'll give you a hiding from one end of the town to the other! Do as Mary says and hold your tongue until you see her tomorrow. Come on, I'll help you on your way.'

Duncan shook his head. 'I can – I can manage to walk to my own door,' he said with dignity, heaving himself to his feet. Then he clutched at the table as his knees sagged.

Matt dragged him upright again and half carried him outside, where the fresh air set Duncan's head reeling. With some difficulty the two of them made their way to Townhead, and Duncan was snoring loudly almost as soon as Matt dropped him into his bed.

The soldier looked down at him thoughtfully. 'Man, Meg'll go berserk when she sees you!' he murmured, then let himself out of the house again.

It was still only mid-evening when he presented himself at the Hospital and asked for Lizzie. When she found him waiting for her in the little ground-floor room she stopped abruptly in the doorway, her Eastern eyes widening.

'So – you're home, are you?'

'Aye. You didn't think to see me, did you, Lizzie?'

113

She smiled faintly. 'No more than you thought to see me. I'm glad you came—' she looked about the room and the smile deepened mockingly '—calling on me.'

'Do you have to stay here?' The place depressed him, made him feel shut in.

'We can go out, unless it shames you to be seen with me.'

He ignored the teasing lilt in her voice. 'I know of a place where we could talk in peace.'

She shrugged, then fetched a worn cloak and they went out into the darkening streets together. Silently he led her to a tenement building by the river and she waited by his side as he paid the landlady for the use of a small room. He left Lizzie there and went out to buy some ale. When he returned she had managed to light the fire and was huddled beside it, fingers spread out to the flames.

'It's cosy in here.' She reached for a mug with a work-roughened hand and drank greedily.

'Duncan tells me you want to see Colin.'

Lizzie tossed her head. 'I'm still his wife.'

'You're no wife to him, for all the church service you went through together. You gave up the right to call yourself wife the day you walked out on him – a helpless cripple! It damned near killed him, do you know that?'

She smiled, her lips wet with ale. 'Did it? So we both nearly killed him, didn't we, Matt?'

The force of the blow threw her off her chair.

She sprawled on the floor, one hand to her face, staring at him. He stood where he was, making no move to help her, and at last she got up and poured out more drink to replace the ale that had spilled.

'D'you think I'm not used to that sort of treatment? It makes no difference, Matt,' she said vindictively. 'You and that horse race took my man from me, and I couldn't settle after that. I'm not the sort of woman who could love a cripple.'

'Because you've never cared about anyone but yourself, you evil bitch!'

Lizzie's eyes flared, then dulled. 'Think that if you want.'

'What else is there to think? First you tried to tempt me, then you fastened on poor Duncan. You'll not cause any more mischief in this town, Lizzie. Leave them alone!'

She laughed, emboldened by the warmth of the drink in her belly. 'What can you do to stop me?'

'You're not dealing with Colin and Duncan now,' he said quietly. 'I'm not a gentleman – so be warned.'

She spat a sulky curse at him, drained the mug and made for the door. He reached it before her.

'Get out of my way, Matt Todd!'

'No, Lizzie!' He grabbed her arm, swung her bodily away from the door and against the damp wall. 'I've had a debt to settle with Colin since the Silver Bells race and now's my chance to pay it. If you try to see him, or get word to him that you're in Paisley, I'll kill you, Lizzie.'

'You're the second to make that threat today.' Her voice was scornful, but a tensing of her body and a sudden heat in her smoky eyes told him that she was keenly aware of his nearness as he held her against the wall.

'I could scream for help.'

It was his turn to mock. 'Lassie, in this building, who'd pay any heed to you? The folk who live here have no wish to call the militiamen's attention to their doings. They know when to turn a deaf ear.'

He was right. In the ramshackle hovels by the river pimps and prostitutes and thieves plied their trades in safety. Nobody would pay attention to a woman's screams, and Lizzie knew it. She let herself go limp and he caught her as she slipped down the wall, holding her to him with an arm about her waist. She tried to push away from him, then suddenly her clawed hands were in his hair, her thin body pressed against him with an animal urgency.

'Matt! Oh, Matt—' she said breathlessly. 'Before Colin, and all the time I was married to him it was you. It was always you I wanted, Matt!'

'Damn you!' said Matt, and released her. She held on fiercely, wrapping her arms about him, pressing herself against him.

'Kill me, if that's what you want to do! Kill me and get it over with! I'd as soon die at your hand as live without you!'

He gripped her arms and she gasped as his fingers bit deep. He looked at the gaunt face just below his, and was suddenly, painfully reminded of the lovely, tantalising girl he had courted long ago, the girl he had left behind when he joined the Army.

There was a tense pause, then 'Will I never be free of you, you Jezebel!' groaned Matt, and dragged her down onto the floor with him.

Their coupling was vicious, an act of hate instead of an act of love. On Lizzie's side there was a deep thirst to be quenched, and revenge for the bitterness of his rejection years before: on Matt's there was all the resentment man had ever felt against woman's ability to tempt and destroy.

Daylight was trying to force its way through the grimy little window before the two of them fell away from each other and slept, exhausted, on the rough wooden planks.

Chapter Three

WHEN LIZZIE OPENED HER EYES the fire was a pile of cooling ashes and Matt was dressing quickly and silently.

'Where are you going?' She raised herself on one elbow, pain stabbing through her bruised body.

'Out of this place.'

'Take me with you—' She began to scramble to her feet. 'I'll follow the regiment – I don't care where – I'd be true to you, Matt, only you—'

But he shook his head vehemently. 'I'd as soon walk with Old Nick himself as with you. And you'd best mind what I told you – keep away from my brother and from the Montgomerys!'

She caught at his sleeve. 'Matt, don't go!'

His face was bleak as he looked down at her. Overnight, new lines had chiselled themselves downwards from the corners of his mouth. 'You wanted me to lie with you when your own man was helpless. You left him and went off with someone else. You're a whore, Lizzie, and last night I used you as a whore. I used you because I wanted to show you what you are. And if you go near Colin or anyone else in Paisley I'll see to it that they all know what happened between us in this room.' There was triumph mingled with contempt in the look he gave her. 'Colin might have taken you back yesterday – but now he'd not dirty his hands on you!'

Without realising what she was doing she reached up with one broken-nailed hand and drew her torn, dirty gown about her throat in a defensive, feminine gesture. 'That's why you brought me here?'

'Just that. D'you think it gave me pleasure to touch you?' he asked bitterly. 'I felt sick! But I had to do it for Colin's sake.'

Her mouth writhed, cursed him, spat on him. He dug into his pocket and tossed some coins on the floor at her feet.

'I'm a generous man – I pay for favours received.'

Silenced, her venom spent for the moment, she gathered the money then straightened again, her eyes fixed on his face. He hesitated at the door, then stripped his jacket off and tossed it at her.

'It's cold outside,' he said, and went out.

The chill morning air struck through Matt's shirt sleeves as he strode away from the building without a backward glance. Deep in his body a familiar pain gnawed. It was a hunger that had wakened in him when he first began walking out with Lizzie all those years ago, a wanting that only her sensuous, insatiable body could ease. But the military way of life had also demanded his attention, and it had won.

During all the time Lizzie was his brother's wife Matt had subdued his desire. Now, when it should have been sated, it burned within him. No other woman had ever been able to rouse him as Lizzie could. Even now, dirty and half-starved as she was, he wanted her. But because she was his brother's wife, and because of what she had done to Colin, he must turn away from her and suffer his own torment in silence.

He hunched his shoulders and walked to his father's house, his eyes fixed on the ground as he went.

By the time Mary called at the Hospital Lizzie was back.

'Now then – I've been thinking about you, Lizzie, and it seems to me that you'd be better taking charge of your own life than hanging onto some man's coat-tails—' the milliner began briskly, and was interrupted.

'You can forget about the sermon, Mistress MacLeod.' Lizzie sneered the name. 'I've decided that I've no more wish to live among the self-righteous mealy-mouthed Paisley folk than I had before.'

Mary gaped, taken aback for once by the sudden change in Lizzie, then noticed the good warm jacket, several sizes too large, about the other woman's shoulders.

'I've seen that before.'

Lizzie gathered it protectively about her. 'It's mine!'

'Oh aye?' Mary asked dryly, then got down to business. 'You've decided to go back to the man you went away with the last time?'

'Him?' Lizzie spat out a curse. 'I'd die before I'd go back to him!'

'So you've finally found the way of the world? Women are daft if they let their happiness depend on a man.'

'From what I've heard, you managed to find a prize for yourself.'

'Andra's a good husband.' Mary refused to be baited. 'But I had my independence long before we wed, and I can look out for myself if need be. Any woman with her head fastened on properly can do the same. Look at the way you worked in the shop – you could turn your hand to shop-keeping again, could you not?'

'If I had to,' Lizzie admitted grudgingly, her eyes suspicious.

'Tuts, it's not a case of having to, it's a case of wanting to. You've no need of Colin or William to buy your bread for you, and you know that fine. You can earn your own living.'

'With nothing to my name but these?' Lizzie indicated the clothes she wore.

'You've got two good hands, and a brain of your own. I started my business with the help of Andra's first wife, and with a lot of hard work on my own account. If you're willing to put in the work I'd mebbe be prepared to put up some money – as a loan, just.'

It was Lizzie's turn to gape. 'And what's to stop me making off with your precious money?'

'I'd set the militia after you if you did. But I doubt if you'd be that daft. Listen to me – Andra has good business friends in Dumfries. If I was to give you a letter of introduction to them, and some decent clothes and money to get you there and give you a start, you could take a wee shop and set up in business for yourself. Mind you, I'd be looking for my money back. But if you put your mind to it there's no reason why you shouldn't pay off the debt in a few years, the same as I did myself.'

It was a gamble, but during the long night, while Lizzie and Matt writhed together on the floor of the dingy room by the river, Mary had carefully thought over everything she had ever heard about Colin's wife, and had gradually uncovered a pattern similar to her own nature.

True, Lizzie had been selfish and cruel, but Mary recognised her intelligence and determination, and felt that it was high time those qualities were appealed to.

She waited patiently as doubt, suspicion and bewilderment chased each other across Lizzie's drawn face.

'You're willing to risk a lot just to buy safety for Colin and your sister's man.'

'I'm not overly concerned with them,' Mary

scoffed. 'I'm thinking of what's best for everyone, including you, for you'll not let anyone here rest easy until you're settled, Lizzie. If you agree to my proposition we'll go right now to my house and I'll give you a decent breakfast. Then we'll go to Glasgow to buy some clothes and get a legal acquaintance of mine to make out a proper business agreement between us. But if you're set on going to hell in your own way—' Mary rose and went to the door – 'I'll bid you good day right now.'

She put a hand on the latch.

'Wait—' Lizzie said from behind her. 'I'll come with you.'

'I knew you were a woman with a good head on your shoulders,' said Mary, and led the way out of the little room.

Duncan's head pounded from the night's drinking and from the tongue-lashing Meg had given him when he finally woke, wincing as daylight splintered into his eyes. Although he hazily remembered promising to see Mary before doing anything else, he hurried along to the Hospital as soon as he could escape from Meg.

His blood ran cold when he discovered that Lizzie had gone. He recalled meeting Matt the night before and telling him about Lizzie and her threats. What if the soldier had killed her to protect his brother?

With visions of Lizzie floating in the River Cart

passing through his befuddled mind Duncan ran to Mary's house. She came into the entrance hall to talk to him, closing the parlour door carefully behind her.

'Get back to your loom and hold your tongue,' she ordered before he could speak. 'The matter's settled and there's no need for you to stay here.'

'But—'

Mary almost pushed him out into the street. 'Duncan, will you go away? Lizzie and me are coming to an arrangement. She'll be out of Paisley shortly, when she's broken her fast.'

'You mean she's here?' he yelped, suddenly realising why the parlour door had been closed so firmly behind Mary.

'Aye, she's here. Now – you can either stay and ruin all my hard work or you can get back to your loom and thank the Lord you've got a friend like me with all her wits about her. I'll tell you about it when I've got the time.' And she shut the door with a decisive slam.

Totally confused, but weak with relief, he slunk back down the hill to the loom-shop. He had to wait until late in the afternoon before Mary came to the High Street house and gave him a brief outline of her talk with Lizzie, ending with, 'So she's away, fed and clothed and looking more like her old self already, the poor soul.'

'It's not right that you should have to put your hand in your pocket on my behalf. I've some money put by that Meg knows nothing about—'

'Tuts, I didn't just do it for you! There's Colin to think of, and Lizzie herself. And if you're able to put anything by without my sister's knowledge then she's failing in her proper duties,' Mary said dryly. 'Don't you go offering me a penny of it or I'll feel bound to tell her you've got it.'

She went to the door, paused, and returned. 'Duncan – you didn't go back to the Hospital last night to talk to Lizzie on your own, did you?'

'D'you think I could have faced her again? No, I got as drunk as a lord and Matt had to help me home,' he admitted, embarrassed.

'Matt?' Her voice sharpened. 'Did you tell him?'

Duncan's shame deepened. 'As I mind it, I did. But you've no need to be feared of Matt. He'd never speak a word of this to Colin or anyone else.'

Mary's face was suddenly blank. 'I'm sure you're right. See that wee bit of money you were bragging about a minute since? Mebbe you should use it to buy Matt a new jacket. Something tells me he could do with one,' she said, and opened the door.

'Eh? Jacket?' Duncan spluttered, but Mary had gone.

'Women!' he thought. He'd never understand them, especially his wife's sister.

Duncan's prediction that silk gauze would become an important industry in Paisley came true, but Peter Todd only lived to see the first hint of it. One April night in 1760 he died in his sleep, and was laid to rest in the family plot beside his first wife and his infant son.

Colin was a rock for Kirsty to lean on in the first grief of widowhood. Often, after the children were in bed at night, she took to sitting in the downstairs room with her step-son, soothed and comforted by the calm presence that reminded her so much of Peter.

Matt was like a lost soul the first time he came home after his father's death.

'It's as though the heart's gone out of the town,' he told Meg miserably. 'Everywhere I look I expect to see him. But there's nothing – nothing.'

Duncan, much as he yearned to get looms into his own shop, agreed to stop on and run the Todds' weaving shop for Kirsty. Jamie had finished school and had become an apprentice at the looms, though Duncan confided to Meg that the boy wasn't cut out for the work.

'He's more like Matt than anyone. He's restless. He only started his apprenticeship to please Peter. Mind you, I think he'll see it through for Kirsty's sake, but he'll likely be off as soon as he can.'

'Kirsty's got more sense than to hold him against his will, surely?'

There was no reply.

'Duncan!' She tweaked a corner of the newspaper clutched in his fists. 'Come out from behind that paper and let me have a proper talk with you! You've surely heard all the news already?'

The Paisley men usually stopped work and got

together to read the paper as soon as it went on sale. Items from all over the globe interested them deeply; in Paisley they knew more about the world's affairs than most working folk in Britain.

'I like to go over it again when I'm on my own.'

Meg laid her sewing down in her lap. 'Do you indeed? And are you not glad I bullied you into learning how to read all those years ago? Where would you be without me, tell me that?'

'Aye, I suppose I didn't get a bad bargain the day I picked you,' he said casually, then yelled as the paper was whipped out of his hands by his exasperated wife.

Paisley became the acknowledged centre of silk gauze manufacture. The town's weavers could match anyone when it came to texture, quality and cost, and by the end of the year it was quite common for the local people to hear English voices in their streets as more and more London merchants sent representatives north to open up new branches. There was work for all, and the looms in the surrounding villages were pressed into service for the Paisley manufacturers.

Over the next two years Duncan at last got his own looms installed. For Kirsty's sake, he continued to spend most of his working day in the Todds' shop, employing a reliable weaver to supervise the looms in his own shop.

Robert and William both put in a year at the new

Grammar School, then were apprenticed, Robert to a weaver, William to a cobbler. Margaret and Thomas were attending the English School, where they learned to read and write, and were taught grammar and geography.

Thomas, who in his mother's words 'soaked up learning like a cloth in a bucket of water', found his schooling quite inadequate, and persuaded his father to let him have extra tuition from Colin.

Although the space left by Peter's death was never quite filled they all adjusted, and life continued smoothly.

'We're like a sack of barley,' Margaret said to William. 'Poke your finger in it – if my mother isn't looking – and when you take your hand away the grain flows back into the space as though it had never been there at all. We do that. We smooth over things and it's all the same again. Well, almost.'

'Except that my grandfather wasn't a finger in a sack of barley,' he said stiffly, then relented. 'But I know what you mean.'

She smiled at him. William was different from the others. He never laughed at her high-flown ideas or belittled her. She slid her hand into his and squeezed his fingers affectionately.

The sense of injustice she had first known when she demanded of her mother at Mary's wedding, 'Why do rich people have houses that are too big for them?', strengthened as she grew older.

Margaret could never accept a system that decreed that some folk lived in poverty while others enjoyed wealth, and as she grew into her teens she was often to be found at the Town Hospital in Sneddon Street, taking the inmates scraps of food saved from her own meals or warm clothing which she and her brothers had outgrown. Her parents approved of her sense of responsibility towards others, but they had to draw the line when her enthusiasm reached the stage where both shop and house were being raided regularly.

'Colin'll be wondering what's happening to his profits,' Meg protested.

'And if much more goes from this house you'd be as well to move us all to the Hospital so that we can enjoy our own possessions,' Robert added scathingly. So Margaret had to rein her generous nature in a little, though she continued to beg and coax unwanted items from all her friends. Margaret always knew of some poor soul in need.

When one of the young hospital inmates was expelled for giving birth to a bastard child, it was Margaret who fought on her behalf, storming into the building to confront the Hospital Mistress and Master.

'I found Jenny in the street, crouched against the side of a house!' she accused them, while the shamed girl wilted beside her, clutching her baby. 'You can't just put her out like that. Where's she supposed to go? How's she to care for her baby?'

'The lassie's sinned in the eyes of the Lord and the community. Forbye, she tried to hide the truth from us. It's a Hospital rule that she can't stay here!' the Master said coolly. 'You've got a good heart, child, but it's a trifle misguided.'

The baby began to wail and Jenny's white, tear-streaked face crumpled. But Margaret was made of stronger stuff.

'Come on, Jenny—' she put an arm about the girl and marched to the door. 'We'll go to where folk care about other folk!'

Outside the big door she hesitated, baffled. A light patter of rain was falling, and Jenny did her best to pull a tattered shawl over the baby's head.

'We'll go to see my Aunt Mary,' Margaret decided, and the two of them made for the milliner's shop and a lukewarm reception.

'There's times when you vex me sorely, Margaret!' her aunt scolded. 'I might have had some lady in here buying a hat!' She covered her ears as the hungry baby's wailing filled the little shop.

'All the better—' said her unrepentant niece. 'The lady might have had a conscience and taken Jenny in. Since there's nobody here but you, Aunt Mary—?' She paused hopefully.

'You needn't think of my house, for Andra's not at all well at the moment and I'd lose the servants if I walked in with a crying bairn. Why not bother your own mother instead of me?'

'Because my father warned me the last time that there was to be no more of it, and it's too soon to change his mind. Please?' Margaret beseeched her.

Mary sighed and shook her head. 'What am I to do with you, girl?'

'It's what you're going to do with Jenny that matters,' Margaret rapped back at her.

'Well – Mistress Brown's a decent widow woman who's fond enough of bairns, and she could probably do with a hand in her wee shop—' said Mary, and so a refuge was found for Jenny and her child.

Not content with her success, Margaret dared to face one of the Hospital directors in the street and take up the matter with him. The shocked man called on Duncan to complain about his daughter's impertinence.

'If we were all as irresponsible and as soft-hearted as your daughter the Hospital would end up as a refuge for all the feckless poor in the town!' he protested.

Duncan eyed him thoughtfully. 'Is that not what it was built for? She's mebbe hasty at times, and for that I apologise to you. But a wee bit compassion for a young mother and her blameless child isn't entirely out of place, surely.'

The director's face flamed. 'It seems that you have no notion of the right way to care for paupers!'

'Mebbe not,' Duncan said shortly, suddenly sickened by the man's manner. 'I only know how to care for folk – and it's the same with my daughter. Now, sir, if you've said your piece, I've work to do—' and he pressed his foot firmly on the treadle and set the loom into noisy action, turning his broad back on the visitor.

When he went home later he soundly rebuked Margaret for her impudence towards a member of the Hospital Board.

'I wasn't impertinent – I asked him in a civil manner how he'd feel if his own daughter had fallen like poor Jenny and was in need of compassion,' she protested.

'Mercy!' Meg's apron flapped over her reddening face. 'Margaret, how could you speak to a respectable gentleman in that fashion?'

'See here, Margaret, if you're going to defend folk you'll have to learn to do it with a smile and a soft word.' Duncan said patiently. 'That way you'll get more out of others without them realising it.'

He was soon to regret his words, for she took them to heart from that day on and redoubled her efforts to help others. When she left shool she worked in the shop and helped Meg in the house. She was a deft spinner, and as thread was sorely needed to fill the eight looms under Duncan's care she persuaded him to employ some of the Hospital women as spinners.

'She's a nuisance at times, but apart from that,' said Mary smugly, 'the girl's got a lot of my nature in her.'

Duncan sighed and nodded.

'That's what worries me,' he said – but he said it very quietly, so that his sister-in-law couldn't hear him.

* * *

Margaret bustled down the length of the hospital sick-room, her blue eyes scanning each bed as she passed. She stopped here and there, to pull a blanket round someone's shoulders, to soothe a fretful child, to hold a cup of water to dry lips.

She reached the end of the room and was about to turn back to the door when her attention was caught by a man tossing in a corner bed.

'Billy? Is it you, Billy?'

She approached the cot cautiously, wondering if she was only imagining a resemblance between the big, cheerful chapman who visited her parents each time he was in Paisley and the flushed, delirious creature twisting and turning between coarse grey sheets.

The sick man looked at her without any recognition for a moment, then his glazed eyes managed to focus and his lips twisted into a faint smile.

'Wee Maggie Montgomery! Lassie, it's good to see a friendly face—' His voice was harsh with fever. 'Would – would you fetch some water? I could drink the Cart dry if I just had the energy to crawl to it.'

The jug by his cot was empty. Margaret sped out of the room and was back in no time with water, then she supported Billy's shoulders while he drank greedily. Her hands felt scorched by the heat from his big body. When he had slaked his thirst she helped him to lie back on the mattress.

'What brought you to this place?'

Billy's head moved fretfully from side to side. 'Just a foolish chill that wouldn't leave me. A few days' rest and I'll be right again.'

Margaret looked about the cheerless room, listened to the cries and moans of the sick. 'This is no place for a man who wants to recover.'

'Where else would I go? No use staying at my usual lodgings if I can't fend for myself. All I need's a bed and shelter till the fever breaks—'

A fit of harsh coughing tore at his chest and Margaret took a linen square from her pocket and wiped the sweat from his face. Then she waited patiently while he struggled to get his breath back.

'So now it's you tending to me?' he said hoarsely when he could speak again. 'The years go by too fast. Mind that day I found you down at the Cross, out of your mind with fear, and I carried you back to the shop on my shoulders? Remember it, Maggie? The day your brother took you to see that old man's hanging.'

'I remember.' It had been buried deep in her mind, only surfacing occasionally in nightmares. She forced her mind to reject memories of the sight she had seen at the Cross that day, and concentrated instead on the kindness shown to her by the man lying in the cot. 'I remember, Billy,' she said gently.

'By God, you near burst my ears with the noise you were making.' He managed a faint chuckle. 'I wish my lungs – were as good as – yours were that day—'

His eyes closed and his voice died away. Margaret stared down at him, troubled.

When she left the Hospital William was waiting for her outside, as he often did. She poured out Billy's story as the two of them walked through the busy streets, ending with 'I think he's awful sick, William!'

'I'll ask Aunt Kirsty to visit him tomorrow. She'll know what's best for him.'

'Yes – do that,' she said with relief, smiling up at him as they stopped outside her parents' door. Margaret was quite tall but William was a good head taller, lean and lithe and always dependable. 'He looks awful sick.'

He had an attractive, crooked grin that lit up his grey eyes. 'Don't fret yourself, just leave things to her. Will you go walking on the braes with me tomorrow?'

'Come to the shop when you're finished work, and if I can be spared I'll go. But don't be hammering any more fingers, or your work'll never get done!' She indicated his left hand with its bandaged index finger. He was learning his trade the hard way, and the number of times he arrived home with bruised fingers made him the butt of everyone's jokes.

The grin widened. 'Jamie says it's because I'm a dreamer. He says I'm handless.'

'You will be if you go on like that,' Margaret told him, and slipped into the house.

'Out with William Todd again?' Robert greeted

her as she hurried in. Thomas sniggered, then turned it into a cough as he met his mother's eye.

Margaret looked down her nose at her brothers. 'I was at the Hospital, as you well know. William walked home with me.'

'He always seems to walk home with you,' Robert scoffed. 'I'll wager he asked you to go up the braes with him – and you know what that means.'

Margaret flushed scarlet, and this time Thomas couldn't disguise his snigger. The braes beyond the town were popular with courting couples.

'You've got a bad mind, Robert Montgomery!'

'That's enough, the lot of you!' Meg ordered as her husband came in. 'Sit at the table and mind your manners!'

Later that night, when Meg and Duncan were getting ready for bed, she said thoughtfully, 'He's a nice lad, William Todd.'

'He's civil enough,' Duncan agreed.

'Margaret could do worse than marry with a decent young man like him.'

Duncan stopped in the act of taking his shirt off, his back to her. After a pause he said carefully, 'What nonsense is this you're talking now, woman?'

'It's not nonsense! They've always been fond of each other, William and Margaret – and it wouldn't be the first time childhood friends wed.'

'Are you serious?'

'You'd have noticed it for yourself if you'd taken the trouble to look.' Meg said with unfair scorn, for she herself had only just begun to wonder about a future romance between the young people.

'You're letting your thoughts run away with you!' Duncan said vehemently, and rolled into bed.

'Are you so old that you've forgotten what it's like to have an eye for a bonny lass?' she teased, but he hunched himself up, turning away from her.

'Margaret's too young for that sort of thing!'

'I didn't mean they were crying the banns already. There's plenty of time – but she's old enough to start thinking of her future.'

'Then she can look elsewhere, for I'll not have her throwing herself away on the likes of William Todd!'

'Duncan! He's an upright, honest lad who comes of fine stock!'

'He's not the right one for our Margaret!' His voice was muffled.

'But—'

'For God's sake will you blow the lamp out and get to sleep!' he barked at her. 'I've got work to do in the morning, and no time to lie here and listen to your nonsense!'

Furious, she put the lamp out and thumped down onto the mattress with her back to him. She was soon asleep, but Duncan lay staring into the darkness, mortally afraid, not only for Meg and himself, but for his daughter. When dawn's grey fingers probed into the room and Meg stirred beside him he had only slept fitfully, and had been plagued by bad dreams.

Swinging his feet to the cold floor, rubbing eyes that felt as though they were filled with dry grit, he swore to himself that from now on he would keep an eye on Margaret. And if necessary he would act to put a stop to her growing friendship with William Todd before things went too far.

Chapter Four

B ILLY CARMICHAEL'S EYES LIT UP when Kirsty arrived at his bedside on the following morning.

'It's good of you to come and see me, lass.'

Her eyes scanned his fever-ravaged face. 'I'm doing more than that,' she said flatly. 'I'm going away right now to arrange for a cart, then I'll get you well wrapped up and take you to my house till you're well again.'

'Deed you will not! You've got enough to do without taking a sick man into your home—'

'Wheesht, Billy,' she ordered. 'The matter's all settled. I'd not let a good friend like yourself stay here while there's room for you in my own house.'

His protests were ignored. Within the hour he was jolting painfully in the back of a cart to the High Street house. Between them Kirsty and Duncan managed to get him upstairs and he was soon in bed, with Kirsty spooning hot broth down his throat.

His recovery took longer than any of them had

imagined. His feverish chill had already turned to pneumonia, and Kirsty had her hands full caring for him and tending her family. Thanks to her careful nursing he passed the crisis and found himself on the road to recovery, though as weak as a kitten. By the time he was on his feet again winter was coming in, and Kirsty steadfastly refused to consider his return to the road.

'D'you think I nursed you back to health just so you could get soaked through and catch another fever?' she wanted to know, hands on hips. 'Make up your mind to a winter spent under this roof, Billy, for you're not fit to go back on the road yet.'

He was secretly happy to give way to her, for the weeks spent under her roof had been a warm reminder of the domesticity he had known before the fever deprived him of his wife and children.

To pay for his keep he returned to his old trade as a cobbler, working in a corner of the weaving shop. At night he sat companionably on the opposite side of the fire from Kirsty, in Peter Todd's old chair, or spent long hours downstairs talking to Colin.

Kirsty was equally content with their arrangement. 'It's good to have a man about the house again,' she confided to Meg.

'No doubt. How's Kate faring?' Slim, red-headed Kate had just started work in a dressmaker's shop.

'She's doing fine. Time flies, does it not? I mind the day your Robert was born as if it was yesterday

– and now they're all going out into the world. There's only Thomas left at school.'

'Aye – Thomas!' Meg laughed and shook her head. Still as round and rosy as he had been since babyhood, Thomas seldom had his nose out of a book. Most of his spare time was spent at Mary's house, where he was allowed to browse through Andrew MacLeod's library. His parents marvelled over his scholastic bent, while Robert and Margaret openly thought of him as the 'strange' member of the family.

'Margaret, now – she's a different problem altogether.' Meg went on slowly, and Kirsty saw a sudden shadow passing over her friend's face.

'What's amiss?'

Meg shrugged and drove her wheel faster. The two of them were alone in the Todds' kitchen, spinning thread for the looms below.

'It's Duncan. I don't know what's amiss with the man. He's like a cat on hot bricks every time he sees Margaret and William together – and you know as well as I do what close friends they've always been. What harm could it do if they decided to wed?'

Kirsty's hand, deftly guiding the strand of thread, stilled for a moment.

'Wed? You're not serious, Meg! Margaret's only just sixteen and William's less than a year older!'

'They're old enough to be thinking of marriage. I wouldn't be surprised if they came to the idea one day. They're fond of each other, and what would be wrong with a marriage between them? William's a fine lad. I can't think why Duncan's suddenly so set against him and Margaret seeing each other. He's started to go on at her, and the two of them are having terrible quarrels over the head of it.'

'That's the wrong thing to do,' Kirsty admitted. 'If Duncan's set against William, Margaret's just the sort of lassie to defy him.'

'That's my own view.' Meg shook her head. 'But why should he be opposed to the boy? William's never done anything amiss in his life – he's a credit to yourself and Colin. I don't know what's got into Duncan at all. He won't talk to me about it.' She sighed, her normally happy face clouded. 'I tell you, Kirsty, it's got me fair worried. I don't know where it's all going to end!'

Duncan himself came to Kirsty a few days later. He closed the trap door then paced the kitchen, his brows knotted with worry.

'Kirsty – I don't know how to begin. The Lord knows I've no wish to rake up the past—'

'Is it Margaret and William? Meg told me,' she said as he gaped at her. 'She can't understand what you've got against the two of them having an innocent friendship.'

'And she'll never know, please God.' He threw his hands out helplessly. 'It never entered my head until I heard Robert teasing her about him, then I realised that they're always together, these two.'

'They always were. It's no more than that, Duncan, and mebbe it'll never be anything else.'

'I can't take that chance, Kirsty! And I can't let them know the truth.' He slammed one fist into the other. 'If I'd had any sense at all I'd have seen to it that they were kept apart from the beginning!'

'You couldn't have done that. All the bairns went about together.'

'I wish I'd never set eyes on Lizzie!' said Duncan for the hundredth time.

'Then you're wishing William away, and that's wrong, for he's a fine boy who's made Colin's life worthwhile.'

She paused, then said slowly, 'If you really think the pair of them'll have to be kept apart, Duncan, Colin must be brought into it.'

'No!'

'Have some sense, man! You know your Margaret as well as I do. Forbid her to see William and she'll fall in love with him just to spite you. And you'll have Colin thinking that his son isn't good enough for your daughter. You'll need his help, can you not see that?'

'It'll kill him!'

'Not now,' said Kirsty. 'He's strong enough and wise enough to take the truth and not let it make a whit of difference to the way he feels about William, at least. Leave it to me – I'll see to it.'

'It's my place to—'

'I know how to talk to him,' she said firmly. 'It has to be done right. How would you like to hear plump and plain from another man that he's your son's real father?'

'Don't make me feel worse than I do already, Kirsty!' he groaned.

'I doubt if anyone could do that.' Her tone was matter-of-fact, but her heart recognised his torment and wept for him. 'Now it's time you got back to your work, for it seems to me that there's more clacking from the tongues than from the looms down there. Go on with you, and leave Colin to me.'

Kirsty turned at the kitchen door to look at Billy, dozing by the fire, a newspaper in his lap. A faint smile touched her lips as she closed the door gently. It was good to see a man by the fireside again. Then the smile faded as she made her way downstairs. She had no stomach for what she must do now.

Colin was working by candlelight when she went into his room, transferring a finished design from rough paper to design sheet. A box of colours stood by his elbow. He looked up and smiled.

'Come away in and sit down. Give me a minute to finish this.'

Before him lay the design paper with a black-leaded page over it. On top he had laid the paper with the design sketched on it, and he was carefully going over the outlines with a blunt steel point. In spite of the furrows which his accident had engraved on his face he was still youthful in appearance and his mop of fair hair was as thick as ever. At last he straightened up and grinned at her, a boyish grin that made him look very like his father and brother.

'I'll colour it tomorrow, then pass it over to Duncan.'

She looked at the simple but delicate pattern of leaves. 'It's bonny.'

'It's a special order. How's Billy coming on?'

'Well enough. He's talking of going back on the road now the weather's turning.'

'You'll miss him,' he said shrewdly, and she flushed.

'I suppose I will.'

He leaned across the table and put a hand on hers. 'Take my advice, Kirsty – keep him with you. Billy's a good man. He'd look after you.'

'Colin Todd!' she blustered, confused and embarrassed. 'I never thought to hear you black-footing like an interfering old woman!'

His grin widened. 'Black-footing's resulted in many a happy marriage. And I know a good match when I see one – where's the harm in putting in a word to help things along?' Then the grin faded. 'But that's not what you came to talk about. What's wrong, Kirsty?'

'D'you think I only come to see you when there's something wrong?'

'No, but you came in that door as if you had the cares of the world on your shoulders.'

Deftly he wheeled his chair round the table until he was beside her. One of the town's carpenters had designed and built the chair for him, and it was

Colin's great delight to be able to move about his room, and even to wheel himself outside in good weather. It had taken a lot of skill to master the chair on rough footpaths, but he had persevered and succeeded.

'Tell me, Kirsty.' His voice was calm, reassuring. His hand touched hers, closed over it. Suddenly she found it difficult to meet his eyes.

'It isn't easy to speak of it—'

'Kirsty, when did you and me ever find it hard to talk to each other?'

She stared into the fire. 'Duncan wanted to see you himself but I'd not let him. It's William and Margaret – Duncan thinks they're getting too fond of each other. He thinks it should be stopped.'

His eyebrows climbed. 'You mean they might be falling in love?' he asked with genuine surprise, then laughed softly. 'And here was me thinking of William still as a bairn. God, Kirsty, the years go by too fast for comfort! But why should it bother Duncan? Is my son not good enough for his—'

He suddenly stopped and she looked up to see the animation ebbing from his face, leaving it strangely blank, like a page still to be written on. She started to say something but he lifted one hand sharply, the hand that had warmly covered hers.

'Wheesht now, Kirsty!' The voice was so like Peter's that she almost expected him to add, 'You're letting your tongue run away with you, woman!' as his father would have done. But when he finally spoke it was in his own quiet voice.

'Duncan? It was Lizzie and – Duncan?'

'What do you mean?' Her voice shook, out of control.

'Kirsty, the Silver Bells accident might have robbed me of the use of my legs, but it didn't affect my brain. D'you think you need to tell me anything about my wife that I didn't know already? Lizzie thought she could keep her own counsel, but I always knew what was going on behind those strange eyes of hers. The only thing I didn't know till now was the man's name. All these years,' he said in wondering tones, 'I thought it was Matt.'

'Oh, Colin—' It was her turn to reach out and take his hand. 'Why did you never say anything? To keep such a secret—'

'It was no hardship,' he said swiftly, briskly, looking more like the old Colin. 'Don't go feeling sorry for me, Kirsty. I've got William and he's my son. I raised him, and I'm proud of him. But Duncan's right – the two of them'll have to stop seeing each other. Tell him I'll find something to say to the boy.'

'You should have told me!'

'What sense would there have been in that?' Colin asked her. 'I didn't know that you knew anything of it. It was Lizzie's secret and I'd not have betrayed her to anyone. Now—' he reached over and patted her hand '—off you go to your bed, Kirsty, and stop worrying. What's done is done. We'll say no more about it – none of us. You can tell Duncan that.'

She got up to go. 'What else d'you want me to tell Duncan?'

Colin smiled faintly. 'Nothing. We've been friends for a long time, him and me. It would be foolish to let a friendship go because of something that happened eighteen years ago.' Then the smile widened a little. 'Mebbe I should be grateful to him for the pleasure William's given me. Now go upstairs and let Billy tell you about the stories in his newspaper.'

She opened the door, then turned. Colin sat motionless in his chair, one finger absently tracing the new design. His head was bent, his hair golden in the candlelight. He looked up and saw her standing there.

'I'm glad it wasn't Matt,' he said.

When Kirsty fumbled her way upstairs in the dark and stepped into the kitchen Billy, who had just wakened, was shocked to see tears on her round cheeks.

'What's wrong? It's not Colin, is it?' He jumped to his feet.

'No, it's – just—' She went to him and his arms opened to take her. She sobbed on his broad comfortable shoulder and he held her close, stroking her hair, until the tears finally ceased.

Then gently, unsure of his reception but unable to deny the longing that had grown in him over the past weeks, he lifted her face to his and kissed her.

*   *   *

'But why?' William asked on the following day.

Colin's fingers tightened on the book in his lap.

'You're just an apprentice, and you're young. It's foolish for you to get too friendly with any girl just yet. Later on—'

'To hear you, anyone would think Margaret and me were talking of marriage!' William exploded incredulously. 'I just like her – she likes me – we get on together, that's all.'

'Are you certain?'

'You know Margaret Montgomery well enough! She's not like the other girls – she's not interested in getting wed and raising a family!'

'Still, it's best that you do as I say and leave it at that, William.'

'But why?'

Lamplight cast deep furrows on Colin's face. 'Mebbe you'd be wise not to ask me that again.'

'It's Duncan Montgomery, isn't it?' Bitterness sharpened William's voice. 'He doesn't think I'm good enough for his daughter!'

'It's not that, it's – for other reasons that don't concern you.'

'Don't concern me? You come between me and Margaret then you say the reason's not my concern?' The boy laughed without amusement then threw himself out of his chair towards the door in an awkward tangle of adolescent limbs. 'I'm going to see Duncan Montgomery. I'm going to make him tell me man to man what he's got against me—!'

'No!' Colin's body, trapped in the wheel-chair, couldn't move between William and the door, but his voice managed to stop the youth in his tracks. He swung round to stare at Colin, his eyes dark angry pools in a pale face.

'William, if you care at all for me and for what we've always been to each other you'll agree here and now to do as I ask,' Colin said quietly. 'I swear to you that I'd not look for such a solemn promise if I could avoid it. But I can't. For my sake, William!'

And William, who loved his father more than anyone else in the world, gave his promise – against his better judgement.

It was some time before Margaret realised that William was avoiding her. She was kept busy with her shop duties and hospital visits, and of course Kirsty's betrothal to Billy Carmichael occupied all their minds.

'I thought we'd see it one of those fine days,' Mary said smugly as she sat in Meg's kitchen. 'Billy always had a soft spot for Kirsty, and she needs a man about the house.'

'She's got Jamie and Colin and William,' Margaret pointed out, and her aunt shot her a withering glance.

'I mean a man to be head of the house. Jamie and William are growing up, and Colin always kept himself to himself. Kirsty's the sort of woman who's the better for having a man around.'

'You make marriage sound the same as owning

a dog,' Margaret said, to her aunt's amusement and her mother's embarrassment.

'Take that shocked expression off your face, Meg,' Mary ordered. 'The girl's more like me than you – she's got some fire in her. Now – what about the wedding bonnets?'

It was decided that Billy should take over Colin's room and turn it into a cobbler's shop. The looms were shifted from the Todd house to an empty weaving shop nearby and Colin moved into the loom-shop where he had more space for his books and papers.

'Such a stramash – I wonder at times if it's worth it all,' Kirsty fluttered as she supervised the transfer of Colin's possessions.

Jamie flashed a huge grin at her as he staggered across the passageway, carrying one end of his half-brother's bed.

'Of course it's worth it.'

'Here – watch what you're doing and don't break the leg of that thing off against the door!' she shrieked, following them into the room. While the men struggled with the bed she stood alone, gazing round. Without the four big looms the apartment was vast and desolate.

'It's strange to see the shop so empty.' Her voice was suddenly tremulous. Her ears rang with the beat of the looms and the sound of Peter's deep, warm voice. She was grateful when Jamie put his arm about her and gave her a warm hug.

'The looms aren't far away, and Colin's carrying on the tradition in his own way, with his designing.'

'Aye.' Kirsty swallowed hard and smiled up at her tall son. Then her eyes travelled beyond his fiery head to the trapdoor linking the shop with her kitchen above.

'And I'll be able to call down to him whenever I want to,' she added, and Colin, catching the words as he manipulated his chair through the doorway, had the wit to smother his sudden apprehension before he caught her eye.

When the move was completed William was despatched to fetch a jug of ale so that they could, in Kirsty's words, 'celebrate the wee flitting.'

Drink could be bought at the howff on the ground floor of the new Town House at the Cross. The upper part of the building consisted of the Council chambers and offices, and the cells.

It seemed fitting that howff and cells shared the same building, for often enough the temporary inhabitants of the cells were men and women who had over-indulged in drink, and it was a simple matter to whisk them upstairs to sleep off their stupor. Everyone thus incarcerated for the night was obliged to pay a fee of four pence – two pence for burgesses – to the jailer.

William had almost reached his destination when someone stepped into his path and Margaret's voice said lightly, 'Good evening to you, Mister Todd. Where might you be bound?'

Colour flamed into his face and he stepped back.

'Margaret! I'm just – just—'

'—Going for ale,' she finished the sentence for him, eyeing the jug in his hand. Then her clear gaze swept up to his face again. 'I haven't seen you for long enough, William.'

'There's been a lot to do at the house, moving the looms out and—' His voice died away and he moistened dry lips with the tip of his tongue.

'I hear Billy's taking you on as his apprentice. And I see you still have that habit of hammering your fingers as often as you hammer the shoes.' She reached out and touched his bruised thumb-nail, then it was her turn to colour as he jerked his hand away from her.

'What's amiss?'

'Nothing.' He clutched the jug in both hands as though it was a shield between them. A puzzled frown drew Margaret's neat eyebrows together.

'When are you coming to the Hospital again?' Then, as he stood silently before her, she asked with growing suspicion, 'Have you been keeping out of my way deliberately?'

'I'd not do that!' the words poured from him, and were checked. 'At least – I'd not want to!'

Her frown deepened. 'Then you've been told to stay away from me? Was it my father? You don't have to heed him, surely!'

William wished that the ground would give way beneath his feet and let him fall into whatever hell might be lurking underground. But the earthen path remained solid and Margaret's eyes were beginning to glint blue fire.

'I – Margaret, don't ask me to explain it, for I can't. It's just that – mebbe they're right, mebbe we were seeing each other too much—'

She gave a short, angry laugh. 'So that's the way of it, is it? You're scared folk might think I've got my cap set at you?'

'Margaret, listen—' It was his turn to put out a hand, with the intention of drawing her into a doorway out of sight while he explained. But she drew back sharply, avoiding his outstretched fingers. Hurt coloured her cheeks.

'Never mind – I'd not want to make a nuisance of myself. I'll wish you good day, Mister Todd – and if we never speak again I'll be well pleased!' she flared at him, then deliberately sidestepped into a pool of dirty water so that she could pass without brushing against him.

He watched her flounce away, back straight, well-shod feet slamming angrily on the path with each step. For the first time in his life he discovered that a heart could ache. He had lost her, and he didn't know why.

Miserable and confused, he stood for a long moment, clutching the empty jug, before turning towards the howff.

Chapter Five

WHILE MARGARET BEGAN THE LONG bitter process of struggling with hurt pride, life held few problems for her brothers. Robert, still serving his apprenticeship, had taken to weaving as easily as his father had. It was what he had been born to, and he loved the life.

Thomas, on the other hand, had no wish to take up weaving. Every time his father referred to the day when he would be apprenticed the boy winced inwardly. He loved books and studying, and he had already made up his own mind about his future. He lived in a perpetual dream, and only came to life at school, or studying with Colin Todd, or when he was in his Aunt Mary's house in Oakshawhill.

In the mornings before going to school, as he waited his turn to draw water at the street well, he would stand in a daze, his mind turning over something he had recently read, or memorising some homework. His blue eyes stared unseeingly at the tenements across the road while his lips moved soundlessly.

After school there were errands to run for his

mother and then, if he didn't have a lesson with Colin, he was free to scurry up the hill to Mary's house, where there was always a welcome for him. His first five minutes or so were spent in the kitchen, where the cook fed him tit-bits, then he and Andrew MacLeod would have a deeply satisfying academic discussion in the library, after which they both selected books from Andrew's extensive collection and settled into comfortable chairs to read in contented silence.

Thomas didn't agree with his sister Margaret that big houses were sinful, nor did he share his mother's awe of Mary's home. He simply saw it as a treasure cave filled with literature and he wasn't in the least intimidated by its many high-ceilinged rooms.

When Mary came home from the shop the three of them had tea then, if Thomas didn't have to hurry home, they all sat in the parlour, Thomas with his homework, Andrew reading or writing, Mary sewing, one or other of them making an occasional remark.

The childless MacLeods developed a genuine affection for Thomas. Mary and Robert got on well enough but saw little of each other. Margaret was so like her aunt in nature that they frequently sparked against each other, but Thomas's placid belief that everyone had a right to live as they pleased made him a relaxing companion.

'Your mother tells me you've had a good report from the school,' Mary said one evening, her needle flying deftly through the material in her hands. Thomas raised his head from the book on the table before him.

'It wasn't bad.'

'You'll soon be finished at the school.'

'Aye.'

'And taking your place at the looms, no doubt.'

There was a pause, then 'I've no mind to be a weaver,' said Thomas. She raised her eyebrows at Andrew, who had looked up from his accounts.

'Indeed? And what does your father have to say about that?'

Thomas swallowed. 'He doesn't know yet.'

'Have you decided what you want to do with yourself, then?'

'Mister Paterson at the school says I could mebbe get a place in Glasgow Academy.'

'That would take money, laddie.'

'I know. But I'd work hard. I have it in mind to be a physician.'

Andrew dropped the pen he was holding and Mary's embroidery needle stabbed into her hand.

'Tuts, I think this thing's got a life of its own!' she said irritably, sucking the wound. 'A physician, did you say?'

'That would mean going to the University,' Andrew put in gently.

'Aye.' Thomas's dark blue eyes glowed in his round face.

'And that's what you're going to tell your father when the time comes?'

'Aye.' The glow dimmed somewhat.

'It's not just what he has in mind for you, Thomas.'

There was a mild warning in Andrew's voice, and the glow dimmed further.

'I know that,' said Thomas, and sighed heavily.

'Well—' Mary's voice was brisk, 'you haven't read all those dry books of Andra's just for the sake of something to do, I'm sure. Plenty weavers read, but I've never seen one that eats books the way you do. You'd probably be too busy with your reading to turn out a decent piece of cloth. Your father'll surely see the sense of that.'

'I hope so,' said Thomas, but without much conviction.

Mary shot a quick glance at him and opened her mouth to say more, but a slight clearing of the throat from the writing desk where her husband sat cautioned her to close her lips again. Andrew was one of the few people who could tell Mary when it was wise to hold her tongue.

'No sense in worrying the boy further – or raising his hopes,' he said when Thomas had gone clattering home in the warm summer evening. 'He's a clever lad, Mary – but he'd make a poor weaver, for sure.'

'Try telling Duncan that,' she said with a sniff, and Andrew looked at her thoughtfully.

'I'd not dare. It might come better from you. As I see it, my task is to keep my mouth shut and my purse at the ready,' he said; then, elderly and frail as he was, he endured his vigorous young wife's grateful kisses with both courage and pleasure.

Mary wasn't one to let an idea simmer for long. A few days later she found Meg and Duncan alone by their fireside and settled herself on a chair, untying her bonnet strings.

'Your Thomas wants to be a physician.'

'A what?' Their two faces stared at her.

'A physician. He has it in mind to go to the Academy in Glasgow, then to the University to study. He doesn't want to be a weaver.'

'And just who—' Duncan began ominously, then collected his wits. 'Mary, it seems you know more about our son than we do.'

'I should, since he spends so much of his time with me and Andra. He's a fine boy, Duncan, and if you take my advice you'll let him have his head over the matter. Meg tells me he does well at the school.'

'Aye, but—'

'When did you hear this nonsense, Mary?' Meg could never get used to her sister's habit of organising each and every one of the family without so much as a by-your-leave.

'Just the other day – and it's not nonsense. Thomas never wastes his time talking nonsense, you should know that yourself. Now, Andra and me've been discussing it, and it seems to us that we should see to the cost of it—' She held up a mittened hand as Duncan shot upright in his chair. '—Since we've no children of our own – Andra being too old and me being too busy anyway – and we're so fond of the boy.'

'Just a minute—' Duncan had rallied and begun to fight back. 'Before you say another word, Mary, I'd always had it in mind to make the lad a weaver, like Robert and myself.'

'I know that, but think about it for a minute. He'd be useless at a loom, for his heart's not in the work and you know better than I do that a weaver needs to be single-minded. Now, Duncan, you'd not want one of your lads to be in a trade he didn't enjoy, would you?'

'Mebbe not, but—'

'Mind you, he still has to prove that he's able, but I'm sure he can do it—'

'To hear you speak anyone would think he's about to open his own surgery already,' Duncan said sourly, and was ignored.

'—So when the time comes for him to go to the Academy in Glasgow, and then the University—'

'The University!' Meg said faintly, and was also ignored.

'We'll pay what's necessary. It would be worth it to have a physician in the family.'

'Aye, that would get your nose in the air, would it not?' Duncan said meanly.

'Yours and all, when it comes to it, Duncan, yours and all. You don't have to mention this wee talk to him, by the way. Let him tell you himself when he feels that the right time's come. I'm just smoothing the way for him.'

She rose to leave, and Duncan made one last attempt to assert himself as the head of the house.

'Before you go, Mary – I'll remind you that I've not given my consent for this daft idea you and Andra have dreamed up between you. I'll have to – Meg and me'll have to give it our serious consideration, you understand.'

She smiled sweetly. 'You do that, Duncan. You think about it, and let me know what you decide.'

At the door she turned and beamed on them both again. 'It pleasures me to know that one of my own flesh and blood kin's to be a physician. We'll all be that proud of him!'

When she had gone they sat in a stunned silence for a while, Duncan carefully re-lighting his pipe, Meg lost in a happy dream. She agreed with Mary – it would be grand to have a physician in the family. But she knew that she daren't get excited about the idea until Duncan had had time to get used to it.

Finally he cleared his throat and spat into the flames.

'I know your sister's always right, Meg,' he said, almost plaintively, 'but does she have to be just as plump and plain about it every time?'

Margaret's pride wouldn't allow her to look for the reasons behind William's betrayal. Something had been knocked awry in her safe, happy world, and she coped with it by putting the blame squarely on William and slighting him whenever she got the opportunity.

Then her fortunes took a turn that swept William from her mind. Mary was in the shop with Meg when Margaret burst in, eyes shining.

'The Chaplain called me in when I was at the Town Hospital just now and – and I'm to be taken on to teach the children!' She grabbed Meg and waltzed her round, then collapsed onto a sack of barley. 'Every morning I've to go along and teach them their letters! Me – they asked me!'

'Oh – Margaret!' Meg clapped her hands to her flushed face, giggling like a girl, but Mary was unruffled.

'I don't see why you should look so surprised, Meg. The girl's the best person to ask, is she not? You'll be an asset to the place,' she told her niece warmly. 'I'm right pleased for you.'

Margaret picked up her apron then threw it down again, too excited to keep still. 'Can I go out for a while? There's so many things to think of—'

'Off you go – I can manage for an hour or two on my own.' Meg felt sudden tears at the back of her eyes as she watched her daughter. It seemed only yesterday that she herself had been on the threshold of adulthood. But in her case it had been the prospect of marriage that brought stars to her eyes.

At the doorway Margaret stopped, darted back

and hugged her mother then her aunt. 'I'll work hard – you'll see—' she said, and was gone.

The sisters smiled at each other when they were alone.

'It's good to see her happy again. For a while there she was awful downcast.' Meg shook her head. 'It doesn't take long for moods to change at that age.'

'Margaret's got the sense to know that bitterness is needed as well as sweetness to make life worth the tasting,' Mary said briskly. 'I'm glad she's found the sort of work that suits her temperament best.'

A sudden thought struck Meg. 'Mary, you didn't—?'

'Didn't what? Arrange the post for her? The very idea! Of course not!' Mary lied virtuously. 'Sometimes, Meg, you vex me sorely with your suspicions. You're getting as bad as that man of yours! You can just measure out the pound of meal I came in for, instead of standing there letting your imagination run away with you.'

Margaret was stifled by the crowded streets. Her feet scarcely seemed to touch the ground as they carried her towards the moors at the edge of the town; then she halted abruptly as William's tall lean figure stepped from a doorway ahead.

Her first instinct was to spin on her heel; she started the move, then checked it. She had to tell someone her news. Until recently she would have gone straight to William. Perhaps this was the time to forget disagreements and start anew—

But even as she began to walk towards him William glanced up and saw her. His head ducked in an involuntary movement and he swung away, presenting his back to her.

Margaret stood where she was, a red tide surging over her neck and face. Jamie, perched on a passing cart, had to hail her twice before she saw him.

'D'you want to come up the braes with me and walk back down?'

'Yes!' It was just what she needed. He caught her upstretched hand and hauled her onto the cart where, sure-footed, she stood beside him on close-packed bales of linen, above the heads of the pedestrians. The cart lurched and Jamie's arm looped about her waist, holding her securely against him.

'Jamie – I'm to teach the children in the Town Hospital!'

'Teach them what?'

'Their letters, you daft loon! I'm to go in three mornings a week and – oh, Jamie, I'm going to teach them such a lot!'

As they left the town behind she dropped down onto the lumpy bales and closed her eyes tightly against the sun's light. Her lids seemed to be made of beaten gold. Beside her, Jamie was propped on one elbow, whistling tunelessly.

At the Bonnie Wee Well, where a spring gushed cold and clear from the rock-face, the carter stopped and they scrambled down onto the grass. By the time the sun's dazzle had cleared from Margaret's eyes the cart was disappearing over the slight rise that lay between them and the bleachfields.

She cupped her hands at the spring and drank its icy water, then rinsed her face and arms. Jamie drank his fill and wiped his mouth with the back of one hand.

Margaret opened her arms to the warm air and danced over the grass, twirling like a leaf in an autumn wind, her skirt twisting about her legs. Finally she dropped to the ground, laughing up at Jamie when he reached her.

'Aren't we lucky to be alive and living in a town as fine as Paisley?'

He sat down, arms clasped about his knees, staring down to where the smoke rose lazily from dozens of chimneys. 'You think so? There's a lot more to life than working a loom and going bowling or cock-fighting. The world's out there—' his hand swept the horizon. 'That's what I want to see.'

'Go for a soldier, you mean? Like Matt?'

'Mebbe. I don't know—' he said restlessly.

'Jamie, what would you do if you could do anything in the world?'

'I'd get onto a cart and ride until the horse was too tired to go any further,' he said promptly. 'Then I'd get another cart and another horse.'

She giggled. 'You could go all the way to the end of the world and come back if there were enough carts!'

'I might. I'd not mind coming back as long as I could say I'd seen the rest of the world.'

'Not me – I've got plenty to do right here.' She stretched her arms above her head. 'Oh – I'm so lucky!'

He looked at her, and saw that the sun had turned her hair into a halo about her pretty, happy face.

'And so bonny,' he said, then leaned forward and kissed her, his lips warm and hesitant on hers.

Sheer surprise made her heart skip a beat. As Jamie's lips left hers she stayed motionless, looking at him with startled eyes. Emboldened, he put his hands on her shoulders and kissed her again, a longer embrace this time.

She liked it – but even her first kiss had to take second place to the excitement the day had already brought her.

'Come on, Jamie—' She jumped up. 'We've got a long walk ahead of us and I've to get back to the shop.'

'Margaret, will you—' he began, but she had started running, and only the warm air heard the last few words '—walk out with me again?'

'Come on, Jamie!' She stopped at the foot of a slope, slipped her shoes off, and ran on without waiting for him, down the hill towards the town below.

The gathering held to celebrate Kirsty's wedding to Billy Carmichael gave proof to the boast that in 1763 Paisley's working class were the best dressed in the country. Most of the women had lace trimming to their vividly coloured gowns and there were plenty of earrings and finger rings in evidence. A few wore the figured silk dresses which were coming into fashion, and the men were dashing and stylish in ruffled shirts and knee britches, with silver buckles shining on their shoes.

Mary's contribution to the occasion was the finest collection of bonnets ever seen at one gathering. Kate and Margaret were highly amused by her little approving nods each time another of her creations swept into the room atop a head.

'You'd think she'd arranged the wedding just to get the chance to show off her bonnets,' Kate whispered, blue eyes dancing.

'You're right – and you and me are next on her marriage list, so we'd best watch our step,' Margaret prophesied darkly.

'Oh, I don't know about that – I'd like fine to have a wedding,' her friend sighed, and Margaret shook her head in disgust.

The house was packed to the rafters, yet everyone managed to sit down to the wedding feast of broth, beef, mutton and fowls followed by puddings swimming in cream, with bread and cheese for those who still felt hungry. After the food had been washed down with generous mugs of ale the furniture in Colin's room was pushed back against the walls and the floor cleared for dancing.

The first person Margaret saw when she went

into the room was William, leaning against the wall, watching the door. When she appeared he pushed himself upright and began to ease his way across the crowded floor.

Then – 'Come on, Margaret—' Robert's hand claimed her and whirled her into a group of dancers. Over her shoulder she saw William stop, as though it had been his intention all along, by Kirsty's side.

It was a grand gathering, a testimony to Kirsty's and Billy's popularity. Half-way through the evening, exhausted and hot, Margaret slipped out of the room and escaped into the coolness of the back yard.

As she walked up the hard earth path by the kail-bed a figure stepped out from the shadows under an apple tree. Startled, she gave a cry and stepped back, almost tripping over a brick by the side of the path. A hand held her arm, steadying her.

'Margaret—?'

She pulled herself free, embarrassed. 'I – I didn't know there was anyone else out here.'

'You mean, you didn't know I was out here.' William moved back in his turn, indicating the distance between them. 'Don't worry, I'll not come too close.'

'No need to make it sound as if you've got the plague!'

'No?' he said bitterly. 'The way you've been avoiding me I thought I must have.'

She looked fully at him for the first time in weeks. His eyes were shadowed, his mouth unhappy.

'It's you that started this nonsense, not me.'

'And I'd finish it,' he said at once, 'if I only knew what to do.'

She darted a glance at the lighted doorway, wishing she had never come through it. 'Mebbe you just have to grow up, William, and stop letting your father make all your decisions for you.'

Even in the dusk she could see his face redden. 'It's not as easy as that.'

'I don't see why not.' Looking at him, talking to him for the first time in weeks, she wanted so much to knock down the wall that had begun to grow between them. 'All you need to do is face your father and make him tell you why he's come between us.'

'I've tried! He says he can't tell me.'

'Can't, or won't? You're not a child any more – you don't have to spend your life pleasing him! When my own father made a fuss about us I soon told him what I thought!'

'But I've never gone against him,' William said wretchedly. 'You don't know how things are between us, Margaret—'

She reached out and took his hands in hers. 'I know you're fond of him, but has he the right to expect so much of you? Is it fair to make you turn away from me when I've done nothing and said nothing to anger him?'

'William? Colin's asking for you,' Jamie called

from the doorway, and she felt William's hands flinch, then loosen in her grasp.

'Well?' she asked in an undertone, 'Are you going? Or are you man enough to stay here, with me?'

She felt his fingers slide from hers.

'Wait for me – I'll come back and we'll talk about it—'

'We'll talk now or never,' she said angrily, then, as he remained silent, she went on, 'Best run in and see what he wants, like a good little boy.'

She stepped aside to leave the path free. He hesitated, then brushed past her and went down the path and into the house.

Margaret kicked angrily at an innocent cabbage and bit her lower lip.

'What's amiss with him?' Jamie reached her side. 'I've never seen William with such a bad-tempered look. Were the two of you quarrelling?'

'I'd not waste my breath quarrelling with the likes of him!' Margaret stormed, then it was her turn to push her way down the path and into the house, slamming the door in Jamie's surprised face as she went.

It was late when the evening drew to its close. As was the custom they all stood to sing the 127th Psalm before going off to their own homes, and the wooden beams rang with their voices. 'Except the Lord to build the house, the builders lose their pain; Except the Lord the city keep, the watchmen watch in vain.'

When the guests had gone William helped his father back to his room and saw him settled for the night, helping him to undress and easing him back onto the pillow with a woman's gentleness.

'It was a grand wedding,' Colin said contentedly. 'And it's good to see Kirsty so happy again.' Then he looked sharply at his son's closed face. 'What's worrying you?'

William hung his father's jacket carefully over a chair, smoothing the material. 'The same thing that's worried me for weeks. I still want to know what you've got against me seeing Margaret.'

The light went out of Colin's eyes and he slumped back against his pillow. 'I've told you – I've nothing against her! I just think you're both young, and it would be a mistake to see too much of each other.'

'There's more to it than that.'

'I've told you all that I'm going to tell you!' There was an edge to Colin's voice that William had never heard before. 'For pity's sake will you take heed and stop pestering me!' Then he added sharply, 'Where are you going?'

'Out for some fresh air!' William snapped.

'Wait—!'

But the boy had gone. Colin fell back onto the bed, one clenched fist pounding helplessly at the sheet over his useless legs.

*　　*　　*

The cool quiet darkness did nothing to ease William's mind. It seethed with pictures of Margaret, laughing as she danced, angry when they faced each other in the garden. And there were bitter memories of that meeting in the street a few months earlier, when she had walked towards him and he, honouring the stupid promise his father had wrung from him, had turned away, only to see her go off with Jamie.

'Mebbe you'll have to grow up, William, and stop letting your father make all your decisions for you.' Her voice echoed in his head.

Four large, sturdily shod feet blocked his path, and he looked up and recognised two of his fellow apprentices.

'Will! Come and have a wee dram with us,' one of them coaxed. He shook his head. Colin didn't approve of drink, and he himself had never felt the need of it. But the apprentices were insistent. Unwilling to pull away from the friendly arms draped about his shoulders, William allowed himself to be steered to a nearby howff.

The door opened, sending a shaft of light, a cheerful hum of voices, a thick aroma of smoke and alcohol to where he wavered on the threshold. The two youths urged him on.

He compared the loneliness and bewilderment he had known recently with the warm unquestioning friendship of the young men on either side of him. All at once his need to belong somewhere was more than he could bear. Let his own people reject him – there were others.

Without looking back William made his choice, and stepped through the doorway.

PART THREE

Chapter One

'PAISLEY—' MARY MACLEOD SAID BREATHLESSLY to her companions as she elbowed her way to the front of the crowd '—is for all the world like a drystane dyke. The big stones are the special occasions, and the wee bits holding them in place are made up of the gossip and the scandals.'

She gained a place right on the edge of the road, pulling Margaret and Kate to either side of her, and added with satisfaction, 'Speaking for myself, I have a great fondness for the wee bits. But there's nothing wrong with a big occasion like this now and then.'

Even Margaret, impatient to be back with her charges in the Town Hospital, felt her blood stir as the shrill piping of fifes and the rumble of drums signalled the approach of the procession. Kate quivered with excitement, her lovely red hair shimmering in the June sunshine.

'I've never seen so many people in the town, even for the Silver Bells race. D'you think King George knows that we're doing all this in honour of his birthday?'

'D'you think he'd care even if he did know?'

Mary's sharp elbow delivered a reprimanding nudge that would have sent Margaret staggering into the roadway if she hadn't been wedged against a stout woman.

'There's an unseemly dryness in your voice, Margaret. Whether His Majesty knows or not it's a grand spectacle for the folk and they've a right to enjoy it.'

'It's too crowded!'

'Havers! A procession's best when you can get a good sight of it, and hear it – and smell it,' her aunt added with relish.

They could certainly smell it. Piles of refuse rotted all along the gutters, and on this day, when the street was crowded, the usual aroma was enriched by the smell of humanity itself. Margaret thought longingly of the braes outside the town, where the air was sweet and fresh and scented by flowers that grew wild among the hedgerows and on the grass and in crannies in the drystone walls.

Then she looked up above the heads of the people opposite and found herself gazing directly into William Todd's serious grey eyes. He was at Kirsty's kitchen window, together with his father Colin, Kirsty herself, and her husband Billy Carmichael.

The other three were craning their necks to see the procession, held as a loyal display for His Majesty King George in this year of his reign 1768. But William stared down at Margaret as though she was the only person in that thronged street.

She looked away quickly. In the past five years she and William had never met informally, never been alone together. Hurt pride and misunderstanding had built an insurmountable barrier between them during those years, but Margaret still regretted the end of their deep friendship, though she would have died rather than let William or anyone else know it.

Mary caught at her arm. 'They're coming! Oh, aren't they bonny lads? See – there's your father!'

The parade was headed by the local militia, their tartan plaids and blue feathered bonnets contrasting with the scarlet cloaks worn by many of the women in the cheering crowd. The officers were on horseback, silver buckles at waist and instep catching the sun.

Duncan and Robert Montgomery walked with the Paisley weavers, the largest contingent in the long procession. They were followed by men from the neighbouring communities – Kilbarchan, Renfrew, Beith and Elderslie, and miners from the Thorn village, each group with its own silken banner carried proudly before it. A breeze caught the banners and filled them till they looked like land-locked sails slashing bold colour against the grey and brown stone tenements on either side of the street.

The men stamped along stolidly to the beat of drums and the chirruping of fifes.

A vivid blue gaze met Margaret's as the Paisley men swept by. Beneath it a wide grin almost split Jamie's face in two, and above it his red head added its own contribution to the colourful parade.

After the weavers came their apprentices, a tousled, cheerful barefoot lot.

'Jackie!' Margaret waved, and her father's new apprentice, a skinny orphan recently hired from the Town Hospital, blushed with pleasure then stared grimly ahead, sticking his bony little ribcage out in imitation of the older boys.

In the wake of the official parade danced the children, ragged and over-excited, some of them tormenting the apprentices who marched in front of them, others cheering squeakily for a King who, in Margaret's opinion, probably cared nothing at all for them.

Then the parade was by, and the onlookers surged after the marchers to the Cross to hear the speeches.

Once the formalities were over, they were all free to mingle, and meet friends who had come into the town for the big occasion.

Jamie arrived at Margaret's side. 'Come down to the river with us – I'm supposed to keep an eye on Kate and Archie, and they want to go for a walk.' He nodded to where his sister was gazing into the eyes of a young uniformed lieutenant and added hurriedly as Margaret opened her mouth to refuse. 'They'll be wanting to be together, and that'll leave me looking like an old nursemaid if I'm on my own!'

They had no sooner reached the water's edge than Kate and Archie wandered off together on the pretext of having a closer look at an interesting flowering bush. Jamie guided Margaret to a spot where a log by the river made a comfortable seat.

'I thought you were supposed to watch out for Kate? They're nearly out of sight.'

'Ach, she's fine,' Kate's brother said with a sudden lack of interest in her welfare. 'We'll sit here and have a talk, you and me.'

She settled herself on the log. 'Talk? We talk nearly every day – there's nothing left to say.'

'There's always something—' His voice trailed off and he worried at a twig, plucking the leaves from it one by one.

There was a short silence, then – 'You're not saying much,' Margaret pointed out with some exasperation.

'I'm just – thinking it out first.'

'There's no thinking needed. Just open your mouth and let your tongue clack on the way it usually does.'

'Och, Margaret!' he rapped at her in a sudden irritated burst, 'It's not easy to ask someone if they'll wed you!' Then his face flamed. 'I mean – I should have said – d'you have to gawp at me like that?'

For once Margaret found herself at a loss for words. Finally she said weakly, 'Wed? Are you asking me to wed you, Jamie Todd?'

'Well, I'd – if you – I—' Jamie gazed around as though hoping to find the right phrases hanging from a tree, then sat down suddenly on the grass and stared at the slow-moving river, avoiding her eyes.

'Yes.'

'You're daft!'

'No I'm not!' Jamie argued hotly. 'I'm a master weaver now, and we've been walking out together for a good long time—'

'But not like sweethearts – like friends!'

'I've heard of friends who've wed each other before this!' he almost shouted, exasperated. 'I know you've a fondness for me. Every woman has a fondness for someone, Margaret. Kate, there—' he gestured to the two figures a considerable distance away, '—she's fond of Archie—'

'I'm not Kate!' Margaret was outraged. 'Just because I like someone it doesn't mean that I want to wed with him. I don't want to wed anyone!'

'Don't be daft, Margaret, every woman wants to get married.' Without realising it Jamie went on adding fuel to the fire. 'Is it William?'

She jumped to her feet. 'Is what William?' she asked in a cool voice.

'Is it him you're fond of? Oh, we all knew you liked each other well enough once, but for years now you've scarcely looked at each other. So I thought that – but mebbe I'm wrong. Mebbe he's the one you care for.'

Then he looked at her face and prudently scrambled to his feet. It didn't seem wise to stay on the ground.

'I've never heard such a foolish notion!' Margaret exploded. 'Of course I've no feelings for William!'

'In that case what's to come between us?' he persisted. 'Margaret, will you wed me?'

'No!' She started to flounce past him but he caught at her hand.

'I'd be prepared to wait while you thought it over.'

'You've got your answer!'

His own temper came to the surface. 'My God, woman, you're stubborn! D'you think I've stayed here in Paisley because I wanted to? It was because I thought you and me might settle down together.'

'I've no intention of settling down with any man!' Margaret snapped, and began to walk back to the town, yelling for Kate as she went.

Jamie fell into step beside her. 'If you turn me down I'm leaving, Margaret. I'll go off to be a soldier.'

'Good fortune go with you. Kate, it's time to go home!'

'I might be gone for years.'

'We'll hold a gathering for you when you come back,' said the light of his life grimly.

'Mebbe I'll never come back. Soldiers can get killed.'

She stopped and gazed up at him as he loomed above her. Jamie was a well-made man, and at that moment, blue eyes aflame and red hair raked by exasperated fingers, he looked invincible.

'Tuts, Jamie Todd, who'd ever be so bold as to kill the likes of you? You'll be back, and we'll all be glad to see you. And isn't it time you attended to your sister instead of leaving it all to me?'

But Kate, pretty mouth twisted in a petulant scowl, was approaching them with Archie in tow, and Jamie had to bite his tongue and give Margaret the best of the argument.

Nine people sat down to dinner in the Montgomery kitchen that night. A babble of voices filled the place, led by Mary's. Since Andrew MacLeod's death a year earlier his widow spent a lot of time in her sister's home, rather than 'rattle around', as she put it, on her own in the big house on Oakshawhill. Robert's sweetheart Annie was another frequent visitor, and so was Gavin Knox, a young surgeon who lived in lodgings in Glasgow and often came to Paisley with Thomas, who had attained his ambition and was now a medical student at Glasgow University.

Jackie, the little apprentice, sat at a corner of the table cramming food into his mouth with the dedication of one who was not used to getting enough. Above his busy cheeks he surveyed the company with two round solemn dark eyes which were hastily lowered whenever anyone looked in his direction.

With his pale face and high-domed head, sparsely

covered with fine straight black hair, he looked more like a small middle-aged man than a child of thirteen, Margaret often thought.

She herself had no appetite and no interest in the talk that flew about the table. She pushed a potato about her plate and looked up to find Gavin's clear hazel eyes studying her. She glared back at him and was pleased when he blinked in embarrassment and looked elsewhere.

She didn't have much time for Gavin Knox. The first time he had come to the house he had tripped on a stool and knocked over a pile of pirns she had just spun, and ever since she had dismissed him as a clumsy slow-moving oaf with little conversation. She could never understand why such a ham-fisted man should wish to be a surgeon.

When the meal was over and the dishes cleared away she escaped to the garden to collect the sun-scented clothes that had been spread out on bushes to dry.

Bees making their final forays of the day droned contentedly as they carved a path through the air between the scented blossoms planted specially for their benefit, and the three skeps sitting in a niche in the stone garden wall. With practised ease Margaret folded the clothes, breathing in their fresh summer fragrance. The tight angry knot within her began to loosen.

'It's a grand evening.'

The knot tightened again as Gavin ducked his

dark head under the lintel of the kitchen door and stepped into the garden.

'It was—' she began ungraciously, then added swiftly, 'Mind where you put your—'

It was too late. As they righted the basket and gathered up the spilled clothes she asked in exasperation, 'D'you walk about the wards like that? It's a wonder sick folk ever get better with the likes of you bumping into their beds and knocking them to the floor! Not to mention the harm you probably do with your cutting!'

'So you've got a tongue in your head after all? I was beginning to wonder.' He picked up a sheet and tried clumsily to fold it. 'It's my personal experience that women are only silent when they're mortally ill or already dead.'

Impatient fingers whisked the sheet from his grasp. 'It's well seen you've got no sisters, then! I can attend to the clothes – is it not time you and Thomas were getting back to Glasgow?'

'We're setting off now. Robert and Annie are walking part of the way with us. I thought – we thought you'd like to come as well.'

'I've other things to do. There's been enough time wasted as it is.' She threw the words over her shoulder as she reached for a cravat that had fluttered to the far side of a bush. Gavin's long arm stretched past her and scooped up the errant garment easily.

'The parade? It meant a day off work for the folk – you'd not grudge them a rest now and again?'

'No, but they could surely find a less frivolous cause.' She twitched the proffered cravat from his hand and dropped it into the basket. Gavin fidgeted with a bush that dropped frothy golden sprays almost to the path.

'You think the King's frivolous? So you're no Royalist?'

She shook out a sheet, making it crack in the still warm air. 'I've no objection to the man, but he lives far away in London. We're hard-working folk in Paisley, and it's only other working folk we understand. If the King was to come here and build a house or plant a field or weave a good stretch of linen I'd see the sense in holding a parade to honour him. But as far as I can make out he does nothing useful at all!'

He was still digesting her comments when she added crisply, 'And you'd best leave that flower alone, for I just saw a bee crawl into it. If the poor thing's forced to sting you it'll be the end of it, and we need our bees. You can carry the basket into the house for me, if you've a mind to be of use.'

Jamie's proposal of marriage irritated her like a stone in a shoe. She slept badly that night, and her usual enjoyment in her work at the Hospital was lacking the next morning. The large gloomy apartment set aside as a schoolroom was even more forbidding than usual; a shaft of sunlight venturing in the high, narrow window only served to emphasise the bleakness of the children's surroundings.

'We'll have a botany lesson!' she announced abruptly, and the solemn, pale faces before her brightened noticeably.

Inside the Hospital walls, surrounded by regulations, the children were always solemn and silent, reminding her, as Jackie did, of small careworn adults. But once they were out in the fresh air they started to chatter, and when they reached the fields near the Hospital they raced around happily, freeing Margaret, the lesson forgotten, to return to her thoughts.

Instead of hurrying off to help her mother and Janet when her morning's work was done she called in at her aunt's shop. Although the two of them were so alike in nature that they wrangled continually Mary was the only person Margaret could safely confide in.

She was alone, and in fine fettle, having just succeeded in selling an expensive bonnet to a difficult customer.

'And she took the one I chose for her, not the one she'd have bought herself,' she said smugly. 'A lacy, frippery thing she wanted, and her with a face like a cow looking over a gate at milking time. Not that I told her that, mind you. I put it a shade more politely, and she's fair pleased with what she bought. So am I, for she's a hard one to please. What news is there from the Hospital?'

'Alexander Orr's in the cells again, they tell me.' Margaret said absently. 'He's got the madness.'

'D'you tell me?' Mary tutted. 'Poor Alexander,

I mind what a fine figure of a man he used to be before the smallpox got him.'

'And wee Geordie Lang's in the sick-room again with a fever.'

Margaret thought of the child as she had last seen him, tossing restlessly in his cot. 'He needs fresh air. The Mistress says he gets enough, for he's apprenticed out to run errands for a tailor in all weathers when he's able. To hear her, you'd think these fevers were Geordie's own fault. But what the laddie needs is to run wild for a few years, the way I did – the way you did yourself, living on a farm.'

'We can't all be hearty.' Mary was busy working on another bonnet.

'The Hospital Mistress would agree with you there. She says he's just suffering from the usual fever, the one that often visits folk in that place.' Margaret felt her mouth twist into a wry smile. 'I asked if she thought it was a sort of poverty fever – and she agreed with me!'

'Now, Margaret, there's a lot done in this town to help the poor – and I should know, for I work as hard at it as anyone.'

'But it's never enough! They need good nourishing food, and more care in the sick-room.'

'And where's the money to come from, may I ask? We all give handsomely as it is. I keep telling you – your grand ideas are all very well, but some folk are born to be poor, just as some are born to be clever, or healthy,' Mary lectured. 'You're only flying in the face of Providence when you try to change the natural way of things. Now that we've dealt with the Hospital – what's amiss with you?'

'Nothing.'

'I'd like fine to think you'd just happened by to exchange a word or two, Margaret, but you never put a foot inside my door unless you've got something important to say. So out with it before another customer arrives. Besides, the lassie's due back any minute from making the deliveries. And that's a bonnet for a councillor's wife, not a chicken waiting to be plucked—'

Deftly she whipped a half-made bonnet from beneath her niece's restless fingers.

Margaret sighed heavily and shot a sidelong glance at her aunt, 'Jamie's asked me to wed him.'

'Has he, indeed?' Mary asked without surprise, 'And what did you say to that?'

'I told him he was daft.'

'Daft for asking or daft for thinking you'd have him? I could have told him to save his breath, for there's more ahead of you than marriage to Jamie. But he's a fine young man, and there was no need to be hard on him.'

'No need? And him with the impertinence to think I'd fall into his arms and thank him for the honour he was doing me?'

'Men always think that, poor simple creatures that they are.'

'And then he said – he said—' Margaret almost

choked at the memory, '—that I'd only refused him because I'd a liking for William!'

'Have you?'

'Aunt Mary! You know fine that I've scarcely said two words to him in years. How could I have a liking for any man who spends all his time drinking himself into a stupor?'

'Poor William,' Mary sighed, her fingers smoothing a piece of ribbon. 'Colin's fair out of his mind with worry over him. I never thought the lad would come to this – going from howff to howff with a bunch of ne'er-do-wells.'

'He needn't have, if he'd any backbone at all.'

'You're too hard on him, Margaret.' But Margaret's mouth was set stubbornly, and Mary changed the subject.

'Have you told your mother about Jamie's proposal?'

'And have her planning a wedding? I have not!'

'That was wise of you. Well now, Jamie's proposed, and you've said no, and that's an end to it. Mind you, it's nice to be asked.'

'Hmphh!'

'Is there no romance in your soul at all, Margaret Montgomery? Oh, you'll come to it one day, when you find the right man. Independence is a fine thing – but when all's said and done, there's nothing like the love of the right man,' said Mary with relish.

'I thought you had more sense than that!'

'Oh, Margaret – when the good Lord created you

he was short on the sweetness and heavy-handed with the thorns.'

'Mebbe so, but I've the sense not to want to spend all my days sitting by some man's fireside,' her niece said sharply, and Mary sighed, shook her head, and said no more.

Chapter Two

ONE AFTERNOON IN OCTOBER, AS autumn bronzed the ferns on the braes and the chill promise of winter made itself felt in the evenings, Mary MacLeod made her way up the Waingaitend and past the Town House. Along the High Street she bustled, stepping high to avoid muddy spots and giving a sharp kick to two dogs who tried to start a fight on the footpath just as she approached on her way to see her sister.

Arriving in the grocer's shop she rattled off a list of provisions, finishing with '—and I've decided to hold a Hallowe'en gathering for the young folk.'

Meg looked at her pityingly. 'Hallowe'en? Who in Paisley would want to know about such daft games?'

'All the young folk. Have you forgotten the times we used to have on the farm?'

'We were just children then.'

'I still recall the state you got into with the three caps, Meg – and so do you.'

For the first time in many years Meg thought

of those Hallowe'en nights at home – the smoke-blackened walls of the farm kitchen and the three wooden basins, one holding pure water, one with dirty water, the third empty. And she herself, on the brink of womanhood, standing blindfold with a rod in her hand. She had just started walking out with Duncan, and the game's outcome was vitally important to her.

She remembered her brothers' and sisters' muffled laughter, the scraping sound of the tubs being shuffled about, the slap of water against wood. She remembered her fear, as she blindly pointed the rod, that in the 'best of three' result she would touch the empty basin, which forecast no marriage, or the tub of dirty water, which represented a dishonourable match.

The breathless excitement of that moment held her spellbound for a few seconds, then she came back to the present with a sharp, 'Och, it was only a bairns' game!'

'I mind you picked the dirty water,' Mary said thoughtfully, and was rewarded when her sister flashed, 'I did not – I picked the clean tub!'

'And made a good marriage, so who are you to sneer at Hallowe'en?' Mary seized her advantage. 'As I was saying – there'll be refreshments for the older folk if they care to come along too. We might as well make a proper evening of it.'

'I'm telling you, Mary—'

'No, I'm telling you, Meg – and I'm never wrong. Just one thing – see and get Margaret to come. She needs a bit of magicking to balance that deplorably practical streak she has. I can't for the life of me think who she takes it from,' Mary said airily, and went off to plan her party.

As she had predicted, her house was filled with people on the last evening in October. Instead of turning up their noses at country customs the young folk clamoured to be taught the old courting games.

'The place'll be like a mire in the morning,' Mary said happily as she shooed them all outside into the darkness to 'pull the Castoc'.

They bobbed blindfolded about her kail-yard, grubbing up the greens; then they trooped back into the kitchen, pink-cheeked and blinking in the light, to where Mary waited to examine each root. The comeliness of the future partner depended on the amount of earth clinging to the roots, and the shape of each vegetable.

'Well, he might be cabbage in shape and a dour-looking man, going by all that dirt, but he'll have a good heart,' she said blandly as she inspected Margaret's offering. Then she looked up at her niece, a wicked gleam in her eye. 'On the other hand, he'd make a good rich broth, and that'll please your practical heart. Now – if you leave it by the door, you'll find that the first man who comes in'll have the same initials as your future husband.'

'Keep your black-footing for the likes of Robert and Annie, or Kate and her lieutenant,' Margaret told her crushingly. 'They've already chosen their partners. Speaking for myself—'

'There's someone coming in right now—' Mary interrupted, and Margaret dropped the cabbage and fled to the safety of the parlour.

Under Mary's supervision the young people roasted peas on live coals to test the strength of future unions, cast apple peel over their shoulders to find out the initial of their loved ones, and enjoyed themselves to the full.

Even Thomas and Gavin Knox threw themselves into the make-believe with enthusiasm; the only two on the outskirts were Margaret and William, who had forsaken his usual drinking friends to attend the party at his father's urging.

For the final test Mary bustled the girls into a line in the hall, each clutching an apple and a comb.

'You go into that wee room there one at a time. Comb your hair before the mirror and eat the apple – mind and hold each piece over your left shoulder before you eat it. Then you'll see your future husband's image in the mirror.'

'I'll not look!' Kate shivered. 'I might see someone I don't like!' But she allowed herself to be pushed into the room, and came simpering out after a few moments, refusing to say what she had seen.

'You too, Margaret—' Mary put an apple and a comb into her niece's reluctant hands when the other girls had finished. 'You have to take your turn.'

'It's all nonsense!'

Mary's eyes widened. 'It takes a foolish tongue to say such a thing at Hallowe'en! This is the night the witches and warlocks have their bit of fun, and who are we to deny them? In you go!' She pushed the girl in, closed the door, and went back to the parlour where all her other guests, young and old, had gathered to hear ghost stories.

The small room was lit by one candle. Shadows flickered in the corners and Margaret's face floated in the mirror like a water lily against a dark background. She heard Mary's footsteps clicking across the hall; a babble of voices rose then sank to a dull murmur as the parlour door opened and shut, and Margaret was alone.

She made a face at her reflected image and decided that she might as well follow the rules of the game and get it over with. She drew the confining pins from her hair and combed it out, letting it drift about her shoulders, then she bit into the apple, daring Mary's witches and warlocks to do their worst.

But no male image, strange or familiar, peered over her shoulder to threaten her future. It was as she had already planned – she would walk through life alone, unencumbered, free.

Margaret pinned her hair up neatly and finished the apple, her mind drifting away from the party and the people waiting for her in the parlour, to the lesson she intended to set the Hospital children in the morning.

Then, suddenly aware that time was passing and

she would have to rejoin the others, she glanced up – and saw a dim figure reflected in the mirror, hovering in the shadows behind her shoulder.

With a stifled gasp she whirled round, the apple core falling from her fingers to spin into a corner of the room.

'Margaret—' the man half-way between the door and the mirror moved forward. 'I didn't mean to fright you. I wanted to talk to you—'

'William!' She jumped to her feet, one hand clasped to her throat where a pulse hammered against the soft skin. 'You – you daft gowk! Has the drink addled what brains you ever had?'

The thoughtless words, born of fright and anger, were out before she could stop them. In the flickering light from the candle she saw his face twist as though a sharp pain had lanced through him.

'William—'

But he was already turning away from her, towards the door. He stopped as it opened and light from another candle flooded the room. Gavin Knox stood there, looking from one to the other of them.

'I thought I heard you cry out, Margaret—'

'I didn't,' she said quickly. 'We were just – talking—'

William brushed past Gavin without a word. She followed in time to see the front door close behind him.

'Did I do something wrong?' asked Gavin from just behind her. She looked up at his rugged, puzzled face.

'No, but I did,' she said, and led the way into the parlour.

On the last day of 1768, two months after Mary's Hallowe'en party, Robert Montgomery and Annie were married.

The most striking figure at the wedding feast was Jamie, resplendent in the green tartan plaid and blue feathered bonnet of the 79th Fusiliers.

'Now do you believe I meant what I said?' he asked Margaret belligerently when he first appeared in his uniform. 'If I can't have you, I'll settle for soldiering.'

She smiled sweetly up at him, relieved that at last the matter was settled. Jamie's proposals had begun to be wearying.

'I always believed you – the trouble was that you would never believe me,' she pointed out, and he scowled.

'You'll grow to be a sour-faced old woman if you don't come to your senses!'

'Mebbe so – but if I do you'll thank providence that you're wed to someone else, and not me,' she said but for a fleeting moment, as she watched him moving about the room, tall and broad and handsome, she wished that she could have been an empty-head like Kate, and happy to settle for marriage.

Then she caught sight of William standing behind his father's chair, his eyes on her, and all thoughts of Jamie were swept away in a wave of irritation.

Why couldn't William be the one who was leaving Paisley? Life would be easier if she knew that there was no danger of meeting him and being reminded how drastically his appearance had changed in the past year or two.

Habitual drinking had dimmed his clear eyes and given his fair skin an unhealthy sallow tinge. His shoulders were rounded and his brown hair, once touched with rich gold lights, was lank and untidy. His mouth never curled into the crooked grin she remembered so clearly – instead, it had a bitter twist to it.

'Poor William,' Mary said into her ear. 'He looks as if he's in sore need of a friend.'

'From what I hear he's got friends in every howff and drinking den in the town.'

'You know what I mean, Margaret. For someone who cares about folk, you've an awful indifference towards him.'

Margaret's face felt warm. 'The people I care about can't help themselves! William Todd's brought all his misery on his own head. He could easily have decided to live his own life, as Jamie's done, and me – and the rest of us. Instead, he's chosen to do everything his father orders him to! What sort of a man would do that?'

Mary's eyes were surprisingly unsympathetic as she studied her niece. 'Mebbe it takes a special sort of son to follow his father's wishes without question and go against his own feelings. Mebbe you should remember that you don't know the whole story. You're lacking in compassion, Margaret.'

Hurt anger set Margaret's eyes ablaze. 'If you're so sorry for him why don't you go and keep him company instead of wasting your time with the likes of me?'

'Because it's not my friendship he's hungering for – and anyway, he's just gone out,' Mary said calmly, and a wave of relief swept over Margaret. She felt more comfortable when William was out of the way. No doubt, she told herself, still stinging from her aunt's criticism, he had gone to join some of his drinking cronies.

Outside, William hunched his shoulders against the chill wind and turned towards Pit Land, a tenement in Broomlands Street with a cock-fighting pit at the rear. It was a popular place, and the room was crowded with men when he got there. Weavers and masons and carpenters and merchants rubbed shoulders, for every man was equal at Pit Land as long as he had money to wager.

Here and there were clusters of brawny, unsmiling men with coal dust etched deeply and permanently into their skin – miners from the nearby Thorn Village, opting to spend their few hours above ground in this airless room, gambling their hard-won wages away.

Tobacco smoke hung like pools of treacle in the lamplight. In a sanded circle at the centre of the room two cocks danced towards each other, necks and wings outstretched, then in a united movement they locked, a tumble of bronze and blue-black feathers and sharp eager talons.

William dug into his pocket and tossed some coins onto the ground. Then he leaned against a post and watched with dulled eyes, little caring what the outcome of the fight was.

Blood sprayed suddenly from the black cock and sprinkled the men immediately beside the ring. The red bird went in for the kill amid a chorus of jeers from onlookers angry at the speedy conclusion to the bout. A hand scooped up William's wager and he threw down more money. The victor and its victim were removed and two more birds, bloodlust in their glaring eyes, were loosed on each other.

The white cock, owned by an Elderslie man, was well-known in Pit Land. It was an undisputed champion, but it was getting old and the challenger had ventured his best bird against it, a gamble that paid off that day.

After a preliminary skirmish to assess its opponent's abilities the other bird, younger and stronger, began to shred its adversary coolly and scientifically. The white cock, covered with blood, retreated almost at once but its humiliated owner, with an angry wave of the hand and a curt 'Let it stay!' deprived it of its right to a swift neck-wringing end. A few minutes later it was a sodden red heap and the owner of the new champion swept up his exhausted bird with a whoop of joy and kissed it, smearing blood from its feathers onto his face.

The scene suddenly came into sharp focus for William. The place reeked of death; the man's bloody face and the bird's bright, hard eyes were demonic in the hazy lamplight. His stomach heaved and he pushed his way out roughly, leaning against the tenement wall and breathing in great mouthfuls of air when he gained the street. Then he wandered into the night, not knowing or caring where he went.

He didn't realise that his feet had carried him out of the town and onto the moors until the splash of a small waterfall reminded him that his mouth was dry. He followed the sound through the dark night, slid down a steep bank and plunged his face into the icy stream, sucking water up greedily.

He was tempted to stay where he was, in that quiet empty place far from the town and its inhabitants. But William hadn't entirely opted from his past. Deep within the bitter shell he had become he still cared for his father, and he knew that Colin would be sick with worry if he didn't go home.

With a sound that was half-groan, half-sigh he resisted the impulse to curl up among the reeds and sleep to the lullaby of the waterfall and began to scramble up the banking.

He was almost at the top when a clump of grass gave way beneath his hand and he slid back, twisting and turning in an effort to stop his descent. His head struck a fair-sized stone by the water's edge; he cried out in pain, then lay still, one arm in the cold water.

Margaret plunged along the footpath. Chill droplets sprinkled her ankles as she splashed into a puddle but she ran on without pausing to inspect the damage to her skirts.

Behind her she heard Jamie call her name, but she rounded the corner into High Street, unheeding.

'William's hurt bad – bad—' The words pounding in her head kept time with her flying feet. People turned to stare at her as she sped by, wisps of dark brown hair escaping from under her bonnet to blow round her pale face, blue eyes seeing nothing of her surroundings.

'Margaret!' Jamie caught up with her as she reached Kirsty's street door. 'It was your mother I was sent to fetch, not you! You should've stayed in the shop and let her come back with me.'

'D'you think I'd be content to stand there giving out pokes of meal when William's mebbe dying?' she stormed, and pulled away from him, into the passageway. He stood where he was, watching her disappear up the stairs, then, shoulders slumped, he went slowly into the room where Colin waited for news of his son.

The kitchen was ominously quiet. Kirsty's spinning wheel lay idle, and its owner was bending over the wall-bed in the alcove.

'Meg?'

'It's me.' Margaret went to the bed at once, her eyes dark with fear of what she might find there.

William lay motionless, his body scarcely mounding the covers, his face whiter than the pillow and even thinner than usual, as though the flesh had collapsed in on the bones. A bloodied cloth was wrapped round his head. To Margaret's terrified gaze he looked as though he was already dead.

'Is he—?'

'He's still with us, though the dear Lord knows how he survived that cold night on the braes.' Kirsty straightened her aching back. 'A carter found him this morning – his head's cut badly and it looks as though he's been lying in a burn all night. He was chilled through. When's your mother coming? I'll need her help with the nursing—'

Gently Margaret lifted one of William's hands. It lay passively in hers. 'I'll do it.'

'Best leave it to Meg and me,' Kirsty insisted but Margaret's head lifted sharply.

'I said I'll do it – night and day if need be! If anything happens to him it's my fault, d'you not see that?' She stroked the inert fingers that lay in hers. 'If I hadn't been so cruel to him for doing as his father wanted, he'd never have turned to drink the way he did – and he'd have stayed at the wedding party instead of going off on his own. If he should die—'

Her voice broke and she bent her head over the still hand clasped in her own grip.

'Margaret Montgomery, your tongue's running away with you! I didn't raise him all those years just to see him put into an early grave.'

'I want to help!'

Kirsty gave her a long level look. 'Very well, but if you're so set on caring for him you'll have to stop crying all over him – he got wet enough last night to do him for a lifetime! Now – dry your face and help me to heat more stones to put against his limbs.'

It was a long hard fight. In spite of her brave words Kirsty thought for several days that they weren't going to save William. The soaking he had endured brought on a rheumatic fever, with swelling and tenderness in every joint. Every movement was agony, and Margaret grew hollow-eyed and pale as she listened to him moaning and babbling in a semi-conscious stupor. The physician prescribed one remedy after another and William was bled, purged, treated with hot poultices and cold poultices, and dosed with everything the man could think of.

'I think that man's killing him with his cures,' Kirsty said unhappily. 'What's wrong with warm flannel next to the skin, and good broth – and peace of mind?'

'There's nothing at all wrong with it, for that's what cured me when I was near death's door.' Billy looked down on the grey-faced man in the bed. 'You should try it, Kirsty.'

'You'll have to do something,' Margaret begged.

'I can't stand to see him slipping away from us like this!'

Kirsty hesitated, looking from one to the other.

'If Colin agrees to it, I will. I'll not see William tormented with that man's cures any longer!'

Slowly, so slowly that it was a few days before they noticed the difference, William began to respond to Kirsty's treatment. Margaret was the first to see it taking effect.

'Speaking for myself, I've viewed healthier corpses many a time,' Mary said bluntly when she called to inspect the invalid.

'He's getting better,' Margaret contradicted her. 'He spoke to me this morning. And it wasn't delirium this time. He's on the mend.'

'I'll just have to take your word for it,' said Mary, but once she was settled by the fire in Colin's room she told him cheerfully, 'The boy's looking better every time I see him. I brought some of my best brandy for him, but he's so well cosseted up there that I decided to give the most of it to you instead. In fact, we'll have a sup of it now to cheer ourselves up.'

His eyes followed her gratefully as she bustled about his room. During the dark days when it seemed as though William was going to die, only Mary had realised how bad the waiting was for Colin, unable to walk upstairs and take his turn at watching over his precious son.

She had taken to visiting the invalid every day

and then going downstairs to report on his progress. Now she handed him a cup of brandy then settled herself on the other side of the fire.

'See and enjoy that now. The Honourable James Erskine and his Honourable wife were in for their dinner last night and I opened this bottle for them. My Andra's finest brandy – but d'you think they appreciated it? Not them! "My," says the Honourable, "a real treat, Mistress MacLeod." And down his throat it went in one swallow before I could get a word of thanks out of my mouth. His wife was no better – the two of them were sitting there going at my good brandy as if it was nothing more than water from the street well. So I winked at the maid-servant to bring out the claret instead and put the brandy by for you. I'd have been better giving these two the sour-tasting elderberry wine Andra's sister sent from Melrose last year, for all the taste their tongues have.'

For the first time since William's accident Colin's rich chuckle was heard, and Mary smiled down into her brandy, well pleased with herself.

Chapter Three

JAMIE JOINED HIS REGIMENT SHORTLY after William began to recover from his illness. On his final day in Paisley Margaret took time from her nursing to walk with him across the moors where they had all played as children.

'It's a shame, you going away without a proper farewell gathering.'

'I'd not want one with William still so poorly.' He gave her a sidelong glance from beneath his lashes. 'I'll miss you, Margaret.' Then, as she walked on without answering, he asked impatiently, 'Will you miss me?'

'I've known you all my life – of course I'll notice when that red head of yours isn't around!'

'Can you not find a gentler way of saying it?'

'Jamie—' she said, exasperated, 'You know fine I'll miss you, without me having to say it!'

His eyes brightened. 'Does that mean—'

'No, it does not.'

'You don't know what I was going to say!'

'Yes I do. You were going to say that if I miss you and I don't have to say it because you know it already, it might mean that I feel strongly for you and that's why I don't say that either. But it doesn't work that way.'

'Och – Margaret!' said Jamie, thoroughly confused.

Braving the January cold, she sat down on a flat rock and pulled her gloves off. She had picked some reeds on the banks of a burn, and now she began plaiting them as she had done as a little girl. The moors had their own bleak beauty under the winter sun, and the air was sharp and clear.

'How can you bring yourself to leave this place?'

'That's easy enough.' He paced restlessly round her, kicking at dry dead clumps of grass. 'It's the folk I don't want to leave – some of them.'

'You'll meet other folk. The world's full of them.'

'Will you write to me?'

'If you write back.'

'Me? You know I was never one for letters.'

'It's not hard,' she assured him. 'Just let your fingers do the work. If they wag as much as your tongue does you'll have no trouble.'

Then her work on the reeds was finished, and it was time to go back home. Margaret searched the grassy area round the rock, but there was no sign of her second glove.

'I'll keep your hand warm,' Jamie said daringly, taking the ungloved fingers in his. She clicked her tongue disapprovingly, but let her hand stay in his warm clasp.

'Can I kiss you goodbye?'

'You can not!'

'Surely a soldier has the right to a kiss before he goes off to the wars?'

'What wars?'

'Margaret,' he wheedled, 'I promise I'll bear in mind that we're just friends. One farewell kiss, that's all I'm asking for.'

She couldn't deny a request from someone who might be on his way to the other end of the world. She reached up and put her arms about his neck, her face lifted to his.

Jamie, resigned to the prospect of a swift peck as Margaret's idea of a kiss, was pleasantly surprised. As her lips met his they softened and parted. For a long moment they clung together, and when they drew apart they were both breathless. Before Margaret could move from his embrace Jamie claimed her mouth again.

Her heart began to flutter and she wondered for a moment why she had so often denied herself the pleasure of Jamie's kisses in the past. Then her practical everyday self took over and she drew back, flushed and breathless.

'Well, that's that,' she observed briskly, as though she had just tossed the dirty dish-water out onto the midden. 'We'd best be getting back now.' And she set off for the town at a rapid pace.

Jamie, striding to keep up with her, was content. He could still feel the soft pressure of her mouth against his, and the warmth of her body in his

211

arms. And her lost glove nestled in his pocket, a fitting keepsake for a brave soldier.

Once William was well on the road to recovery a continual stream of visitors tramped up the stairs to see him; Robert and Annie, flushed with the joy and self-importance of their marital status; Kate, perching on the bed and chattering like a bird about her own approaching marriage to her young lieutenant, unaware that each enthusiastic bounce sent waves of pain through poor William's tender joints; Thomas, the gravity of a medical student sitting strangely on his round young face; Mary's sharp, witty tongue bringing the gossip and scandal that made up the 'drystane dyke' of Paisley life.

But his favourite visitor, and the most frequent, was Margaret. By some unspoken agreement neither of them spoke about the misery of their separation. They behaved as if nothing had ever come between them and Colin and Duncan, both shaken by the young man's brush with death, left them in peace.

It was mid-March before William was well enough to go out, walking slowly up and down the garden with his arm about Margaret's shoulders for support, his pale face lifted to the spring sky. The only reminder of the rheumatic fever that had almost killed him was a slightly crooked left elbow.

When he was fit enough to travel, he went down to Beith to convalesce on the farm which was now owned and worked by Meg's brothers. As she watched him go Margaret felt a sudden pang that she hadn't experienced when she waved goodbye to Jamie. William was part of her life again, and his going left an empty space in her days.

But an epidemic of influenza in the Town Hospital soon gave her plenty to do. Hours spent nursing William had given her the patience to work with sick people, coaxing them to take nourishment, watching over them in their delirium, soothing them when they were weak and afraid.

Those who died were immediately replaced by new inmates grateful for the opportunity to walk through the big doors even as the bodies were carried out the back door for hasty burial. Poverty was like the River Cart itself – it flowed endlessly, and filled every available space. But while the river gave Paisley new growth and a reason for its existence, the flow of unwanted humanity contributed nothing.

There were plenty who saw the Hospital as unacceptable, humiliating charity and preferred to beg in the streets and sleep huddled under walls rather than apply for a place.

'More fools, them,' Meg said irritably as her way along the footpath was hinderered by one of those unfortunates one day. 'Littering the public way when they ought to be in the Hospital – I don't know what they think they're about!'

'Have you visited the Hospital?' Margaret asked. 'It gives shelter, but it's a cheerless place – and some poor souls still have enough pride left to want to manage on their own.'

'Pity they don't have the pride to look for honest work.' Meg had worked all her life, and she had little time for folk who didn't earn their own way.

Margaret's eyes flashed blue fire. 'There's not enough work for them all – and some of them are sick. Have you forgotten poor old Rab Dalrymple?'

Meg had the grace to look embarrassed. Rab, an old shepherd, had been forced to give up his work during the winter because of increasing blindness. No work meant no home, and Rab had gone to the Town Hospital. But hunger for the fields and hills where he belonged gnawed at him, and one bitterly cold day he went out, feeling his way along the house walls and out into the countryside, where he was found the next day, frozen to death.

Margaret was haunted by memories of Rab and people like him who were sacrificed because they didn't fit into the community. But there was little she could do about it except work longer hours at the Hospital, helping where she could.

During the epidemic she was sometimes joined there by Thomas and his friend Gavin Knox, the 'clumsy physician', as Margaret always thought of him.

The clumsy physician arrived at Margaret's side one evening as she left an old woman's bedside in the big sick-room, her cloak in his big capable hands.

'Put this on and I'll walk back with you. Thomas'll be a wee while yet.'

She pushed a strand of hair back from her forehead. 'So will I. I've still to—'

'You've done enough for tonight,' he interrupted crisply. 'You'll make yourself ill if you keep working at this rate, and that'll not help anyone.'

She opened her mouth to argue, then shut it again. He was right – her very soul ached with exhaustion. Meekly, she allowed him to put the cloak about her shoulders and lead her out onto the Hospital steps, his hand beneath her elbow.

'Lift your chin up and breathe deeply,' he ordered, retaining his hold on her arm. 'I find it the best way to recover when I've been working too hard on the wards.'

'I've not been working too hard.'

'Yes you have. Your colour's gone and your eyes—' He halted suddenly and scooped her chin into his free hand, turning her startled face up to his. '—You've got nice eyes, but they're shadowed. You should pay heed to what I'm telling you. It was foolish to spend weeks nursing William Todd back to health then go straight to the Hospital sick-room without giving yourself a rest.'

She pulled her chin free of his grasp, and would have freed her arm too if he hadn't held it in such a grip that it would have meant an undignified struggle.

'No need to lecture me! It's those poor sick folk back there who need help, not me.'

'They're getting it. You're not stepping out as I told you.'

'I'm tired!' she snapped at him, and regretted the words as soon as she saw his eyebrows climb towards his untidy dark hair.

'Isn't that just what I said earlier?'

She could have kicked him. Instead she asked icily, 'Did you never think of joining the militia, Mister Knox? You'd have made a grand officer with your fondness for giving orders.'

He grinned, unruffled. 'You can call me Gavin. I might have gone for soldiering if I hadn't set my heart on medicine instead. Mebbe you're not the only one who wants to help folk. D'you like dancing?'

'Dancing?' The abrupt change of subject took her by surprise.

'Dancing. You've surely heard of it? Folk do it sometimes, to music.'

'Folk that have nothing better to do with their time!'

'So you don't care for it? That's a pity, for there's a public dance to be held in the Saracen's Head in three weeks' time. I'd be honoured if you'd agree to be my partner.'

Sheer surprise brought her to a standstill. As it happened, they were outside the Saracen's Head, the main assembly rooms in the town.

'Well?' Gavin prompted.

'But I – I don't know how to dance.'

'You can learn. I'm told that a Mister William

Banks has just opened a dancing school in Waingaitend.'

Panic seized Margaret. 'I'm – I've never felt the inclination to go in for such frippery.' She lied. Part of her wanted to go to the dance, to wear a fine new dress and learn the social arts. But the other part of her was terrified in case she made a complete fool of herself in front of a man who was, after all, a stranger to her. He fell into step with her as she walked on.

'If you feel that you'd not have the skill to master the steps there's no sense in agreeing to go to the dance with me,' he murmured.

'I didn't say I couldn't master the steps if I put my mind to it! I just said that I – I wasn't sure if I'd enjoy the dance.'

'Have you never been to a dance before?' he asked, and she had to shake her head, like a bumbling country girl who knew nothing of society, she thought angrily.

'Then you must let me partner you to this one,' he insisted, and Margaret, afire with mixed feelings, gave in.

Kate thought that the new formal dances from England were the height of elegance, but Margaret's worst dreams were realised. She was not a natural dancer and she hated every step and every lesson at Mister William Banks' dancing classes.

'I'm not going back,' she threatened each time she came home, but when Kate called to accompany her to the next lesson Meg thrust her out into the street and off she went, tightlipped. If it hadn't been for the thought of having to admit defeat to Gavin she would never had gone on trying to master the complicated steps.

Her only pleasure in the whole business came when she put on the gown that Kate had specially made for her. Margaret, who had never been over-interested in clothes, possessed a fashionably long, slim figure, and even she was impressed by her own appearance on the night of the Assembly.

Her gown was of pale green silk over a hooped white underskirt embroidered in the same pale green. The over-gown's low neckline was trimmed with white lawn and the sleeves ended at the elbows in a foam of green ruffles. Her shoes were of white satin, and her brown hair was simply dressed and tied with ribbons to match the gown.

When Meg escorted her into the kitchen where Gavin waited, his hazel eyes blazed with surprised admiration.

'You look almost beautiful!' Thomas said in awe, and Jackie, Duncan's little apprentice, stopped in the doorway, mouth agape, the stoup of water he had been bringing in for Meg tilting in his grasp and almost spilling onto the clean floor.

She stood before them, rosy-cheeked under their admiration, feeling strangely unlike herself, yet liking the sensuous kiss of silk against her skin and the whisper of her skirts as she moved.

When they reached the Saracen's Head light was pouring through all its windows, illuminating the area outside, which was crammed with carriages and horses. In the building's main rooms voices and laughter mingling with the lusty music of a Scottish reel.

'Would you care to dance?' Gavin roared over the noise, and led Margaret onto the crowded floor.

At first it seemed that everything was going to go well. The musicians were playing for a Scottish reel, and Margaret began to enjoy herself as she swung round to the beat of the music, her hands tight in Gavin's, her green silk skirt billowing about her. They danced the next dance, a strathspey, then Gavin led her to a seat and went off in search of a cooling drink.

As he came back, weaving skilfully through the crowds, a cup in each hand, she studied him through discreetly lowered lashes. He wore a deep blue coat with silver buttons, a flowered waistcoat, yellow shirt and breeches, and there were silver buckles on his shoes. His own dark hair, unpowdered, was tied back with a ribbon. He was, Margaret had to acknowledge, a fine-looking man. She took the proffered cup and sipped at it. The evening was going to be more bearable than she had supposed.

But the formal English dances proved her wrong. During the first, she managed to be deep in conversation with someone, watching with growing panic as Gavin adroitly steered Kate through the intricate steps, smiling down into her flushed, excited little face. But there was no escape the second time, and her heart sank as he led her onto the floor and the music began.

Three minutes later he caught up with her as she fled outside on to the balcony, to hide her shame in the darkness.

'Margaret?'

'Let me be!'

His hands turned her about to face him. Beyond his shoulder she could see through the lighted window to where dancers circled and bobbed with stylish ease.

'Are you ill?'

'Ill in the head, to try those daft dances!' Her voice shook with humiliation.

'You were doing fine.'

'You didn't think that when I trampled on your foot, did you? I heard what you said then, Gavin Knox!'

'Well – it hurt at the time. But—'

'At the time? You'll probably be lame for a week – and so will everyone else who was dancing near me!' She realised that she was wringing her hands, and pushed them down by her sides. 'I'm going home—'

'No you're not! You came to the dance with me, and I'll take you home when it's over,' he said firmly, his big body trapping her in a corner.

'I'm not one for dancing – I told you that in the

beginning,' she wailed. 'Why couldn't you have paid heed then and found some elegant Glasgow lady to go with you?'

'I didn't want any Glasgow lady – I wanted you to be my partner.'

She felt tears thicken her throat and plunged on in an attempt to finish before they choked her altogether. 'It's that dancing class that's to blame! Mister Banks won't teach men and women together, and I'm taller than Kate so I always had to be the gentleman and – and I'd have been better dancing with the girl Thomas invited, for I've I – learned the steps all the wr – wrong way!'

The final words came out in a sort of wail, then there was silence, broken only by Margaret's sniffs of self-pity. Gavin drew in a deep breath and stared over her head at the wall behind her. 'Are you laughing at me?' she demanded to know. It was too dark for her to make out his expression.

'No!' The denial was too prompt, too abrupt. Margaret put her hands on his shoulders and stood on tip-toe, peering into his shadowy features.

'Am I to believe, then,' she said tartly, 'that you always have a silly grin on your face?' Then she released him and stepped back, chin tilted belligerently. 'Get on with it, then – get it over with!' she ordered, as if he was one of the children in the class at the Hospital.

She had never heard Gavin laugh so heartily. He roared and whooped and gasped for breath, first supporting himself with one arm about her shoulder – for all the world as though she was one of his drinking friends, she thought indignantly – then gathering her into his embrace.

She endured it stoically, her nose pressed against his jacket buttons, waves of mirth rumbling in his chest and vibrating against her cheek. Finally, just as she was wondering if he was ever going to stop, the peals of laughter eased to hiccups, then slowed.

'Your pardon, Mistress Margaret,' he said at last, his voice still shaky with amusement.

'So I should hope—' she began indignantly, then the words died away as she looked up and saw his face just above hers.

'You look beautiful—' Gavin said huskily and bent his head to hers.

'I – I don't approve of kissing men I scarcely know,' said Margaret weakly when she was free to speak again.

'I should have known that. You'll grow to like it—' he said, and kissed her again.

She should have resisted. Indeed, she fully meant to resist, but somehow time passed and she did nothing about it, other than sliding her arms about his neck and letting her mouth soften and melt beneath his.

In the two weeks after the Assembly Margaret made a point of being out of the house when Thomas and Gavin Knox came from Glasgow.

Memories of those moments spent in Gavin's arms tormented her. She had lost her head – she had behaved like an empty-headed female, and she was afraid that he, like Jamie, would leap to the conclusion that a kiss meant more than it should. But as the days passed and the physician made no attempt to seek her out, her confusion lessened and the Assembly faded into the background.

William came home earlier than was expected. Country air and farm food gave him back his health quickly, and he was soon hungering for Paisley again, for the familiar routine of work and above all for Margaret.

She was wandering alone on the braes, enjoying a rare afternoon's freedom, when a cart rumbled past, bound for Paisley. The man on the box grinned when he saw her perched on the bank of a burn, her skirt kilted about her knees and her bare toes splashing in the water.

'It's yourself, Maggie Montgomery,' he called, and she recognised him as a former schoolmate. 'It's a grand day.' Then he jerked the whip-handle over his shoulder. 'William Todd's coming your way.'

She shaded her eyes from the sun and looked up at him. 'William? He's in Beith, surely.'

'I brought him back myself. He got down just over the hill there to walk the rest of the way—' His voice faded as the cart rattled on.

She scrambled to her feet and ran up the rise, not waiting to put her shoes and stockings on.

Her heart jumped as she saw a figure in the distance, a man walking with an easy swing, unhampered by the weight of the bag slung carelessly over one shoulder. A warm breeze brought her the sound of a melodious whistle as he walked.

She cupped her hands about her mouth. 'William!'

He stopped, looked round, saw her, and began to run. Her hair was in a curly mass about her face, her skirt caught about her bare legs as she sped towards him, but it didn't matter. As they met he dropped the bag and picked her up, whirling her round as though she was a feather's-weight.

'William – put me down! You'll hurt yourself!'

'I will not. I'm as strong and hearty as ever I was, thanks to your aunt's cooking.' He set her down but kept her within the circle of his arms. 'She fed me so well I began to fear that she was fattening me for Christmas.'

'You look so – oh, you just look grand, William.'

He did. His skin had taken on an even gold tan and the gold lights had come back to his soft thick hair. His grey eyes sparkled and the body lightly touching hers was strong and firm.

'And I'm—' she tried in vain to smooth her tangled hair, laughing up at him. 'I must look like a tinker child. What a way to welcome you home!'

He shook his head, hugged her close. 'You're even more lovely than I remembered,' he said into her wind-blown curls. 'And it's the best welcome a man could hope for.'

Then he scooped up his bag and they turned towards Paisley, his arm firmly about her.

Chapter Four

SUMMER BLOSSOMED, THEN GAVE WAY to autumn. Weavers with work to do in the late afternoons had to light tapers to see by. Kate married her young lieutenant and in October Robert's wife Annie gave birth to their first child, a son.

Jackie McNab, the orphaned apprentice in Duncan's employment, decided that the time had come to better himself and plucked up the courage to ask Margaret if she would teach him to read and write 'proper'.

'But I taught you along with the others in the Town Hospital, Jackie.'

His thin little face was crimson, his mouth trembling with the need to say the right things, to convince her of his sincerity.

'But I have to learn more if—' He shuffled his knobbly bare feet and squirmed with self-consciousness, '—if I'm to be a proper master. Now that there's drawlooms coming into the town there's a new need for learning—' His brown eyes begged for her understanding.

Despite Meg's good food, Jackie was doomed to

carry always the signs of a half-starved infancy. He was small for his age, and rickets, that common childhood ailment, had warped his bones and made him look clumsy, though he was agile enough, with a speed of movement learned from the need to dodge blows and keep out of trouble.

'So you want to learn to work a drawloom, do you?'

His face glowed. Jackie's real idol wasn't Duncan, but Robert, who wove cloth on one of the big new drawlooms with an intricate overhead harness that had to be worked by a drawboy.

'If you'll teach me about letters and numbers I'll learn well—' he said huskily, scarcely daring to hope, and she wanted to take his slight body into her arms and mother him.

'You'll have to work hard, Jackie McNab,' she said instead, with a briskness that was meant as much for herself as for him, and was bathed in a huge smile of gratitude and pure love.

'I will!' gulped Jackie, and was as true as his word. Each evening he studied his books by the light of a taper in the corner of the silent loom-shop where he slept. And whenever Robert called at the house, wreathed in the confident aura of a family man with a son of his own, Jackie tried to be there, tucked into a corner of the work-shop, devouring the talk that floated round his ears with the blue-grey tobacco smoke from the men's pipes.

'Gauze is on its way out,' Duncan would announce firmly above the thump of his loom.

'If you're right, there's something to be said for cotton, now they've got that new yarn in England,' his elder son said just as firmly. 'I hear it makes for a better cloth.'

'Let England get on with it, then. We've got our own way of working.'

Robert's fist crashed onto the deep window-sill where he sat. 'Listen to me, man – a Lancashire weaver can make seven shillings in a week!'

'And a Paisley weaver can make the same if he puts his mind to it, without being beholden to anyone. D'you want to see us turning to those manufactories they've started in the south? All the looms under one roof and the weavers working for one employer and not able to call their souls their own? That's not for me!'

'But we have to move with the times!' Sooner or later Robert would come out with Jackie's favourite phrase.

Later, when the day's work was done and he was studying alone in the loom-shop, the little apprentice would clamp his slate-pencil between his teeth in imitation of a pipe, pace the floor, thump his fist on a loom and tell the silent wooden structures about him, each with its half-made cloth stretched between its rollers, 'Man, we have to move with the times, I'm telling you! Move with the times!'

When all was said and done, Jackie had never been happier in his entire life. Every morning he began his day by cleaning and oiling the looms, sneezing as he removed fluff, spiders' webs and, sometimes, snails attracted by the damp dark places beneath the treadles. Then it was time to have breakfast with the family.

Afterwards he brought in water from the street well and swept the back yard, then he took his place in the loom-shop, doing whatever he was bid, and watching the finished cloth gradually take shape between the huge rollers.

If the weavers were keeping pace with the work in hand they very often took the afternoon off, leaving Jackie free to work on his lessons or run off with apprentices from other shops. They bowled, ran races, went to the braes to paddle in cold swift-running burns. Sometimes they went swimming at the Hammells, the River Cart waterfalls close to the town centre, or visited the cock-fighting pit behind the Deer Inn in Broomlands Street. There was always something to do. Ragged and mischievous, rebelliously against authority other than that imposed on them in the loom-shops, the apprentices and drawboys often brought the wrath of their elders down about their uncaring ears, but Jackie tended to be a follower, not a leader.

The market was another popular venue with the apprentices. One of Jackie's closest friends was a carrot-headed drawboy named Charlie Brodie, famed for his ability as a sneak-thief. A walk round the market in Charlie's company usually resulted in some treat or other – pies or fruit or sweets that had magically slipped into Charlie's tattered shirt as he passed a stall.

'Want one, Jackie?' he asked one afternoon as he saw the younger boy's gaze fall on a pile of apples, large and rosy, promising crisp white flesh and sharp-tasting juice that would trickle down a boy's chin.

Jackie's mouth watered. 'I wouldn't mind.'

'Easy.' Casually, Charlie sauntered closer to the stall, looking around, while Jackie watched, his stomach tight with excitement and his tongue already tasting the fruit. Two scarlet globes seemed to glide from the stall into Charlie's grasp. One disappeared into his shift, but as the other one was about to follow a large hand whipped out and caught him by the arm.

'You thief, you! I'll teach you to steal from me!'

Charlie immediately ducked and twisted, but the woman held on and he only succeeded in ripping the sleeve out of his worn shirt. The first apple fell to the ground; he threw the other to Jackie, who automatically put out his hands and caught it. As soon as its firm roundness slapped into his palms he realised his mistake, but it was too late.

'Get that one an' all!' the stall-holder bellowed above Charlie's enraged screeches of innocence. Faces turned towards Jackie, hands reached out to grab him, and he turned and ran for his life. Head down, the apple still clutched in his hands, he butted his way across the market, eeling between stalls until he gained the High Street.

He fled across it, miraculously avoiding the carts and carriages, and ran down Waingaitend with some idea of finding a hiding place in the bushes and trees by the river.

Terror squeezed his heart and all but stifled him. He could have thrown the stolen fruit away and run into one of the tenement entries, protesting his innocence if he had been caught empty-handed. But he could no longer think clearly. All he wanted was to get away, to hide, to be safe from pursuit.

He reached the bottom of Waingaitend and ran by the Town Hospital, too frightened to see Margaret coming down the steps.

She almost fell over him as he fled past, and put out a hand to stop him. Jackie felt her fingers brush his shoulder, and with a thin, choked scream of despairing terror he swerved away, into the roadway and into the path of a large farm cart filled to overloading with refuse collected from a nearby tenement yard.

'Jackie!' Margaret's shriek broke through his panic and he looked up to see the carthorse above him, hooves flailing as the carter dragged back on the reins. Again, Jackie hurled himself to one side, the apple thrown away at last to let his arms curl protectively about his head.

He fell clear of the chopping hooves, which tore lumps of dried mud from the road as they descended, but his bid for safety didn't carry him far enough.

As the cart lurched to a standstill one of its huge

231

iron-bound wheels ran over his outstretched leg, crushing it as if it was a twig.

With a wrenching scream that echoed in Margaret's ears for the rest of her life, Jackie's thin body arched up then fell back, his fingers clawing into the hard-packed earth.

People came running to group around him as he lay there. Margaret was among the first to reach him, heedless of the unnerved horse's hooves as she dropped to her knees by the boy.

The apple, thrown well clear, had rolled into a puddle of stagnant water. It only lay there for a few minutes before a small child scooped it up and carried it off.

There was little they could do to save Jackie's leg. The weight of the cart, taking refuse to fertilise the fields, had crushed and mangled the bone beyond any hope of repair. It would have to be amputated.

Nausea swept over Margaret when Doctor Scobie pronounced his verdict. Jackie had been carried into the Hospital, where he lay, mercifully unconscious, in a cot in the big sick-room.

'Amputation's the boy's only hope,' the doctor repeated, frustrated by his own uselessness in the face of such terrible injuries.

'And what sort of hope is that for anyone?' Margaret asked dully. 'When will it be done?'

'In the morning. I'll have to find a surgeon willing to undertake it.'

A surgeon. The word penetrated Margaret's misery, bringing with it pictures of a square face under dark hair, a clumsy big body and broad capable hands.

'Gavin's one of the finest surgeons you could hope to meet—' Thomas's defence of his friend echoed in her head.

'Wait – I think I know of a surgeon who'd see to Jackie—' she said, with rising hope, and fled from the Hospital, glad to be out of the place and doing something to help the injured boy.

It was only natural, now, to look to William for help. Within the hour the two of them were huddled in a cart, rattling over the town bridge and through the new streets recently built on the opposite bank, each one called after the trades that had brought prosperity to Paisley. Usually Margaret delighted in those fine names – Silk Street, Cotton Street, Gauze Street – but that day she had no time to spare for them.

William watched her anxiously. 'Margaret, from what you say of his injuries, the boy might not recover even if the King's physicians themselves took on his case. You're mebbe expecting too much of Thomas's friend.'

'I'm not looking for a miracle. I just want to know I've done all I can for Jackie. Gavin might – he might—'

She stopped, fighting back tears, and he put an arm about her and held her close against his shoulder.

233

Dusk was hovering over Glasgow's fine broad streets by the time they arrived at Thomas's lodging house. Margaret scarcely took time to introduce herself to his landlady before hurrying upstairs with William following close behind her. She rattled on the door panels with impatient knuckles, then burst in without waiting for an invitation.

The little room seemed to be overflowing with books. They fell over each other on a shelf on the wall, sprawled in heaps on the table, lay scattered over the floor.

Thomas, in shirt sleeves, was sitting at the table, and Gavin lounged comfortably in a chair by the fire. The two men looked up, startled, then jumped to their feet.

As Margaret poured out the story of the little apprentice's accident the medical student and the surgeon exchanged glances. They let her finish without interruption, then Gavin took her over the details of Jackie's injuries again, interrupting her several times, making her describe the wounds as accurately as possible. When she had finished there was a long silence while he deliberated.

'From the sound of it there's not much I can do to save the leg—' he began and William interrupted him.

'If you're not willing to try, we'll walk the streets of Glasgow till we find someone who is!'

A muscle twitched in Gavin's jaw, and his eyes seemed to frost over as they met William's glare.

'I was about to say that I'll do my best. I'll come to Paisley first thing in the morning.'

'Now! Come back with me now!'

An irritated frown furrowed his brow. 'I'm on my way to dine with friends right now, and it's an engagement I can't cancel. Besides—'

She flew at him and he took a step back under the unexpected onslaught. 'Be damned to your dinner-party!' The oath sprang easily to her lips in her agitation, though it was the first time in her entire life she had used it. 'There's a child lying in the Hospital, needing your care right now!'

Appalled by his sister's behaviour, Thomas sprang forward, but it was William who reached Margaret first, pulling her away from Gavin and into the shelter of his own arms.

The surgeon smoothed his blue embroidered silk coat.

'The child needs to rest tonight – and so do I, for I've been working in the wards all day and I'd not trust my own judgement at the moment,' he said coolly. Then he added, in a kinder voice. 'You have my promise that I'll be in Paisley first thing tomorrow. Go home now, Margaret, and get some rest yourself. We'll all need to be strong tomorrow.'

When Margaret arrived at the Hospital early in the morning Gavin and Thomas were already there, closeted in a small side-room with Jackie. Clear-eyed and calm, the surgeon gave her a brief nod by way of greeting when they came into the Mistress's room with Doctor Scobie.

'There's nothing for it but to take the leg away.'

Despite herself Margaret felt her lips tremble. 'But – all he's ever wanted is to be a master weaver. A weaver needs his two legs!'

'He needs to be alive, too.' Gavin's face darkened. 'It's a matter of trying to save the boy himself now. Thomas, you know what we'll need.' He took his coat off and dropped it on a chair. 'Margaret, do something useful – take the children outside, away from this business.'

Not many people could dismiss Margaret Montgomery as easily as that and hope to get away with it. But Gavin was no longer Thomas's clumsy, amiable friend, or even the man who had kissed her at the dance. He was a professional trained man with an air of authority about him that she had never seen before. Meekly, she did as she was told.

Thomas felt a stab of envy as he watched his sister lead her charges out of the building. It was the first time he had assisted at an operation under such circumstances, and his skin prickled with apprehension as he went into the room where Jackie lay on a large table. Gavin was setting out his instruments, his face mask-like as he concentrated his mind on the work ahead.

Thomas splashed whisky into a cup and lifted

Jackie's head. The boy choked, coughed, then swallowed the liquid that trickled into his mouth. Patiently Thomas fed the cup's contents to him, drop by drop.

When Jackie's eyelids fell and his breathing took on a thick, slow note, Thomas put the empty cup aside and bared the injured leg, drawing in his breath sharply as the shattered mass of bone and bloody flesh was revealed.

The two male inmates who had volunteered their services for payment of sixpence each paled and turned their heads away, but mercifully they both retained their determined grip on Jackie's small body as ordered.

Gavin's eyes were calm and his hand, as it gripped Jackie's thigh just below the groin, was steady. For a second he paused, then the knife descended.

The small paupers, revelling in their freedom, scampered along the river's banks, noses reddened by the chill wind. Margaret found a sheltered area and paced up and down, tormented by thoughts of what must be happening back at the Hospital. Finally, unable to banish the terrible pictures from her mind, she resorted to a childhood trick, thrusting her ungloved hand into a thorn bush, letting the pain of a dozen small scratches shock her back to her surroundings.

The minutes dragged by, and she felt as though she must have aged years by the time the sun indicated that it was midday and she was able to gather up her charges and shepherd them back to the Hospital.

They went willingly enough, their appetites whetted by the fresh air, eager for the piece of bread and the small plate of broth that made up their midday meal.

Gavin, Thomas, and Doctor Scobie were all in the Mistress's room. Thomas, gratefully sipping at a glass of brandy, smiled wanly at Margaret.

'He's survived the operation – and a fine job Gavin made of it,' he added proudly.

'It was that,' the physician chimed in and Gavin, his shirt sleeves and waistcoat spotted and blotched with blood, nodded in offhand acknowledgment of their praise.

'It wasn't a difficult task. But there's many a fine piece of surgery hidden in a grave.'

Margaret's heart was touched by an icy hand, 'You mean he'll die after all?'

He eyed her thoughtfully. 'Don't expect too much, Margaret. The boy's not strong and I've no great hopes for his future.'

Fear for Jackie, the shock of the accident itself, and the surgeon's seeming indifference suddenly welded together within her to red-hot fury.

'So you think you've had a wasted journey? You think we should have got someone else to cut the boy's leg off – or mebbe we should just have left him to die in the street, seeing he's only an orphan and a pauper? I'm sorry if we've taken you away from the important work of tending to a rich man in a fine Glasgow hospital, but you've no need to worry, for I'll pay your fee whatever the outcome. You'll not be out of pocket – not even if your doctoring kills Jackie!'

'Margaret!' Thomas's face was crimson with anger and embarrassment. Doctor Scobie was scandalised, the Hospital Mistress pursed her lips disapprovingly, but Gavin merely raised one eyebrow.

'You're angered with me,' he said unnecessarily. 'There's no need. I care for the boy's welfare, but it doesn't do to get upset over any patient, rich or poor. If I let myself do that every time I'd not be a good surgeon, you see. And I want to be good at my work.'

'I've no doubt you will be, one day – when you've tried your hand on folk that don't matter to anyone – like Jackie!'

'Margaret!' This time Thomas's voice was a whip-lash, cracking across the small room.

'Leave her be,' Gavin advised him calmly. 'She needs to speak her mind. Though you're being hard on me, Margaret. Best prepare your mind for the worst, as I do in these circumstances.'

'Why not?' she asked bitterly, unable to stop the tirade now that it had begun. 'What chance does he have now, in any case – a crippled pauper!'

Gavin got up unhurriedly and crossed the room, 'Just so,' he agreed, and went out, closing the door gently behind him.

Thomas's fingers ground into his sister's arm, forcing her down on a chair.

'Will you hold your tongue, for the love of God – and take a sup of this, for it seems you need it more than I do!' The cup containing half of his brandy was thrust into her hand, and he stormed out of the room.

He found Gavin outside on the steps, leaning against the Hospital wall, his hands in his pockets.

'Thomas,' he said thoughtfully when his friend tumbled out of the building and arrived by his side. 'The more I see and hear of your sister, the more I think she'd make a grand wife for some ambitious man.'

'If,' said Thomas, his voice tight with rage, 'anyone'd be stupid enough to want her!'

Chapter Five

Formally, Margaret proffered Gavin's amputation fee – three shillings and four-pence – on the day after the operation, and formally he accepted it.

She watched the coins disappear into his pocket with stunned disbelief. She had fully expected him to refuse payment on the grounds of his friendship with the family. Then she would have been able to force the coins on him and thus ease her troubled conscience.

She glared up at him, and reddened as she glimpsed a sparkle of malicious amusement in the hazel eyes that met and briefly held hers. Then he was serious again, looking down at Jackie.

'He's survived the shock of the cutting, at least.'

'He seems to be comfortable.' She caressed the sleeping child's face lightly with one finger.

Gavin said nothing, and she knew what he was afraid of. Thomas had taught her that gangrene was the surgeon's greatest enemy. All too often infection set into a wound and killed the patient.

Nobody knew why, Thomas said, his round face perplexed.

'D'you like tending the sick?' Gavin asked as they left Jackie's bedside.

'I like seeing folk getting better. Thomas is lucky to be going into medicine. I wish I could have done that.'

'Hospital work's not for the likes of you,' he said decidedly. 'They can be dirty places – it's a wonder to me that anyone gets well at all in some of them. I've seen dogs running in from the street to forage round the beds for food. And the women that work in the wards – lazy old hags willing to buy drink for any patient who'll share it with them.'

'Mebbe someone should change things.'

He shook his dark head. 'I doubt if that'll ever happen. The folk that care the most are too busy trying to cure the sick to do anything else, and the rest are indifferent.'

In the days that followed he came to Paisley whenever he could to see his patient. Jackie regained consciousness of a sort, though he was too confused to take in what had happened to him. Margaret was glad of that, for she dreaded the day when the boy would discover that he was crippled. In his conscious moments he fretted because they wouldn't let him get up despite his pleas that Mister Montgomery needed him in the loom-shop, but Margaret's presence soothed him a little, so she sat by his bed for hours, listening to him babble about the years ahead, when he would be a drawloom weaver with apprentices of his own.

On the fifth day Gavin came to meet her as she went into the sick-room. His face was pale.

'Margaret, before you go in to him – I've changed his dressings and—'

She knew then that the fight was lost. The poison that had crept into Jackie's wound claimed its victim with hideous efficiency, and when the end came Margaret could only be thankful that Jackie's sufferings were over.

Gavin pulled the dirty sheet over his patient's face and walked out without a word, leaving Margaret to tell the Mistress the news and beg some brandy from her.

She found Gavin in the empty schoolroom, staring at the wall. She put the cup into his hand, and his fingers curled automatically about it.

'You did your best.'

'It wasn't enough.' He drained the cup in one gulp.

'Gavin—' she said awkwardly. 'I was wrong to speak to you the way I did that first day.'

'You said what was in your mind.' His head was bent, both hands gripping the empty cup as though he was warming himself with it. 'I can never accept a death,' he said, more to himself than to her. 'I should have got used to them, but I never do. This one – it was wasteful. The operation went well. He would have lived.'

'He'd probably have become a beggar if he had,

poor boy. He'd have hated that – perhaps it was as well it ended this way.'

'I'm not thinking of that!' Gavin said fiercely. 'I don't care what might have become of him. He died because of something we haven't found yet. Because we know how to cut folk, but not how to care for them properly after the cutting. And I can't for the life of me think what we're doing wrong!'

Then he put the cup down and went back to Glasgow and his duties there, without another word.

Jamie came home just when Margaret most needed the sight of his cheerful grin and blazing red head.

'You're sure you've missed me?' he asked jealously during one of their moments together.

She beamed at him affectionately. 'The whole town misses you. You're like a stone in a pond, Jamie Todd – you cast ripples everywhere you go.'

'I'm not talking about the whole town, just about you!' He paused, then added, carefully casual, 'I see you and William are as cosy together as a couple of old women gossiping at a street corner.'

'And why not?'

Jamie scowled. 'Mebbe I should have stayed home. Mebbe if I had you and me would be—'

'Would be quarrelling most of the time instead of enjoying the times we can be together, like this,' she finished the sentence swiftly. 'Admit it, Jamie – you'd not change your soldiering life for anything.'

'I'd not go as far as to say that—' he began, then grinned and shrugged his broad shoulders. 'Well – mebbe you're right. There's things to do and places to see, and the restlessness in me's eased a little now.'

Then, as they rounded a corner and came on a group of sturdy girls, hair tucked under linen caps and round brown arms and legs bared to the chill wintry sun as they gathered water to wash the linen that was spread out to whiten, he added with a wolfish twist to his grin, 'But I'll admit that Paisley has some bonny sights!'

'This is a bonny pattern.'

William, on one of his many visits to his father's room, lifted a sheet of paper that Colin had left lying on his cluttered work table.

Everything Colin needed lay on that table – colours for his designs, volumes he used when he taught his young pupils, sheets of paper scrawled with verses, the half-dozen books that Colin happened to be reading – they huddled together in what seemed to be chaos to the observer, though he himself knew exactly where every item was and resisted all Kirsty's efforts to tidy things up for him.

His thin face flushed with pride at William's praise, though his voice was casual. 'I'm pleased with it – but I'll no doubt have to make some changes before it gets to the loom. The weavers are still complaining that I expect too much of them at times. Mebbe one day some clever man'll invent looms that can take my designs as I mean them to be.'

'Nothing surer.' William sat down on the other side of the fire that kept the December chill at bay, and sprawled his long legs over the hearth rug with the air of a man well-pleased with himself. 'I've been thinking about my future.'

'Aye?' Colin's loving eyes travelled over the younger man's face, noting with relief how well and happy William looked now that he had stopped drinking and found peace with himself and his surroundings.

'Aye. I like working with Billy Carmichael well enough, father, but my apprenticeship's long over now and it's time I started out on my own. See—' he held his hands out, laughing. 'Not a mark on them that wasn't put there by honest toil. Mind when I started work? I was never done hammering my fingers or cutting them instead of the leather. I've mastered my trade at last.'

'How's your arm?'

William punched the crooked elbow, the only reminder of his bout of rheumatic fever, with his other fist. 'It doesn't bother me at all,' he said carelessly, intent on telling his news. 'Now – I was out at Renfrew last week, and there's a wee shop there to rent. It would make a nice beginning for a man setting up in business for himself.'

'What would you use for silver?'

William grinned disarmingly, sure of his reception.

'That's why I've come to you – though you'd always be the first to hear of any plans I might have anyway,' he added hurriedly. 'If you could lend me the money to start off with – it'd not be much, just enough for my rent and my materials, I'll work all the hours God sends to pay it back and get myself properly started.'

'It can be a hard life, setting up a new business. I know, for I did the same when I was about your age.'

William brushed the warning aside with a wave of one hand. 'I know that, but I'm not afraid of hard work. It would do me good – I'm getting too lazy working for Billy, for there's not enough to keep me as busy as I'd like. He could manage with another apprentice, he doesn't need a time-served man, to tell the truth.'

He stopped, eyeing Colin anxiously. The older man deliberated for a few moments, eyes fixed on the flames in the grate, then he looked up and nodded.

'You can have as much as I can afford, and welcome.'

William jumped up and shook his father's hand vigorously. 'I'll only take what I need to see me started, and not a penny more. I want to work for

247

what I get.' He paced the floor, the words tumbling out as he planned aloud.

'I could be in business by February at the latest, and my debt could be paid off by next year at this time. By then I'll know how soon I can afford to find a wee house and get wed—'

Colin's laughter, rarely heard, interrupted him. 'Hold on, man!' he protested. 'One minute you decide to set up on your own and the next you're a married man? You're letting your tongue run away with you.'

'Oh, but I've got it all worked out. I'll not ask Margaret until you've got your money back, but by then—'

'Margaret?' his father interrupted, the laughter suddenly wiped from his face, his hands clutching at the arms of his wheel-chair. 'What Margaret?'

William stopped pacing. All at once it seemed as though the temperature in the warm room had dropped sharply. A gust of wind rattled at the window.

'What Margaret do you think? Margaret Montgomery, of course,' he said, then his gaze hardened. 'Father, you're not going to start all that nonsense again, are you?'

'Have you spoken to her of marriage? What makes you think she'd have you?' Colin's voice was harsh in its urgency and William frowned.

'I told you I'd no intention of asking her until I've got something to offer her. But I think – I hope – she'll accept me when the time comes.'

'You can't marry Margaret Montgomery.'

The bleak words seemed to take shape and stand between the two men like a barricade. William's young face flinched, then set in a cold mask.

'So you're planning on coming between us for a second time, are you? D'you not think that you and Duncan Montgomery have caused enough trouble between Margaret and me? We're grown now – we don't have to heed our fathers any more.' He leaned forward, each word clear and definite. 'I'll not let you tell me what to do with my life now – and if I have to, I'll find the money I need from someone else – so don't think you can try to buy my obedience!'

Colin's face, youthful in his happiness only minutes earlier, was old and drawn. 'Listen to me, William. Believe me. You can't marry Margaret Montgomery!'

William's hands clenched into fists by his sides. 'I'll not listen! And I'll not let you and her father conspire against us this time. I was willing to wait for another twelve month before I spoke to Margaret, but not any more. I'm going to her tonight, and I'm going to ask her if she'll give me her promise that she'll be my wife as soon as I can offer her a home.'

'And if she refuses you?'

William's mouth twisted. 'If she refuses me of her own free will I'll accept that. But I hope she'll say yes – and if she does, father, I'll bring her back here with me and we'll throw your small-minded bigotry right back in your face!'

'William – I'm begging you to leave things as they are!'

'I love her, and I've wasted enough time. If you've got good reason for coming between us a second time then for God's sake tell me what it is—' William strode to the door where he paused, one hand on the latch '—or mind your own business from now on!'

For a moment there was silence, then William's tension was released in a long breath.

'You see? There's no real reason at all, is there? Just some bee you and old Montgomery got in your bonnets. I'm going to Margaret.'

His thumb pushed the metal tongue down, releasing the latch. His wrist tensed to pull at the door.

'She's your sister.'

Even the flames in the hearth seemed to stop moving. William's fingers tightened on the door handle but he wasn't aware of its edge cutting into his palm. He felt as though he had been pushed off the edge of the world and was cart-wheeling through space.

'What?'

Colin's voice was bleak. 'Margaret Montgomery is your sister.'

William opened his clenched hand with difficulty and walked across the room to the window. Kirsty was spreading her washing over bushes to dry. Her rounded arms, damp from the wash-tub, seemed impervious to the bitter wind.

Billy came from further down the garden, a muddy spade in his hand, and said something to her as he passed. The two of them laughed together.

William turned away from the scene, avoiding Colin's gaze, and picked up the design he had been looking at earlier.

'How can she be my – my sister?' he asked through stiff lips.

'Because Duncan Montgomery's your father.'

There was a pause, then – 'Go on!' William's voice was rough, ugly. 'Or am I supposed to try to guess what happened? D'you want to turn this nonsense into a child's game?'

'It isn't nonsense, William. I wish to God it was. Your mother, Lizzie, was my wife, but it was Duncan who fathered you, not me.'

'How did it come about?'

'I don't know the full story of it. I never wanted to know.'

'Well, I do!' The design was crushed into a ball, thrown aside. 'It's my existence we're talking about! Why wait till now to tell me?'

'I thought you were my own flesh and blood until a few years ago, when Duncan saw the danger of you and Margaret becoming too close. It makes no difference to me. You were never his – always mine!'

'"When Duncan saw the danger—"' William

repeated, stunned. 'Duncan saw it? But it was you that came between us – you that used my affection for you to get my promise that I'd not see Margaret again.' He ran a hand over his hair, bewildered. 'You damned near killed me, to cover up what he'd done to you – and to me?'

'He wanted to be the one to speak to you, but you'd not have listened to him, and neither would Margaret. D'you not see that? It had to be me. It was the only way I could think of to protect you and her from the truth!'

'But you've kept your friendship with him! With the man that betrayed you with your own wife!'

Colour flooded Colin's face but his voice didn't waver. 'What's the sense in raking up the past and hurting innocent folk who know nothing about this?'

'It was all right to hurt me, was it? To put me through hell and then do this to me when I finally come out the other side and try to make something of my life?'

'If you hadn't fallen in love with her you'd never have had to know—'

William laughed bitterly. 'I might have realised the fault would lie with me at the end of it!'

Then he asked, low-voiced, 'Is there anything else I should know while we're about it?'

Colin's fingers had teased a thread from the blanket about his knees, and twisted it about his index finger until it was a livid white.

'Lizzie – your mother – she didn't die when you

were small. She went off with another man. I've
no idea what happened to her after that.'

'The bitch!'

'You'll not speak of her like that?' Colin flared
at him. 'When all's said and done she's still my
wife and your mother!'

William's laugh sounded as though it had been
blessed in Hell. 'My mother? An hour ago I had
no mother! An hour ago I was a happy man!'

'William, it's breaking my heart to see you
like this!'

'Is it? Who else knows about – about me?'

'Only Kirsty.' Fear jumped into Colin's eyes.
'You'll not tell Margaret or her mother? It would
kill Meg if she knew—'

'You think I'd want to tell anyone about this?
You think I'd want anyone to know that I'm
the fool that was going to ask his – his half-
sister—' William choked the words out '—to be
his wife? They'd all have a good laugh over
that one in the drinking houses and the loom-
shops!' His hands clenched on the back of a
chair.

'Go and see Duncan,' Colin urged, at his wit's
end. 'Talk to him. Ask him all you want to
know—'

'No! If I found myself alone with Duncan
Montgomery I'd not be able to keep my hands
off him. He's made a bastard of me – he'll not
make me a murderer as well.'

'William, listen to me—' Colin implored, but the

hard young voice flowed on, each word striking at Colin's heart.

'"The sins of the fathers shall be visited on the children." Is that the way it goes? I could never believe the Almighty would be cruel enough to make that come true, but He has. My Heavenly Father! That makes three fathers I've got today – and not one of them able or willing to give me any comfort!'

He lunged towards the door.

'Where are you going?'

William looked back at the man huddled in the wheel-chair, a look so devoid of feeling that Colin's breath caught in his throat.

'As far from Paisley as I can,' he said, and went out of the house where, after a lifetime, he felt that he no longer belonged.

'But why go away now, just when – when everything's all right again?' Margaret asked, perplexed.

'Because I'm tired of Paisley, the way Jamie got tired of it. There's other places to see.'

'William Todd, you'd hate soldiering and you know it!'

William's face was set in a stubborn scowl. 'There's more than soldiering.'

'What, then?'

'All sort of things. Don't nag at me, Margaret! I'll go to Edinburgh first, to Unc—' he stopped abruptly, then went on '—to Matt's farm. Then

I'll find work in the city, or mebbe I'll take ship for some other country.'

Matt Todd had left the Army years earlier and was farming outside Edinburgh.

'There's something you're not telling me,' Margaret said suspiciously. Then her face darkened. 'Your father's not starting his nonsense about us again, is he?'

'No!' William exploded, then drew a deep breath. 'No, of course not. I just want to stretch my legs. Leave it at that, Margaret – a woman can have no notion of the way a man's mind works!'

There was a ruffled silence while she eyed him narrowly and he glowered at a beetle struggling up a blade of grass.

'I know how your mind works,' Margaret said at last. 'I know you'll not be able to stay away from Paisley for long. You'll be back soon enough.'

The toe of William's boot flicked the beetle off the grass stem. It soared through the air and disappeared from sight into a clump of reeds.

'I'll never be back,' said William. 'Never!'

PART FOUR

Chapter One

RAIN FELL STEADILY FROM A grey sky. It pattered on the earthern streets and, with the help of horses' hooves, cart-wheels and feet, turned them to quagmires. March of 1770 had come in like a lamb, blue-skied and rich with the promise of spring; now it was going out like a lion, laying down a grey, damp carpet to welcome April.

Even the red tents sheltering the kail-wives and their wares at the open-air market looked drab and colourless. Customers hurried through their business and turned homewards without stopping to talk. The place was almost deserted.

'You should have stayed by the fire,' Margaret told Gavin as they splashed along the High Street and turned towards the market. He pulled his hat more firmly over eyes half-shut against the rain.

'A wee bit water never hurt anyone. And it looks as if it might be easing,' he said optimistically.

If it had been up to Margaret she would have stayed at home, snug and dry, but her mother needed some vegetables for the evening meal. At least she and Gavin were warmly dressed and well shod.

She went from stall to stall, prodding the merchandise with an experienced finger, bargaining with the kail-wives who were, for the most part, bare-armed and bare-headed in spite of the rain. Gavin followed her patiently. Living in lodgings as he did, he enjoyed the domestic side of life in the Montgomery household.

Margaret finally decided between two large solid cabbages and paid the woman.

'That'll please my mother. You'll be staying for your dinner, I suppose?'

'I will. I enjoy your mother's cooking.'

'I've noticed,' she said dryly, and stopped at a stall to peer at some cheeses.

Gavin stepped across a puddle. 'Mistress Paterson feeds me on herring and potatoes every day. First thing in the morning, then again in the evening with a mug of small beer.'

She looked up at him, blinking against the rain. 'You seem to be thriving on it.'

'I am that,' he agreed cheerfully. 'It's a fine nourishing diet, but a change now and then's more than welcome.'

'Mistress!' An old woman wrapped in a greasy, tattered cloak that had long since lost its original colour and warmth tugged at Margaret's sleeve. 'Mistress, have you mind of Beth Lang?'

'Beth? I mind her fine.'

'You've to come to her right now, for she needs

you,' the woman said, and scuttled off over the wet slippery ground like an aged crab. Without any hesitation Margaret pushed her basket into Gavin's hands and followed her down one of the narrow lanes leading to the maze of alleys and closes and tall houses by the river.

The area was the oldest part of the town and its tall buildings had long since deteriorated into dirty, neglected slums. This was where the poor who could still afford some form of shelter congregated. Rubbish was piled high on footpaths and streets, the gutters flowed with stinking water, many of the windows were empty holes in the walls, open to the wind and rain.

Margaret followed the old woman into a lane so narrow that her shoulders almost brushed the walls on either side. Something squelched underfoot and she recoiled instinctively. When she looked up again her guide had vanished. Just ahead was a doorway, two crumbling steps up from the street. She went through it into a dark ill-smelling passageway, felt her way along the slimy walls, and almost fell through an opening. The stench of the small room caught at her throat.

The place was lit by one tiny window. Half its panes were broken and the gaps stuffed with rags in a vain attempt to keep the wind out. The existing glass was too thick and too dirty to allow much light to filter through.

As Margaret's eyes accustomed themselves to what there was she made out a rough table and a bench. The old crone stood beside a younger woman who held a whimpering baby in her arms. A man snored in one corner, his face to the wall. A pile of rags in another corner moved, and she realised that several children were lying there in a heap.

'There she is—' The old woman pointed to the darkest corner of all, where someone shuddered and trembled on a heap of straw.

'Beth?' She dropped to her knees, heedless of the filthy floor. The girl, in the grip of a spasm that made her entire body shake violently, groaned as Margaret tried to take her into her arms.

'Margaret! In the name of God where are you?' With a wave of relief she heard Gavin's voice from the passageway.

She called to him, and saw the shock on his face when he arrived in the doorway.

'Gavin, it's Beth from the Town Hospital – she's sick—'

'She's been taken with the fever,' the old crone said, though by now Beth's teeth were chattering so hard that they could all hear her, even above the man's snoring and the wails of the baby. Gavin knelt, brushing Margaret's hands aside with an impatient, 'Out of my way till I see to her.'

She stood up. The last time she had seen Beth the girl was employed as a servant in one of the big houses, and doing well.

'What brought her to – to this place?' she asked the women, who shuffled uneasily.

'She'd need of a roof over her head, and enough to pay for her keep,' the younger woman said reluctantly, her voice hoarse and slow. 'But now the money's gone and she's sick. You'll have to take her back to the Hospital.'

She began to cough, a bubbling cough that racked her body. The baby, fearful of falling, caught hold of her hair with tiny grasping hands and cried louder.

'She told us about you.' The old woman took over the story. 'She'll have to get out of here.'

The other woman straightened, spat, and sucked air into her lungs, the coughing fit over. The sick girl's breath whistled in her throat.

'She'll have to get out of here,' Gavin agreed, his voice grim.

'What's wrong with her?'

'She's dying.' He straightened up and tore his coat off. 'And it's no wonder, in this place.' He wrapped the coat about Beth then lifted her in his arms. 'Out of here, Margaret, if you value your own life!'

He pushed past the two women, Beth's tangled fair hair swaying as her head lolled against his shoulder. The old crone, her good deed done, spat an oath at him, but the younger one allowed herself to be elbowed aside without complaint, her gaze fixed avidly on the table where, Margaret saw, Gavin had put the basket containing her mother's cabbage.

'Here – make the children some broth with this—'

she said before she followed him out, thrusting it into the grimy hand that was already reaching out to claim it.

Gavin was waiting in the street, breathing deeply to flush the fetid air from his lungs. In the grey light of day Beth looked as though she was made of grey-blue wax.

'Show me the way out of this rabbit warren.'

'Gavin, will she—'

'Hell's teeth, woman, stop chattering and do as I tell you!' he roared at her.

They made an incongruous trio; Margaret in her good warm clothes, Gavin, his waistcoat and shirt black with rain-water, and Beth, unconscious in his arms, her ragged gown half-covered by the elegant bottle-green coat he had wrapped about her. But few people turned to stare as they passed, for they were in a part of the town where folk minded their own concerns and it was not wise to be too inquisitive.

As they turned into New Sneddon Street a passing carriage stopped and Mary MacLeod's sharp nose appeared at the open door.

'Margaret! What in the world are you up to now?' she demanded of her niece.

'She's saving a life,' Gavin snapped back, wrenching the door open and stepping up into the carriage as though the girl he held weighed no more than a rag doll. 'Drive us to the Town Hospital.'

'No!' Margaret scrambled up behind him. 'I don't

want her to wake up and find herself in the Hospital sick-room. That's where her brother Geordie died of the poverty fever.'

'The – what?' he asked, bewildered. Then Beth began to cough in great harsh spasms that twisted her thin body, and he said tersely, 'I don't care where we take her as long as she finds a warm place to rest.'

'Then we'll go to my own house,' Mary decided promptly. As the wheels began to turn she sat back and murmured to her niece, 'He's mebbe a bit on the sharp side, but I like his style!'

'You might not be able to save the girl, Mistress MacLeod.' Doctor Scobie's long sad face looked longer and sadder as he walked into Mary's parlour an hour later.

'I'll make a brave try at it, though. What ails her?'

He pursed his lips in a way well known throughout Paisley. 'Well, now – her brother was never strong, as I mind. And it seems that she has the same tendency to be affected by humours in the atmosphere—'

'She's half-starved and worn out,' Gavin interrupted from behind him. The older physician looked ruffled.

'Mebbe, mebbe, but even so—'

'But why was she in that place at all, when she left the Hospital to work in Councillor Brodie's household?' Margaret wanted to know.

'Why is anyone in a hovel like that?' Gavin's face was dark with anger. 'Who owns the place?'

'I'll – I'll be on my way,' Doctor Scobie said uneasily, picking up his bag and giving one last regretful glance at the cupboard where Mary kept an excellent Madeira. 'I'll call tomorrow morning, Mistress MacLeod – that is, if the girl's still with us by then—'

'I'll let you know if she should leave,' the lady of the house assured him graciously, and rose to accompany him to the door. 'And I'll make sure Beth's still alive tomorrow,' she added when she returned, 'for I don't believe in giving in to doctors and their opinions. Now – you were asking about these tenements down by the river. All the property down there's owned by Councillor Johnny Brodie.'

'The man that employed Beth?' Margaret asked, stunned.

'The very one. A bad-tempered, greedy wee runt of a man, he is – but a great one for making money and keeping it.'

'Come on, Margaret—' Gavin's hand clamped round her wrist. 'We've got things to discuss with Councillor Brodie!'

'Now don't go upsetting the man,' Mary squawked primly after them, a glint in her eyes.

'I've a feeling poor Johnny's in for a shock,' she added to her late husband's portrait, hanging above the ornate fireplace. 'And it serves him right!'

*　　*　　*

Councillor Brodie lived in a large and comfortable house only five minutes' walk from Mary's. His thin eyebrows rose at the sight of Gavin's dishevelled appearance.

'You find my wife and I enjoying a quiet hour at home. You'll take some claret?'

'Thank you, no.' Gavin ignored the chair he had been waved to, and stayed on his feet. Margaret declined an invitation to sit on the sofa by Mistress Brodie, so the councillor was forced to remain standing with his guests. He was a small man, intended by Nature to be thin but blessed, because of his wealth and self-indulgence, with a pot-belly which, together with his skinny limbs, gave him the look of a beetle that had learned to walk on two legs.

Gavin swept aside the usual formalities. 'We're looking for a girl named Beth Lang. I believe she's in your service.'

Brodie's jaw dropped and his wife looked up briefly from her embroidery. 'I mind the name, Johnny. She came from the Town Hospital, did she not?'

'To take up employment in your house.' Margaret's voice was angry, and Gavin laid a restraining hand on her arm.

'That's her. I dismissed her,' said Mistress Brodie serenely, and returned her attention to her work.

'There you are, then. She was dismissed.' The councillor was clearly beginning to wish that they would go away and leave him in peace.

'Why?' Gavin turned his attention to Mistress Brodie. She looked him up and down, decided that he was a fine looking young man, recalled that she had two daughters as yet unmarried, and smiled on him.

'Theft.'

'Never!'

'Hush now, Margaret,' Gavin reproved. 'And when would this be, Mistress Brodie?'

'Some two weeks since. I thought you'd have seen her back in the Hospital, Margaret, and got the whole sorry tale from her.'

Margaret kept her voice under control with an effort. 'She didn't go back. What's she supposed to have taken?'

'I recollect it now,' the councillor butted in, annoyed at being ignored in his own parlour. 'She's the one who took the ribbon from Lizzie's room.'

Margaret turned to him. 'You found it in her possession?'

'No, but she must have taken it, for it disappeared and the only other servant's from a good Paisley family, so it wasn't her,' the councillor's wife nodded complacently.

'You turned a girl into the street because of a missing ribbon?' Gavin asked slowly.

'It was our Lizzie's best new ribbon!' Mistress Brodie pointed out.

'We could have sent the girl to the cells and had her flogged for theft,' her husband chimed in. 'But we were generous. We just told her to go.'

'Where did she go?' Gavin pressed.

'That's not our concern.'

'I'll tell you anyway. She took lodgings in a house you own by the river, and now she's mebbe dying. There's a whole family still there, living in a way you'd not force on a pet dog.'

The councillor retreated a step or two towards the sofa. 'The girl's a thief – no responsibility of mine. And if you can't be civil to me in my own house I'll thank you to leave!'

'Civil!' Margaret began, but Gavin's fingers bit painfully into her wrist and she stopped.

'D'you ever visit the houses you own by the river, Councillor?'

'I've no need. A man sees to collecting the rents for me.'

'Would you come with us now and see where we found Beth Lang?'

'I will not, for I've important town business to attend to. And I'll have no more of your insolence, Mister Knox!' Brodie retreated right behind the sofa. His wife, who was easily his height and fat all over, rose to her feet as though prepared to defend him with her embroidery needle if necessary.

'We'll leave, since you request it in such a civil manner,' Gavin's voice was suddenly silky. 'Come on, Margaret.'

'That was a fine performance!' she snapped at him when the councillor's door closed behind them.

'Why didn't you let me speak? I'd have given him something to think about!'

'So will I, in my own way. Best leave him to me, for I don't live here and he can't harm me the way he might try to harm you or your father.' Gavin looked up at the afternoon sky, which was beginning to clear, then said again, 'Come on, Margaret,' and set off along the road, her hand clasped firmly in his. 'We've got work to do before night falls. We'll go to the Hospital first.'

In the next hour, working with an air of efficiency and authority she had never seen before, he hired a cart and persuaded the Hospital Mistress to find room for the family living by the river.

'The youngest'll be dead in a matter of weeks, and the mother's in a bad way too, so they'll not take up room for long,' he told her with cruel honesty. 'But we might be in time to save the rest of the family.'

When they returned to the room where they had found Beth he marched in and pulled the man to his feet, ignoring his fuddled protests.

The women and children began to cry in fear and panic as he half-carried his feebly struggling burden out to the waiting cart. Before he could re-enter the room the younger woman slammed the door and started to drag the table against it. Margaret tried to stop her and the woman clawed at her, hissing like an enraged cat; then she shrank back as the rotted wood of the door exploded under the weight of Gavin's foot.

'For pity's sake, can't you see that you're being saved, not murdered?' he roared in exasperation, and the children's sobs redoubled.

'You're frightening them! Why don't you try kindness?' Margaret shouted at him over the din. 'How would you like it if a stranger burst into your home and began to drag you out?'

'I'd like it fine – if I lived in a sty like this!' he retorted, and threw a handful of coins down on the table. The noise stopped at once as the women and children stared at the money. Then, as if by magic, the table was bare and the children were being hushed and gathered together.

Gavin grinned at Margaret. 'You see? Money can do more than kindness,' he said smugly, and ushered his charges out to the waiting cart.

'Mister Brodie'll easily find more tenants to replace them,' she said helplessly when the family had been driven off, clutching their few possessions.

'Not in this room.' He led her back into the building. 'Look at it – the walls are running with water—' His fingers sank into crumbling plaster and with a short sound of disgust he rubbed his hand on his coat and moved to the window. Tall as he was he had to hoist himself up to peer through what glass remained. The breeze ruffled his dark hair. 'The river runs right by this wall. It's oozing in through the foundations.'

He dropped to the floor, then went down on one knee to examine the boards. After a moment he stood up and stamped hard. A plank crumbled under the weight of his foot and the room smelled worse than ever.

'I thought so.' He looked round and his eyes fell on her. 'Give me that thing you've got round your neck – I'll buy you another!' he added as she hesitated. Dumbly she handed over her small headshawl and watched as he wrapped it round one hand then began to rip the floorboards up. The stink in the room was indescribable now, and she clapped a hand over her mouth and ran to the door. Outside, she breathed fresh air in deeply before venturing back into the room.

'Stay where you are,' Gavin rapped as she arrived in the doorway. He was examining the large cavity he had made in the floor. Rotten boards were piled by his side.

'A sewer runs right under this floor. It's a wonder these folk didn't fall through the rotted boards. Well, if Mister Brodie won't come and see it for himself we'll just have to take the proof to him.'

Gingerly, he tied a rag round a piece of flooring and dipped it into the hole he had made. It came out saturated with thick stinking slime.

'Now – we're going to pay another visit to the Brodies,' said Gavin coldly.

Chapter Two

WHEN THE COUNCILLOR'S MAIDSERVANT AN-
SWERED the door Gavin shouldered it wide
and marched through the hall, Margaret at his
heels. Straight into the parlour he went, ignoring
the maid's cry of, 'But the master has callers—!'

Councillor Brodie and three other men sat round
the table; Mistress Brodie and one of her daughters
plied their needles diligently on the sofa. Six pairs
of eyes looked up as Gavin swept in. Six noses wrinkled as the smell from the rags reached them.

'There—' He dropped his unpleasant burden on
the table before Brodie, '—is your lodging house,
Mister Brodie.'

The man's face paled and he stood up, pushing
his chair back so violently that it crashed to the
floor. His wife and daughter squealed.

'Don't go, gentlemen,' the surgeon added smoothly
to the other three men, scrambling to their feet.
'You're welcome to hear what I have to say. This
rag comes from a bed used by children in a house
owned by Councillor Brodie here. A sewer runs
under the floor. The river seeps into the building

through the walls, and wind and rain have access through broken windows. You can judge for yourself what the stink's like. The children's mother's dying and their father drinks all the money that comes in – apart, I'm sure, from Mister Brodie's rent – to forget the misery of it all.'

Mistress Brodie fainted onto her daughter's shoulder. The colour had flooded back into her husband's face, and his eyes had begun to bulge. His companions were discreetly melting across the room and out of the door.

'I'll have the law on you!' the councillor raved, pointing a shaking finger at Gavin.

'You do that – and I'll see to it that the whole town knows how you treat your tenants. I'll make you a laughing stock in this place.'

'I'll set the militia on you – the pair of you!' Brodie screamed. Dirty mud from the rag oozed over his polished table and the papers strewn across it. Gavin leaned over to prod at the man's fat belly.

'You're welcome to try,' he said with quiet menace, his finger forcing the councillor a step back at each word. The man almost tripped on his overturned chair and only an undignified skip kept him upright.

'I just wish,' Gavin said with real regret as they stepped out of the councillor's gate, 'that I could have pushed him into that sewer. He belongs in it.'

Margaret was almost dancing with glee. 'You did enough! Oh, Gavin – I was proud of you!'

Then her smile faded. 'But your clothes are ruined – and look at my skirt! We're like a couple of tinkers!'

He examined a jagged tear on his coat sleeve and shrugged. 'Mebbe my landlady'll be able to mend it.'

'Come on home – I'll see to it.' She walked on, thinking about the family who would be trying to come to terms with their new life in the Hospital at that very minute, and had got to the end of the lane before she realised that Gavin wasn't with her.

He had perched himself on a low wall and was staring intently at a small and ugly pig that was nosing happily round a pile of refuse. Gavin had broken off a twig from a branch overhanging the garden wall behind him and was twisting it absent-mindedly between his fingers.

She went back to see what was of such interest to him but could find nothing – only the contented pig.

'I've been thinking, Margaret,' Gavin said, his eyes on the black twig with its tight-curled sticky buds. 'I've been thinking it would be a good thing if you and me were to wed.'

'You're daft!'

When she had said that to Jamie by the river he had angrily defended himself. But Gavin, lounging on the wall in the day's dusk, merely said, 'I think I must be. What's your answer?'

'But – why should marriage come into your

head in a place like this?' She indicated the lane, the muck-heap, the rooting pig.

'I didn't plan to mention it here,' he said with a hint of exasperation. 'But I suppose one place is as good as another for the purpose. We get on well enough and I like your sharp way of treating folk, though I realise that most men wouldn't. And there's a lot of sense in that pretty head of yours. I'm ready to settle down – and I have no wish to settle with anyone but you.'

'But I scarcely know you!'

'I've been coming to Paisley with Thomas for a good year now. Besides, we can get to know each other better when we're married, and living in the same house,' he pointed out. 'The more I think of it the more the idea pleases me. You're going to refuse me, aren't you?'

She glared at him. 'If I am I'll do it myself. No need for you to stick your nose in!'

He rubbed the offending feature and grinned. 'You're free to make up your own mind, and you always will be. But as your brother's closest friend I feel it's my duty to advise you to give my proposal some thought. I'm a good catch.'

Then he got up, scratched the pig behind one ear with the branch, and walked on down the lane, saying over his shoulder. 'Come to that, it would be a fine match for both of us.'

It was a ridiculous proposal – unromantic, ill-timed; never, surely, had a woman received a more disinterested offer of marriage, Margaret thought angrily. She ran after him and caught him up as he reached the corner.

'We'd fight – all the time.'

'Well – most of the time, perhaps. I'm counting on that, for I never wanted a dull marriage.'

'If I wasn't happy I'd not stay.'

'I'd hold the door open for you myself. Well?'

Exasperation, disbelief, bewilderment milled together in her mind, together with the dawning realisation that her life would never be the same again, now that Gavin had walked into it. And the further realisation that she didn't want him to walk back out of it.

'Well?' his maddeningly calm voice prompted.

'But Gavin – you've never said you love me!' she almost shrieked at him, stamping her foot. 'Why can't you say you love me?'

His expression, polite interest with just a hint of anxiety underlying it, wavered and crumbled as though it had been a mask, giving way to a look that made her heart flutter and her head spin. She swayed, and might have fallen if he hadn't swept her into his arms.

'And risk the rough edge of your tongue? Oh, Margaret,' he said against her neck, 'are you entirely blind? Don't you know that I've loved you since that night you danced all over my feet?'

'I didn't—' she began to say before his lips stopped hers.

'Don't you know how impatient I've been, and how afraid that you'd send me away if I spoke at the wrong moment?' he asked when he finally lifted his head. 'I thought I'd lost you when William Todd came back from Beith, for the two of you were together so much—'

She ran her finger-tips from the corner of his mouth to where his hair curled on his temple, and the sensation brought a melting joy she had never known before. 'William's one of my closest friends, nothing more.'

Her fingers buried themselves in his hair, sliding round to the back of his head, pulling him down to meet her eager lips again. The pig found a choice morsel and nibbled at it happily, its little eyes fixed on the couple who stood, locked in each other's embrace, at the corner of the lane.

'My mother,' said Margaret shakily, when she was free to speak again, 'will be pleased.'

He grinned down at her, his tawny eyes openly alight with happiness. 'She will. But d'you think our news'll be enough to take her mind off the loss of that fine cabbage we were supposed to bring back?'

Chapter Three

B Y THE TIME MARGARET AND Gavin married, three months later, Beth Lang had recovered from her ordeal in the slum by the river, and had been taken on as Mary MacLeod's companion.

'It's pleasant to have a young person about the house again,' the milliner said on one of her visits to Margaret's new home. 'I've been lonely since Thomas went off to Glasgow. Though I'm right glad—' she added with more than a touch of malicious pleasure, '—to have you two so near me now.'

Margaret flushed crimson and thumped the teapot down with more energy than necessary. Gavin had agreed to her wish to stay in Paisley, where she could continue her work in the Town Hospital, but only on condition that they took a house fit for a surgeon. Despite her protests, he had bought a house on Oakshawhill, almost the twin to Mary's.

'And that's a nice respectable maid-servant you've got,' Mary went on mercilessly.

'It was Gavin employed her, not me,' her niece

snapped. 'I could have managed the house fine on my own!'

Gavin gave up trying to hide his amusement. 'Poor Ellen has to run morning noon and night, trying to get through the housework before Margaret does it for her. I found the two of them nearly at each other's throats yesterday over who was to get to scrub the kitchen floor.'

'I can't sit still and let someone else clean my house for me!'

'Now, Margaret,' he said with that air of calm possessiveness that both maddened and warmed her. 'You do plenty, what with the Hospital and helping your mother in the shop and entertaining our visitors. That's more than enough for someone in your—'

He stopped short as his wife glared at him.

'—condition,' Mary serenely finished the sentence, setting her cup down and brushing a crumb from the lacy ruffles at one wrist.

'I told my mother in confidence!'

'Tuts, Meg never said a word – it was the smug look she's had on her face for the past seven days that gave it away. Gavin's right, though – you'll have to learn to let other folk take on some of your work.'

A wet, cold October left Colin with a heavy chest cold, and Meg with an agonising bout of rheumatism that forced her to stay at home. That same month the widow who lived with her family in the rooms behind the shop re-married and moved with her family out of the town altogether, leaving the burden of the shop on Margaret's shoulders.

'Colin'll have to find someone else!' Gavin insisted, worried about her health. 'What about the girl that worked there before?'

'Janet? She's gone from bad to worse, married to that lout of a husband,' Meg fretted. 'She's got a family by his first wife to see to, and her own children – not that I'd be able to trust her on her own now.'

'William!' The worried frown cleared from Margaret's brow, to be replaced by a broad smile. 'He's the very one to look after the shop.'

'He'll not come back,' Meg scoffed. 'He's happy working for Matt. He wouldn't even come home for your wedding.'

'But he'll do it for his father's sake. And there's no denying—' the cloud drifted over Margaret's face again 'that Uncle Colin's getting frail now. I'm sure William'll come home – and I'll go to fetch him myself!'

There were moments, during the bumpy carriage ride to Glasgow and the bumpier coach journey to Edinburgh, when Margaret regretted her decision. When they reached the capital Gavin had to carry her in his arms into the coaching inn, where he coaxed some brandy and water between her ashen lips.

'But don't ask me to eat, for I never will again!' she said miserably into his comforting shoulder, her stomach heaving at the aroma drifting from the kitchens.

By the time the brandy was finished she felt a little stronger, and after a night's sleep and a good breakfast the following morning she was herself again and impatient to make the final short journey out to the farm where Matt lived with his wife Mirren.

Their visitors got a warm welcome. Matt, strong and handsome as ever in spite of his greying head, sent a boy to fetch William, who was out in the fields.

'I think he'll want to go back with you, for Colin's sake. But he'll be missed here, for he's a good worker.'

'You should come back yourself, for a visit,' Margaret urged, but he shook his head.

'This place won't run itself. And to me, Paisley was never the same after my father died. I'd see his ghost everywhere. Have you had news of Jamie?'

'The last we heard he was in London, and wondering if he might be sent out to the Americas.'

Matt's big body heaved in a nostalgic sigh. 'There's nothing like soldiering to set a man up,' he said, then grinned at Mirren and added, 'Mind you, there's something to be said for a settled life and the right woman to share it.'

'You're right,' Gavin said from the window-seat,

his gaze reaching across the low-ceilinged kitchen to enfold Margaret in its warmth.

Then he looked out of the window and saw a tall, lithe, well-muscled young man come into the cobbled yard, two farm dogs twisting round his feet as he walked.

'What is it? Is it him?' Margaret saw his change of expression and hurried to the door. Then with a glad cry of 'William!' she was running across the yard.

Gavin watched from the window as William stopped in his tracks; surprise, disbelief, and something else that was controlled so swiftly that Gavin hadn't time to register what it was, chased each other across his tanned face. Then Margaret threw herself into his arms, almost knocking him over, and he caught her and held her close.

In that moment, as he saw his wife's dark brown head blend with William's short, loose curls, bleached by an outdoor life into a tumble of bronze, Gavin knew a stab of uneasiness, and something even stronger. Something that had until then been alien to him.

Jealousy.

'There's nothing in Paisley for me. I'm better where I am.'

Margaret put her spoon down, her face stiff with astonishment as she faced William across the table. 'But your father's not well! He needs you!'

'Did he ask for me to go back?'

'You know he'd never do that. He doesn't even know we're here.'

'That's all right, then.' William kept his head bent over his plate, though he wasn't eating. 'He can get a woman in to tend the shop. There's plenty'd be pleased to get the work. I've my own life to live here.'

'But we all want you to come home, where you belong,' Margaret persisted, and his head was suddenly thrown back, the gold lights in his hair catching the lamp's glow, his eyes angry.

'I don't belong there! I never did!' he said, and pushed his chair back.

'William! Tell him—' she appealed to Matt as the door to the yard slammed behind William, but the older man shook his head.

'He makes his own decisions. I don't know why he's so bitter, but it's deep in him. Best not tamper with it.'

She rose from the table and followed William out to the yard, stumbling as her eyes tried to accustom themselves to the change between lamplight and darkness. A dog growled at her and William's clipped voice silenced it.

'William? Stop this nonsense and come back to Paisley with us!'

'It's not nonsense!' he rapped back in the same tone that had dealt with the dog. 'I'm not one of your Hospital children to be ordered about!' Then he added, his voice changing. 'Why did you have to come here and meddle in the life I've made for myself?'

'I just want you to come back to your father – to all of us—'

She reached out to touch his arm and felt the stuff of his coat slide by her fingers as he pulled back. Then a soft gold light spilled over them as the farm door opened. The glow touched his eyes and gave them the same tawny light that Gavin's had. She saw them move over her, stop at the spot where pregnancy swelled her gown.

Gavin, silhouetted in the doorway, called at her, and William said, low-voiced, 'Go to him, Margaret. Go back to Paisley with him and leave me to my own devices!'

Then he was gone, merging into the shadows, the dogs at his heels, and she was alone.

As Robert Montgomery had predicted, silk was becoming one of Paisley's main cloths, though linen was still of considerable importance. On her return from Edinburgh Margaret managed to get a small incle loom set up in the Hospital so that some of the women there could weave ribbons, another popular new product.

She also found a woman to work in the grocer's shop, and Meg herself was soon back behind the counter, wincing when she had to stoop to ladle grain from the sacks on the floor.

Colin couldn't shake himself free from his chest cold. It settled, and they were all reminded, as they heard his harsh cough, of his father's chronic bronchitis.

Margaret persuaded Beth Lang, Mary's companion, to take over her work at the Hospital temporarily. She and Gavin battled over her decision to return to teaching once her baby was born, and she won.

'But it's not seemly for a woman to leave her child to someone else's attentions!' Meg fretted.

'I'm needed at the Hospital. I'll not be away from the house all that much, and Ellen's well able to watch over the baby when I'm not there.'

'Isn't it a blessing,' said Mary slyly, 'that you've got a maid-servant?'

'Since Gavin insists on employing one, Aunt Mary, I might as well make use of her,' her niece said sharply, and Mary smirked into the ribbons and lace of the hat she was making.

It was a relief to Gavin when Margaret stopped going to the Hospital and the shop every day. He worked hard, and it made all the difference to him to find her waiting for him when he came home.

Their marriage was very happy, for all its minor storms, and they looked forward together to their baby's birth.

The tranquillity he prized so much was shattered when he arrived home one evening in late November to find Margaret pacing the parlour floor, shaking with rage, while Mary sat by the fire and watched her with a worried frown.

'I'm glad you're back. See if you can talk sense

to this woman,' she appealed to him. 'It's not good for her to get herself into such a state.'

'Gavin!' Margaret clutched at him, her bright eyes and the tension that almost sparked from her body alarming him. 'You'll have to make them see reason! You're a surgeon – they'd surely listen to you!'

'Who? For the love of God, Margaret, sit down and tell me what's amiss?' He pushed her gently down onto the sofa and sat beside her. 'You'll do yourself and the baby no good!'

'That's what I told her. But it's the Society—' Mary began, and he groaned.

'Not the Society for the Reformation of Manners again! Margaret, haven't I advised you to keep well away from them?'

'D'you think that would make any difference? Looking the other way's not the answer!'

'Sometimes it's the only thing a sensible person can do!'

The Society for the Reformation of Manners was a group of well-to-do Paisley people who took it upon themselves to seek out and chastise the sinners in their midst. Compassion and understanding were not emotions that they recognised, and both Margaret and Mary had clashed with them on more occasions than Gavin cared to remember.

'You think we should just let them get on with their foul work unhampered?' There were tears in her eyes. 'Gavin, they're going to flog Janet through the town tomorrow if we don't stop them!'

'That's the woman who used to work for Colin and Meg.' Mary offered. 'It seems she took some cloth from a loom-shop and sold it.'

'But surely that doesn't warrant a flogging?'

Margaret took a deep breath, then said in a flat, calm voice that worried Gavin more than her former hysteria, 'It does as far as the Society and the Council are concerned. Janet's to be driven through the town tomorrow, and given ten lashes at each end of New Street, then another ten lashes at the Cross. Then she'll be put out of the town to fend for herself.'

'And her children,' Mary finished the story. 'That no-good man of hers got out of harm's way the minute he heard that she'd been taken.'

'You've spoken to the Society, Mary?'

'We both have – Duncan and Meg too. But Johnny Brodie's in control of them now – and he's waited for nearly a year to get his revenge for that business over his house down by the river.'

Gavin groaned again. 'Councillor Brodie!'

'They've hired a man from outside for the work.' Margaret's voice was still flat. 'They're paying him three guineas.'

'What? That's more than I'm paid to amputate half a dozen limbs!'

'The Society seems to think it's worth the cost,' Mary said dryly. 'Well, I've done all I can – I'll have to get back home. Take my advice, Margaret

– tell yourself that you can only do your best and no more.'

When she had gone Gavin gathered Margaret into his arms.

'Mary's right – what more can anyone do?'

'You're a surgeon,' she repeated. 'They might listen to you.'

He gave in. 'I've little hope of succeeding, but I'll try – after I've had something to eat.'

She was in bed, wide awake, when he got back. He sat on the bed and took her hand.

'Councillor Brodie's done his work well. Not one of them would change his mind. They as good as told me to mind my own business.' The humiliation he had suffered at the hands of Brodie and his cronies choked him. 'Make up your mind to it, Margaret – you can't always expect the whole town to dance to your tune, and that's a fact.'

Without another word she threw herself over in the bed, turning her head away from him, listening to the sounds of him undressing.

For the first time, they slept without holding each other.

'I wish I could stay with you today, but I'm needed in Glasgow,' Gavin said after a silent breakfast on the following morning. He hesitated, then took her into his arms. Her lips were cool and unresponsive to his kiss.

'Stay in the house today. Don't go out.'

'That won't save poor Janet from her flogging, will it?'

He shook her gently. 'Margaret, nobody can help Janet now. Can you not see that?'

She could, and she would have been happy to stay at home, closing her mind to the day's events. But it was impossible. When the crowd gathered to witness the flogging she was on its outer fringes, watching as Janet was driven up in the back of a cart, her wrists lashed to the rail before her.

The woman, younger than Meg and Mary, looked years older than either of them. Her face was lined, her straggling lifeless hair was grey. Margaret, who hadn't seen her for years, was shocked by the effect life had had on the girl who used to work behind the grocery counter. A carriage bearing some of the Society's members, Councillor Brodie among them, followed the cart.

As the man paid to administer the punishment raised his whip Margaret suddenly came to her senses. Gavin was right – she couldn't help Janet this way. She was only adding to the mob that had come to jeer and gawp and be glad that it wasn't happening to them. She turned, and would have hurried back to Oakshawhill if the crowd hadn't surged forward to get nearer to the cart, closing round her and carrying her with them.

The whip descended. Janet's curses rose to a scream, and to Margaret, fighting to keep her feet as she was carried forward, it became old Hector Lyle's public hanging all over again. She felt her throat constrict and closed her eyes against the faces round her, especially the sight of Janet flinching as the whip came down again and again on her back.

The darkness behind her lids flashed red lightning and threatened to draw her down into its depths for ever. Afraid that she might lose her footing and be trampled, Margaret opened her eyes again and saw a crimson thread of blood run down Janet's chin as the woman sank her teeth into her lower lip. Her face, turned towards Margaret, was knotted with pain as the lash landed for the tenth time. Then the whip was laid aside and a small cup of spirits held to Janet's lips. She sucked at it greedily as the cart jolted into motion down the slope that led to the foot of New Street.

Jostled by the crowd, unable to fight free, Margaret was forced to follow and witness the next ten lashes.

'For God's sake have some mercy!' she heard herself scream at the men in the cart as Janet's thin shawl was torn to shreds and fell, wet and red, from her back. But nobody heard her in the noise of the crowd, half of them jeering at the victim, the other half shouting encouragement to her and abuse to the stony-faced Society members in their carriage.

When at last they reached the Cross, and the

final ten lashes were administered Janet's defiance had gone, and she slumped over the cart's rail, her body jerking as the lash hit it. The man who wielded it was clearly softening the blows, for now that the sport of it was gone the crowd's mood towards him was becoming threatening.

Then it was over, and Janet was released and allowed to fall to the floor of the cart. The militiamen in attendance kept back the crowd as her friends lifted her and carried her away. The Society officials hurriedly left the scene, and the crowd dispersed, leaving Margaret free, at last, to go home.

All she wanted was to go to bed, to hide herself from the day's events in sleep. But when she reached the front door Gavin opened it, his face a mask carved out of ivory.

'Where have you been?'

She dragged her shoulders straight, walked past him to the parlour.

He followed her in and shut the door as she sank down onto a chair by the fire. 'You went to the flogging, didn't you?'

'Of course I did.'

He was white to the lips. 'I knew fine you'd disobey me. I came back as soon as I could – I was out of my mind with worry!'

'I'm not a child! I can look after myself!'

'I wish I could be as sure of that! Listen to me – the woman stole from a weaver. In this town that's a sin, and she knew it. She was punished according to the law and it's not your business to interfere. D'you hear me?'

'I do – and you sound as twisted as Johnny Brodie! I'll not stay in my own parlour to listen to such talk!'

She stormed to the door, anger revitalising her exhausted body. But he was there before her, his hands on her shoulders, his face twisted with rage.

'You'll not mention me in the same breath as that man!'

'Take your hands off me,' she ordered coldly, and his arms dropped to his sides. Choking with rage, they glared at each other. It was Gavin who made the first move towards reconciliation.

'Margaret – you know well enough that if the law's broken there has to be a punishment.'

'So Johnny Brodie can make money from other folk's misery and get away with it, while the likes of Janet are beaten until the blood runs for trying to find the money to feed their children?'

'I'm not proud of the way the law works. There are changes needed, but it's up to the men who run the country to see to that, not you and me. I've got enough to do, worrying about my own wife's well-being, and my child's well-being too—'

She swept away from him, back into the centre of the room. 'Your wife – your child!' she mocked, anger flaring again. 'No need to worry about your possessions, Mister Knox. Your child'll do fine, for he's to be born to folk with enough money to buy food for him. We won't have to steal to keep him alive!'

'Margaret—' He reached for her, but she evaded him.

'I wish you'd stop talking about your precious child as if I've nothing to do with him at all – as if I'm nothing but a – a box to hold your son!'

Hurt grimaced across his face then the anger flooded back again. As he advanced towards her the door behind him opened cautiously and Ellen poked a scared head in.

'Mistress Knox—'

'What d'you want?' Gavin rounded on her and she recoiled before the look on his face.

'A visitor to s – see the mistress. Will I tell him—?'

'Tell him to go to He—'

'Tell him to come in, Ellen,' Margaret ordered grandly.

'You'll do nothing of the—' Gavin began, but the embarrassed visitor had already been scooped into the room by Ellen and was hesitating in the doorway, his country clothes and weathered brown face giving him a strangely alien look.

'I decided I should come home—' he began.

'Oh—! And a welcome sight you are!' Margaret's

anger melted into tears of joy as she brushed past her husband and went forward, hands out-stretched.

Gavin stayed where he was, his eyes as cool as his voice when he said formally, 'Welcome back to Paisley, William.'

Chapter Four

IT SEEMED AS THOUGH MARGARET'S marriage sailed into a sheltered harbour with the birth of her daughter in March 1771.

There had never been a bonnier, better-behaved baby than Christian, who had her mother's neat-featured face and Gavin's thick dark hair and gold-flecked hazel eyes.

At last Margaret settled happily into domesticity, even deciding to share the Hospital work with Beth so that she could spend more time at home caring for Gavin and their daughter.

With William back, Paisley was its old self. The only person she missed now was Jamie, whose letters were few.

'Kirsty's worried about him,' William said on one of his frequent visits. 'When he does manage to put pen to paper, he says very little. There's something amiss.'

'I've no doubt he'll weather anything that comes his way,' she said comfortably, knitting wires flashing between her skilful fingers, one foot rocking Christian's cradle. 'How's your father today?'

'Keeping to his bed. I was shocked to see how he'd changed.'

'He'll be the better for seeing you. You were right to come home.'

'Mebbe.' Then he changed the subject. 'I've ordered a good stock of snuff for the shop. I hear the men at the Hospital are to be given their snuff penny again.'

Her face lit up. 'Poor souls – a penny a week's not much, but a wee bit snuff gives them such pleasure.'

Two months after William came home Colin Todd died in his sleep. It was as though, as Kirsty said, he had been waiting to see his son home again before he let go.

Margaret paced the parlour restlessly on the evening of the funeral day. Gavin was closeted in his small study, Ellen was entertaining a friend in the kitchen, Christian slept peacefully, and none of them needed Margaret's presence.

She picked up her knitting wires, but tossed them down again almost at once. Her spinning-wheel was discarded just as promptly. She went to the window, but the darkening street outside was empty, with nothing to fix her eyes and her mind on except trees tossing and bending in the rising wind. Finally she fetched her cloak and put her head round the study door.

'I'm going to see William. Ellen'll listen out for the baby.'

'You're going out on a night like this?' The first spatter of rain on the glass underlined Gavin's words. 'Kirsty and Billy are there – he doesn't need you.'

'I'll not be long.'

'If you wait five minutes I'll walk down with you.'

But she had no wish for his company on her errand. 'You get on with what you're doing. I'm able to walk down the hill on my own. I'll not be long,' she said again, and went out before he could argue.

By the time she reached the High Street house the rainstorm had started in earnest and the sky was black. The door had been left on the latch and she slipped into the passageway, a sixth sense leading her to Colin's room instead of up the stairs to the kitchen.

The room was dark, but she could see William, sitting in the wheel-chair, silhouetted against the window. His head turned briefly as the door opened and closed.

'Margaret?'

'I'm here.' She sat down at the table.

'I'm glad you made me come home for – for the end.'

'You'd have come anyway.'

'No.' After a long pause he said, 'I went away because of a quarrel we had.'

Surprise sharpened her voice. 'You and your father? But you've never ever said a harsh word to each other!'

'He didn't – but I did. The thing about words is that you can't take them back.'

'But it was all right in the end, surely?'

'I think so,' he said. 'We never spoke of it again. I was too shamed, and mebbe he didn't feel that there was time for further bitterness in his life. God knows he'd supped more than his fair share of it.'

'You came back, and that's all that would matter to him.'

She heard his breathing check and then change to a soft, uneven rhythm, and guessed that he was crying. Her hands fluttered in her lap hesitantly before folding about each other. Comfort was for hurt children; men needed solitude in their grief.

She waited until, a full ten minutes later, his breath steadied and he scrubbed a hand over his face, then she got to her feet and touched his shoulder.

'I must go home now.'

He turned his head and she felt his lips brush her fingers before she went as quietly as she had come, leaving him alone in the dark.

Lamplight spilled from under the parlour door when she reached her own house again. Gavin was hunched in a chair before the dying fire.

'So you're back.'

'I said I'd not be long.' She knelt on the hearth, sifting powdery ash from the fire with the poker then lifting coals from the gleaming brass scuttle to lay on the embers.

'Did you see him?' Gavin's voice was sullen.

'William? Yes, I saw him.'

'And comforted him, I've no doubt.'

She laid down the tongs, sitting back on her heels. 'Nobody can give him much comfort at a time like this. He'll have to get over his loss in his own time and in his own way.'

'That's what I tried to tell you – but you insisted on going to him all the same.'

She got to her feet. 'Of course I did – as I'd have gone to anyone who's suffering as much as he is just now. And if you're going to make such a fuss about it I might as well go to my bed as stay here.'

He was out of the chair and at the door before her.

'Was Kirsty there? Or Billy?'

Irritation began to edge her voice. 'What has that to do with it? Gavin, what's come over you? Every time William's as much as mentioned you begin to jump about like a cat that's fallen into a wash-tub!'

'It's not me that does the jumping – it's you! When he's here you fret about his comfort, when he's not here you wonder if he's all right—' Then his angry tirade stopped as she began to laugh. 'What is it now?'

'It's just you – you should see yourself, like a wee boy that's been left out of a game! Gavin, you're surely not jealous of William? He's like one of my own brothers – the best of them, for Robert was a bully and Thomas too fond of his books for my liking. William was the gentle one, the one I felt safe with. But you're the man I wed, Gavin. If you think of William as a threat, you've as much notion of common-sense as your daughter has of Latin right now.'

Gavin eyed her doubtfully. 'Did he ever ask you to marry him?'

'Never.'

'If he had, would you have accepted?'

The laughter was still in her voice. 'I've no idea, for I never intended to marry, as you know yourself. And as he didn't ask me, the thought was never in his mind either. Oh, Gavin—' She slid her arms about his neck, drew him close and spoke against his throat, feeling his skin warm and pulsing beneath her lips. 'I'll make my own friends where I choose – just as I chose my own husband. And I'm too well pleased with him to look elsewhere.'

Then she squeaked as he lifted her off her feet and turned to the door.

'Put me down – I've just built up the fire!'

'You have that,' he agreed huskily, carrying her out of the room and across the dark hall to the stairs. 'And now you'll have to take the consequences!'

Kirsty's kitchen was warm, noisy and filled with the smell of broth and fresh-baked bread. Meg and Mary, Kate and Robert's wife Annie had come to take tea, and the patch-work rugs on the floor were lively with babies – three-months-old Christian propped up on cushions, Kate and Annie's older children crawling and toddling near their mothers.

Margaret took a moment to wonder, as she often did at her own presence in the middle of such a domesticated crowd. Motherhood must addle the brain – but it was a pleasant affliction, she admitted to herself, poking Christian with a gentle toe and watching the smile that was so like Gavin's break over the baby's face.

Then she lifted her head, listening, thinking that she had heard the street door open, a familiar voice calling. But it was impossible to be sure of anything with such a clatter of tongues vying with the whir of Kirsty's spinning-wheel.

So it came as a complete surprise to them all when the kitchen door flew back on its hinges and a tall figure appeared in the doorway. He looked drawn, and considerably older than when they had last seen him, but there was no mistaking the fiery hair, the wide grin, the blue eyes.

'Now then—' said Jamie Todd. 'Here's a bonny sight to welcome a man back home among his own folk!'

'Prison!' Margaret said, aghast. 'Jamie Todd – I always knew you'd fall into bad ways! Haven't I said it time and time again?'

'Not to my knowledge.' Jamie, sprawled comfortably in the Knox parlour, was unrepentant. 'It's not as if it was a real jail, Margaret. Just an Army one. Insubordination, they said.' He rolled the word around his tongue with relish. 'The truth of it was, I got tired of being ordered

302

about by namby pamby officers who didn't know what they were talking about half the time.'

She eyed him closely. For all his joking there was a new awareness at the back of his eyes, deep lines etched into his face, a cynicism that had never laced his smile before.

'There's a lot more to it than that. Something bad happened to you, Jamie.'

For a fleeting second she saw bitterness chill his eyes, then it was gone.

'I'll just say that I wanted to see the world – and there are some things out there that I'd as soon not have seen,' he said lightly, and she knew that that was as much as she or anyone else would get out of him.

'And what do you plan to do next? There's plenty young men in the town talking of going to the Americas to find a new life.'

He stretched his legs out and contemplated the toes of his boots. 'No, I've had my fill of travel for the moment. And it's time the looms were back in my father's shop. After all, weaving's what I was trained to do.'

He hadn't lost the ability to surprise her. 'You'd settle down here and be a weaver?'

'I'm in the mood for that. Paisley has its attractions for me now—' a sly smile sparkled at her '—and that bonny Beth Lang that stays with your Aunt Mary's one of them.'

'Just you watch yourself, Jamie Todd! I've already

decided that Beth would make a fine wife for William.'

'Let William look out for himself, then,' said Jamie, half in fun, half earnest. 'The girl I wanted belongs to someone else now – and a weary traveller's entitled to find his comfort where he can.'

Chapter Five

'PLEASE GOD, NO!' MARGARET PRAYED aloud as she threw herself out of bed and ran, sure-footed in the darkness, to the crib. By the time Gavin had lit the lamp the baby was in her arms, still making those terrible choking, wheezing sounds that had wakened the two of them.

'Give her to me—' Gavin took Christian over to the light. Her face was congested, her frightened eyes stared up at him, her small fists flailed at the air. 'Go and boil a kettle, Margaret!'

She ran barefoot, terror choking her throat just as the croup was choking her baby. Through her mind, as she poked the glowing kitchen range into life, splashed water into the kettle and swung it on its hook over the fire, tramped a never-ending list of names of infants who had died in the town from the dreaded illness.

Throughout that long night she and Gavin took turns to walk the floor with Christian, filling every pot they could find so that the kitchen became humid with steam to loosen the mucus in the little girl's lungs. Slowly she improved, and by dawn the immediate crisis was over and she slept, exhausted.

It happened again on the next night, and the next. Before their eyes Gavin and Margaret saw their baby sicken and lose ground.

'If anything should happen to her—' Margaret said fearfully one morning when dawn's grey light found Christian slipping into her first sleep of the night, her dark hair wet with sweat, her mouth blue-tinged. Gavin reached out and drew her close.

'Nothing's going to happen to her – nothing!' he said fiercely, but when she looked up at him she saw her own terror mirrored in his tired face.

'Gavin—'

'Sshhh—' he led her back to bed, though it was almost time for him to get up and go to Glasgow. 'I've been thinking, Margaret – some folk say that sea air can be beneficial. I've a cousin living down in Ayr – we could take Christian to spend a few days with him.'

'D'you think it would help her?'

He shrugged helplessly. 'I don't know – but I'll try anything.' Then he lifted her face to his and kissed her gently. 'Leave Ellen to see to the wee one today and go out for a while. You'll make yourself ill if you stay in all the time with her – and I couldn't bear it if something happened to you as well.'

Against her own wishes she did as she was told, turning her steps towards her parents' house. But

Meg was out somewhere, and Margaret couldn't face Kirsty, who had lost a baby to the croup herself. Without making any conscious decision she found herself walking into the grocer's shop.

William was serving a customer. She nodded and went through to the back. The rooms where she had been born and raised were sparsely furnished, for he had few needs. There were a lot of books, two chairs flanking the fire, a rag rug, and little else. The mantelshelf was bare of ornaments.

Shivering, she knelt down to stir the fire into a blaze. The shop door closed and she heard William come into the room behind her.

'Margaret?'

She kept her eyes on the fire. 'William – my baby's going to die.'

He drew in his breath sharply, knelt down beside her so that he could look into her face. 'No!'

'She is – she is—' Margaret insisted, and the tears that had been aching to flow for the past three days finally surfaced in a passion of grief and fear beyond her control.

To her relief he didn't try to stop her. He gathered her into his arms and rocked her as she would have rocked Christian, holding her against his shoulder, letting her sob herself into hiccuping silence before he mopped her face, eased her gently into a chair, and bent to lift the kettle that simmered all day on the range.

Then he wrapped her hands round a cup of tea and made her sip the hot liquid.

She sniffed and gave him a watery smile. 'I've wanted to cry for days now – but I couldn't, in front of Gavin and Christian.'

'Who told you she was going to die?'

'Nobody. I just know. William, if you saw the state she gets into just trying to draw a breath—'

'Hush—' He leaned forward and put a hand against her cheek, his grey eyes holding her own. She felt as though his strength was flowing into her. 'Hush, Margaret. She'll not die – not Christian. She's not the dying sort – and I should know, for I was close to it myself a few years since and it was you that drew me back from the edge.'

'It was Kirsty's skill, not mine.'

'Mebbe, but you gave me a reason to get better – then,' he said quietly, but her mind was on Christian and she scarcely heard him.

'We're taking her to Ayr for a while. Gavin says the sea air might help her.'

He nodded, memories clearing from his eyes. 'Mebbe. It's been a bad summer here. All that rain – the burns are rushing down from the braes and the Cart's risen well up its banks. The air's damp and chill.'

The shop door rattled and he had to leave her. She took advantage of his absence to finish the tea and wash the tearstains from her face. When she heard the customer go out she went into the shop, clear-headed and calm again.

'I'd best get back to Christian. Thank-you for

being such a good friend, William. There's nobody I can turn to as easily as I turn to you.'

A muscle jumped in his face but he said nothing, busily shifting a new sack of meal into position and opening it.

'When I get back from Ayr I'm going to give those rooms of yours a good clean-out,' she added briskly. 'Oh, they're neat enough, but they need a woman's touch. We'll have to think of finding a nice wee wife who'll look after you properly.'

He looked at her, opened his mouth to speak, closed it again – then the door rattled once more, letting in three women laden with baskets, and Margaret left him to his work and went back home, comforted and refreshed.

She never found out what he had been going to say.

Ayr was a revelation to Margaret, who had lived inland all her life. Situated on the Firth of Clyde, it had its own harbour and fishing fleet, rich farmland around it, and beaches where waves rolled majestically in to break on great stretches of sand.

At Gavin's insistence the three of them spent almost all their time out of doors. They collected shells to take home, and when Margaret kissed Christian her skin tasted of the salt-laden winds that blew in from the sea.

All day and every day, no matter what the weather was like, they walked for hours. She and

Gavin talked and talked, played with the baby, grew closer together – and best of all were the nights, when Gavin made love to her in the big comfortable bed, and together they listened to the murmur of waves breaking on the shore, and to the easy, regular breathing of their healthy, contented little daughter.

'You'd think the sky would have run out of rain by this time.' Margaret peered from her parlour window at the dripping trees. The rain, driven by a wind, lanced at a sharp angle, and the few people to be seen were almost bent double as they battled along against the worst bout of September weather in living memory.

Meg, waiting by the fire for Duncan to come and escort her home, bounced Christian on her knee. 'There'll be damage done to roofs and chimney-pots tonight,' she prophesied. 'It's not a night for man or beast to be out.'

'Gavin's supposed to take his turn at the night watch tonight.'

'You tell him to stay by his own fireside – even the robbers'll stay home if they have any sense.'

It was a town rule that all the able-bodied men had to take their turn at patrolling the streets at night. Many of them paid others to do the work for them, and as often as not this led to more law-breaking, for substitutes had been known to turn a blind eye, for a share of the profits, to any crime they came across.

'Here he is—' Margaret said as Duncan's burly figure bowled along the road at a brisk pace and collided with the gate-post.

He refused her offer of refreshment. 'We'd best get back home, for it's getting worse outside,' he said, and took Meg off, the two of them clutching each other as the gale whirled around them.

Gavin insisted on going through with his town watch duties. Well-fed and warmly wrapped up against the worsening weather, he stopped her protests with a kiss.

'You're the one who's always going on about duty,' he said, then the door slammed behind him on a gust of wind, and she was alone.

When Christian was put down for the night Margaret settled by the parlour fire with a novel borrowed from the town's new book-lending club. The wind's whistling round the eaves and the warmth of the fire began to lull her to sleep, and she jumped when Ellen showed William in, his clothes and hair dark with rain. He shook his head when she urged him to take his coat off and get dry.

'No sense in settling down, for I'm off in a few minutes.'

'Off where?' she asked, with sudden foreboding.

'To Edinburgh, for a start. I've come to make my farewells.'

'But why, William? You're settled here again!'

He picked up her book, riffled through it without

glancing at the pages, set it down, fidgeted about the room. 'Now that my father's dead there's no reason for me to stay.'

'But your friends are here! And there's the shop—'

'You're all busy with your own lives, and I'd sooner farm than be a shopkeeper.' He went to the window, parted the curtains to peer out at the wild night.

'How long have you been planning this?'

William let the curtains drop and turned to face her. He looked very tired. 'I've known for a while that I was wrong to come back. I've told Kirsty and Jamie. It's best that I go.'

'But not tonight!' The words broke from her in a cry. 'Not like this, without giving me time to say a proper farewell. You can't be so cruel!'

'Sometimes being cruel's the best way. Goodbye, Margaret—' he said, but she moved before the door, blocking his way.

'William, you've been special to me all my days. It was you I went to when I thought my baby was dying. It was you that gave me the strength to go on. Have you forgotten already?'

'No, for that was the day I knew that I had to go away—' Then, as she stayed where she was, back against the door, his voice hardened. 'Margaret, stop this nonsense and let me by!'

'Not until I find out why you're leaving us!'

For a moment she thought that he was going to pull her clear of the door, and one hand reached behind her back to anchor itself to the handle. Then the anger went out of his eyes, leaving a dull hopelessness echoed in the slump of his shoulders as he walked over to lean on the mantelshelf.

'All right, I'll tell you.' His voice was empty, lifeless. 'You'll not rest until you know, and it's my last chance to say it aloud. And when I have, you'll be glad to see me go.'

Suddenly she was afraid for him. 'William, whatever it is that's bothering you, you must know I'd never think ill of you!'

He turned, looked at her, and said clearly, 'You think not? You see, Margaret – I love you.'

Rain beat at the window. A puff of smoke eddied round his legs as the gale gusted down the chimney.

'It isn't a brotherly love. It's the strong love a man feels for a woman, and it's destroying me. Every time I hear your voice or see you smile or watch the turn of your head it tears the heart out of me. I want to hold you and have you for my own, but I can't do that – I never could. So I'm going out of Paisley, to a place where I'll not be tormented with the nearness of you.'

'But – you never said anything in all the time before Gavin—'

'I told you—' he said harshly, 'I couldn't! That's why I went away. I was contented enough until you came after me and told me I should come back. So I did – just to be near you. I should have had more sense—'

He moved suddenly, but she was faster, her hands on his shoulders, holding him.

'William – don't just leave me like this, without—'

His eyes moved to a point above and behind her and she turned, her hands sliding from his wet coat, to see Gavin in the doorway, his eyes dark and expressionless as he surveyed them.

Wet hair was plastered to his forehead and rainwater ran down his face and dripped to his shoulders. As he moved into the room and dropped heavily onto a small chair mud dropped in sticky clumps from his boots.

Margaret was too agitated to think of the picture she and William must have presented to him. 'Gavin – he's leaving tonight for Edinburgh! Tell him he can't just go away like that!'

Gavin's voice was tired. 'He'll not go anywhere tonight, for the river's in spate and that wind would blow anyone off the bridge if they were daft enough to venture onto it in the first place.'

As he reached for the claret, which stood on a small table, lamplight caught the side of his face and she saw a broad ribbon of blood from hairline to chin.

'Gavin!' William was forgotten as she ran to her husband. He put his hand to his cheek and looked at the blood on his fingers with disinterest.

'Pour some claret, for pity's sake, for I'm weary to the bone. It was – a chicken, as I mind. It was trying to roost under a roof and the gale blew it off

314

just as I was rounding the street corner. It struck me in the face.' He took the proffered glass, drained it, managed a twisted grin. 'For a minute I thought it was the Devil himself attacking me, for it's a night when a man can believe in Hell. The poor bird must have got as big a fright as I did.'

She explored the wound with gentle fingers. The panicky bird's beak and claws had gashed his cheek in several places between the corner of his eye and the angle of his jaw. A few drops still oozed from the deeper scratches. She refilled his glass and thrust it into his hand.

'I'll fetch water and some clean rags.'

The front door banged as she was coming out of the kitchen with a bowl of water, but she didn't give it a thought until she got back to the parlour and saw that Gavin, still huddled in his chair, eyes closed, was alone.

'Where's William?'

Gavin started, and looked up. 'I didn't see him go.'

She set the bowl down and ran back to the hall. The heavy front door flew open as soon as she turned the handle, hurling her back into the hallway. Wind and rain surged in, wrapping her skirts about her legs and soaking her. She screamed William's name into the night and the sound was blown back down her throat, almost stifling her. She put her shoulder against the door to close it, but it resisted until Gavin's weight was added to hers.

He shot the bolt across, locking the wild night

out. 'Leave him be. He'll go nowhere tonight, I told you!'

Later, in bed, her head pillowed on his shoulder, she listened to the storm outside and thought of William.

'You don't think he would try to go away in this, do you?'

He cupped one breast, kissed its soft curve. 'Of course not. He'll have had the sense to go back home.'

Reassured, she gave herself up to his loving.

Chapter Six

'YOU'RE NEVER INTENDING TO GO out of Paisley tonight, surely?' the stable-owner asked as his final customer appeared from the storm. 'Man, you'd be daft to try it!'

But William was adamant, and an extra coin or two showed the man the sense of his argument. He led out a sturdy, reliable horse, saddled it, and vanished back into shelter.

The animal was reluctant to leave its stable and William, an indifferent rider, had difficulty in persuading it to move out into the street. The force of the wind, once they were clear of the protective house walls, sent the horse staggering before it managed to brace itself and go forward.

Gavin was right – the Abbey Bridge would be an impossibility in such bad weather. But there were two fords, one at the Sneddon, near the Town Hospital, the other at the Saucel, on the other side of the Cross. William checked a move on the horse's part to go back to the stable and dragged on the reins, turning its head towards the Saucel.

Rain sluiced in sheets against his face, making it difficult to keep his eyes open. He seemed to be completely alone – even the beggars that usually slept against the house-sides had managed to find better shelter that night. The wind shrieked like a pack of enraged ghouls and tried again and again to pluck him from the saddle. He gripped tightly with his knees, determined to get out of Paisley that night.

Clumps of roofing thatch, slates, tatters of cloth and small twigs whipped by him as he rode. His hat was torn from his head and his hair flailed about his face. The wind changed direction and now the rain stung his face like a thousand tiny needles.

He heard the river long before he saw it, roaring defiance to the night as it plunged dementedly between banks that could scarcely contain it. The ragged, racing clouds let the moon through for a minute just as he reached the ford, and William saw that the normally slow-moving river, swelled by weeks of rain and fed by a hundred little burns running down from the braes, had become a maddened foam-flecked thing that seemed to be trying to toss the bulk of its water back into the sky.

His terrified mount threw its head up as he urged it down the banking. William's teeth sank into his tongue and he tasted the salt of his own blood.

'By God, you'll go on!' he roared, consumed with terror at the thought of being trapped in Paisley for another night. It was as though the town was a living entity, reaching out to pull him back as he tried to escape for the second time.

The horse backed into a tree and thin branches whipped painfully about his wet uncovered face. Enraged by the stinging pain he caught at a branch and tore it free, more pain scalding through his crooked elbow as he did so; then he used the weapon to whip the horse back into the water, screaming curses that were torn away by the gale the moment they left his lips.

The animal went forward, its hooves slipping in the mud. As the river foamed round its legs it panicked and swung round, scrambling up the soft banking, throwing William off. He managed to get to his feet and found himself thigh-deep in water. Free of his weight, the horse gained the bank and disappeared, headed purposefully back to its stable.

William fought the river's pull, rubbing rain from his face and trying to judge the distance to the opposite bank. In normal weather it wasn't far and the water was no more than knee-deep; in earlier days, before the bridge was built, sturdy women had earned their living by carrying people on their backs across that same ford. Now, swollen and angry, it was an unknown element.

He planted his feet firmly against the river-bed, peered across the tumbling white-flecked water, and saw a light ahead. Someone had set a lamp in a window in the New Town. The sight cheered him. If he could keep moving towards that light he would be safe. He could, if necessary, find shelter on the opposite bank for the night and leave for Glasgow early in the morning before the town was awake. He went forward slowly, tensing his muscles against the pull of the river, testing the river-bed with each step before going on.

Suddenly his foot slipped and the torrent was on him like a hungry dog, bowling him over, bruising him, burying him beneath the surface.

He came up choking and spitting, treading water in a futile attempt to find something solid beneath his feet. He couldn't see the lamplight any longer and he had to fight down panic as he thrashed about, his feet reaching desperately for the river-bed and failing to find it. Then he realised that he must have been carried over the Hammills, the small waterfall between the Saucel ford and the bridge. Now he was in the deep pool where he had often gone swimming as a boy.

Weighted down by his clothing, he kicked out and managed to swim, letting the current carry him for the moment while he concentrated on clearing the pool and reaching shallower water.

But before that happened the Cart wrenched free a mass of flotsam caught between two boulders and hurled it angrily over the Hammils into the pool. A heavy piece of timber hit William with great force on the back of the neck.

His body relaxed, gave up its struggle, and let the river take it, turning over and over as it went.

*   *   *

William Todd was found early next morning, wedged among a pile of debris that had lodged at the Sneddon ford, on the New Town side of the bank.

Jamie came running up Oakshawhill with the news, his boots splashing through great puddles, his face so white that the untidy mop of hair above it looked as though it had been set on fire.

As soon as she opened the door and saw him Margaret knew what he had come to tell her.

Chapter Seven

GAVIN'S SMART NEW CARRIAGE BOWLED along the road that led from Barrhead to Paisley. On the wide driving-seat beside him Margaret smoothed the skirt of her handsome new green silk gown then braved the sun to look up at her husband, his hands steady on the reins. Happiness enfolded her as snugly and neatly as the long-sleeved gloves on her hands.

Gavin had been visiting a patient, and she had left Christian, now a busy toddler, with Ellen, and gone with him in order to spend some time with Kate, who lived in Barrhead. Beneath the seat, protected from the sun, was a mass of red and pink and white and yellow roses specially picked from Kate's garden; her husband Archie, now retired from the Army, was a keen horticulturist in his spare time.

From the road she could seen burns splashing demurely downhill to join the Cart, neat within their banks and bearing no resemblance whatsoever to the undisciplined torrents of the great storm nine months earlier. White and pink flowers massed the hawthorns, frothy elder-flowers had come into bloom, ragged robins clustered in red clumps by the roadside, creamy-white honeysuckle held out inviting blossoms to the bees and butterflies, who were not slow to sample the heady nectar offered to them.

The air was thick with scented warmth, and even when they came into the town, passing the riverside area where the manufacturers had their warehouses and then taking the turn into New Street, they were bathed in the perfume of the roses near their feet.

'Stop here a minute—' Margaret said suddenly and Gavin drew the carriage up without comment at the gates of the Laigh kirkyard, then jumped down and lifted her from her seat as though she was as light as Christian, instead of a grown woman and almost seven months pregnant.

The Todd family plot was at the back of the graveyard, away from the comings and goings of the street. Colin's and William's graves still had a new look, though the summer had covered them with fresh green grass to take away the stark rawness of brown earth.

Clumsily, Margaret bent and laid a spray of white rosebuds on the mound that covered Colin, then a second spray on William's resting place. She stood for a moment, head bowed. She often came here to talk to William and be comforted by the memory of him. She missed him sorely. She always would.

'Come on,' Gavin said quietly from behind her. 'They'll all be waiting for us.'

They were – Jamie and Billy, Meg and Duncan and Robert. Margaret stopped short in the doorway of the High Street loom-shop, astonished.

'It looks just the way I mind it as a wee girl!'

Almost all the floor space had been taken up by four looms. The floor had been freshly swept, linnets chirped in a cage hung at the sun-splashed window, a great box of the pinks that many Paisley men grew in their weaving shops stood on the sill.

'Now then—' Jamie's grin spilled over them all as he went to his loom, which stood just where his father's had been. He settled himself on the 'saytree', the long bench, and ran his fingers lightly over the wood before him. Then he looked up at the open trapdoor above.

'Are you ready?'

'I'm more than ready!' Kirsty called from the kitchen, where she was seated at her spinning-wheel. 'It's long past time for this house to hear the beat of a loom again. Get to your work and save the chattering till later!'

He winked at the others. 'Aye, mother.'

His foot pressed on a treadle. A set of warp threads lifted and Jamie sent the shuttle flying through the gap to the other side of the machine. Then he moved his foot to another treadle, and another set of threads lifted to form an arch in their turn. The shuttle sped back through it and Jamie warmed to his work, swaying to a steady rhythm beaten out by the thump and clack of treadles and shuttle.

Margaret felt Gavin's arm go round her, and leaned her full weight back against him, secure in the knowledge that he would always be there.

She stood within his embrace, watching as the good strong cloth on the loom began to take shape and grow, inch by inch.

Bibliography

The Paisley Thread	– Matthew Blair
Paisley Weavers, Pen Folk, Etc.	– David Gilmour
Statistical Account of Scotland, Volume VII	
Vanduara	– William Hector
Paisley Weavers of Other Days	– David Gilmour
From Cottage to Castle	– Andrew Coats
Edwin Chadwick. Public Health Movements 1832–1854	– R. A. Keats
The Paisley Shawl	– Matthew Blair
The Paisley Pamphlets	– Renfrew District Libraries Services

The Dancing Stone

This book is dedicated with gratitude and affection to all the librarians and all the readers I met during Scottish Book Fortnight, 1996.

E.H.

1

Although moonlight washed the street, the pend leading
to the back yard was an ink-black cave with no floor,
walls or roof. Caitlin, who walked through it every day
and had thought that she knew it well, hesitated, one
foot poised on the line where moon-silver met menac-
ing black, then stumbled as Bryce surged confidently
past, drawing her after him into the darkness with a
grip on her wrist.

'I can't see!'

'Ye don't need tae see,' he said gruffly. Then, as
she tripped and slipped over the unseen cobbles, he
released her wrist to put his two strong hands about her
waist and swing her round. Her back came up against
the house wall hard enough to make her gasp out a
protest, but before the words were formed Bryce was
kissing her, his open mouth covering hers and denying
her breath. She struggled, suddenly panicking, and
managed to push him away.

'What's amiss?'

Caitlin sucked in air. 'You are, Bryce Caldwell.
D'you have to behave like an animal?'

'That's not what ye said when I pulled ye intae that
close in Causeyside,' he said, hurt. 'Ye were all for
kissin' me then.'

'I know, but . . .'

'But what?'

Although the September night was mild, Caitlin shivered. 'This is . . . different. It's too dark to see you.'

'We don't need tae see each other. Feelin's enough.' His hands slid round her back, drawing her away from the wall and close against his body while his mouth sought and found hers again.

He was right; after walking out with him for the best part of a year, she well knew how he fitted into her embrace, the touch of his hands and body, the smell of him. Now that her eyes were becoming accustomed to the darkness she could just make out the curve of the pend's roof over his head. Beyond those age-blackened bricks lay her small bedroom with its two windows, one looking to the street, the other to the lane leading to the yard and workshop, and behind her, across the width of the storeroom that had recently become a weaving shop, her mother and stepfather would be sitting companionably in the kitchen at that very moment, one on either side of the fire. She relaxed at the thought and gave herself up to the pleasure of Bryce's kisses.

When he finally drew back they were both breathless, and Bryce was trembling from head to foot, a sure sign that it was time for Caitlin to go into the house. Fond though she was of him, she had a good sense of right and wrong, and although she had firmly resisted all his attempts to get her to go further than cuddling and kissing, it didn't stop him from trying to introduce new intimacies whenever he got the chance.

'It's getting late,' she began, her fingers busy straightening and buttoning her jacket, and he groaned.

'You always say that just when we're gettin' cosy together.'

'It's true, though. We've both got work to go to tomorrow.'

'Has Todd said anythin' about the new workshop?'

The sudden change of conversation took her by surprise. 'What new workshop?'

'The one your Alex wants tae buy down by the river.'

'This is the first I've heard of it.'

'Aye, well, you're no' involved with the workshop, so nob'dy'd think tae say anythin' tae ye.'

His condescension stung, and her voice was sharp when she shot back at him, 'Nobody said because there's nothing to say. You're just havering.'

'I am not. Alex came from Glasgow this very mornin' tae talk tae Todd about it. He has it in mind tae buy some old mill over by the river an' set it up as a workshop with Todd in charge.'

'And sell this place?' Kirsty, Caitlin's mother, had inherited the house and the adjoining cabinet-maker's business from her father. Caitlin's half-brother, Alex, had since bought it from Kirsty; as the owner he had the right to sell, but Caitlin couldn't see him letting the family inheritance go.

'Alex says that the business is doin' so well that it needs tae expand. Todd'd run the new place, an' he an' the missus'd live in the wee house that goes with it. That means that I'd take over the runnin' of this place, and that means . . .' Bryce reached for her again, his breath warm on her cheek, 'that you an' me could get wed an' live here.'

Alarm twinged through Caitlin. 'You're taking an awful lot for granted!'

'Come on, lass, we've been walkin' out for years.'

'For ten months. And anyway, what makes you think I want to marry and run a house and look after you? I've got my own work to do.'

'Carin' for a man an' raisin' bairns is a woman's proper work,' Bryce assured her. 'We're the right age, Caitlin, an' we're well suited.' He pulled her close again, his voice muffled by her neck when he said, 'An' there's nob'dy else I'd want tae be wed tae but you.'

With surprising speed, he managed to unfasten the jacket she had just buttoned. One hand moved inside it, sliding over her blouse to find and cup a breast.

'Bryce . . .' she protested as he squeezed the soft flesh gently.

'Caitlin,' he groaned in answer against her mouth. 'Oh, my wee darlin'. Can we no' just . . .'

Without realising it, Caitlin had moved further along the pend during her attempts to say goodnight. Instead of leaning against the brick wall, she had reached the weaving shop's timbered door, and when it opened she swayed backwards, off balance, into the sudden void behind with a yelp of fright. Bryce almost tumbled after her; he pulled back with a startled oath as Caitlin was saved from toppling down the two steps into the shop by hands that caught at her shoulders from within the room.

'Are you all right?' Murdo Guthrie's soft, lilting voice said just above her head.

'D'ye have tae go creepin' round the place?' Bryce snapped.

'I didn't know that anyone was in the pend. I'm sorry if I frighted you.'

'So ye should be!' Bryce snatched Caitlin from the other man's grasp and tucked her possessively under one arm.

'I'm sure that Murdo was as startled as we were, Bryce,' Caitlin said swiftly, embarrassed at being caught spooning with her sweetheart. 'You're working late tonight, Murdo.'

'I was working on a piece of cloth that Mr MacDowall wants for the end of the week. I'll bid you a good night.' Murdo Guthrie brushed past them, his head and shoulders taking on a silvery outline as he stepped out of the pend and into the moonlight.

'Daft Highland devil!' Bryce snarled.

'Shh, he'll hear you!'

'What if he does? When I get tae be master here that one'll be out on his ear.'

'Alex won't allow that, and he's the one who employs Murdo.'

'I'll find a way.'

'What harm has Murdo Guthrie ever done to you?'

'None – yet. And he'll no' get the chance tae try, I can promise ye that. Not tae me or tae you.'

'Why should he harm any of us?'

Bryce hunched his shoulders. 'He's a sleekit Highlander, and ye cannae trust any of them. I don't like him skulking in the store at all hours, so close tae the house.'

'He told us that he was doing some work for Alex. All the man wants is to earn a living.'

'Takin' his side, are ye? Have ye a fancy for him, then?' Bryce sneered, and she felt her face begin to burn.

'Don't be so daft, I scarcely know him. I'm only saying that he's probably as decent as any of us.'

'But he's a Highlander . . . ,' Bryce began, and Caitlin gave up.

'I'm going in.'

This time, alerted by the sharp note in her voice,

he didn't try to detain her. 'I'll see ye tomorrow night?'

'I'll mebbe have to work on at the shop, for we've got a lot to do.'

'Suit yersel',' Bryce said huffily and turned away, stamping over the cobbles and throwing his hefty body round the corner into the street without offering, as he usually did, to walk the last few steps to the kitchen door with her. She didn't bother to call him back.

Caitlin had expected to find her mother and stepfather alone in the kitchen, but to her surprise the room was full when she went in through the back door. Her younger sister, Mary, was still up, sitting on the hearth rug with her head resting against her mother's knee and her eyes heavy with sleep, while Alex, Caitlin's half-brother, had turned a chair around from the table and straddled across it, his arms folded along the chair back.

'What's amiss?' Caitlin asked at once. It was rare to see twelve-year-old Mary still up and about and Alex in Paisley at that time of night.

'Nothin's amiss, lass.' Todd Paget's fireside chair stood with its high back to the door. A cloud of tobacco smoke drifted up into the air as he spoke.

'Nothing at all.' Alex smiled at her. 'I just came to see Mam and Todd about an idea I've had.' His normally solemn face was animated and his blue eyes sparkled. One look at the way his ruffled red hair glowed in the lamplight told Caitlin that Bryce hadn't been havering after all. Alex's hair always seemed to take on added colour when he was excited or elated.

'Is it about the new workshop?'

Kirsty Paget's needle had been dashing through a

length of blue cloth as though her life depended on finishing the seam she sewed. Now the needle stilled as she gaped at her daughter. 'How did you come to know about that?'

'From Bryce Caldwell.' Alex supplied the answer. 'I saw the man's ears wagging when I was talking to Todd earlier.'

'So it's true that you're thinking of buying an old mill here in Paisley?' Caitlin took off her hat and started to unfasten her recently buttoned jacket.

'Did he tell you the asking price and all?' Alex wanted to know dryly. 'Aye, it's true. Our customers have taken a liking to having furniture made specially for them, and I could do with expanding the workshop.'

'But you've already got your own wee place in Glasgow. Surely the two workshops can supply all the furniture you need?'

'I'm selling the Glasgow premises, for my father wants me to spend more time in the emporium,' Alex explained. 'The way he sees it, I'll be running the place one day, and he wants me to start getting used to the idea of being there.'

Alex's natural father, Angus MacDowall, owned a large furniture emporium in Glasgow. A cabinet-maker by trade and an artist by nature, Alex had introduced hand-decorated handmade furniture into the business, and it had done so well that MacDowall had publicly acknowledged the young man as his son and heir and set him up with his own cabinet-maker's business in Glasgow. In return, Alex had taken on his father's surname. Father and son had commissioned the small Paisley workshop Kirsty owned to make furniture exclusively for them.

'My father originally thought of asking you to run

the Glasgow factory, Todd, but I didn't see Mam wanting to move to the city.'

'You're right there,' Kirsty said firmly, and Alex grinned at her.

'You could have started up your own clothes shop in the city, Mam. Look at the success you've made of Jean's wee place.'

'That was a matter of helping an old friend, and in any case, it's Caitlin and Rose who've made the real success of Jean's shop. I'm content with what I've got – and where I am.'

'But you'd not be averse to moving just a few hundred yards or so, would you?' Alex coaxed. 'The mill's only at Hunterhill, so you'd still be near enough to the shop and Mary would still be near her school. There's a fine big gatehouse on the premises with plenty of room for the four of you. It's not been lived in for a good while, so it needs work done to it, but I'd see to all that for you. You could have the whole place done out just the way you want it, Mam,' Alex wheedled. 'And Todd would have more room to work, for the mill's several times larger than the wee workshop out the back. It's got three floors to it, as well as a good-sized yard.'

Todd shot a glance at his wife, then asked, 'What about this place?'

'We'll keep it, of course, since it's been in Mam's family for so long. Your journeyman could run it, and you'd be close enough to keep an eye on him.' Alex got to his feet. 'I must go or I'll miss the train back to Glasgow. I'll take the two of you to see the mill tomorrow or the next day.'

Mary, her eyes sheltered from the light by the material Kirsty was stitching, had fallen asleep against her mother's knee; while Todd went to the street door with Alex, Kirsty roused the girl and sent her upstairs, yawning and rubbing her eyes.

'Is that you doing my work, Mam?'

'I'd finished the darning, so I thought I'd just put a stitch or two into it for you.' Kirsty smoothed the material gently. 'It's bonny. I didn't get as much done to it as I'd wanted.'

Todd came back into the room, looking down at his wife with a bemused and slightly troubled expression on his normally placid face. 'What d'you think, Kirsty?'

She folded the cloth on her lap, tucking the needle securely through several layers of cloth. 'I'm too tired to think anything, so I'm going away to my bed, and so should you two. We can talk about it in the morning.'

Todd nodded, but Caitlin took the sewing from her mother and settled down in Todd's chair. 'I'll just get a bit more work done before I go to my bed.'

Alone with the ticking clock and an occasional crackle from the fire in the well-polished range, Caitlin considered the implications of Alex's news as her fingers bustled the needle in and out of the skirt she was making for one of her customers. The prospect of moving to another house didn't bother her, for she had only come to this one, and in fact to the town of Paisley, seven years earlier when her mother had inherited the house and workshop.

Caitlin's father, Matt Lennox, had been alive then; he had died almost four years ago. After three years of widowhood, Kirsty had married Todd, who had been journeyman to her father then to Matt. The marriage had met with approval from Kirsty's children, who liked Todd and appreciated his gentle, placid nature, so different from Matt's sudden bursts of temper.

9

On her return to Paisley, Kirsty had renewed her friendship with a former school friend, Jean Chisholm, who ran a second-hand clothes shop. After helping Jean with the shop, Kirsty had used her skills with a needle to introduce clothes alterations into the business. Some time after that, Rose Hamilton, the youngest daughter of a wealthy local family and an independent soul with no wish to emulate her sisters and her friends by following the usual path to marriage and a household of her own, had come in as a partner, buying the empty premises next door and expanding the original shop to include dressmaking for those who could afford it.

When Caitlin left school, her talent as a seamstress and her flair for design had helped to develop the dressmaking side of the business. She loved her work, and she and Rose shared plans, hopes and dreams of future expansion, which was why Bryce's plans for their future made her uneasy. He was a good worker, and no doubt, with Todd still in the area to keep an eye on him, he would run the workshop efficiently. He deserved the chance to better himself, but Caitlin had no desire to marry him, or anyone else, yet, although as Bryce had pointed out, they were both of marriageable age, he twenty-one and she nineteen.

Finding, after a short while, that the seam she was working on had begun to waver before her tired eyes, she put the work aside and turned off the gas lamps before going upstairs. As she passed the master bedroom, she heard her mother and Todd talking in low voices, no doubt discussing Alex's offer.

The moon, still high in a sky free of clouds, washed her small room with its silvery-blue light. Brushing her hair by the window, looking down into Espedair Street, empty at this hour of pedestrians and traffic, Caitlin remembered the way the light had haloed Murdo

Guthrie's head and shoulders as he'd stepped from the pend into the street, and she wondered if that same ethereal effect could be achieved with materials. A very dark blue cloth, perhaps, overlaid with silver lace, if she could find some among the collection of clothing in the back shop. The bulk of Jean's stock consisted of cast-offs from the women who lived in Paisley's big houses, and the best of materials was to be found among them.

She put the brush aside and slipped into bed. While her mother and stepfather talked on in the adjoining room, she fell asleep in the space of a minute.

2

Young Mrs Harper had set her heart on a costume with a long jacket in horizontally striped material, just like the drawing she had come across in her new fashion magazine. The model in the sketch was tall and slender, while Mrs Harper was small and of the type described in Caitlin's circles as 'a sonsy, well-set-up lassie'.

Caitlin, who in childhood had suffered nightmares after coming across a drawing of a hapless native trapped in the coils of a large snake, was keenly aware that that was just what Mrs Harper would look like in the stripes she craved. She had scoured the fashion magazines Rose brought to the shop, finally coming across the ideal outfit on the morning after Alex's visit.

Rose and Kirsty both approved of the choice, a smart high-waisted jacket with narrow, vertical embroidered panels running up the sleeves, bodice and collar.

'Much more slimming than the one she wants,' Rose said. 'What colour?'

'Something light – ivory,' Kirsty said, and Caitlin nodded.

'That's what I thought, too, with blues and reds in the embroidery. But it means having the embroidery done specially.'

'Isa Harper can afford it. I just wish,' Rose said for the hundredth time, 'that we could employ our own hand-embroiderers instead of having to farm the work out. That way everything could be done on our own premises instead of having to leave good materials in the embroideress's house. With all those children she has, I always worry in case the cloth gets torn or something's spilled on it.'

They were all in the small fitting room. Jean Chisholm, enjoying a cup of tea in peace before returning to her usual place behind the shop counter, sniffed loudly. 'If things had been left the way they were, nob'dy would have to traipse expensive material through the town,' she pointed out, and Rose smiled sweetly at her.

'If it had been left the way it was, Jean, you'd still be running your wee second-hand clothes shop and you'd not have me as your partner. Just think of the pleasure you'd have missed.'

Jean sniffed again, though the glimmer of a smile tugged at the corners of her mouth as she went through the curtained archway leading to the sewing room and the shop. Suspicious of Rose when she first suggested a partnership, she had grown to like the younger woman, but they still enjoyed the occasional tilt at each other.

'You know that we need more room, Kirsty, now that you and Caitlin have opened up the dressmaking side of things,' Rose persisted as the curtains fell back into place behind Jean's narrow back.

'It's you that's done most of the opening up, showing your new clothes off to your friends,' Kirsty said, and Rose preened herself.

'If you'd spent all your life feeling more like a giraffe than a person, you'd want to show off a bit too.'

Too tall, too thin and angular, Rose had until quite recently driven her socialite mother to despair with her inability to dress stylishly. When Caitlin had started working in the shop the situation had changed, for she had a natural affinity for colours, shapes and materials. The first person to recognise Rose's potential for elegance, she had designed and made several garments for her. They had aroused such interest and envy among Rose's friends, and so many of them had begun to make use of Caitlin's services, that Rose now referred to herself as Caitlin's sandwich-board woman.

Today Caitlin and Kirsty wore the shop uniform that Kirsty herself had introduced – a white blouse with a black bow at the throat and a black skirt. Rose's outfit was similar but topped by one of Caitlin's designs, a long, loose silk waistcoat made up of diamond shapes in all the colours of the rainbow. It was Rose's favourite garment and one she wore frequently.

Rose's insistence on going into commerce instead of making her parents happy by marrying well had made her something of a curiosity among the women of her own social class. Friends and acquaintances such as Mrs Harper tended to visit the shop, ostensibly to call on Rose while passing, but in actual fact to view the place she had chosen to become involved with and to spend most of her time in.

After looking round the shop with disdain and deeming it 'quaint', most of them swept back out to their waiting carriages, nose in the air, then enquired of Rose at some social function within the next two weeks if she could arrange for 'that little woman' who had made her gown, blouse or costume to make something for them. When that happened, Kirsty or, more and more frequently, Caitlin would call at their houses, armed with pattern books and samples of material.

A few hours after she, her mother and Rose had agreed on the perfect outfit for Mrs Harper, Caitlin, pink with triumph, hurried back to the shop from the large and elegant house opposite Brodie Park where the woman lived with her husband.

'Hello, Aggie,' she said affectionately to the dressmaker's dummy that always stood outside the shop, dressed in a different outfit every day, as she hurried past the shop door, choosing instead to use the door leading directly to the sewing room, Jean's original shop.

As usual, Teenie Stapleton was crouched over her sewing machine like a champion jockey riding a thoroughbred to victory on the race course. Her feet were rocking the treadle so hard that they were a mere blur of motion, and her turbaned head was bent so close to the material whizzing beneath the needle that she seemed in permanent danger of stitching her nose as well. Teenie was extremely short-sighted and, despite the wire-framed spectacles Rose had insisted on getting for her, she always worked with her face almost on the table so that from behind, her body seemed to be headless. Her sewing machine, Kirsty's machine on the table set against hers, and every surface in the room were hidden beneath heaped clothing and pieces of material. She paid Caitlin no heed at all.

After dropping her bag of samples and patterns on the floor, Caitlin stretched her back then took off her coat and hung it up neatly. Finally, she cleared a space on Teenie's table and rapped her knuckles sharply on the wood. 'Teenie!'

The machine roared to a standstill and Teenie lifted her head, her magnified grey eyes huge in her small face. 'It's yoursel', lassie.'

'Is Rose in the fitting room?'

'Aye, with your mother and a customer,' Teenie said, and went back to her work.

The customer was buttoning her blouse while Kirsty carefully folded a woollen coat and Rose made notes in a large exercise book. 'Next Thursday afternoon?' she said as Caitlin went in.

The woman's face fell. 'We're visitin' my man's old auntie on the Wednesday night, hen, an' she's that particular. He likes me tae look my best when we see her. Could ye no' . . . ?'

'I'll make certain that the coat's ready for you on Wednesday afternoon,' Kirsty promised, and the woman beamed.

'I'd be grateful, pet.' She reached out and stroked the coat gently. 'This'll fairly make her sit up and take notice,' she said, with a giggle of anticipation. 'I'll pay half now and the rest when I get it.'

'Miss Chisholm in the shop'll attend to that. I'll take you through.'

'Poor woman,' Rose said, when Kirsty had escorted the woman out. 'I hope the new coat stuns her auntie into silence for the entire visit. I've got an aunt just like that – she treats all her relatives like servants and her servants like slaves. She's the only person I've ever seen Mama grovelling before.' She made a final note in the book and slammed it shut with one of her usual quick movements. If Jean Chisholm, who was of a nervous disposition, had been in the room, she would have jumped at the noise, but Caitlin, used to Rose's ways, was unruffled.

'Mrs Harper's agreed to the costume we chose, with the embroidery and the velvet hat.' Caitlin, who had gone home to change into her visiting clothes before going to Brodie Park, took a long smock from a hook on the wall and began to put it on.

'Well done! I've heard that her husband's taking her off on a cruise next summer. If she likes the new costume well enough she might come to you for her holiday wardrobe.'

'How can we cope with an entire wardrobe when we've scarcely got room for the work we're already doing?' Caitlin gestured at the small room where they stood; like the sewing room, it was gradually being taken over by clothes that were half made, being altered or waiting their turn to go on display in the main shop.

'We'll just have to make room. If only the butcher next door would move out, we could rent his premises.'

'There are three generations working in that shop,' Kirsty said from the doorway. 'I don't see them closing down.'

'Then we must think of another way of expanding. We need a proper storeroom for materials instead of having to go out and buy what we need bit by—'

Kirsty cut her short. 'Rose, I've heard more than I want to about expansions in the past few hours. Caitlin, I need a hand with some sewing.'

'I'll come as soon as I've written Mrs Harper's details into the workbook. She's agreed . . .' Caitlin began eagerly, but her mother had already gone.

'I'll see to the workbook.' Rose took it from her. 'What's amiss with Kirsty today? She's jumping about the place like a hen on a hot griddle, and it's not like her to be so sharp.'

'She's fretting about Alex's plan to buy the old mill. Did she not tell you?' Caitlin asked when Rose looked puzzled.

'She did not.'

Caitlin's heart sank. 'She must have wanted to keep it to herself. Mebbe you'd best say nothing,' she said hurriedly, but it was too late. Rose had already forged past her and into the sewing room. 'Kirsty, what's that carrot-haired son of yours up to now?' she was saying when Caitlin scurried in behind her.

Rose pounced as soon as Alex arrived at the shop that afternoon, looking every inch the businessman in a grey pinstripe suit with a watch chain across his flat, waistcoated midriff. 'What's this I hear about you buying property in Paisley? I didn't know that there was a mill for sale.'

'It's only just come onto the market. It's been lying empty for a while, and I've had my eye on it, waiting for the owner's decision to sell.'

'Have you put in a definite offer?'

'Mebbe,' he said calmly, then turned to Kirsty. 'I've hired a cab. I thought I'd call for you first, then for Todd.'

'I'll come with you.' Rose reached for her coat. 'I'd like to have a look at the place.'

'You'll do nothing of the sort. I want Mam and Todd to see it without being influenced by your opinion,' Alex told her, and swept his mother from the sewing room, leaving Rose almost apoplectic with rage.

'The impertinence of the man! Who does he think he is?'

Teenie, used by now to Rose's outbursts, continued to thunder away on her machine, while Caitlin said apologetically from where she sat at her mother's sewing machine, 'You know Alex – he hates talking about his business ploys until they're settled.'

Rose sniffed loudly and stamped into the fitting room, her brown curly hair escaping from its restraining pins as it always did when she was upset or angry. Caitlin shook her head at the material flashing beneath her needle. Like Jean, Alex had been suspicious of Rose when they first met, and she had taken a dislike to him. They were both ambitious, stubborn and proud, both determined to fight for whatever they wanted against the odds. In Rose's case the enemy was her overpowering mother, who had done all she could to push the youngest of her three daughters into marriage as soon as she had completed her education, and in Alex's case it had been his stepfather, Matt Lennox, determined to dominate his family and see his own son prosper rather than Alex.

They had both won their personal battles, and in the process they had developed a cautious respect for each other. Over the years, respect had mellowed until, despite the fact that they still argued and disagreed frequently, both Teenie and Jean Chisholm had talked of them being almost like brother and sister.

Caitlin didn't agree. It seemed to her that if her half-brother and her friend would only desist from their arguing and fault finding, they might find themselves becoming even closer than siblings. In her view, it was bound to happen eventually.

Kirsty didn't return to the shop that afternoon, and when Caitlin arrived home midway through the evening she found Mary alone in the kitchen, busy with her school books.

'They're in by.' She jerked her head in the direction of the front parlour. 'Your dinner's being kept hot; I'll clear a space and put it out for you.'

'Have they said anything about the mill?' Caitlin asked as she ate at one side of the big kitchen table while Mary scribbled busily at the other.

'Not a word, but they still think of me as a wee lassie,' said Mary, who, as her mother often said, had made the move from child to elderly woman during her first year at school. The classroom had opened up a new world for her; she had learned to read almost at once, and lived now for books and school. The creative skills shared by Kirsty, Caitlin and Alex had passed Mary by; her interest lay in facts and figures. She was a fine housekeeper, well able to cook and clean, but in her case housework was approached with an almost mathematical precision as she first estimated the time necessary for each task, then set out to complete it faster.

During the family's first years in Paisley, Mary had been a timid child with a tendency to cling to her mother and sister. No little surprise, Caitlin thought as she looked at her sister's bent head, considering the troubles that had beset them. Fergus, the baby of the family, had died under the hooves of a carthorse in the pend; Alex had been driven from the family home and business by his stepfather's harshness; Ewan, Matt's son by an earlier marriage, had run off with Todd Paget's betrothed; and finally Matt had died.

It had seemed to Caitlin in those dark days that the move to Paisley had brought her family nothing but worry and misery, but time had improved their lives. The shop had prospered, and Alex had settled down well with his father in Glasgow. Todd's serenity, the very opposite of Matt Lennox's tensions and tempers, had enriched the entire household, and under his influence Mary's timidity had melted away.

The younger girl had gone off to bed when Kirsty and Todd finally came through to the kitchen, both looking as though they bore the cares of the world on their shoulders.

'You didn't like the mill,' Caitlin guessed.

'There's nothing wrong with it,' Todd said. 'It's just . . . a big step for both of us to take. That wee workshop at the end of the yard'd be lost in the mill.'

'You could do with some extra space.'

'Aye, but . . .' He looked apologetically at the two women, then burst out, 'I'm no' an ambitious man – nothin' like Alex. I'm no' sure that I could run a big place.'

'Of course you could,' Kirsty's voice was firm. 'Once you got into the way of things it'd be no bother to you at all. And you'd have more men under you and less to do yourself.'

'Aye.' Todd, who was allowed to smoke in the parlour but never did because he was afraid of spoiling his wife's good furniture and curtains, reached automatically for his pipe, tobacco pouch and matches. 'I'll just go out by for a wee smoke.'

'Stay in here; it's cold out tonight.'

He shook his head. 'I'll be out of the wind, for I've a mind tae go down tae the workshop.'

'Then put these on.' Kirsty lifted his scarf and jacket from the nail on the back door. 'I don't want you catching a chill.'

'I'm no' a babby,' Todd protested, but did as he was told, winking at his stepdaughter. Matt Lennox had suffered badly from rheumatism brought on by his move to the damp climate that had made Paisley's textile industry so successful, and as a result Kirsty tended to fuss over her family's wellbeing, especially in cold, damp weather.

'Would you be willing to make the move, Mam?' Caitlin asked when they were alone. Kirsty, making the tea that was a cure for all ills in Scotland, sighed.

'To tell the truth, I didn't want to come back to this house when I heard that my father had left it to me, for as a lassie I knew such unhappiness here after my mother died. But Matt was eager to come to Paisley, and it's a woman's place to do whatever her man wants.'

Then for a while I blamed the house for the bad things that happened when we settled here, but now I'm not so sure that I want to leave.' She poured hot water from the kettle into the teapot then looked round the kitchen, her eyes misty with memories. 'The house is contented again, more like the way it was during my mother's time. It has a good feeling to it.'

'It's the people that make a house, not the other way round,' Caitlin said gently.

'Aye, I suppose it is. Your poor father was never really happy here, for all the hopes he'd had of the move. And if the head of the house isn't settled, nobody else is.'

'Todd isn't happy with the thought of a move.'

'All Todd's ever wanted was to earn a living and to know that those around him were contented. The thing is, Caitlin, if we decide to stay here, what are we going to say to Alex? He's set his heart on buying that mill and opening it as a wee factory.'

'It's early days yet. You and Todd should take time to think about it before you decide.'

'Aye, I suppose you're right. I just wish Alex hadn't found that mill, then we'd not have this worry.'

Todd returned a few minutes later. 'Murdo's still workin' away in the old store – I saw a chink of light through the shutters when I came back up the lane.'

'Poor man, he must be tired. Ask him would he not come in for a drink of hot tea.'

'It's no use, Kirsty, you know he'll never sit with us. I'll take a mug out tae him and mebbe keep him company for a wee while if he's in the mood for a bit of a crack.'

Todd was still out when Caitlin went up to her room, and there was no sound of the loom's steady clack beneath her feet. Undressing, she wondered whether the two men were talking or just sitting in as companionable a silence as anyone could enjoy in Murdo Guthrie's brooding company.

Alex had found Murdo sweeping floors in Angus MacDowall's store, and on discovering that the Highlander was a hand-loom weaver and therefore a rare find in 1913, he had brought him to Paisley. Kirsty's mother and grandfather had been weavers, and her grandfather's loom, found lying in pieces in a corner of the storeroom by the pend when the family first came to Paisley, had been carefully restored. It was Kirsty's dearest hope that one day it would work again, and it was as much for her sake as his own that Alex had turned the store into a weaving shop and commissioned Murdo to make material to upholster some of the furniture now made by MacDowall and Son.

Kirsty, overjoyed to hear the thump and clack of her grandfather's loom again, had immediately offered the freedom of her kitchen to the weaver, hoping that he would become part of the family. But Murdo, a silent and withdrawn man, chose to keep himself to himself, and not even Kirsty's kindness could reach him. He tolerated Todd's company on occasion, but nobody else's. Kirsty fretted about his wellbeing, while Bryce mistrusted him because of his secrecy and his soft, lilting accent, so unlike the harder, flat tones of the Lowlander. As for Caitlin, she wasn't quite sure whether she felt sorry for the man in his loneliness or feared his dark presence.

For the past few years Caitlin had been attending evening classes at Paisley's Technical College and Art School in George Street, studying drawing and design. Shortly after Murdo's arrival in Paisley he, too, began taking evening classes; she had seen him at the school but had never had the courage to approach him. Nor had she told anyone else that she had seen him there, feeling that she had no right to gossip about him.

Sometimes she heard snatches of music from the store below. Todd had told her that he had seen an old mouth organ lying on a shelf in the store, but Murdo had merely shrugged when asked about it. Whenever she heard the music, sometimes melancholy, sometimes surprisingly lively, Caitlin longed to go to the store where she could listen properly. But, knowing that if she as much as put a hand on the door latch the music would stop and the instrument would be slipped out of sight, she kept her distance and continued to puzzle over the enigma that was Murdo Guthrie.

3

A sudden pounding on the door knocker made Kirsty jump just as she was moving the heavy soup pot onto the range. Soup splashed over the rim and sizzled dry on the hot metal, leaving a stain.

'For any favour!' she muttered irritably, bustling into the hall to throw the door open. 'You didn't have to knock the door down,' she snapped. 'A wee tap would've brought me just as quick.'

The burly bearded man standing on the pavement was in no mood to apologise. 'I've other deliveries tae make, missus, and this wind's been cuttin' through me all day.'

Kirsty eyed the horse and cart at the gutter. From between the cart's wooden bars, a child stared sullenly back at her, and she saw that its small fingers, locked around two of the spars, were dark blue with cold.

'If you're making a delivery, you'll have to take it through the pend to the workshop yard.' She began to close the door, with some thought of hurrying upstairs in search of a pair of woollen gloves that she could give to the child before it was driven away, but the man put out a hand with a grubby handkerchief wrapped about the knuckles to stop her.

'There was nothin' said about any workshop.' He

brought his other hand close to his eyes and scowled at a piece of paper almost lost in its grip. 'Would Mr Lennox be at home?'

Kirsty stared. 'Mr Lennox has been dead these four years nearly.'

'Are you the widow then?'

'I'm . . . Yes, I'm his widow.'

'Then you'll do,' he said shortly, turning his back on her and stomping across the pavement. 'It's on the cart,' he said over his shoulder, 'and ye'll have tae fetch it down for yersel', for I'm havin' nothin' more tae dae wi' it.'

'What is it?' She followed him across the flagstones.

'This.' He jerked his head, and Kirsty, studying the boxes and trunks and brown-paper parcels scattered over the wooden planks, took a moment to realise that he meant the child.

'What're you . . . ?'

'No sense in askin' me, missus. All I know is that I was paid tae bring it tae Mr Lennox at this address. And a time of it I've had an' all,' he added, glaring through the bars as though studying an animal in a zoo. The child glared back at him. 'Kickin' an' screamin' and carryin' on, an' every time I stopped it was off an' away an' had tae be fetched back. I'd've left it tae run, but there's still a shillin' tae pay.'

Looking closely, Kirsty saw to her horror that one of the child's wrists had been lashed to the bars. 'You've never tied the poor wee soul to the cart!'

'I had tae, it was the only way tae keep it from runnin' off.'

'Untie him . . . her,' Kirsty still had no idea whether the dirty little scrap of humanity was male or female, 'at once!'

'I'll have my shillin' first,' the carter demanded.

'You will not.'

'I will!'

'You'll untie that child or I'll fetch a policeman.'

He flourished the hand with the handkerchief under her nose. 'You dae that, missus. No doubt he'll cart it straight tae the jail for bitin' decent hard-workin' folk. An',' he added in the child's direction, 'he'll put it intae a black cell wi' nothin' tae eat but hard bread.'

'For goodness' sake!' Kirsty didn't know what to do for the best. If she went off to fetch Todd the man might drive away, and heaven knew what might happen to the poor child then. 'I'll fetch your shilling if you'll untie that rope,' she compromised.

'But—'

'Untie that rope or there'll be no shilling!' she almost shouted at him. He hesitated, eyes swinging back and forth between her and the little face pressed between the bars, then finally gave a reluctant nod. Kirsty hurried into the house, convinced that she was throwing her hard-earned money away but at a loss to know what else to do.

When she returned, the child had been freed and was standing on the pavement. One end of the rope was still tied about its wrist, and the carter grasped the other end at arm's length. The shabby skirt hanging to the child's ankles proclaimed that this was a girl.

When Kirsty held the money out the man snatched at it, at the same time pushing the rope's end into Kirsty's hand. 'Here ye are – an' ye're welcome tae it, missus.' He plucked a brown-paper parcel from the cart and handed it to Kirsty, together with the paper he had been holding, then he scrambled onto the cart and stirred the horse into action, leaving Kirsty and her delivery on the pavement.

'What's your name, pet?'

The child tucked her mouth into a thin firm line to indicate that she had no intention of answering. She was filthy, from the top of the shapeless felt hat jammed over her head to eyebrow level to the toes of her scuffed shoes. Two women passing by stared openly at her, then at Kirsty, who was still holding the rope. One seemed about to remonstrate, but the other caught her by the wrist and almost dragged her away. 'Don't get drawn into anything, Nancy,' her voice floated back. 'It's none of our business . . .'

Kirsty dropped the end of the rope as though it had caught fire, and took the child's hand instead. It was like touching a block of ice. 'Poor wee lamb, you're frozen. Come in and get warm.'

The small fingers in hers stiffened, and for a moment she thought that the child was going to resist. Filthy though she was, Kirsty nerved herself to pick her up and carry her indoors if need be. Then the child began to shuffle reluctantly, one foot at a time, across the pavement and into the house.

In the hallway, Kirsty knelt to unfasten the rope from the little girl's tiny wrist, exclaiming at the red marks on her soft skin. The poor little thing must have been trying to free herself by pulling at her bonds.

'Does it hurt?' Her lips were gripped between her teeth, but from where Kirsty knelt, on a level with the child's face, she saw the child's eyes for the first time, wide and clear blue and tilted up at the outer corners. She only got a glimpse before they were hidden beneath long-lashed lids.

In the kitchen the child immediately ducked out of sight beneath the table. Lifting one side of the chenille cloth that covered the table when it wasn't in use, Kirsty tried to coax her out but with no success.

'Just stay there, then, until you feel ready to come and speak to me,' she said helplessly and turned her attention to the paper she had been given. It was an envelope, addressed in a hurried scrawl to Mr Matthew Lennox, Cabinet-maker, Espedair Street, Paisley.

Opening it, Kirsty took one look at the signature then caught at the edge of the table for support. She read the few words on the single sheet of paper, read them again, then said in a voice only just above a whisper, 'I'll just . . . Stay where you are, pet, I'll be back in a minute,' and blundered towards the back door.

In the workshop, Todd's smile at the sight of her disappeared as he took in her expression. 'Kirsty? Has somethin' happened?'

'I need to talk to you – outside,' she added, acutely aware of the sudden interest being shown by Bryce and the apprentice. He came at once, joining her in the yard and closing the door against inquisitive ears.

'It's not Mary . . . or Caitlin?'

'No, no, it's nothing to do with them. Read this.' She thrust the letter at him.

'Not out here, it's too cold, and you're shiverin'. We'll go intae the house.'

'Not the house – not until you've read the letter,' she insisted, then, as he opened his mouth to argue, 'The wash house'll do.'

'For any favour, woman, what's wrong with the kitchen where it's warm?' he protested, but she would say no more, and he had no choice but to follow her along the lane and into the stone wash house that had been built on at the back of the house. Once the door had been closed against possible eavesdroppers, Kirsty, comforted by the familiar smells of soapy water, bleach and starch, sat down on the little chair mainly used to hold piles of clothes and handed the letter to her husband.

As she had done, he glanced at the signature first. His brown head, the hair just as thick as when she had first met him, though now it was well scattered with grey, came up swiftly. 'Ewan?' He stared at her. 'Ewan . . . after all these years?'

Kirsty's heart fluttered uncomfortably in her throat. 'Read the letter, Todd,' she ordered huskily, 'and read it aloud, for I'm not sure that I've made sense of it yet.'

'"Dear Father, . . ."' he began, and looked at her again, perplexed.

'He'll have no idea of Matt's death since we didn't know where he was to tell him. Read it, Todd!'

'"Dear Father, you'll be surprised to hear from me again, and maybe not much pleased, but I have nobody else to turn to. This is Rowena Lennox, born in wedlock on 28 July in the year 1909. Me and Beth wed each other, so at least your grandchild is not a bastard. As cir . . . circum . . ."' Todd, never a scholar, stumbled slightly over the word but finally managed it, '"cir – cum – stances have turned out, we are not together now, and I must go away for a while. I hope that you and Mam will care for the child in my absence and trust that you will not hold my sins against her, for none of them were of her making. I will write when I am more able. Your dutiful son, Ewan Lennox."'

Todd read the letter again, this time to himself while Kirsty watched his lips form each word, then he looked up.

'Ewan and Beth – they had a child.'

'They did, and she's in our kitchen right now, under the table. A carter brought her to the door. He'd tied her to his cart.'

'Why did you put her under the table?' Todd asked, thoroughly confused.

'I didn't, she went there of her own will!' Kirsty didn't know whether to laugh or cry. In the space of an hour, her ordinary, contented life had been turned upside down. 'She's . . . She'll not say a word. The carter says she bit him. What are we going to do, Todd?'

He shook his head slowly, still bemused, then went to peer out of the small window overlooking the yard and workshop. Realising that, like her, he needed a moment to collect his thoughts, Kirsty bit back the words that flooded forth and waited, hands tightly clasped in her lap, until her husband turned back to her.

'I suppose the first thing is tae try tae get the bairn out from beneath the table,' he said, 'then try tae find out what's been happenin', and where Ewan might be.'

Mary came home from school while they were both trying to coax Rowena from beneath the table. Todd had attempted to pull her out but had given up the idea when she lunged at his outstretched hand like a dog, sinking small but sharp teeth into his knuckles.

Not one to be easily ruffled, Mary listened to the tale of how Ewan's daughter had arrived at the door tied to a cart then lifted a corner of the tablecloth and peered underneath. 'She'll be hungry,' she said when she straightened up. 'She'll come out when the dinner's ready.'

Rowena did indeed crawl out when the aromatic broth was ladled into bowls, but only for long enough to take her bowl and the hunk of bread Mary offered her before disappearing beneath the table again. Normally the cloth was taken off and the plates put on the scrubbed boards, but today Kirsty decided to leave it where it was for once rather than deprive the child of her protection.

'Best to pretend she's not here,' Caitlin suggested when she arrived home. 'She'll be feeling strange in a place she's never seen with folk she's never met.'

It wasn't easy to behave normally while at the same time straining their ears to catch every movement from below. They ate in silence, darting glances at each other then looking away whenever their eyes met. 'It's a fancy sort of name, Rowena,' Mary finally ventured in a loud whisper.

'It's a name Beth always liked.' Todd, who normally had a large appetite, had been stirring his broth around his plate. 'She got me tae take her tae the theatre at Smithhills once tae see a play. I mind that one of the lassies in it was cried Rowena.'

Kirsty put down her spoon, her own appetite suddenly gone, and got up to dish out meat and potatoes. When everyone else had been served she put a plateful on the floor, and a small and very dirty hand darted out and pulled it beneath the cloth. After a moment the empty soup bowl was pushed out against her feet. That night Rowena had the heartiest appetite in the house.

She came out when the meal was finished and stood against the inner door, surveying them all with clear blue eyes that seemed able to pierce through skin and flesh and bone and look right into their minds and souls. They had agreed, in whispers and nods and winks, to behave as though she wasn't there until she got used to them, so the two girls busied themselves with washing and drying the dishes at the sink while

Kirsty swept the hearth and Todd settled in his chair with his pipe and newspaper.

When the dishes were done, Mary took it upon herself to pour milk into a mug and hand it to Rowena. The girl hesitated, then took it and drank deeply and noisily. When she eventually took her face from the mug Kirsty's heart melted at the sight of the milky moustache decorating the little face. She longed to lift the child and give her a hug, and longed even more to put her into a bath and clean her up, but she knew that she must bide her time.

'So,' Todd said comfortably when the mug had been emptied and the little girl had sidled over to put it by the sink, always keeping the table between herself and the others, 'you're Rowena, are you?'

She nodded, her chin wagging up and down.

'And ye've come tae stay with yer grandma?'

Mary giggled, her eyes flying to her mother's face. Kirsty, settling into her own chair opposite Todd, felt her jaw drop.

Rowena nodded again, then said in a surprisingly strong voice, 'Till my daddy comes for me.'

'And when'll that be, then?'

'When he can.'

'What about yer mammy, pet?'

Rowena stared at him, her eyes suddenly darkening. For a moment Kirsty thought that she was going to burst into tears, then her chin jutted out. 'She went away. It's just me and my daddy, and he's coming for me when he can.'

'While ye're waitin' for him ye might as well sit by the fire,' Todd suggested casually, then began to study his newspaper again, with great interest. Rowena fidgeted in a corner for a while, then, as Kirsty and Caitlin got on with their sewing and Mary spread her school books on the table, she sidled over to sit on the hearth rug. Soon the heat of the fire made her eyelids droop.

'You'll be ready for your bed?' Kirsty ventured. The little girl hesitated, her eyes darting round the room as though in search of escape, before nodding.

'A wee wash first, though.'

Rowena's face seemed to close down. Her mouth tightened, and she shook her head firmly.

'She'll have to have a bath,' Kirsty appealed to the rest of the family. 'She can't get in among clean sheets in that state.'

'It won't be easy,' Todd warned.

'Easy or not, she isn't getting into bed like that. She could be covered in fleas for all we know.'

'If she was, we'd all be scratching ourselves by now,' he pointed out, getting to his feet. 'I'll fetch the tub from the wash house, for she's too wee tae go intae the upstairs bath. Best wash in front of the fire. Put more water on tae heat, Caitlin,' he added over his shoulder as he opened the back door.

Rowena watched the preparations with mistrust. When the bath was ready, Todd and Mary went upstairs to pull the truckle bed from its storage place beneath Mary's bed and make it up, while Kirsty and Caitlin set about undressing and bathing Rowena.

As Todd had predicted, it wasn't an easy task. She fought tooth and nail, and by the time she was bathed, dried and dressed in a nightgown Mary had grown out of, Kirsty, Caitlin and the hearth rug were all soaked. Leaving Caitlin to empty the tub and start clearing up the mess, Kirsty carried the squirming child upstairs. It was like holding a barrowload of monkeys.

When they put her into the bed she jumped straight out again, and for a while it looked as though they were going to have to leave her to sleep on the floor. Then Mary scurried from the room and returned with a photograph, which she thrust below the child's nose. 'Look, Rowena, d'you see who that is?'

Rowena's blue eyes, sparkling with fury, swept over the picture. She stopped struggling and snatched the piece of board from Mary's fingers. 'That's my daddy. That's mine,' she said fiercely, clutching it to her chest, defying any of them to take it from her.

'Of course it's yours, that's why I gave it to you. Now,' Mary pulled the blankets back, 'take the picture to bed, and you and your daddy can have a good sleep.'

They left a lamp burning, and when Caitlin looked in five minutes later, Rowena was sound asleep and the corner of the photograph, which Ewan had had taken not long before leaving Paisley, could just be seen peeping from beneath the pillow. Caitlin stood by the bed for a moment, marvelling at how fierce the child had been when she was awake, and how innocent and vulnerable she looked in sleep, with her face washed and her hair dried and brushed. A rich chestnut colour, it was fine and silky. Beth Laidlaw, the beauty who had scandalised Paisley by running away with Ewan just days before her marriage to Todd Paget, had had hair of that texture, though hers had been black. The little girl's blue eyes had been inherited from Ewan, though the uptilted corners had come from Beth. She had her father's wide mouth, but beneath her baby chubbiness her mother's clearly defined cheekbones could be seen.

'She's asleep. There's little doubt as to whose bairn she is,' Caitlin said when she rejoined her family, and her mother and stepfather nodded.

'The only question is, what's happened to the two

of them?' Kirsty was unpacking the parcel Rowena had brought with her, shaking out the few clothes it held. 'There's not much here, and no letter to explain anything.'

'What are we going to do?' Mary asked from the table.

Todd puffed at his pipe. 'There's not much we can do but keep her until Ewan comes to claim her.'

'D'you think he will?' Knowing Ewan, and his dislike of responsibility, Caitlin was doubtful.

'She's determined that he will,' Todd answered, 'and that's enough tae be gettin' on with. The thing is, what are we goin' tae dae with her in the meantime?'

'The shop has more need of Caitlin than of me, so I'll stay at home tomorrow. I'll bring out my old sewing machine, and you can send some work round to me, Caitlin.' Kirsty hesitated, then went on, 'I think Beth's family should be told and given the chance to take her in.'

'What, old Mr Laidlaw and that sour-faced daughter of his? D'ye think they'd want her?' Todd asked in astonishment.

'They have the right to know what's happened. After all, she's Mr Laidlaw's grandchild as much as mine – even more, since Ewan isn't my flesh and blood – and I don't want any of them saying that we never asked them.' Kirsty looked round at her family, then added firmly, 'I'll take her over there tomorrow.'

4

Kirsty had been shaken by Todd's memory of the night he took Beth to the theatre. Still trying to come to terms with the realisation that she was a grandmother, albeit by marriage rather than by blood, she had forgotten until he'd spoken of Rowena's name that the child asleep in Mary's room had been borne by the woman he had once worshipped and planned to marry.

Getting ready for bed, she thought of Todd as she had first known him. He had seemed to her to be a mere lad then, though she later discovered that he was older than he looked. Almost all of his conversation in those days had been about Beth and his great fortune in being chosen by her as her future husband. When Beth had eloped with Kirsty's stepson, Ewan, just before her and Todd's wedding day the young journeyman had almost gone out of his mind with grief.

Kirsty had thought that those difficult days were long over and forgotten, but Rowena's arrival, she reflected unhappily as she climbed into bed, must have triggered off memories within him of the two people who had betrayed him and destroyed his dreams.

A few minutes later Todd turned the lamp off and slipped into bed beside her, leaning over to give her his usual goodnight kiss before settling down.

'What's amiss?' he asked, peering into her face. 'Is it the bairn coming? We'll manage, lass, don't fret about that. We can surely find food and board for a wee scliff of a thing like that.'

'I was just thinking . . . She might have been yours, Todd, if things had gone the way they should.'

'Mine?' The bed bounced as he settled by her side. 'Never mine,' he said, amused. 'Not with my looks. Anyone can see that that wee one had two bonnier parents than me.'

'Will it bother you to have her in the house?'

'Not a bit of it,' he said comfortably. 'Is that why ye're thinking of askin' the Laidlaws tae take her in? Tae spare my feelin's?'

'No,' she lied. 'I just think that they should have the chance.'

'They'll say no, Kirsty. I'm certain of that.'

Silence fell. Kirsty opened her mouth to speak several times, then closed it again. But the question nagged at her and finally she had to ask it. 'Todd, d'you ever think of Beth and what there might have been for you if she'd stayed in Paisley?'

'I have, on occasion. And each time I've thanked fate that things turned out the way they did.'

'D'you mean that?'

He fumbled beneath the sheet for her hand, which he took firmly into his. 'Beth and me were never right for each other, but I was too befuddled by her tae see that. If it hadnae been your Ewan, it'd have been someone else. It's as well it happened when it did, before her and me went up the aisle together.'

Kirsty squeezed his fingers, then said after another silence, 'She never cried . . . Rowena.'

'Is that not more of a blessin' than a curse?'

'It's not natural, Todd. She's only four years of age.

You'd think she'd be crying her poor wee eyes out at being deserted by her parents.'

'If and when she's ready, she'll cry and we'll comfort her,' he told her patiently. 'Now stop frettin' an' go tae sleep, for ye're goin' tae have yer hands full in the mornin' with that one.'

Five minutes later he was asleep, while Kirsty lay wide eyed by his side.

Rowena ate her breakfast at the table instead of beneath it, but even so she remained aloof, scarcely answering when spoken to, keeping her head down and darting swift glances at her new-found relatives when she thought they weren't looking at her. After the others had gone off to work and school, Kirsty washed the dishes then helped the little girl on with her coat, which had been brushed but was in need of a good wash. As she smoothed down the sleeves, she noticed with a pang that there were still faint marks on the delicate skin of Rowena's wrist where the carter's rope had chafed. Deciding that the felt hat was only fit for the dustbin, she brushed the child's hair before tying it with a ribbon. It was soft and thick and crackled beneath the brush.

'I'm going to take you to see your grandfather, Rowena, and your aunt and uncle. They've got a nice shop just across the road, and they'll mebbe want you to live there with them.'

Rowena's eyes were immediately hostile. 'If I go away from here, my daddy won't know where I am.' It was the longest sentence she had spoken so far; when she had barked it out she folded her lips tightly together in what had already become a familiar gesture.

'I'll tell him when he arrives, and he'll only have to cross the road to get to you.' Kirsty buttoned on the shabby shoes she had tried in vain to polish, then stood up. 'I want you to be a very good girl, Rowena.'

It had been a while since she had felt nervous going into the tobacconist's, but as she crossed the cobbled street with Rowena's hand small and unfamiliar in hers, Kirsty felt her stomach lurch slightly. During her childhood, old Mrs Laidlaw, who had owned the shop then, had been the scourge of the local children. In Kirsty's teens, when deep loneliness after her mother's death had driven her into the arms of her father's apprentice, Mrs Laidlaw had been the first to detect the signs of her pregnancy and had told her father, who had almost beaten the lad to death and banished Kirsty from Paisley.

On her return more than eighteen years later, she had been relieved to find that Mrs Laidlaw was in her grave and no longer able to torment her. But her childhood friends had insisted that old Mrs Laidlaw was a witch with the power to curse folk, and even in maturity, with a husband and a family of her own, Kirsty had had reason to think that the tales might be true and that Mrs Laidlaw had cursed her all those years ago. Although she herself had gone, her granddaughter, Beth, had taken her place behind the shop counter and had dazzled Ewan and spirited him off, breaking Todd's heart and leaving Matt, already crippled by rheumatism, to mourn the loss of his beloved son for the rest of his life.

After Beth's disappearance, her elder sister, Annie Mitchell, had returned to Paisley with her husband to run the shop and share the flat above with her father. Mr Laidlaw had been in indifferent health for some time and was rarely seen in the shop, but on that day he was sitting in a corner, a woollen shawl round his shoulders and a rug over his knees. From behind the counter, his daughter eyed Kirsty coldly. In spite of the fact that nobody had ever been able to dominate Beth Laidlaw, her family had long since determined that the elopement was entirely Ewan's doing.

'Yes?'

Kirsty pushed the little girl forward slightly, her hands on the small shoulders. 'This is Rowena – Beth and Ewan's wee girl. She arrived yesterday.'

The old man in the corner gave a muffled exclamation, while Annie Mitchell, who possessed none of her sister's beauty, flicked a glance at the two blue eyes that could just be seen above the top of the counter, then drew herself upright. Her face seemed to close in on itself. It was for all the world, Kirsty thought, fascinated, as though the woman possessed the ability to button up her features.

'What's that to us?'

The chill in her voice and in her eyes reminded Kirsty so strongly of old Mrs Laidlaw that she almost lost her resolve. It took all her determination to stand her ground. 'It seems from the letter Ewan sent with her that he and Beth are no longer together. He's asked us to look after Rowena until he comes for her. Since she's your sister's child I thought—'

'She has no sister!' the old man said in a creaky voice, thumping the floor with a walking stick clutched in one knotted hand.

'But—'

'My father's right, I have no sister. As far as we're concerned, Beth died the day she walked out of here.' Annie Mitchell spat the words out as though they were poison. Hostility twisted her features, ageing them and emphasising the resemblance to her grandmother. 'We want no more of her or her paramour – or her brat for that matter!'

41

'I only thought—'

Mr Laidlaw thumped the stick again. 'Get out of my shop!' It was the second time he had given Kirsty such an order. The first had been when she had tried to apologise to him for what Ewan had done.

Annie Mitchell swept round the counter and threw open the door. 'You heard what my father said – leave this shop at once and take that . . . that devil's child with you!'

Before Kirsty knew what was happening, Rowena wrenched her hand free and shot across to the shelves against the wall. Swinging one arm forward, she swept a hand along the shelf at shoulder height, sending a shower of pipes and packets of tobacco to the floor.

Annie Mitchell screeched, then screeched again as Rowena spun round and rushed straight at her to deliver a hefty kick on her shins.

'Old bitch!' the little girl shrieked, then as the shop door opened she spun again, full circle this time, and plunged out onto the pavement, crashing into the customer on his way in and almost knocking him over.

'Rowena!' Her heart in her mouth, Kirsty ran after her, careering into the startled customer in her turn but managing to catch the child by the shoulder just in time to prevent her from crossing the road under the hooves of a carthorse. The animal half-shied, the carter shouted angrily and Kirsty, with memories of the day her youngest child had died beneath a horse's iron-shod hooves in the pend, clutched at a lamppost with her free hand, a wave of nausea sweeping over her.

Rowena, scarlet faced and heedless of the near accident, twisted round beneath her grandmother's restraining hand and screeched 'Old bitch!' at the top of her voice. Annie Mitchell, peering through the window, reeled back in horror, as did an elderly woman passing by on the opposite pavement.

'Get into the house!' Kirsty, shocked into action, hurried the child across the road and fumbled at her door.

'Some children'd be the better for a good smacking,' she heard the passer-by say as the door opened. She rushed Rowena through it and closed it thankfully behind them.

'You promised you'd be a good girl!'

Rowena stood foursquare in the hall before her. 'You were going to give me to that old bitch!'

'I was not. I just wanted your auntie and your grandfather to know that you were here.'

'I hate you,' Rowena yelled, and stamped into the kitchen. When Kirsty followed her, she had again taken refuge beneath the table.

'Come out and I'll give you a biscuit.' When there was no reply, Kirsty added, 'You can't stay there for ever.'

'I'm staying here until my daddy comes. He told me to stay here, and I'm not going to live with that nasty smelly man and that old—'

'Nobody said you had to live with them. You'll stay with us,' Kirsty said wearily, accepting the inevitable. When Rowena remained silent, she went to make herself a very strong cup of tea.

'If Ewan's told her to wait here for him, at least we know that she'll not try to run away,' Caitlin said helpfully that night when Rowena had been put to bed. 'She seems to be more fond of him than of her mother.'

'What I want to know is, how long will it be before he comes for her?' Kirsty had had a bad day; Rowena had refused to speak to her, and she knew that it would be a while before she was forgiven for having taken the child to Mr Laidlaw's shop. She heartily wished that she had never thought of it.

'However long it takes, we're all the family the bairn's got.' Todd's face suddenly creased into a grin. 'I wish I'd seen Annie Mitchell's face when the wee one cleared the shelf then kicked her.'

'I wish you'd seen it too, instead of me.'

'What's going to happen to the shop if you have to look after her?' Caitlin wanted to know.

'If she's going to stay, Rowena must learn to fit in with the rest of us. I'll have to take her to the shop with me – just in the mornings at first, until she gets used to it.'

'What if she behaves in your shop the way she behaved in the Laidlaws'?' Mary put in.

After a quick look at his wife's face, Todd said hurriedly, 'She won't. She was upset today because Annie Mitchell called her names. She might be wee, but she's as sharp as a needle. Nothing gets by her. If she's treated right, she'll behave hersel'.'

'One thing's for sure,' Kirsty said wearily, 'there'll be no move to the old mill for us now. How can we put our minds to settling into a new house and a new factory at a time like this? Besides, moving to another strange house would unsettle her.'

'Alex won't be pleased.'

'Alex'll just have to put Bryce in to run the new place or find another overseer, for I'm not moving.'

Todd said no more, but Kirsty thought that she saw relief in his face as he sucked thoughtfully at his pipe.

Alex was not at all pleased. He argued for an entire

evening, but Kirsty's mind was made up and she refused to change it.

'It's too much for Todd and me to deal with, Alex. There's the wee one to consider now. I'll find it difficult enough caring for her and doing my work at the shop without making the move to a new house as well.'

'But there's more room in the mill house, and we could make a wee garden at the back for her to play in.'

'Matt and me brought five bairns here, and there was room for us all. In any case, the other house is too close to the river. I'd be fretting every minute of the day in case she fell in and drowned.'

'She seems a sensible lassie from what I've seen of her.'

'You've not seen her at her worst. I'd not put it past her to drown herself out of spite, and then what would I say to Ewan when he came to fetch her?'

'You think he will? If you ask me he's gone back to his old life now he's shot of her and Beth. You surely mind how much Ewan liked his freedom.'

'If you're right it means that Rowena's going to be with us until she's grown, and to my mind that gives all the more reason for us to stay here. Put Bryce into the new place and find another journeyman for Todd.'

'Bryce is too young.'

'He's not much younger than you are.'

'Four years, and not that long past his apprenticeship. I know he's a good worker, but there's still a restlessness about him,' Alex fretted, and Todd nodded agreement.

'Alex is right. The lad's a touch impulsive. He'd mebbe try tae be too clever too soon, just tae impress Alex.'

'Then take on a new manager.'

'Trustworthy men aren't that easy to find,' Alex told his mother sharply. 'That's why I wanted Todd. I'd not have had a minute's worry with him running the new place and he would still be close enough to keep an eye on what Bryce was up to here.'

Caitlin, keeping well out of the discussion but listening to every word, felt relief wash over her. She knew what Todd meant about Bryce being too eager to impress. He would be disappointed to hear that Todd was staying on in Espedair Street, but since he wasn't going to get the house after all, he would have to relinquish all hopes of marriage.

'You realise that this means giving up the idea of buying the mill?' Alex was saying.

'That's your decision, son.' Kirsty put her hand briefly on his. 'I'd have liked fine to please you, but I must think of my responsibilities towards that wee lassie upstairs.'

'Don't act hastily, Alex. Give yourself time to consider things,' Todd advised. Like Caitlin, he was relieved by the way things had turned out.

When he was leaving to catch the Glasgow train, Alex paused at the door. 'Ewan often caused trouble when he was living under this roof,' he said bitterly. 'Who'd have thought that he'd still be doing it? And him not even here!'

It was Mary, calling at the shop next day to hand in some work that Kirsty had completed at home, who told Rose Hamilton that there was to be no move to the mill house.

'My mam says that she's got enough to worry about just now, and it wouldn't be fair on wee Rowena to move her to another strange house.'

46

'You'll be sorry about that.'

Mary shrugged. 'I'm not bothered.'

'So Alex'll be putting someone in to manage the new place?'

'He says it'd be too much trouble.'

Sudden interest sharpened Rose's blue eyes. 'You mean that he's not going to buy the mill after all?'

'He tried to make out that it was Mam's fault, but she'd have none of it,' Mary said in her old-woman way, and departed.

Caitlin, busy with Mrs Harper's new costume, was vague when Rose questioned her. 'Alex'll get over the disappointment, and so will Bryce. I think Todd's pleased, though. He didn't care for the thought of overseeing a bigger place and more men. D'you think this material would do for the lapels, or should I see what else I can find? I wonder,' she said thoughtfully, 'if Alex would let us use the ends of the cloth Murdo weaves. It's good, strong material, and it's thrown away once it's cut off the loom.'

That evening Rose went to a supper party with John Brodie, the young lawyer who had drawn up the partnership between herself and Kirsty and Jean Chisholm. Family friends since childhood, they often accompanied each other to social events, much to the delight of both mothers. Rose looked on John as nothing more than a friend and, especially that evening, as a shrewd business partner.

By the end of the evening she had persuaded him to view the mill with her the following morning.

Twenty-four hours later, Rose had bought it.

5

Alex MacDowall strode up the long driveway, across the sweep of gravel fronting the Hamilton house, then surged up the steps to rap on the door.

The uniformed maid who answered his knock smiled politely at the well-dressed visitor, then stiffened visibly as he barked at her, 'I want to speak to Rose.'

'I'll enquire as to Miss Rose's whereabouts, sir, if you give me your n—' she began, then fell back with an outraged gasp as Alex put the flat of his hand on the door, pushed it wide and stepped past her into the large entry hall.

'The name's Alex MacDowall, and you needn't bother enquiring. Either she's in or she isn't, and if she isn't I want to know where I can find her.'

'Alex?' Rose said from the landing, then came swiftly, lightly down the stairs.

He went to meet her. 'You bought the mill!'

Arriving in the hall, she glanced up into his face. 'We can talk in the dining room. It's all right, Morag.'

The maid bobbed a curtsey then fled to the safety of the door behind the stairs as Rose led her visitor into a large panelled room dominated by a polished table running almost its full length.

'Sit down, Alex.'

He stayed on his feet, tossing his hat onto the table and ignoring the portraits ranged along the walls, the huge windows opening onto the terrace, the bowls of flowers and leaves placed at careful intervals along the table, their colours reflected in its rich depths.

'You bought the mill,' he said again, 'the mill that I had earmarked for myself.'

Rose pulled out one of the many high-backed chairs at the table and sat down. 'You changed your mind about buying it.'

'I did nothing of the sort!'

She frowned. 'But surely Todd and Kirsty have decided to stay in Espedair Street.'

'That has nothing to do with it. I was still considering the mill.'

'The factor told us that no definite offer had been made.'

'Damn it, Rose, you knew I had my eye on it!'

'Mary told me—'

'Oh, I see.' Alex took a few steps towards one of the windows, then swung back to face her, his voice cutting. 'You took Mary's word for it – and since when has my schoolgirl sister been my business partner?'

Rose's long face flushed. 'I assumed—'

'You've a habit of assuming things, Rose,' Alex told her icily. 'It comes of having more money than sense.'

Her face crimsoned, and she jumped to her feet, but he swept on.

'Years ago when you cost my mother her job here, you assumed that she would come crawling back when you wanted her to. Then you assumed that you had the right to poke your nose into the way Jean Chisholm ran her wee shop—'

'The three of us have done well with that shop!'

'Thanks to the hard work Jean and Mam and Caitlin have put into it.'

'That's most unfair, Alex! If it hadn't been for my money, we could never have expanded.'

'And if it hadn't been for your money and your God-given assumption that you should get everything you want, I wouldn't have lost that mill!'

Rose slammed her palms on the table. 'Don't blame me, Alex MacDowall – you lost that mill because you hesitated and I didn't!'

'I lost it because you took Mary's word for Gospel instead of speaking to me. I lost it because you and your friend Brodie went to the factor behind my back . . . and no doubt,' he sneered, 'you both used your family names as an additional lever.'

'We did nothing underhand. John's a lawyer.'

'John,' Alex spat the name out contemptuously, 'is your lapdog and so besotted with you that he'd do anything to please you, as you very well know.'

'You . . . How dare you.' She came round the table towards him like a whirlwind. He took a step forward to meet her just as the door opened and Mrs Hamilton's small, dumpy figure bustled into the room. She stopped short, one hand flying to the triple row of pearls at her throat.

'Rose? Who is this . . . person?'

'This is Alex MacDowall, Mother.' Rose's voice was clipped, her eyes still locked with his. 'And we have business to discuss.'

'We have nothing to discuss,' Alex corrected her, snatching up his hat and giving her mother a brief nod of the head. 'Mrs Hamilton . . .'

As he went towards the door the woman scuttled hastily to one side, out of his way.

'Alex . . .' The door closed behind him, and Mrs Hamilton blocked Rose's move to follow him.

'Who was that rude man?'

'I told you, Mama. It was Alex MacDowall.' Rose went to the window and watched Alex stride away along the drive.

'MacDowall.' Mrs Hamilton pursed her lips. 'Do we know his family?'

'I work with his mother, Kirsty Lennox.'

Mrs Hamilton winced, as she always did when she heard the word 'work' on her daughter's lips. 'I'm not even going to ask why they have different surnames. He strikes me as a very disagreeable person, Rose, and I trust that you will not encourage him to call at my house again.'

Alex was out of sight, hidden by the bushes lining the driveway. Rose turned from the window. 'I don't believe he will, Mama,' she said bleakly. 'In fact, I'm quite sure of it.'

'You'll never make this place a fashion house.' Caitlin stood in the middle of the mill's first floor, turning round slowly to take in the space, the pillars, the large but grimy windows.

'Of course we will.'

'We?'

'You're surely not going to leave me to run the place on my own. I'm hoping that you'll come in as designer.'

Caitlin gaped, then said weakly, 'Designer? But I've not got the experience.'

'You're taking design at night school, aren't you?'

'Yes, but . . .'

'And you're good at designing already. Look at Mrs Harper and the others – they've been pleased with the clothes you've made for them. That's one of the reasons why I bought this place. You need to get the chance to do more designing, and the best way to learn is to do it. You will come in with me, won't you?'

Caitlin nodded, scarcely able to believe her good fortune.

'Once it's cleaned and painted and some decent flooring has been installed, it'll be perfect.' As Rose paced, the ends of her long woollen scarf drifted out behind her. 'This floor can be the sewing room – just think how many machines it will hold! Our offices and the fitting rooms will be on the ground floor, as well as two pleasant salons where clients can wait to be seen.'

'Why two?'

'One for the comfortably off, and one for the ladies who fancy themselves to be too important to mix with the others. Instead of you having to go to their homes, they will come here to you. And the top floor will be the store. Just think of it, Caitlin. You'll be able to buy all the cloth and ribbons and everything you need beforehand instead of by the yard as you require it. Our ladies will be able to choose colours and materials, and we can have our own embroideress, or two, or more.'

It was unusually cold for October and the mill, unheated for some time, was chilly. Caitlin wrapped her arms about herself for warmth and exhaled a cloud of steam when she said, 'It'll have to be warmer than it is now.'

'Mmm.' Rose studied the antiquated stove in the middle of the floor. 'I doubt if this ever gave out much heat. We'll have to put in a good system that'll heat the whole place.'

'That,' said Caitlin, 'will take a lot of money.'

'Don't you worry about that. I'll manage, and John's agreed to put some of his money in as well.'

Rose had changed in the past week, Caitlin thought, watching her pace the floor. She had become . . . She searched for the right word and decided that brittle best described her friend. She shivered and thought longingly of the comparative warmth of the back shop as Rose went on.

'The yard below will be ideal for the clients' motor cars . . .'

For the first few weeks after her arrival, Rowena had asked on several occasions when her daddy was coming for her, but after that the questions stopped. She was still very much an outsider, speaking only when she had to and refusing to have anything to do with the children who sometimes played in the street.

Each day she went with Kirsty to the shop, where she sat in a corner twisting bits of cloth round empty bobbins or stood for hours watching the sewing machines at work, her vivid blue eyes peering over the edge of the table.

'She's like a wee old woman, listenin' tae every word that's said and watchin' every move,' Jean Chisholm marvelled. 'It's not natural for lassies of her age tae be so quiet.'

'I'm just grateful that she's behaving herself and hasn't bitten anyone,' Kirsty said with relief. Occasionally Rowena ventured into the front shop, where a number of customers had tried to make friends with her. Kirsty had held her breath, anxious in case the child should take it into her head to unleash one of her rages, but Rowena had studied each face gravely before turning away to slip, shadow-like, into the back shop.

Although she had kept well away from him at first, Todd turned out to be the only person able to make any headway with her. In the evenings she tended to sit on the floor at his feet, and on occasion he took her to the workshop, where she played with odd pieces of wood and the sweet-smelling drifts of curled shavings by the workbench.

Bryce found her presence unnerving. 'She slips in and out like a ghostie,' he complained to Caitlin. 'Ye don't know she's there until ye feel those eyes of hers on the back of yer skull. There's somethin' sleekit about her – mebbe old Satan's put his mark on her.'

'Don't be daft, she's just a wee girl.'

'She doesnae behave like one,' said Bryce, who came from a large and noisy family. Then he added, with a sideways glance, 'Our bairns'll no' be like that, I can tell ye.'

'Are you not a wee bit ahead of yourself with such talk, Bryce?' she said sharply, and he shrugged, undeterred. 'No sense in leavin' things too late.'

A slight chill touched Caitlin every time he said such things. Now that the mill was well on the way to becoming a fashion house, she was looking forward to working there and more determined than ever to retain her independence.

Rowena was doing what her father had told her to do – keeping quiet and minding her manners. If she did as she was bid, he had said before lifting her onto the cart and walking away from her, her grandparents would let her stay with them until he came to fetch her back.

It had been difficult at first. The carter had shouted at her and slapped her when she wept for her father, and in her opinion he had fully deserved to be bitten. Her daddy had warned that her grandfather was a cross old man who would smack her arse if she misbehaved and might even put her out on the streets, but she herself had found him to be gentle and quiet voiced. Confused, she at first suspected that he was setting some sort of trap for her, but as time passed without him raising his voice, let alone his hand, she gradually came to trust him as much as she would allow herself to trust anybody.

Days turned into weeks, and weeks into months. The end of November found Rowena still waiting for her father to come for her as he had promised. With December looming, Kirsty took time away from the shop when she could, bent on ensuring that her house would be spotless when the new year arrived, and sending Rowena out of the way to play in the back yard. Tiring of her own company on one such day, the little girl wandered to the work yard, where she slipped in through the open door. There was no sign of her grandfather, and Bryce and the apprentice were busy with a difficult piece of furniture.

Rowena made for the corner where the wood shavings were piled, burrowing into them and relishing their fresh, clean smell. She scooped up handfuls, scattering them over herself until she was almost completely covered and peering out at the workshop through a thin veil.

Neither of the men had noticed her arrival or heard the rustling in the corner. It wasn't until Rowena sneezed, just as Bryce was reaching for a hammer from the shelf above the shavings, that he realised she was there.

The sudden explosion of sound from just in front of his feet startled him. Letting out an instinctive yelp, he sprang back as Rowena rose from the corner, scattering shavings everywhere. Then he yelled again as the hammer slipped from his fingers and landed painfully on one of his feet.

A burst of laughter from the apprentice, a lad with a strong sense of humour, added to the journeyman's shock, pain and humiliation.

'You!' Bryce forgot about his sore toes. 'Ye wee bugger, ye!' He reached for Rowena, who in her four years had become wily in the ways of self-preservation. She eeled out from beneath the clutching hands and fled towards the door. Going after her, Bryce managed to catch a good handful of her long chestnut hair. He hauled back on it, and Rowena, within inches of freedom, screeched with pain and rage as she was almost lifted from her feet.

'Hold on there,' the apprentice protested. 'She's just a wee lassie!'

'She's a wee devil – and the spawn of devils, from what I've heard. It's time someone taught her a lesson.'

Bryce caught the child by the shoulders and spun her around, then lifted her off her feet, shaking her until her head juddered on the slender stem of her neck. Both arms were pinned to her sides by his grip, and she wasn't close enough to bite, but her feet were free, so she lashed out with them as though running in midair. Bryce's 'Right, milady,' gave way to a startled 'Oof!' as the tip of a sturdy boot, with all the muscle Rowena could muster behind it, caught him in the pit of the stomach. He doubled up, dropping her. She landed hard on the floor, winded, but managed to roll over, get onto her hands and knees and scramble rapidly towards the door. Once there, she got to her feet and fled without a backward glance.

'Get a hold o' her!'

'She's only a wee lassie,' the apprentice said again, then grabbed at Bryce's sleeve as the older man lunged for the door. 'For pity's sake, man, what d'ye think ye're at?'

'I'll teach her tae make a fool of me!'

It was the apprentice's view that Bryce had made a fool of himself, but he had the sense to keep that to himself. Aloud he said, 'The master's fond of her – ye'll only get intae trouble if ye go after her. Ye dropped her with a right bang as it was. It's tae be hoped that ye didnae hurt her.' As Bryce glared at the door then at him, the apprentice added, 'Leave it be. Mr Paget'll be back soon. We'd best get this place put tae rights an' say nothin' about it.'

He seized a broom and began to sweep the scattered shavings up, watching anxiously out of the corner of one eye. To his relief, Bryce finally shrugged and limped back to the workbench, rubbing his stomach gingerly.

'With any luck she'll run through the pend and under the wheels of some motor,' he said. 'Then we'll be rid of her.'

With any luck, the apprentice thought, putting the broom away and returning to his work, she wouldn't tell anyone about what had happened.

Rowena had indeed bolted through the pend and onto the pavement, only to stop short as she saw Annie Mitchell at the door of the tobacconist's shop, turning to help her father down the single step to the pavement.

The child immediately ducked back out of sight, then peered round the corner. Old Mr Laidlaw was making heavy weather of negotiating the step. When he was safely on the pavement and supported on one side by his daughter's arm and on the other by his walking stick, he began moving slowly along the pavement on a course that would take him past the pend, though on the opposite side of the road.

Slowly Rowena retreated through the pend, keeping close to the brick wall and trying to make herself as small as possible in case the couple parading along the pavement glanced over and saw her. On the day she'd been taken to the tobacconist's her gran had referred to this old man, who had shouted at her and banged his stick on the floor, as her grandfather. This meant that she had two grandfathers – and old Mr Laidlaw might be the one her father had warned her about.

The last thing she wanted was to be sent to live with him and his sour-faced daughter, which meant that she had no option but to return to her gran and face whatever punishment she might get for making Bryce angry.

Her hand, brushing along the brick wall, suddenly swung into space. Startled, Rowena turned and saw that a door was set in the wall. From behind it she could make out a strange thumping beat. She pushed tentatively with both hands, and the door opened just enough to allow entry. Rowena stepped through, and suddenly there was no floor and she was falling for the second time. For a moment she lay where she landed, cold, hard damp-smelling earth beneath her cheek. The thumping stopped, and hands lifted her and set her back on her feet.

'Are ye all right, lass?'

Although light came through the windows, the place was shadowy compared to outside. Rowena blinked, adjusting her eyes to the difference.

'Are ye hurt?' asked the man hunkered down in front of her.

She moved back, twitching herself out of his grasp.
'No.'

'You fell down the step with a right wallop,' he
said. Then: 'Where are you from?'

His voice was soft, with a lilt in it that she had
never heard before.

'The house,' she said, ready to run if he tried to
touch her again.

'You're biding with the Pagets?' he asked. Then,
when she gave a quick nod of the head: 'So you've
come to see what I'm up to in my wee room here, have
you?' He got up and gave her a slight bow. 'Welcome
to my weaving shop,' he said, then reached for a plain
wooden chair against one wall and brought it forward.
'Sit yourself down,' he invited, and went to sit on a
bench behind a large wooden contraption that filled
most of the room.

6

———

As Rowena scrambled onto the chair with some difficulty – her entire body was beginning to ache after her two falls – the strangely spoken man began to work his machine and the rhythmic beat began again. She watched, fascinated, noting how he operated wooden treadles with his feet and how his body swayed from side to side on the bench as he reached out, first with one hand and then with the other, to pull at strings on either side of the framework before him.

Each time he pulled, a collection of wooden rods holding threads lifted and a small something shot through the threads, passing just in front of him, to hit the opposite post with a sharp clack. Then the rods closed down behind it, lifting again when he pulled at the other string.

Curious, Rowena wriggled down from the chair and ventured closer to man and machine. The rods and the swift little thing, she gradually realised, created the thump-and-clack rhythm she had heard from outside. It was as though he was part of the wooden machine. He didn't stop work or look at her when she came closer, but said easily, 'I'm making cloth. See how the yarn's lifted? These threads are the warp, and the weft's carried across them by the shuttle. There's a box of shuttles behind me, if you care to look at them.'

She peered into the box at the little wooden things, her stomach contracting with homesickness as she saw that they were quite like the little wooden boats her father had sometimes carved for her. Occasionally, when he had been in a good mood, he had taken her to sail the boats in the small burn near where they lived. After her mother had gone away, though, there had been no more playing with boats.

She blinked against the tears that had come to her eyes at the memory and slid a quick glance at the man, wondering if he had witnessed her weakness. He was still swaying, still working and seemingly oblivious to her, but even so she kept her head down over the box, staring hard at the little boats. Soon the battle against the tears was won. Each boat, she saw when her vision cleared, was hollow in the middle, and each hollow carried a reel of coloured thread. There were all sorts of colours in the box – reds and greens and blues and yellows and purples.

The man stopped work, and the machine fell silent as he got to his feet, stretching his arms until his fists almost brushed the ceiling. 'Will folk be wondering where you are?' His voice was soft and unhurried, like clear water running over stones.

She shook her head, and he sat down on the bench, this time with his back to the machine, reaching for a shabby cloth bag on a nearby shelf. 'You'll have a wee bite to eat, then,' he said, bringing some bread and a thick slab of cheese from the bag. He broke off a piece of bread and handed it to her, followed by a chunk of cheese cut from the slab by a knife he produced from a pocket.

She looked at the food, then at her host, uncertain

of what to do. He bit off a piece of cheese, then a piece of bread, and Rowena did the same, not realising that she was hungry until she tasted the food. They ate in companionable silence, then he drew a bottle from the bag.

'It's only cold tea, and I have no mug, for I didn't know I'd have company.' He unstoppered the bottle, wiped the neck carefully with a handkerchief, and offered it to her. While she drank, one of his big hands helped to support the bottle, and when some of the liquid slopped round the sides of her mouth and ran down her chin, he used the cloth to wipe it away. Then he drank from the bottle himself before setting it aside and taking something else from the bag.

'We'll have a wee bit of music to finish with, then you'll go back to your gran.' He put the instrument to his mouth, cupping both hands round it, and blew into it.

Rowena stood before him, her eyes on his, her ears drinking in the music he made. The notes, like his voice, were slow and soft; they spoke to her of home and her mother, long gone, and her father, who still hadn't come for her. Loneliness, and the longing that had almost overcome her when she looked at the little boats, began to creep back again.

As always when he played his mouth organ, Murdo Guthrie was lost in memories of his own, but they suddenly fell away when he happened to glance at the child standing before him and saw that her small round face, slightly grubby but as open and innocent as a flower, was beginning to melt into tragedy. Swiftly, he broke into a new rhythm, a dance so quick and light and mischievous that the mist gathering in the little girl's clear blue eyes vanished and her mouth curved upwards at the corners into a smile.

Her feet shifted and her body began to twitch as though it wanted to break free and dance across the hard-packed earth floor. Just as it seemed that it would, the door opened and Murdo immediately stopped playing, the notes cut off as sharply as if he had taken a honed knife to them.

Kirsty, busy turning out the room she and Todd slept in, wasn't aware of the passing time until Caitlin arrived from the shop with a message from Jean.

'What time is it?'

'Half past eleven.'

'Mercy!' Kirsty swept past her daughter and down the stairs to the kitchen. 'You'll all be in for your dinners in half an hour and me with not a thing started yet. Set the table, Caitlin, while I peel some potatoes.'

'I must go back to the shop before I have my dinner.' Caitlin scooped cutlery out of the drawer. 'Where's Rowena?'

'Out at the back,' Kirsty was at the sink, running water into a basin.

'She wasn't there when I came through the pend.'

'She'll be with Todd then,' Kirsty said, then added as an afterthought, 'Let the table be, and run to the workshop, just to make sure.'

Caitlin opened her mouth to say that the child would be fine, then closed it and went out, leaving the cutlery in a pile on the table. Her mother was overanxious where Rowena was concerned, but Caitlin could understand why; she had lost one of her own children during a moment's inattention, and she would have no wish to lose Ewan's child as well. Better for her to be reassured.

But Rowena wasn't in the workshop. 'I've not seen

her,' Todd said, adding, 'Mind you, I've been out for a good part of the mornin'. Did the bairn come lookin' for me?' he asked Bryce.

'We've not seen her.' He glanced at the apprentice. 'Have we?' The lad gave a quick shake of the head without looking up from his work.

'Was she playing in the back yard when you came back?'

'No. I thought she was in the house with Kirsty.' Todd began to look concerned. 'D'ye think she's run off?'

'If she was going to do that she'd have done it by now,' Caitlin assured him, though she herself was getting anxious. 'I'll look in the wash house.'

Finding the wash house empty, she hesitated at the back door, then, unwilling to face her mother, hurried to the pend. Rowena wasn't in it, nor was she to be seen on the pavement, when Caitlin went out onto the street and looked both ways. Starting back to the yard to enlist Todd's help, Caitlin paused, hearing strains of music waft from beyond the weaving shop's partially open door. Hoping that Murdo Guthrie might have seen or heard something of the missing child, she pushed the door open further, and the music stopped at once.

'Murdo?' Caitlin stepped down into the shop, nervous about intruding into the Highlander's domain. 'I wondered . . .' She stopped as the man began to rise from the bench and the little girl standing before him whirled round. Both looked guilty, but Caitlin, weak with relief, paid no heed. 'Rowena! Oh, Rowena, we thought . . .'

As Caitlin went into the room, Rowena moved back, her face closing in on itself, until she was against Murdo's legs. He put a reassuring hand on her shoulder 'She heard the sound of the loom and came to call on me. There was no harm in it.'

'Of course there wasn't,' Caitlin said swiftly, struck to the heart by the way Rowena had cringed as though expecting to be punished. She stayed where she was, extending a hand as though trying to reassure a nervous dog. 'We just wondered where she'd got to, that's all. Your dinner's nearly ready.'

Rowena started to shake her head, then Caitlin saw the hand on her shoulder push her gently forwards. The little girl twisted to look up at the man, and when he nodded she stepped obediently towards Caitlin, who exclaimed as she stepped into a ray of light from the window and it touched the beginnings of a bruise on the side of the small face. 'What happened to you?'

'She fell down the stairs coming in the door,' Murdo said, and Rowena nodded firmly, and said, 'I hit my face on the floor.'

'We'll put something on it to make it better before you have your dinner.'

Murdo cleared his throat. 'I've mebbe spoiled her appetite, for I gave her some of my bread and cheese.'

'I'm sure she'll manage to eat something else.' Caitlin hesitated, then said, 'And you'd be welcome to join us.'

The firm shake of his dark head was very like Rowena's. 'Thank you, but I'm fine with what I have,' he said courteously.

Rowena hung back for a moment as she was led to the door. 'Can I come another day to see the cloth being made?'

'Mr Guthrie'll not want to be bothered—' Caitlin began, but his soft lilting voice said from behind her, 'She'd be no bother, if your parents will allow her to come in now and again.'

'We'll see.'

Rowena paused on the step, twisting her head over her shoulder. 'I'll be back,' she announced to the weaver, then went with Caitlin into the house, where she ate every scrap of her midday meal.

'If you did without the panelling . . . ,' John Brodie suggested.

'How can I? We're talking about the salon where clients will wait to be seen. You know these women as well as I do, John. Can you see them sitting comfortably in a room with whitewashed stone walls?'

'Panelling will swallow up more money than you can afford.'

Rose stopped pacing her father's library and glared at him. 'You sound just like a pompous lawyer.'

He was hurt. 'Not pompous, surely. But I am a lawyer – your lawyer.'

'And my friend,' Rose said sweetly.

'I most certainly hope so, but as your lawyer,' John pressed on, fully aware that she was trying to divert him from the business in hand, 'it's my duty to try to make you see reason. You only have a certain amount of money to spend on the mill.'

'I must have that panelling!'

'Then you'll have to give up something else.'

She swooped down on the table, planting both hands on its surface and leaning towards him. 'Such as?'

'The heating costs a great deal. I know,' he said as she began to speak, 'you have to keep the place warm for your clients.'

'And for the staff.'

'What about staff . . . and furniture?'

'The clients must have somewhere to sit, and our employees must have sewing machines and chairs, not

66

to mention cloth to stitch and thread to stitch with!'
She spun away and started pacing again, with the long
mannish steps that Caitlin had tried so hard to tame.
When she concentrated, Rose could move like a lady,
but her long legs tended to carry her along swiftly when
she was angry, excited or worried. Today she was
moving over her parents' thick, expensive carpeting
so quickly that she had to change direction every few
steps to avoid bumping into furniture.

'I wish I'd never bought the place!'

'I did point out at the time that it might not be a
good purchase.'

'Nonsense,' Rose said at once. 'It's ideal. It will be
perfect.' She swept back and forth for a moment, then
said, 'I could leave the old gatehouse as it is for the
moment.' She had had plans to renovate the building
by the mill gate and turn it into a home for herself.

'Since you've not allocated any money to the gatehouse yet,' John pointed out, 'leaving it as it is won't
make much difference.'

'John, are you determined to vex me? You're talking
like a lawyer again!'

'I'd certainly advise against trying to raise any
further loans, unless they come from friends or family.'
Then, as the grandfather clock in the hall chimed, he
said, 'Good Lord, is that the time already?' and began
stuffing his papers into a briefcase. 'I'm sorry, Rose,
but I really must go. We'll talk again tomorrow.'

Mrs Hamilton came downstairs just as they crossed
the hall. 'John, my dear, surely you're having lunch
with us?'

'Nothing would please me more, Mrs Hamilton,
but unfortunately I have another appointment,' he
apologised.

'Next time, then.' When John had left, she followed

Rose into the library and began to fuss over the writing
table, rearranging the blotter and pen set. 'John's such
a charming boy, so well brought up,' she said, giving
her daughter a sidelong glance. Rose, staring out of the
window and twiddling her fingers, wasn't listening.

'Mama, I was wondering . . .'

Mrs Hamilton was more shrewd than she looked. 'If
it's about money for this new venture of yours, Rose,
you can save your breath. Not a penny of mine will
be thrown away on it.'

Rose turned towards her, hurt. 'I'm talking about a
loan, not a gift. I'd pay it all back, with interest.'

'Not a penny.'

'Then I shall ask Father.'

'You may certainly ask, but he and I are firmly
agreed on the matter,' her mother said with obvious glee, 'and he won't change his mind any more
than I will.'

'So you've discussed it.'

'Of course we discussed it – after John's mother
told me what you were up to. It was very hurtful,
Rose, to have to hear of my own daughter's actions
from someone else.'

'I was going to tell you.'

'If you need money, why don't you take your
grandmother's inheritance back from that shop?'

'I can't. Jean and Kirsty couldn't afford to lose it
all.'

'You see? I knew at the time that it was a foolish move, but you assured me that the money was
still yours.'

'It is still mine, but it's tied up in sewing machines
and materials and wages.'

'Your poor grandmother would turn in her grave if
she knew how you had thrown away her inheritance.'

Rose summoned up all her patience. 'I did not throw it away, Mama, I invested it, and it pays me a good dividend.' She ignored her mother's exaggerated wince at her use of masculine terms like investment and dividend. 'It has already earned me enough to buy the mill, but at the moment I need a little more for renovation and furnishing.'

'Then you must look elsewhere for it, my dear.' Mrs Hamilton said, and swept out of the room, pausing at the door to add, 'It seems to me, Rose, that the only way you'll ever learn the value of money is by losing it!'

Alone, Rose chewed on a fingernail, wishing that she could talk her problems over with Alex MacDowall. Although they disagreed on almost everything else, they were alike when it came to business, often trying out new ideas on each other, confident of receiving practical advice free of sentiment or extreme caution. On several occasions Alex had thrown cold water on Rose's grandiose ideas, and she had had to admit, in hindsight, that he had been quite right to do so.

But her impetuous action in buying the mill without making certain that he no longer held any interest in it had destroyed their friendship. Just when she needed him most, he would have nothing to do with her.

She struck the heel of one hand hard against her forehead. 'You're a fool, Rose Hamilton,' she muttered, 'such a fool!'

7

Kirsty's hope that Ewan would contact his family at New Year, even through a brief note, came to nothing, and 1914 arrived without a word from him. If Rowena, too, had expected her father to make contact, she didn't mention it; since she'd begun visiting Murdo Guthrie in the weaving shop every day she had settled down, and now she rarely asked when Ewan was coming to fetch her.

At first Kirsty was uneasy about the child's sudden interest in Murdo Guthrie. 'We know nothing about the man,' she fretted to her husband. 'He could be a thief – or a murderer, even.'

'I doubt a villain'd be content tae live in a lodgin' house and spend most of his working hours at a loom. Alex is pleased enough with the man's work, and Rowena's no fool for all that she's so young. She'd not spend time with Guthrie if she didnae trust him. If anyone should be frettin' about her preference for the man it's me, for she never comes intae the workshop now, and I have tae say that I miss seein' the wee soul playin' about the floor.'

'She should be with children her own age.'

'Ye've tried that, and it didnae work. Things are hard enough for the bairn, Kirsty, havin' tae fit in with

70

folk she knew nothin' of until that carter brought her here. Now that she's found someone she can be easy with, let her be.'

'I don't know what Ewan'll think when he comes for her and mebbe finds her sitting in that dark room with a stranger.'

'If he comes for her,' Todd corrected, a slight edge creeping into his voice. 'Face facts, lass, there's not been one scrape of a pen from him since she arrived. He's not tried tae find out how she is, let alone told us if or when he'll come tae fetch her. It seems tae me that Ewan's the one who'll need tae dae some explainin' if he ever turns up, not you.'

By mid-January a new heating system had been installed in the old mill and an army of women had cleaned the place out. The painters arrived to whitewash the walls inside and out before builders began partitioning off rooms on the ground floor. Broken paving stones in the yard were replaced, the fencing repaired and painted.

Most of Rose's time was spent at the mill. At first she bubbled over with enthusiasm during her spasmodic visits to the shop, but as time went by the others began to notice that she had become unusually silent, often staring into space and having to be spoken to twice before she heard anything.

'If ye ask me,' Jean said to Kirsty, 'that mill's causin' trouble for her. Buyin' it's been a poor day's work; I'm sure that this time the lassie's bitten off more than even she can chew.'

'But she can surely start small and work up, the way everyone else does.'

'Rose Hamilton?' Jean said, astonished. 'Have ye ever known Rose Hamilton tae behave the way every-one else does?'

Caitlin said nothing to the others, but she, too, was concerned about Rose's silence, and she had become unsure of her own future. After being told by Rose that she was to become an important part of the new fashion house, she had pinned all her hopes and ambitions on the prospect, working extra hard at night school and studying books on design borrowed from the public library. She had even started working on a design portfolio in secret so that when the day came she would have something to offer to her clients.

Rose appeared at the shop one afternoon just after it had closed. Teenie had already gone home, and the others were preparing to leave when she arrived, sombre faced, and asked them to give her a few moments in the back room. She looked round the circle of faces, biting her lips to summon up the courage to speak.

'We've always worked together, the four of us, and it's only fair that you should all know what's happening at the mill. The truth is that although I've put every penny I can scrape together into the place and borrowed all that I could as well, it needed more doing to it than I first thought.' She looked down at her hands. 'I had a long talk with John this afternoon, and the fact is that there's still not enough money to furnish the place and take on the seamstresses we'll need, not to mention buying in the materials.'

'Are ye lookin' tae take back the money ye put intae the shop?' Jean's face was pinched with apprehension.

'Oh no,' Rose hurried to reassure her. 'I'd not dream of doing something like that to you. In any case, there would be no sense in losing everything we've built up here just so that I can start elsewhere,' she added, and Jean gave a gusty sigh of relief.

Kirsty offered her suggestion about starting in a small way and building the new business up, but Rose, jumping to her feet to stride as best she could about the small sewing room, rejected it out of hand. 'If the place starts small, it'll stay that way.'

'I don't see why that should be.'

'Kirsty, this is Paisley, not Glasgow or London. If we're going to give this town a fashion house it must be a proper fashion house from the start. Folk'll come if they think it's going to be worth their while, but starting small would be just like opening another shop. If I try that, they'll all decide to stay away until such time as it expands, and without their custom that will never happen.'

'Mebbe you should just sell it and settle for this place,' Jean said.

'John already suggested that, but it's too late. The ground floor's already been divided into separate rooms, and the panelling's being installed at this moment. The place could never be used as a mill again, and as it is now it's of no use to anyone but me – and please don't tell me that I should never have bought it, Jean,' Rose added, trying to smile but not succeeding, 'for I couldn't bear it just at the moment.'

'The thought never entered my head!'

'Of course it did, and you're quite right. I should have waited until I found a large shop that didn't need as much doing to it as the mill. But there's no sense in going over what should have happened now. Instead of waiting I went ahead with my idea, and now I've got to open the fashion house or have folk pointing the finger and crowing over me for being such a fool.'

Kirsty bridled. 'If you mean Alex, he'd not do such a thing.'

Normally Rose would have flared back at her, but today she just turned a wan face towards her friend. 'I didn't mean just him, though I'd not blame him if he did. I'm sure I would, if the boot was on the other foot.' She straightened her shoulders. 'But as I said, I'm determined that nobody's going to get the chance to point a finger, even if I've to sell my body to raise the money I need.'

To Caitlin's surprise the shocked gasp came from her mother and not from Jean, who merely asked, 'How much d'ye think ye'd get for it?'

Rose glanced down at her bony frame. 'Not nearly enough,' she admitted, and laughed for the first time in weeks. Then, sobering, she said, 'There's only one way I can raise more money.' For the first time she looked directly at Caitlin. 'I've always planned the fashion house as a partnership between you and me, Caitlin, with me providing the money, welcoming the clients and dealing with the running of the place while you designed the clothes and supervised the making of them, but as John pointed out . . .'

She faltered slightly, putting a hand to her mouth. Caitlin, who already knew what her friend was going to say, couldn't bear to let the misery go on for another moment. She swallowed hard, then said levelly, 'As things stand, Rose, you must find a designer who can put money into the business by buying a partnership.'

Rose's mouth fell open. 'How did you know?' she said into the shocked silence.

'It was easy enough. We've all known for weeks that you were worried, and I'd an idea that it must be to do with money. John's quite right. It makes sense to look for a designer who wants a partnership and is able to buy into the business. That's just what you need at the moment.'

'What I need,' Rose said fiercely, 'is you and your lovely designs. But you're right.' She gave a small, hopeless shrug. 'I can't afford you, Caitlin, though you have my firm word that as soon as the business starts to prosper you'll be brought in as the second designer.'

Caitlin, painfully aware without looking at her mother and Jean of the sympathy in their eyes, smiled brightly at a spot somewhere beyond Rose's right ear. 'I'll look forward to it,' she said, then bounced to her feet and made for the door. 'I think I'll just finish off the work I was doing on Mrs Forsyth's skirt before I go home, Mam.'

The three of them had the sense to leave her be. Long after they left, she worked on in the small lamplit room, finishing Mrs Forsyth's skirt then moving restlessly on to the work left in her mother's sewing machine. As the hours passed she pumped the treadle and rushed the cloth along beneath the pounding needle as fast as Teenie ever had, her face set and her eyes dry, although deep inside she was weeping and raging with grief for her lost hopes and dreams. Finally, exhausted and cold, she locked up the shop and walked slowly home through the dark night to face her mother's pity, and Todd's and Mary's.

But when she got to Espedair Street it was to discover that her family was involved in a drama of its own. Rowena, who should have been in bed long since, stamped around the kitchen in her nightdress, her face buttoned into a fearsome scowl, with Kirsty trying in vain to coax her to eat her supper. Todd studied his newspaper in his fireside chair, keeping his head well down, and Mary pored over her books at the table, her hands clamped over her ears. Even during her holidays Mary kept up to date with lessons.

'Just a wee mouthful,' Kirsty was saying when Caitlin went in. Rowena tightened her mouth until it almost disappeared and shook her head.

'What's amiss?'

'She wants to go to a ceilidh,' Mary said calmly.

'A what?'

'A cay – lay,' Mary pronounced the word distinctly. 'You know, one of these parties that the Highlanders like to hold in their church hall.'

'Is that what they call them?' There were a number of Highlanders in Paisley, and most of them attended the Gaelic chapel in Oakshawhill. Caitlin knew that they held social events in the small hall adjacent to the church; sometimes if she and Bryce happened to be walking through the area of an evening, they heard lilting music, the sound of voices and even the stamping of feet coming from the small hall. On these occasions, Bryce always wrinkled up his nose and muttered something about heathens.

Mary turned a page of her book. 'Murdo Guthrie told Rowena that he was playing his mouth organ at the next ceilidh, and now she wants to go.'

'She came in with her head full of it,' Kirsty said despairingly, 'and flew into a right temper when I said no.'

'These parties are just for the Highlanders, Rowena,' Caitlin tried to reason with the little girl. 'Mebbe one day when you're older they'll let you go to one, but you're too wee just now.'

Rowena crossed her arms over her chest and scowled. 'Am not!' she said, and Kirsty tried to take advantage of the moment and pop the spoon into her open mouth. But Rowena was too quick for her. She buttoned her lips up again and the spoon almost went flying.

'Think of it, Rowena – Murdo'll be too busy playing

his mouth organ to look after you. You need to be with someone.'

'We'll all go, then.'

'Not me,' Todd said hastily. 'I cannae understand the Highlanders at all, and I'm surely not puttin' mysel' in among them. The rest of ye can go if ye've a mind.'

'Not me,' Mary snapped shut her book. 'I'm going to bed.'

'Mam?'

Kirsty looked at her daughter as though Caitlin had just invited her to jump into the River Cart fully clothed. 'I don't understand the Highlanders either. I'd not dream of going to one of their hoolies.'

'Ceilidhs.' Mary threw the word back over her shoulder as she went out of the room.

'What sort of daft-like word is that, for a start?'

'It's Gaelic, Mam, the language Murdo and his friends speak when they're at home. Gaelic can't hurt you.'

'It's not going to get the chance.'

Rowena remained mute, her eyes fixed on Caitlin, who sighed. 'I'm not promising anything, but I'll ask Murdo about the ceilidh,' she said reluctantly. 'But only if you eat your supper and go to bed like a good girl.'

The scowl was wiped off Rowena's face as if by magic, to be replaced by a smile so sweet that it almost took Caitlin's breath away.

'She's got her father's charm,' she said wryly when Rowena had eaten and been taken off to bed by Kirsty. Todd grunted and turned a page of his newspaper noisily, and she had the sense to hold her tongue and say no more. Ewan's warm smile could indeed have charmed the birds from the trees, while Beth's did little more than display her neat white front teeth.

The only people who ever saw a real smile from Beth were the men she was intent on winning over.

Caitlin wondered, briefly, who was at the receiving end of one of Beth's smiles now. The woman always needed to be on a man's arm, and she had surely deserted Ewan for someone able to offer her more than he could.

'You shouldn't encourage the lassie, Caitlin,' Kirsty scolded when she came back into the kitchen. 'It's just giving in to her.'

'It was the only way to get her to go to her bed. I was in no mood for one of her scenes tonight.' Caitlin caught the swift look that passed between her mother and stepfather and knew that Todd had been told of what had happened in the shop.

'I think I'll go to my bed,' she said as Todd cleared his throat as if to speak. She couldn't face a discussion about her future.

'You've not eaten anything.'

'I'm not hungry,' Caitlin said, and escaped before Kirsty could argue.

'Leave her be,' Todd advised as his wife made to follow Caitlin out into the hall. 'The lassie's hurtin', and she needs time on her own.'

Kirsty returned to her chair reluctantly. 'I wish there was something we could do. She's a good girl, Caitlin, and she works so hard in the shop. She deserves the chance to use more of her designs, and I know that Rose wanted to work with her.'

'Aye, well ... Money rules us all, if we let it. And right now Rose Hamilton's allowin' it tae lead her by the neb like a bull bein' taken tae auction.'

'It's her way, I suppose. Rose grew up with money; she's used to buying what she wants.'

They sat for a while in silence, then Kirsty said, 'You don't think that Alex . . . ?'

'I'd keep Alex out of it, if I was you. He's hurtin' tae, because of Rose buyin' the mill.'

'But surely he'd want to help his own sister!'

Todd turned a page of his paper. 'It's up tae yersel', Kirsty, though for my part I'd just as well keep right out of it and let things lie where they fall. Between you and me,' he added, peering at her over the top of the paper, 'I'm just glad tae know that I'm stayin' put and not havin' tae move intae the mill and start all over again. I owe that much tae wee Rowena, at least.'

Upstairs, Caitlin wept into her pillow, her tears hot and fierce and angry. She would have given anything to have been able to bawl and rage and stamp around as Rowena did during one of her temper storms, kicking furniture and slapping at the wall. But she had to satisfy herself with a silent rage, stuffing the sheet into her mouth and every now and again punching at her pillow until a tiny but ominous ripping sound warned her that she would have to give up even that luxury. The last thing she wanted was for her mother to see the room covered with feathers from a torn pillow in the morning.

She cried until she was emptied of tears, then got up and washed her face in the china bowl by the street window. The night sky was cloudy, and the moon shone only fitfully on the silent cobbled street below. As she got back into bed she heard Kirsty and Todd coming upstairs, moving about their bedroom, talking quietly. Then silence fell again, and Caitlin found that she hadn't rid herself of all her tears after all.

She was determinedly cheerful in the morning, and

nobody, at home or in the shop, where she made a point of working in the sewing room all day, was tactless enough to comment on her swollen eyes. Teenie had obviously been told what had happened, for she, like the others, treated Caitlin with tender consideration. Rose was about the shop quite often that day. There was a haunted look about her, and she kept her distance from Caitlin, who could finally stand it no longer.

'Is it your mother?' she asked abruptly when Rose, coming into the back shop and finding her alone, shied back and tried to retreat without being seen.

'What?'

'You've given in at last and hit her over the head with something?'

Rose, trapped in the doorway, ventured a step forward. 'I don't know what you're talking about.'

'I'm talking about you creeping round this place as if you've hidden a body and you're waiting for the police to come and arrest you.'

'I wish I had,' the other girl said mournfully. 'At least I'd feel better than I do now.'

'For goodness' sake . . .' Caitlin put down the garment she was about to cut into and faced her friend. 'Rose, you've got no choice but to find a designer who can put money into the fashion house. I understand that. It makes sense.'

'But it's not fair! It was always going to be me and you running the place together. That's what I wanted!'

'It's what I wanted too, and there's no point in denying it, for I know that I've been walking round all day looking like a dumpling.' Caitlin briefly put a hand to her puffy eyes.

'You couldn't look like a dumpling if you tried.'

'Don't try to flatter me, Rose Hamilton, I'm not a bairn. I'm old enough to deal with disappointment now and again. And you've said that you'll take me into your fashion house as soon as you can.'

'I will – the very minute I can afford your wages.'

'Until then, can you stop looking so haunted?'

Rose gave her a dazzling smile and a swift hug. 'You're such an angel, Caitlin.'

It was a relief when she went out, for the backs of Caitlin's eyes had begun to prickle ominously. Alone, she gave an almighty sniff and blinked hard, telling herself sharply, *Behave, for goodness' sake!* There was always work for her in the shop, certainly enough to keep her busy until Rose could afford to take her into the fashion house. For one thing, she still had her portfolio to work on.

She sniffed again and blew her nose, then picked up the scissors and got on with her work.

8

Caitlin and Murdo Guthrie both attended classes at Paisley College later that week. As she spotted him going out of the main door just ahead of her, Caitlin said a swift goodnight to the girl she was with and pushed her way through the other students. Reaching the steps, she saw him cross George Street and begin to stride towards Causeyside Street, moving fast. She had to run to catch up with him; he didn't hear when she called his name, and she had to put on a spurt of extra speed and shout again before he swung round, a surprised glower on his broad face.

He halted, looking puzzled when he saw who it was. 'You're looking for me?'

'Yes.' Breathless from her run, and from embarrassment, she would have given anything to have been free to walk away in the other direction, but she had made a promise to Rowena. 'It's . . . it's about Rowena.'

He stiffened slightly, his face expressionless. 'She's no bother, but if your mother would prefer her not to come into the weaving shop . . .'

'It's got nothing to do with that. In fact, it's good of you not to mind her visits.'

'She's a decent, quiet wee lass,' he said, and Caitlin wondered what Kirsty would say if she heard that.

'She doesn't get in the way, and she likes hearing the music.'

'That's what I wanted to ask you about. Rowena mentioned that you were playing at a ceilidh.'

'Aye, next week at the chapel hall. I do, on occasion, though I'm not one for the dancing.'

'Rowena's got it into her head that she wants to go to it.'

His brows lifted slightly. 'She never said a word of it to me. Not that I'd have the right to say yes or no.'

'She's determined to go, and I said I'd speak to you about it. Mebbe it's only for adults,' Caitlin said hopefully.

'A ceilidh's for anyone that wants to go,' he informed her. 'Those that have bairns are always welcome to take them along, for it's just dancing and a bit of singing, and a bit of a talk. I'm sure you'd be welcome to bring her if you'd a mind.'

'I don't know . . .' she faltered, and again he stiffened.

'Of course not everybody in this town cares to mix with Highlanders.' Although his voice was usually soft, she discovered that it could also sound as hard and sharp as a honed steel blade. 'They think all Highlanders are tarred with the same brush, and that we're all tinkers and mebbe thieves or worse, and they'll not mix with the likes of us.'

He turned and began to walk away from her, and again she had to run to catch up with him. 'I didn't—'

'It can happen when you have to leave your home and all that, you know, and go to new places where the customs are not your own,' he said tightly, without looking at her. 'That's why the folk meet for their ceilidhs, so's they can be with those who know what their lives used to be like.'

'Murdo!' She clapped a hand on his arm and he swung round to face her. 'D'you have to be so . . . so stubborn?' she asked, finding a flash of anger of her own. 'I meant no criticism of you or your friends. I know that you've suffered from some folks' behaviour, and I'm truly sorry about that. It's because of it that I wondered if me and Rowena would be welcome – or do Highlanders think that all Lowlanders are tarred with the same brush too?'

He blinked, then had the grace to look embarrassed. 'Forgive me, I've been behaving badly towards you,' he said. 'You and Rowena will be made welcome among us, have no fear of that. I'll meet you outside the church at seven o'clock on Friday and take you in with me. Goodnight, Miss Lennox.'

He turned and walked away, not looking back. Watching him, Caitlin realised that the whole thing had been arranged without her having the chance to agree or disagree.

Rowena was overjoyed when she heard the news the next morning.

'Mind, you'll only go if you're a good girl until then,' Kirsty warned, making the most of the opportunity, and the child tucked her hands firmly behind her back and nodded agreement.

Caitlin had hoped that the others might attend the ceilidh as well, but they all refused. Given Bryce's antagonism towards Murdo and all Highlanders, she decided against inviting him.

Against Todd's advice, Kirsty told Alex about Caitlin's disappointment when he next visited Paisley. He listened, his long lean face expressionless, until she had finished speaking, then said, 'And you're expecting me to pay Caitlin's way into Rose's business?'

'I'm expecting nothing.'

'But you're hoping that I'll agree to hand over the money.'

'She's your sister, after all.' Kirsty felt her hackles rising. She knew that Alex could be as stubborn as the next man when he put his mind to it, but at the moment all her sympathies lay with Caitlin.

'Sister or not, what you're really asking me to do is to put money into Rose Hamilton's new venture.' His green-blue eyes, very like Caitlin's, became dark and stormy.

'The money's not for Rose, it's for Caitlin.'

'It'll be to Rose's benefit – and she's the one who snatched that mill from beneath my very nose.'

Kirsty's temper snapped. 'For goodness' sake, Alex, why should a daft quarrel between you and Rose spoil your sister's life? Have you no thought for Caitlin? Even though you're with your own father now, she's still a part of your family.'

'Family's one thing, Mam, and business is another. If Caitlin needed the money for something else – anything else – I'd do all that I could to help her. But this matter concerns—'

'It concerns your hurt pride, and you care more about that than you do about your own flesh and blood.' Kirsty snatched up an armful of clothes and pushed past him towards the back door. Ignoring his call, she slammed the door behind her and stormed into the wash house, where she pushed the clothing down into the steaming water in the tub then snatched up the long-handled wooden tongs and used them to ram the clothes below the surface. She didn't turn her head when the door opened.

'Mam, can you not see—'

She rounded on him, her face flushed with the

water's heat, the tongs steaming and dripping in her hand. 'Don't fash yourself, Alex, I'll find another way to help my daughter,' she said. Then, as he tried again to say something: 'I'd not want to be more beholden to you than I already am.'

For a moment he stood by the door. Then, he said, 'Please yourself,' and went out.

Kirsty pushed the tongs viciously at a sleeve that had dared to scramble back to the surface, then jerked away as a few drops of near boiling water spattered over her arm.

Rowena had been exceptionally good all week; now, as Caitlin walked along Causeyside Street to the town centre, known as the Cross, she skipped ahead, disappearing into the darkness, continually having to stop and wait for her aunt or run back to her.

'You'll be tired out by the time we get there,' Caitlin scolded gently, but the little girl just shook her head, ignoring the proferred hand, and danced off again. Rowena was not one for holding hands.

They had reached the Cross and were heading for Moss Street when they met Bryce and a group of his friends. Caitlin's heart sank as he halted in front of her. Rowena, about to scamper ahead, sidled against her aunt's legs instead, and to her surprise Caitlin felt a small mittened hand slip into hers.

'On ye go, I'll catch up with ye,' Bryce ordered his friends. Then he said to Caitlin, 'I thought you'd work tae dae this evenin'.'

'Rowena was too restless to go to bed, so I said I'd take her for a walk to tire her,' she improvised hurriedly.

'Is that right?' He glanced at her dark blue skirt and wrapover jacket, and Caitlin was thankful that she had decided against dressing up for the ceilidh. Even so, he said, 'You look very smart.'

'You know that I like to dress well. Sometimes it encourages folk to buy their clothes from Jean's shop.'

'I'll walk with you,' he offered.

'There's no need. We'll be turning back soon, and your friends are waiting.' The other young men had halted and formed a tight group beneath a gas lamp, eyeing Bryce and Caitlin from under the skips of their caps and murmuring to each other.

'Ach, let them wait. We can put the bairn intae the house and have a wee while on our own.' His voice dropped to an intimate murmur and heat began to kindle in his eyes.

'I promised her that it'd just be the two of us tonight,' she protested, and Rowena chimed in, 'Come on, Aunt Caitlin, we'll be late.'

'Late for what?'

'Late getting back,' Caitlin said swiftly. 'It'll soon be past her bedtime.'

'I could get rid of them,' Bryce jerked his head in the general direction of his friends, 'and meet you outside your house later.'

'Not tonight. I've still got that work to do after we get back.'

He began to argue, but Rowena, edging round to stand in front of Caitlin, glared up at him and said loudly, 'Go away!'

'Rowena!'

Rowena ignored her. 'We don't want you!'

Bryce's face darkened, and he bent down towards her. 'Wee lassies should mind their ain—' He yelped as Rowena's foot connected squarely with his ankle. A burst of noisy laughter came from his cronies as he skipped away from her.

'She's a bonnier fighter than what you are, Bryce!' one of them shouted.

'Rowena!' Caitlin said, scandalised, then 'Bryce!' as he snarled, 'Wee bitch!'

He glared at her, his face crimson with pain and mortification. 'What are ye yellin' at me for when she's damned near maimed me?'

'She's too wee to hurt you that badly, and anyway she's sorry, aren't you, Rowena?'

'Go away!'

'We're the ones who're going. Come away at once.' Caitlin dragged her away.

'I'll see you later, then.'

'Not tonight, Bryce.' She threw the words over her shoulder. 'You'd better go home and get a poultice on that sore leg of yours.'

She almost ran into Moss Street, dragging Rowena after her, convinced that Bryce was following. But when she glanced back there was no sign of him.

'You don't deserve to go to the ceilidh,' she scolded as the two of them started up School Wynd. 'You were a very bad girl.'

Rowena's head was well down, so that her muttered, 'He's a bad man,' only just reached Caitlin's ears. She recalled the way the small, childish body had trembled against her legs even while Rowena was ordering Bryce to go away. 'What d'you mean? Has Bryce been bad to you?'

Rowena, concentrating on climbing the steep hill, said nothing, and Caitlin, remembering the venom in Bryce's face and voice when he swore at the child, decided to let the subject drop for the time being.

Murdo was waiting for them outside the Gaelic chapel hall. 'You came, then?'

'Why wouldn't we?' Caitlin asked sharply, still jumpy from her meeting with Bryce. He said nothing, but turned towards the hall door. Rowena, deserting her aunt, hurried to his side and grasped one of his fingers firmly. The two of them walked into the hall together, with Caitlin trailing behind.

The place was already busy, but people obligingly made room for the newcomers on one of the benches lining the walls.

'This is Mhairi.' Murdo indicated the woman sitting beside Caitlin. 'She'll look after you, won't you, Mhairi?'

'I will indeed. Off you go now, man, for my toes are itching to dance.' Mhairi leaned forward and smiled past Caitlin at Rowena. 'You've got a bonny wee lass there.'

'She's my brother's child.'

'Indeed? I've not seen you here before.'

'We've never been to a ceilidh before.'

Mhairi patted Caitlin's knee. 'Then you've got a treat before you, my dear.' She was small and plump, with a round rosy face and bright blue eyes, and snow-white hair escaping in soft little curls from the knot at the back of her head. Caitlin took to her at once and didn't mind answering her probing questions. After all, she was a stranger in the midst of people who clearly knew each other well. When Mhairi had satisfied herself as to who the newcomers were, she turned to convey the information in Gaelic to the others, who had been eyeing Caitlin and Rowena with open curiosity. 'You'll not mind me telling them, my dear. We always like to welcome folk.'

They did. There were smiles and nods and some hand-shaking before the musicians on a small dais at one end of the hall began to play, setting off an immediate scurry to find partners. Almost at once the floor was filled with dancers of all ages, from quite small children bouncing about in pairs or by themselves to elderly men and women whirling, and in some cases hobbling, round the floor. The clothing, too, was varied, with some well dressed and others wearing patched and darned garments; it made no difference to their enjoyment. Even those still on the benches were moving to the lively music, while Mhairi thumped her feet on the wooden floor in time to the beat and slapped her open palms so hard on her thighs that Caitlin was sure the woman's legs would be covered in bruises in the morning.

By her side, Rowena twitched then bounced on the wooden bench, finally slipping down to the floor to jig on the spot, her eyes on the dancers, her small face entranced as she tried to follow their steps. Now and then, as the dancers swung apart, Caitlin caught glimpses of the musicians. There were two fiddlers, an accordionist and a stick-thin lad with a flat drum not much larger than a good-sized dinner plate strapped to one hand. In the other he held a short baton, laced through his fingers so that he could flick either end rapidly against the drum. He and the other musicians were grinning from ear to ear, but Murdo, standing to one side of the group, was as sombre as ever. Not that it was possible to smile while playing the mouth organ, Caitlin thought.

Within a few moments a middle-aged man had whisked Mhairi from the bench and into the thick of the dancers. Every now and again Caitlin caught sight of her stamping and spinning with the best of them. The dances ranged from fast, with a great deal of hooching from the dancers, to slow, with elegant, almost ritualistic steps. Now and again, to give the dancers a chance to catch their breath, a singer stepped onto the dais. During an interval for food and drink, Murdo appeared by Caitlin's side. 'Are you enjoying yourselves?' He had taken his jacket and cravat off and loosened his shirt at the throat; his face was flushed, and damp strands of slightly overlong brown hair clung to his forehead and cheeks.

'I am, but mebbe it's time Rowena was in her bed.'

Rowena, thirstily drinking lemonade and eyeing some children shyly over the rim of her mug, whirled round at once. 'I've not done any dancing yet. Show me how to dance, Murdo!' She ran at him and tugged on his trouser leg while Caitlin marvelled at the child's easy informality with this silent, somewhat frightening man.

'How can I dance when I'm playing the music as well?'

'I'll show you how,' a young lad offered, and Rowena beamed at him. Once she was on the floor there was no question of taking her home early, and soon Caitlin, too, was drawn to her feet to stumble through unfamiliar steps. Rowena picked up the rhythms faster than she did, but nobody seemed to mind when, on occasion, her ignorance spoiled the rhythm of the dances.

'You'll come again,' Mhairi said when they were leaving the hall at the end of the evening. 'You'll be more than welcome – the two of you.'

The small hall, filled to capacity, had been warm, and the cold wind cut through them when they stepped outside. A few snowflakes danced at them from the darkness. 'I'll see you safe home,' Murdo said, and scooped Rowena up, ignoring Caitlin's polite protests.

The little girl put her arms round his neck and almost at once began to snore softly against his shoulder while, in silence, he and Caitlin walked to Espedair Street together.

9

'Whatever you want, lass, is fine by me,' Todd Paget told his wife placidly.

'It's your money as well as mine. You have to be in agreement, Todd.'

'I am. The only thing I'm wonderin' is what your Alex'll have tae say when he hears about it.'

Kirsty's mouth tightened slightly. 'I don't see that it's any of his concern. He'd his chance to help his sister and he refused. I can't understand him, Todd. In the old days Alex would've given any one of us the shirt off his own back if need be. I don't like the way he's changed.'

Todd puffed gently on his pipe. 'It's hard work, runnin' a big Glasgow shop and thon workshop as well. He's had tae grow up, that's all.'

Kirsty couldn't let the matter go at that. 'D'you think that working alongside his father's hardened him? When I first knew Sandy he was such a gentle lad, but it's a different man who's come back into our lives.'

'Can ye blame him?' By now Todd knew the story of Alex's parentage well. 'After bein' near murdered by yer father then thrown out of the town with nothin' but the rags on his back, the man had tae fight for everythin' he has. Folk that've had it hard cannae survive without changin'.'

'But Alex hasn't had to suffer nearly as much as his father.'

'Even so, he's a grown man, Kirsty, and ye have tae let him make his own decisions, even when ye cannae agree with them. Ye have tae let him go his own way as he sees fit.'

'I suppose you're right,' she said sadly, thinking of the caring lad her Alex had once been. Then, her chin coming up, she added, 'And I must go my way as I see fit, so if you're willing, I'm going to help Caitlin, for she deserves it.'

'Fine.' Glad that the discussion was over, Todd reached for his newspaper. For a while the kitchen was silent, then Kirsty looked at the clock.

'Should they not be back yet? It's long past Rowena's bedtime.'

'They'll be enjoyin' themselves.'

She opened the back door then shut it at once, shivering. 'It's starting to snow. Mebbe you should take a walk along the road, Todd. You might meet them.'

He sighed inwardly but put the paper aside, knowing that his wife wouldn't be content until he did as she wished. As he got to his feet, the back door opened and Caitlin came in, Murdo Guthrie looming behind her with Rowena in his arms. For a moment both Kirsty and Todd were taken aback at sight of the weaver on their doorstep, but Kirsty recovered swiftly. 'You'll have a cup of tea with us, Mr Guthrie.'

'I'd not want to keep you from your beds.' Murdo began to ease Rowena carefully from his shoulder.

'Ye're no' keepin' us back at all, man,' Todd told him heartily. 'Come in, come in.' Then, hopefully: 'Ye'd mebbe sooner have a dram than tea?'

But Murdo refused to go over the doorstep. 'I've an early start in the morning, so I'll bid you goodnight,' he said, and handed over the child's small body before melting into the darkness.

Todd closed the door with his free hand, shaking his head as he turned to the women. 'I swear I don't know what tae make of that man.'

'Give her to me, poor lamb.' Kirsty claimed the little girl. 'You're just vexed because you missed the chance of a wee whisky.'

'What're ye talkin' about, woman? I can have a dram in my own kitchen whenever I want tae!' Todd reached for the bottle on its shelf.

'This bairn's exhausted! You should have brought her home sooner, Caitlin.'

'I couldn't get her to come away.'

'Well, she can sleep in her wee semmit and drawers for once, for I don't want to disturb her more than I must. The tea's fresh made,' Kirsty said over her shoulder as she carried Rowena out of the room.

'Mebbe I'll just have a cup with ye.' His point made, Todd replaced the whisky bottle and fetched mugs from the draining board by the sink for himself and his stepdaughter. 'Did the bairn enjoy hersel'?'

'She did that.'

'And did you have a good time an' all?'

Caitlin sank into a chair. 'I did. I really did.'

'Then that's all that matters,' Todd said comfortably, pouring tea.

When Kirsty came downstairs to report that she had managed to stow Rowena safely in her bed without rousing her, Caitlin got to her feet, too tired to face her mother's searching questions about the ceilidh. But Kirsty put out a hand to stop her.

'Sit down a minute. There's something me and

Todd want to say.' Kirsty took a seat at the table, smoothing her skirt nervously, darting glances at her husband as though hoping that he might deliver the news. But Todd just smiled serenely back at her and sipped at his tea.

'It's your idea, Kirsty. You tell the lassie.'

'It's like this.' Kirsty took a deep breath and plunged into her speech. 'We both know how disappointed you were when Rose decided to bring in a designer who could put money into her fashion house.'

'I was, but it's all right now. I'm going to join her as soon as she can afford my wages, you know that.'

'Wheesht when I'm speaking to you. You'll get my words in a muddle,' Kirsty rapped nervously, then took another breath as her daughter subsided. 'The thing is, you're a good hard-working lass, and me and Todd think you should have your chance. So we're going to pay Rose the money she needs so that you can work with her as her partner.'

It was the last thing Caitlin had expected to hear. She sat upright in her chair, her tiredness gone, staring at her mother then at her stepfather. 'But how . . . where'll you get the money?'

'Don't look at me, it was all your mother's idea – though I'm all for it,' Todd added swiftly.

'Mam?'

Now that her idea was out in the open, Kirsty's nerves had vanished, and she was beaming. 'It's the money Alex and his father paid to me for the workshop.'

'I can't take it!'

'Of course you can. Money's for using, not for lying idle in a bank.'

'But that was meant to keep you and Todd in comfort when you stop working.'

'Tuts, lassie, that'll not happen for a good long time yet. Todd'll stay in the workshop and I'll stay with Jean until we're both too old to be of use to anyone, and by then you and Rose'll have paid the money back.'

Caitlin looked from one to the other. 'It doesn't seem right,' she said weakly, but already a faint glow had begun to tingle and grow deep inside her.

'Of course it's right. It's what you want, and what we want for you. Is that not right, Todd?'

'Right enough,' he agreed amiably.

Caitlin's knees were weak when she stood up. She hugged her mother, then Todd, who gave an embarrassed chuckle. 'I don't know what to say.'

Kirsty gave her a slight push towards the door. 'There's nothing to say. Just get off to your bed – and mind that that mill's part yours now, so you'll have to make a go of it.'

'I will!' At the hall door, Caitlin turned. 'What'll Alex say about you giving his money to me?'

'It's not his money,' her mother told her firmly. 'It's ours, in payment for the workshop. What we do with it is no business of Alex's.'

Despite her exhaustion, Caitlin was still awake long after the house had settled into silence for the night. Apart from her excitement, the music she had heard during the evening echoed through her mind, sometimes fast and light-hearted, sometimes slow and sad. She finally got up and lit the paraffin lamp on the small table, then brought out her sketchbook and leafed through it. The designs already on its pages had been part of her collection for the distant future, but now, it seemed, they might become reality within the next twelvemonth.

Inside her skull the fiddles rippled up and down

the scale and the accordion wove its ribbon of sound, underlaid by the swift, exciting beat of the drum, and all of them were linked by the sound of Murdo Guthrie's mouth organ. Looking through the window into the dark night, she saw the dancers' flushed smiling faces, hair and skirts and coat tails twisting and flying, remembering the moments when these same laughing faces had stilled as they listened to the other music, slow and lonely, recalling memories of places far from Paisley's streets.

She turned to a blank page, reached for her crayons and began to draw.

Jean was shocked when Rose, on hearing Caitlin's news, rushed out and brought back a bottle of champagne.

'Ye'd think it was Ne'erday all over again!'

'It's even better than Ne'erday,' Rose told her, beaming as she filled the motley assortment of mugs normally used for their tea. 'Ne'erday's only the beginning of a new year – this is the beginning of a new life. A toast!'

'But it's not ten o'clock yet. It's far too early tae be drinkin'. We'll all be fleein' by noon, and us with a shop tae run.'

'It's only the once, Jean, an' it makes a nice wee change from tea.' Teenie eyed her mugful thirstily.

'You'd not grudge us a celebration on a day like this, surely.' Rose clinked her mug against Jean's, her smile almost splitting her long face in half. 'To all of us and what we've achieved so far, and to me and Caitlin in our new venture!'

'Ach, why not?' said Jean, and downed her mugful. 'Right enough, it sets up a nice wee glow,' she admitted, and joined in a second toast when John Brodie, summoned from his office, arrived with another bottle and insisted on filling the mugs again.

'To . . .' he paused, then asked, 'Have you thought of a name for the new place yet?'

'The House of Rose,' Teenie suggested, but Rose shook her head.

'No, it has to be both names or something else entirely. We'll think of something.' Then she raised her mug. 'To us again!'

'I was wondering,' Rose said later to Caitlin, 'if MacDowall and Son might be willing to make the chairs and small tables we'll need for the salons.'

'You're going to ask Alex?'

Rose flushed. 'It's only fair to give the business to folk we know, and it means that we can describe just what we want. I'd like to see some of his hand-painted chairs in our salon, and you never know, the clients might like them too and give him some orders.'

'I don't know, Rose . . .'

'Ask him and see. Nobody can deny that Alex is a businessman through and through,' Rose said with a slight edge to her voice, 'and I doubt if he'll turn down the chance of selling some of his work, even to me.'

Caitlin had reached the corner of Espedair Street on her way home that night when Bryce, who had been leaning against a wall, straightened up and moved into her path.

'I thought you'd be finished work long since.'

'I have, but I wanted tae speak tae ye.'

'I've got something to tell you, too.' She had been walking on air all day, longing to run into the street and shout her news to the entire town. 'Bryce, you'll never guess what's happened!'

'I know fine and well what happened.' His face was dark, his voice tense. 'Ye didnae know that ye were seen, did ye?'

'Seen where?'

'Walkin' along Causeyside Street last night with that . . . that Highlander!' He spat the word out as though it had a foul taste. 'And it was long past the time ye told me ye were tae be in by. Where were ye?'

As she stared up into his angry eyes, Caitlin came back to earth with a bump, elation ebbing and anger taking its place. 'What business is it of yours where I was last night and who I was with?'

'It's my business if ye're seein' him behind my back!'

'If you must know, Rowena wanted to go to the ceilidh at the Gaelic chapel, so I took her.'

'Ye were dancin' with that weaver? An' me standin' here like a fool waitin' for ye tae come out walkin' with me?'

'You were here last night?'

'I said I'd be waitin' for ye.'

'And I told you not to bother.'

'Aye, because ye'd work tae dae, you said. Some work!' He turned away and spat into the gutter. 'Dancin' with the likes o' him!'

'I was not dancing with Murdo Guthrie – he was playing his mouth organ all evening.'

'Then he walked ye home.'

'Rowena was tired and he carried her back home for me. Did your loose-mouthed friend not tell you that it was her in his arms and not me?' Caitlin made to walk past him into the pend, but he caught at her arm.

'I'll not have ye goin' out wi' him, Caitlin!'

'I've not been out with him at all. I told you, it was for Rowena.'

'I'll not have my lassie seen out wi' the likes o' him.'

'I'm not yours, Bryce.'

'Ye are,' he said almost pleadingly. 'Ach, Caitlin, everyone knows we walk out together.'

'Then you'll just have to tell everyone that they're wrong, since we're not walking out together any longer. And you can tell them that it was your stupid jealousy that put an end to it!' Furious now, she pulled away from his grip. 'I've got more to do than argue with you,' she said curtly, and pushed past him into the pend without looking back.

When Alex next came to Paisley, Caitlin seized her chance and offered to walk to the station with him when he left. It was hard for her to introduce the subject of the proposed fashion house; she made several attempts at it, but they all trickled away into silence, and they had almost reached the station entrance when he said, 'I know fine that you've got something on your mind, and if you don't hurry up with it I'll be halfway to Glasgow and none the wiser.'

'It's not me, it's . . .'

'Well?' His brow crinkled in a frown. 'You're never scared of me, Caitlin. I might have taken on my father's name and moved to Glasgow, but I'm surely still your brother.'

She took a deep breath. 'We'd like . . . Rose and me would like you to make some furniture for our new fashion house.'

His eyebrows shot up. 'You're still going into that business with her?'

She beamed at him. 'I'm going to be the designer.'

'But I thought she was looking for a designer who could be a paying partner—' he began, then stopped abruptly.

'How did you know about that?'

'It was just something Mam mentioned,' Alex said vaguely. 'So Rose decided she didn't need the extra money after all?'

'She's still getting it. Mam and Todd are buying the partnership for me.'

'What?' Alex, about to start down the steps to the station, halted abruptly. Caitlin, already part of the way down, turned with one hand on the rail.

'It was their idea, not mine, but they were determined to do it.' She stopped, then said in a small voice, 'You didn't know that they were giving me the money you gave to them.'

The lamplight in the street behind him meant that his face was in deep shadow, so she had no way of seeing his expression. 'The money for the workshop belongs to Mam and Todd, and they can spend it as they wish,' he said, and began to descend the stairs again.

Caitlin scurried down ahead of him. 'You're not pleased, though.'

'It's none of my business, though I think you're taking a risk, going into a new venture from the start.'

'I don't think so. Rose and I know what we're doing, and I'm sure it'll work. We're both determined to make it work.'

The train had been signalled, and the few people already waiting on the platform were moving towards the edge. 'You really care about this idea of hers, don't you?'

'More than anything in the world. Imagine me getting the chance to design clothes for folk instead of just altering them!'

'And is it you who thought of asking me if MacDowall

and Son would make some furniture for the place? If so, you'd be advised to see what Rose thinks before I give you an answer, for I doubt if she'd approve.'

His refusal to believe anything good of Rose began to annoy her. 'You're quite wrong, Alex. It was Rose's idea, and she asked me to speak to you about it.'

'Do you want me to do it?'

'Of course I do. We couldn't do any better than have some of your hand-painted furniture in the place.'

A whistle blew, and looking back beneath the bridge she saw the engine coming, steam puffing from its funnel.

'What sort of furniture?' Alex had to raise his voice above the noise as the train thundered into the station then slowed with a screech of brakes.

'About six decorated chairs for the main salon and one or two small tables to match. That's all we can afford to begin with.'

'I'd want to visit the mill and see the setting before I started working on the furniture.'

'Of course, though you'll need to wait until the workmen have finished with it. Does that mean you'll do it?'

'I'll do it – for you,' he said, and made for the nearest carriage.

When the train had gone, Caitlin ran up the steps and almost danced home, smiling at everyone she passed on the way, light-headed with the relief of knowing that the ordeal was over and he had agreed. He would visit the mill, he would meet Rose there, and perhaps the two of them would settle their differences. If that happened, Caitlin's life would become as close to perfect as it ever had.

Alex made a point of returning to Paisley within a

few days, choosing a time when he thought his mother would be at home and knocking at the street door instead of taking his usual route through the pend to the back yard. He wanted to see Kirsty rather than Todd. When she opened the door, her apprehension changed to surprise, then alarm at the sight of her son on the step.

'What's amiss?'

'Nothing at all. I just came to see you.'

'Then why not come round the back?'

'Because I wanted a word with you on your own.' He stepped inside and closed the door.

'Something is wrong!'

'No it's not, Mam. Can we go into the kitchen, or are we going to have to talk out here in the hall?'

'You know fine and well that the street door's for visitors and bad news,' Kirsty scolded, and bustled ahead of him into the kitchen, which smelled pleasantly of home baking. 'Everyone else comes round the back.'

The big table was covered with flour, and Rowena, swathed in an apron, was kneeling on a chair and working away at a lump of dough.

'We're making buns for Grandad's dinner,' Kirsty explained. 'You go on with it, pet, while your uncle Alex and me have a wee talk.'

But at the sight of the visitor the little girl had already dropped the dough, grey and greasy from her manipulation, and was scrambling down from the chair, trying to pull the apron off at the same time.

Kirsty helped her, wiping her hands carefully while Alex held his tongue and waited with what patience he could find.

'Go and play upstairs,' Kirsty coaxed, but Rowena shook her head and made for the door leading to the yard. She was called back and pushed into a warm coat before finally being released outside.

'She's still that timid with folk she doesn't see every day,' Kirsty fretted, reaching as usual for the teapot. 'That'll be her away to the weaving shop, to that Murdo Guthrie.'

'There's no harm in her spending time with him as long as she doesn't get in the way of his work. Mam, Caitlin tells me that you and Todd are buying her a partnership in Rose Hamilton's new venture.'

Kirsty, who had just finished pouring boiling water onto tea leaves, paused with her back to him, the kettle still poised in one hand. 'Aye, that's right,' she said at last.

'There's no need for you to put your hand in your pocket. Since Caitlin seems to have set her heart on it, I'll give her the money.'

'It's already been paid over.' Kirsty put the empty kettle down and brushed a drift of flour into the middle of the table with the back of one hand to clear a space before taking clean cups from the cupboard.

'Then I'll give you your money back.'

'You'll not bother,' she said flatly.

'But . . . Look, Mam, she's my sister and I should never have refused you the way I did. I was angered with Rose Hamilton and I stupidly took it out on you and Caitlin. Now I want to put things right.'

Kirsty said nothing, concentrating on pouring milk into one cup then the other. She filled each cup with tea then stirred sugar in as though getting everything right was of the utmost importance.

'So how much was it?'

Kirsty pushed his cup towards him and sat down. 'That's our business, Alex. You'd already refused to help, so we did what we thought best.'

'But that money was meant to make you feel more secure about your future.'

'We do feel secure. Rose and Caitlin'll pay the money back to us, and mebbe some extra besides.' Kirsty sipped at her tea, then put the cup down and looked levelly at her son. 'John Brodie explained everything to us and drew up the papers. Isn't that how a lot of business folk make their wealth?'

'Yes, but they don't invest every penny that they own. Let me pay the money back to you, then it'll be me that takes the risk. I can afford it better than you can.'

'You refused to help Caitlin when I asked you to. Why should you help her now?'

'I've already admitted that I took my anger with Rose out on Caitlin. It was a daft thing to do and I'm sorry about it.'

'I'm glad to hear you say that, son,' Kirsty said with almost formal dignity.

'And now I'm going to make amends.'

'Alex, Todd and me decided to use our money to help Caitlin, and that's the way things are going to stay. You don't need to do anything. We'll get the money back in good time.'

'Are you certain of that?'

'As certain as anybody can be about anything. You don't understand, do you?' Kirsty said almost kindly. 'There's business, and there's family. You refused to pay the money over because, as you saw it, it would help Rose to set up in the mill that you'd wanted for yourself. That's business. Todd and me just wanted to help Caitlin, and that's family.'

'But I'm family too, and I want to put things right!'

'There's no need,' she said, as though trying to

explain something to a child. 'It's all been seen to, and we're going to let things stand as they are.'

He argued, reasoned, argued again, but nothing he said would change her mind. Finally, realising that time was passing and he was due to return to Glasgow, he left the house.

As his train rattled towards the city he stared out of the window without seeing the tenements that presented their shabby backs to the railway line. When his natural father had suddenly come into his life, offering work, his name, and a secure future, Alex had seized the chance to escape from an increasingly difficult life with his dominating stepfather. In his own eyes he had remained part of the Paisley family, but now a gulf seemed to be opening between his present life and his past.

He would have liked to go straight to the small factory where he spent a good part of his day. There he would find solace in the familiar surroundings of timber and tools and sawdust, the calmness of craftsmen going about their business, the pleasure of creating furniture from wood that had grown over centuries in huge forests. But he and his father had agreed to meet an important new client, so instead he had to walk from the station to the large and imposing emporium with 'MacDowall and Son' in bold letters over the door and above the windows on both outer walls.

As he made his way to the offices on the top floor, the counter assistants, supervisors and even some of the regular customers who knew him nodded and smiled. Their recognition was usually soothing, but not today.

Angus MacDowall was waiting in his office. 'I've just sent a lad down to the factory. I thought you might have forgotten our meeting.' Despite the hard life he had known in his earlier years, and despite the extra flesh that age and comfortable living had laid over his bones, he was as straight backed and quick in his movements as a much younger man.

'I had to go to Paisley.' Alex hung up his coat and hat and glanced into the mirror by the hatstand.

'Nothing wrong, I hope?'

'No.'

Angus eyed his son closely. 'Is your mother in good health?'

'She's very well.'

'Good.' Apart from a few brief meetings when he had first gone to Paisley to find Alex, Angus had had no other contact in recent years with his son's mother. Once they had meant everything to each other, but only for a short time; after that, their lives had gone along widely divergent lines, and they had become strangers, with only Alex's existence to remind them of what had been.

Angus consulted the gold watch chained across his slightly rounded stomach. 'They're late.'

'Father, have you ever made a mistake?'

'Me?' Angus grunted an abrupt laugh. 'I've made more of them than you've eaten hot dinners.'

'I'm talking about mistakes you regretted.'

'So am I.'

'And when you felt regret, how did you go about making amends?'

Angus leaned forward, hands on his large handsome desk. 'Are you going to tell me what this is about?'

'I don't believe I am.'

'Quite right.' Although they respected each other highly and, in their own ways, cared for each other, the relationship between father and son had always been more businesslike than familiar. They both preferred it that way; when it came to open warmth, Alex had his Paisley family, and Angus his daughter, Fiona, Alex's half-sister, now married and living in Fort William.

'If you want my opinion, lad, you can never make amends,' Angus said bluntly. 'Best to let the matter be, whatever it is, and make up your mind to be more careful with your decisions in future.'

Then the door opened; the awaited clients were ushered in, and the matter was dropped.

10

Todd waited that night until he and his wife were alone in their bedroom before saying, 'Ye've been awful quiet all evenin', lass. Has somethin' happened tae upset ye?'

'Alex was here.'

'Alex? But he never came tae the workshop.'

'He didn't stay for long. I sent him away with a flea in his ear,' Kirsty admitted, 'and now I'm wondering if I did the right thing.'

'I'll not be able tae advise ye as tae that till ye tell me more about it.' Todd, already in bed, patted the pillow beside his. 'Come over here.'

'I've not brushed my hair yet.'

'It can wait.'

When she joined him, he put an arm about her and drew her close to his warm body, listening to what she had to say without comment until she finished.

'I've been vexed with the way he refused to help Caitlin, I'll admit that. But even so, mebbe I dealt with him too severely today. D'you think I was acting out of spite, Todd – doing to Alex what he did to me and Caitlin when he refused the money in the first place?' Then, when her husband said nothing: 'I just felt that someone had to make him see the difference between

110

an act of business and helping out one of your own family.'

Todd had rested his chin comfortably on the top of her head. 'If an itch bothers ye, scratch it,' he told her. 'It seems tae me that Alex set up a right itch in ye when he refused tae lend the money in the first place. And today ye had a good scratch.'

'But what if I've driven him away from me?'

'I doubt if the matter's gone that far. It's a poor sort of son who'd deny his own mother just because he didnae get everythin' his way,' Todd gave a huge yawn, '—an' your Alex is a better man than that any day of the week.'

In less than a minute he was breathing slowly and regularly, the matter discussed and his mind at rest. Unwilling to disturb him, Kirsty stayed where she was, her mind reaching back over the past to long before she had met Todd or her first husband, Matt. She had been only sixteen when she had given birth to Alex; her father had packed her off to live with his sister, who had agreed with him that the child would be put up for adoption immediately after its birth. Instead Kirsty had run away with her newborn baby and had had a hard struggle to support the two of them before meeting and marrying Matt Lennox.

She hadn't even known that Sandy's full name was Angus MacDowall until the day he had turned up at Espedair Street, wealthy and successful and eager for a son to run his large furniture store with him, and eventually take it over. It had almost broken her heart when Alex had chosen to throw in his lot with his father, though she had known, and still knew, that Angus could offer him a far better future than he could expect with her. But he had been her son, her precious first-born. Now, despite Todd's reassurance, she felt that things had changed for the worse.

Todd snored slightly, then settled again, his arm tightening about her. The hollow between his neck and shoulder was warm and safe and, despite her worries, Kirsty, too, drifted into sleep, her hair unbrushed and the lamp still burning on the table.

By the beginning of February the former mill had been painted inside and out, and the ground floor had been divided into several rooms. New, larger windows had been installed throughout, the yard where weeds had struggled up through broken cobbles had been relaid with flagstones and the railings round the property had been cleared of rust and painted. On the evening of the day the workmen finished, Caitlin, John and Rose toured the mill, breathing in the smell of fresh wood and paint.

'This salon,' Rose spread her arms out, revolving slowly, 'will be for the very wealthy, and the other one will be for the rest, though we won't let the rest know that there's any difference.'

'We'll just furnish this one until you start bringing in clients,' John put in warningly. He had brought a sheaf of papers with him and was making lists of all that still had to be done. They had agreed to retain the space on the first floor, which had once held machinery, as a sewing room, with two large cutting tables in the centre – 'One to start with,' John said – flanked by sewing machines. At one end stood the new stove, which would pipe its heat through the entire building, and at the other, doors opened into two small rooms that had once been occupied by overseers. One, it had been decided, would be occupied by a forewoman, when they could afford such a luxury, while the other would be used for specialists, such as embroiderers.

A flight of stairs took them to the top floor; here the small windows had been retained, shelving had been installed round the walls to hold bolts of cloth and cupboards stood along the centre of the room, waiting to be filled with small items such as threads, needles and ribbons.

In its original state the mill had appeared poky to Caitlin, but now that it had been cleaned and the walls whitewashed and larger windows installed, she was appalled by the size of the place. 'We'll never fill it!' she said as they went back downstairs.

'We will, given time,' Rose said confidently. 'We can build up gradually.' She settled herself on a broad stone windowsill in the main salon. 'Now, I'd like to open in April, with a small fashion display on the first day to show some of Caitlin's designs.'

'April?' Caitlin, leaning against the wall, straightened up. 'That's too soon!'

'It's a good time of year to start a new business.'

'But you're not giving me enough time to provide all the new designs we'd need for a display!'

'I was thinking of using some of the designs you've already done as well as a few new ones. If we ask some of the people we've already made clothes for to wear them in the display, it would show what we've – you've – already achieved. They would love it – think of the fun they could have! And who knows, it might tempt them to order more clothes.'

'It sounds quite interesting – not that I know anything about clothes,' John added hurriedly.

'As to new clothes, if you could manage to make one or two items, Caitlin, I'm sure that John and I could persuade some of those empty-headed girls we meet at parties to model them for us,' Rose rushed on, 'especially if we allowed them to buy the garments they model at a reduced price. And we'll frame some of the other designs and hang them on the walls for the guests to look at. I'm sure we'd bring in a few orders on that first day.'

'First of all,' John interrupted, 'we have to find out if Caitlin will be able to do everything in the time you're allowing her.'

Caitlin's mind was racing. She had been doing some further work on the sketches inspired by the ceilidh, and it excited her to think that she might be able to develop them quite soon. 'I might get it done on time, if I start right away. You'd need to find the models quickly.'

'I will,' Rose promised. 'You and I will need to go to Glasgow next week to shop for materials.'

'We'd never manage to make all the clothes at Causeyside Street in the time, not with the orders that are lying there already.'

'Then we'd best get some sewing women for this place as soon as possible and buy in machines for them.' John made a note. 'I'll put advertisements in the *Express* and the *Gazette* for experienced seamstresses. How many?'

'Six,' Rose said, just as Caitlin said, 'Three.'

John looked from one to the other. 'Three to begin with. Furniture . . . As I said, we could start by furnishing just one salon and one fitting room, and perhaps you two could share the larger office until we're established. I believe that your brother's going to make the furniture for this room, Caitlin.'

'Yes. He hopes to visit Paisley next Friday morning to see the place and talk about what we want.'

'That's decided, then.' Rose stood up, dusting her

hands and beaming at her partners. 'I can't wait to see Mama's face when we tell her that we open in April!'

Rowena's interest in dancing, awakened by her night at the ceilidh in the Gaelic chapel, took up most of her attention and kept her out of mischief. With her quick mind she had memorised some of the basic steps, and she practised them tirelessly in the kitchen, in the weaving shop whenever Murdo had time to play his mouth organ and, as winter lost its grip and the weather began to improve, on a large flagstone set into the small patch of grass in the back yard.

The flagstone quickly became her special dancing stone, where she happily hopped and skipped and twirled to music that only she could hear. Occasionally she managed to coax Murdo from the weaving shop during his midday break to play the mouth organ while she danced.

Although most of Caitlin's evenings were spent with books and her sketch pad, working and reworking new designs for the fashion house, Rowena persuaded her to go to another ceilidh. This time Mary went too, and admitted, as they walked home at the end of the evening, enjoying herself.

'I'd wondered how it would be, with Highlanders so different from us Lowlanders, but they're nice enough folk.'

'Especially that lad you kept dancing with.'

'Mmmm.' Mary refused to be drawn. 'Murdo Guthrie's a strange man,' she said, staring at his back. He and Rowena, deep in conversation, were walking a few yards ahead. 'I wonder what's happened to him in his life.'

'I've wondered that myself, but I doubt if he'll ever tell us.'

'Mebbe that's why he gets on well with Rowena. Mebbe she's the only one to take him as he is, without question. They're alike – both trying to fit into a place that isn't theirs. That can't be easy.'

'I feel a bit like that myself with the new fashion house,' Caitlin admitted. 'Now that I'm having to go to Rose's house some evenings to meet the lassies she's bringing in as models for the opening, it's as if I'm in a different country, among folk I don't understand.'

'Away you go,' Mary told her roundly. 'There's nothing strange or different about rich folk.'

'But they don't speak like us, and they lead such different lives.'

'That's the sort of folk you'll be dealing with all the time once the fashion house opens.'

'I know. There's times I wonder if I've done the right thing, going in with Rose.'

'Of course you've done the right thing! I wish I could see inside a big house like hers.'

'It's lovely, and you'd like her big bedroom with its thick carpet and its velvet curtains right down to the floor – you could put our whole house into that one room, Mary. And the maid that brings us tea and wee sandwiches is nice enough. It's the times I meet Mrs Hamilton in the entrance hall or on the stairs that I hate.' It was a relief to tell someone. 'She looks at me as if I was after the silver or as if I smelled bad.'

'She does, does she? Cheeky old witch,' Mary snorted. 'Just you put your own neb in the air next time she tries that.'

'I can't. When folk look at you as if you're dirt, it makes you feel like dirt.'

'You're far too soft, Caitlin Lennox. You'll have to

learn to be just as snooty as they are. No, not snooty,'
Mary corrected herself. 'Calm and ladylike, with just a
hint of subservience, because they need to think they're
superior. It keeps them happy. But at the same time
you have to remind them that you know more about
clothes than they do, and they're dependent on you to
make them look stylish.'

'How do you know about that?'

'You can learn a lot from books.' Mary linked her
arm through Caitlin's as they swung round a corner.
'I'll teach you,' she said confidently.

Rose and Caitlin had arranged to go to the mill together
on Friday morning to meet Alex, but when Rose arrived
at the shop she found Caitlin in a panic.

'It's Mrs Gilbert – she tried to alter her new jacket
herself but she only succeeded in spoiling it, and she's
due to wear it at a special luncheon party in Glasgow.'

'So someone must go to the house to try to put things
right.' Mrs Gilbert had a tendency to try to make her
own alterations, despite the fact that she usually got
everything wrong. 'Can't Kirsty go, or Teenie?'

'I'm the one who made the jacket, and you know that
she's promised to let us make her winter clothes.'

'Yes, I know. We'll need her custom.' Rose sighed,
then said, 'I'll just have to meet Alex on my own.'

'You don't mind?'

'We can't leave him to cool his heels outside, can
we? Someone has to do it, and I certainly can't do
anything about Mrs Gilbert's jacket.'

'I'll be at the mill as soon as I can.'

'Or sooner, if possible,' Rose said, feeling like a
condemned woman about to take her final walk to the
scaffold.

*   *   *

Alex MacDowall paused at the mill gate, taking in the newly painted exterior of the building he had once intended to buy. There were even tubs of flowers flanking the entrance. Then his heart sank at the sight of a familiar bicycle propped against the wall by the door. He had hoped against hope that Rose wouldn't be present.

He took a deep breath, pulled down the front of his jacket and walked across the courtyard to the door. The two steps up to it, which he recalled as having been hollowed in the centre from use, had been replaced.

He had to wait for so long for an answer to his knock that he began to wonder if there was anyone in the building at all. But finally Rose opened the door, saying abruptly as soon as she saw him standing on the step, 'Caitlin's been delayed. She had to go and see an important customer, but she'll be here as soon as she can get away.'

He nodded, then as she stood in the doorway, looking at him warily, he said, 'Would you prefer me to wait on the step for her?'

He had meant it to be a light remark, but he regretted it when her face went beetroot red. She took a swift, clumsy step back, opening the door wide. 'Of course not. Come in.'

'I'm sorry, that was boorish of me,' he said as he stepped into the big square entrance hall. Since they had been thrown into each other's company, there was no sense in starting off on the wrong footing.

'Yes, it was, but I should have been prepared for it.' They eyed each other with hostility for a moment, then Rose's shoulders slumped. 'And now, I suppose, it's my turn to apologise. You and I always seem to bring out the worst in each other, Alex. I knew as soon as Caitlin was called away that you and I would end up quarrelling. Can we start again?' She stuck out her right hand.

He shook her hand formally, his lips twitching. 'I'd certainly agree on a truce, if only for Caitlin's sake.'

'John had hoped to be here as well, but he's been detained at his office. You should probably see what we've done to the place first.' Rose opened the nearest door to reveal a spacious room, well lit by three windows overlooking the mill race. At that moment the room held a kitchen table and three upright chairs, making an elaborately carved triangular cupboard in one corner look out of place. 'This will be Caitlin's design office, though she and I will share it until the smaller room can be furnished for me. We've allowed space in here for another two designers, when we can afford them.'

As they went through the ground-floor rooms, then upstairs to the other two levels, they began to relax a little. Rose's nervousness was replaced by her pride in the restoration and her plans for the future, while Alex was impressed, despite himself, by the skilful way in which the mill had been adapted to suit its new purpose.

Back in the design room, Rose opened the corner cupboard to reveal a decanter, a bottle and some glasses. 'Can I offer you something to drink? We have sherry, or there's whisky if you prefer it.'

He chose whisky.

'The cupboard and its contents are from my parents' home,' Rose explained as she poured. 'My father says that our clients may enjoy a small glass of sherry when they visit, and their husbands, should they be brought in to approve their wives' purchases, will need the whisky. With a wife and three daughters, he knows about such things.' She handed him his drink in a handsome cut-glass tumbler. 'I suspect that he has a certain admiration for what we've achieved – not that he'd admit it, of course. In any case, my mother would be furious if he dared.'

Alex took a deep swallow of the whisky then raised his eyebrows. 'He must admire you to present you with such a fine malt.'

'I thought that Caitlin would have been here by now.' She crossed the floor to stare out of the window at the mill race, then turned swiftly with what he always thought of as a Rose-like movement, so that her dark blue skirt belled out and the bright colours of the loose multi-coloured silk waistcoat she wore shimmered in the light from the window. 'Before she comes, Alex, I want you to know how much I regret having gone behind your back to buy this place as I did.'

'There's no—'

'Yes there is,' Rose interrupted. 'I've wanted so much to apologise, but I've not had the chance until now. I'd have written, but I find it difficult to put my true feelings down on paper.' Her face was scarlet; he felt sorry for her, knowing how much Rose Hamilton had always hated having to admit that she had been in the wrong.

'I could have behaved better myself at the time. In any case, it's all in the past now.'

Again, she held out her hand to him. 'Then can we consider ourselves to be friends again?' Her face was bright with relief. 'I've missed our arguments.'

'The Glasgow folk are a bit on the mild side for me,' Alex admitted. 'Not one of them possesses a temper like yours.'

The main door opened and Caitlin called out.

'We're in here,' Rose answered, releasing Alex's

hand and moving back towards the window as Caitlin came in, breathless from running and full of apologies for her absence, looking anxiously from one to the other. 'You should use a bicycle, like me,' Rose told her. 'It's much easier than running everywhere.'

'I'd have to learn to ride one first, and you've got me working so hard that I haven't the time for that.' Caitlin beamed at her brother. 'So, Alex, what do you think of our fashion house?'

'I have to say that now I've seen it I believe that this place suits your purpose better than it would have suited mine. When do you hope to open?'

'In April.' Rose took his empty glass back to the cupboard. 'Though we still have to think of a suitable name.' As she closed the cupboard doors and turned back to face them, Alex's attention was caught again by the way the light shimmered on the colourful diamond shapes that made up her waistcoat.

'Harlequin,' he said without stopping to think. The other two looked at each other.

'Harlequin? Isn't that some sort of fool?' Rose asked doubtfully, and he wished he had kept his mouth shut.

'If so I didn't know it. I thought Harlequin was a performer who wore bright colours. It was your waistcoat that brought the word to my mind.'

Rose looked down at the silky material. 'Of course – you based it on Harlequin's costume, didn't you, Caitlin? It's a perfect name!'

'It certainly denotes colour and design,' Caitlin agreed.

'And the theatrical side of it is apt too.' Rose laughed aloud. 'My mother certainly thinks I'm some kind of fool to want to risk every penny I have.'

Alex felt his face warming. 'I didn't mean—'

he began, but Rose stopped him with a wave of the hand.

'Don't spoil it by trying to explain. The House of Harlequin . . . Harlequin House of Fashion. How clever you are!'

'If you're certain of it, I'll paint a sign to put above the door. Something bright and eye-catching.'

'How soon could you show us the design for it?'

'Next week?' he suggested. It was like old times, Caitlin thought. Clearly Alex and Rose had settled their differences during their enforced time together.

'And we could use the same design on our paper-work.' Rose smiled on them both. 'Now there's no reason why we shouldn't open in April.'

'Perhaps there's just one reason,' Alex said. 'If you want furniture made and painted for an opening in April, isn't it time we discussed it?'

11

There had been a flood of applicants in response to John Brodie's advertisement for sewing women. Every one of them had to be interviewed, and Caitlin found it very hard to narrow the decision down to just three.

'They all need the money.'

'That's not our concern,' Rose told her firmly. 'If we give work to every single person who needs it we'll end up with an army of people who aren't up to our standards.'

'Couldn't you make the final decision? After all, you're running the business.'

'And you'll be working with the seamstresses, so you must decide whether or not they're suitable.'

Caitlin looked down the list, trying to fit faces to the names, and finally settled on three women, two in their early twenties and the third, Grace Watson, ten years older and with experience in a Glasgow dress shop.

John had acquired three sewing machines and a big cutting table, all second-hand but in good condition. They were installed immediately in the old mill, and Kirsty agreed to work on the new clothes there with the two most experienced women, while the third moved into Jean's shop to do some alteration work under Teenie's watchful eye. Caitlin divided her time between shop and mill, while John and Rose undertook the task of furnishing the other rooms, visiting auction rooms and house sales in an attempt to keep down costs.

There were times when Caitlin regretted telling Mary about her worries over dealing with clients. Her sister pored over fashion magazines in the shop, borrowed books on etiquette from the library, and at every opportunity made Caitlin parade up and down the parlour with a pile of books balanced on her head. She also introduced exercises involving smiling, speaking, sitting and standing, turning, picking things up and putting things down. Mary was an excellent tutor, though hard to please; nothing short of perfection would do, and at times Caitlin rebelled.

'How can anyone be expected to walk about with a pile of books on her head?' she wailed one evening when they crashed to the floor yet again.

'In some countries the women carry big jugs of water on their heads.'

'Try to make me do that,' Caitlin threatened, making for the door, 'and I'll empty the jug over you. I'm going for a walk.'

'We'll go together. The fresh air might cheer you up.' Mary scooped up a bundle of books and held them out. 'You can balance these on your head while we stroll along.'

Caitlin glared and took the books, steadying them atop her brown head before pacing from window to fireplace for the umpteenth time.

Although Caitlin was busy working at her designs and trying to learn how to deal with the gentry, and Rose spent a considerable amount of time in search of furniture at economical prices, the two women managed to spend several hectic days in Glasgow, choosing materials for Caitlin's new designs and selecting cloth, thread and the dozens of other items required for the new fashion house.

Afterwards, delighted with the success of their day, they visited the MacDowalls' small factory to look at the chairs and tables Alex and his staff were making for the salon.

Before they returned to Paisley, Alex insisted on taking the two of them for high tea. 'And cream cakes. You deserve something special after the day you've had,' he insisted when they tried to argue. He picked up a sketchbook as he shepherded them out of the building. 'In any case, I want your opinions on the sign I'm planning to make for you.'

The restaurant he took them to was extremely smart, and Caitlin found herself glad of Mary's ruthless training as she followed Alex and Rose to their table. The two of them suited the stylish decor, Alex in a grey lounge suit with matching waistcoat and bowler hat, and Rose in a green checked woollen costume that fitted her tall, slender figure admirably.

Alex had planned a black background, which would stand out against the building's whitewashed walls, with 'Harlequin' painted across it in multicoloured letters. The harlequin diamond pattern filled in the top of the A and the centre of the Q.

'It's wonderful,' Rose enthused. 'You must give me a copy of it so that I can have it copied on cards and letterheads.'

Alex took an envelope from his pocket. 'I took the liberty of getting the printer we use to give me some samples.'

Caitlin was glad to see how comfortable her brother

and her friend seemed to be in each other's company; not, perhaps, as relaxed as before their furious quarrel, but certainly at ease. She cared deeply about them both and hated to see them at odds.

As March gave way to April, it seemed to Caitlin that hours became minutes, days became hours and time began to rush downhill like an out-of-control steam engine, with her trapped inside. Sewing machines thundered through her sleep, and in her dreams she chased designs that leaped from the pages of her scrapbook and danced away, out of reach and out of sight.

In her waking hours, though, she could see that everything was beginning to come together. Under Kirsty, Teenie and Caitlin's supervision, the new seamstresses had given a good account of themselves, and her designs for the opening day fashion display were taking shape. Rose had persuaded several clients to model clothes designed for them by Caitlin and a considerable number of invitations had been sent out. John had ordered enough stationery to last their first year. In secret, Caitlin marvelled over the cards with her own name neatly printed beneath the Harlequin logo and the words 'Fashion Designer' below.

Lights blazed in every mill window on the night before the opening. Todd and John Brodie had brought the sewing machines from the shop earlier so that the costumes could be completed, and John had volunteered to transport glasses, cutlery and china from his home and Rose's. Alex had arrived that afternoon from Glasgow, bringing the salon furniture and the sign with him. After the tables and chairs had been installed and the sign put in position, he sent the van driver away, planning to stay the night in Espedair Street and attend the opening the following day.

While her elders worked, Rowena scampered happily through all the rooms, supposedly helping but in fact getting in the way. Kirsty and Todd took her home when she began to droop.

'You get back to help the lassies,' Todd told his wife when Rowena had been put to bed. 'I'll keep an eye on the bairn.'

'Are you sure? It doesn't seem right to leave you here on your lone.'

'Ach, away ye go, woman – I'm happier with my pipe and my paper, and ye know ye're fair dyin' tae get back and see what's been goin' on behind yer back. Anyway, they've need of ye.'

They had indeed. While Alex and John got the ground floor rooms ready and hung Caitlin's designs, carefully framed, on the walls under Mary's watchful eye, all five sewing machines were kept busy in the sewing room above. In the small rooms to one side, Rose and Jean helped six giggling young women into the garments they were to model, and Caitlin was kept busy darting between seamstresses and models, checking, advising, making last-minute alterations and worrying.

It was close to midnight by the time everything was finished.

'You've brought in an awful lot,' Kirsty said doubtfully, surveying the glasses and teacups laid out on trestle tables covered by great stretches of white linen. 'D'you think you'll get enough folk to use it all?'

'Their noses'll bring them, if nothing else does,' Rose told her. They were all more than ready to go home. The models crowded into the Hamiltons' car, which had been waiting outside for Rose, and John

127

managed to squeeze Mary, Jean, Teenie, Kirsty and Caitlin into his car, promising to come back for Rose, who had been persuaded to leave her bicycle at home for once. Alex opted to walk but returned almost at once, startling Rose, who was making a last-minute check of all the rooms before leaving.

'I just noticed when I was looking back at the place that the sign's crooked. D'you have a ladder? I sent mine back in the van.'

'Only the one you and John used to hang the designs on the walls. It's not big enough for outside.'

'It'll do.' He made for the smaller, unused office.

'Leave it, Alex,' she said. 'We'll get a proper ladder in the morning.' But he was already struggling out of the room with the ladder.

'I'll not be able to sleep until I get it right. Give me a hand,' he ordered, and Rose rolled her eyes before doing as she was told. Between them they got the ladder out into the April twilight. Alex put it in position then hurried back into the building for the hammer and nails. Rose stepped back and eyed the ladder uneasily.

'It's too small – and it's rickety into the bargain,' she protested when Alex came out.

'I'll manage.' He stuffed the nails into one pocket and the hammer into another. 'It's just a wee adjustment.'

'At least wait until John comes back.'

'Stop fussing and hold the ladder steady,' he ordered, and started to climb. Rose clung to the struts, feeling the whole contraption shake as he made his way to the top. Glancing up, she saw to her horror that he was balancing himself precariously on the very top step and working on the sign with both hands.

'Alex!'

'Wheesht, you're distracting me,' he said breathlessly, positioning a nail and hammering it home with blows that made the entire ladder creak and shake. 'Walk back a bit and see how it looks now.'

'I'm not going to let go of this ladder!'

'For goodness' sake, I'm balancing myself against the wall. I'm quite safe. Will you do as you're told for once?'

Reluctantly Rose released the ladder and backed off across the yard.

'Well?'

In the semidarkness she could barely make out the sign. 'It's grand.'

'Are you sure?'

'I'm positive!' she shouted at him.

As he twisted round to say something to her over his shoulder, the ladder began to sway beneath him. Rose screamed his name and rushed over to throw her weight against the supports.

'I'm all right.' He began to scramble down, then stopped and asked irritably, 'Rose, how can I get to the ground with you lying across the treads?'

As soon as she knew that he was almost on the ground again, and therefore safe, she stormed into the building. When Alex had put the ladder away he went looking for her and found her huddled on one of his hand-painted chairs in the salon, shaking.

'What's the matter?'

'You're the matter, Alex MacDowall, great daft lummox that you are! You could have got yourself killed!'

'Don't be daft. I'd not have had far to fall even from the top of that ladder.'

'You could have landed on top of me and killed the two of us, or you could have fallen onto the flagstones and broken your neck or your skull. What sort of opening would I have had with folk having to step over your blood to get in the door?'

'Rose . . .' Bewildered, he put a hand on her shoulder, but she twitched away, furious with him for having given her such a fright and with herself for giving in to weakness – and with him again for being there to witness her weakness. 'Just g-go on back to Espedair St-street!' Her childhood habit of stuttering at times of stress returned.

He moved away, and hearing the clink of glass against glass, she looked up to see that he had opened one of the bottles and was pouring something into two glasses.

'That's supposed to be for the g-guests tomorrow.'

'Your need's greater than theirs. Anyway, there's plenty for tomorrow.' He put a glass into her hand. 'Drink it down properly and never mind sipping at it.'

She did as she was told. He had given her brandy; it made her cough, but at the same time it burned down into her stomach and restored her backbone.

'Feeling better?' Alex asked, and she summoned up a faint smile.

'I'm sorry.'

'That's all right. It's nerves, with the place opening tomorrow.'

She took another drink. 'It has nothing to do with nerves. I don't have many good friends, and I can't afford to let one of them kill himself.'

He gave a brief, embarrassed laugh. 'It'd take a lot more than a shaky ladder to put an end to me,' he said, and began to wander round the room, giving her time to steady herself. 'This is very elegant, now that I see it all put together.'

Caitlin had opted for cream curtain material in all the ground-floor windows, trimmed with deep red and held back with red sashes. The chairs and small tables were also cream, and Alex had painted sprays of deep red roses over the back and arms of each chair. Delicate and yet sturdy, the furniture fitted in well with the airy, panelled room and the pastel-patterned rugs scattered over the polished wooden floor.

Alex tossed a wry smile at Rose. 'It's hard to remember now that it was once a mill and that I was planning to turn it into a wee factory.'

'Alex, what if my parents are right and I'm making a terrible mistake? What if Harlequin fails?'

'It won't fail. Just keep telling yourself that.'

She shook her head. 'But if it did – it's not just me; Caitlin and Kirsty stand to lose more than money if things go wrong.'

'You're just doubting yourself because you're tired. D'you want another drink?'

'Best not. John will be here in a minute.' She put her empty glass on the table, then said, 'You've got a streak of dust across your cheek from that sign. Here.' She took a handkerchief from her bag and held it out. 'Spit,' she ordered, and when he had moistened the cloth she scrubbed at his face.

He screwed his eyes up. 'That stings!'

'You can't go through the streets with a dirty face.'

'Why not? Enough,' he protested, then reached up to stay her hand as she rubbed harder. 'It's like being wee again, with Mam trying to skin me with the face flannel.'

'And I suppose you made a fuss then, too, bairn that you are. There, that's you clean and tidy again.' She put the handkerchief aside.

131

'Have you taken the skin off?'

'No, but there's a red mark.' She touched his cheek, smoothing the skin beneath her fingertips. 'It'll fade . . .' she began. Her voice died away and her smile faded as Alex put his hand up to cover hers and hold it against his cheek.

His cheek tensed beneath her fingers, and she was close enough to hear him swallow and to see his throat muscles move smoothly beneath their covering of skin.

'Rose . . . ,' he said. Her hand was still trapped by his, but her thumb was free; of its own volition it moved to caress the line of his jaw.

The air between them seemed to crystallise; it seemed to Rose that they were standing at some unseen crossroads, where her next movement, or his, could change the entire course of their lives. She caught her breath. Then John's car turned in at the gate, car horn parping, and the moment was gone.

Alex declined the offer of a lift to Espedair Street. He closed the yard gates behind the car, and when Rose twisted round in her seat to wave, she saw that he was standing, hands in his pockets, watching them drive away. He didn't return the wave.

Strains of 'Alexander's Ragtime Band', one of Rose's favourite pieces of music, wafted through the crowded ground floor from a gramophone in one of the fitting rooms. The brief fashion display was over, and now the models were mingling with the guests to allow them a closer look at the gowns. Rose, striking in a dark-blue layered skirt beneath a long, loose tunic in broad vertical stripes of deep red and paler blue, moved from group to group, notebook and pencil in hand.

'Nasty American noise,' Caitlin heard an elderly woman say as she went by.

'Not at all, Mama. It's the latest fashion, and such fun to dance to,' chirruped the girl with her. 'Let's go over there. I want you to have a closer look at that little afternoon gown.'

They moved away, and John Brodie appeared by Caitlin's side. 'Perhaps "Clair de Lune" would have charmed Mrs Bruce,' he murmured. 'But on the other hand, I think her daughter, Adele, may well become a client. She adores dancing, the wilder the better. Is that one of your designs Rose is wearing?'

'Yes.' Once, Rose had said airily that she looked on clothing merely as a way of avoiding the embarrassment to others of appearing naked in the street. Now almost all of her clothes were specially designed for her by Caitlin.

'She looks wonderful. When I think of the clumsy, gawky person she used to be . . .'

'She's still the same Rose.'

'I know, but now she looks so . . .' John cleared his throat, then asked, 'Does Rose ever mention me, Caitlin?'

'Frequently.'

'I don't mean as a lawyer or as a friend. I mean, does she ever talk about me in another way? Dammit, Caitlin,' he said as she looked blankly at him. 'Does she ever show any interest in me as a man?'

'Oh.' She had known full well what he meant, but it embarrassed her to talk about Rose behind her back. 'You know Rose – her mind's usually on things to do with the shop or Harlequin.'

'So she hasn't said anything about me?'

'Not really.'

'Or about any other man?'

133

'She's said nothing, John.'

He coloured. 'The fact is, Caitlin, I used to think very little of Rose other than her being more of a good sport than other women – and having a damned good business brain, too. But now . . . well, I rarely seem to be thinking of anyone else. D'you think that if I was to take her out somewhere quiet for dinner or a drive, I could venture to—'

'What on earth are you doing in a fashion house, John Brodie?' A plump, heavily scented young woman squeezed herself between them, her back to Caitlin.

'I have an interest in Harlequin, Isa, as you well know.'

'I did hear something of it. Did you see me in the fashion display?' Mrs Harper swept on.

'I did indeed, and you were quite amazing.'

'Oh, you flatterer!' Mrs Harper said coyly, and Caitlin bit her lip hard, wondering how John could keep such a straight face. Rose's friends had done quite well as models, but her idea of using real clients of various ages and sizes to augment the display had caused some anxious moments, particularly with Mrs Harper, who had graciously agreed to model the costume made for her by Caitlin seven months earlier. Unfortunately the woman had put on weight since then, and fitting her into it had been, as Jean remarked afterwards, like trying to fit a small shoe onto a large foot. They had succeeded, but Caitlin's heart had been in her mouth when the woman's turn had come and she had paraded round the salon, her high-waisted jacket and straight skirt straining at every seam. Mrs Harper, she noticed, had changed her outfit immediately after the display.

'You know Caitlin Lennox.' John reached out and drew her to his side. Mrs Harper inclined her head graciously.

'Ah yes, you're the seamstress who made my costume.'

John frowned and opened his mouth, but Caitlin spoke first, Mary's instructions ringing in her ears – *Neck straight, a very slight inclination of the head, lips curved in a faint smile that doesn't reach the eyes.* 'I designed your costume, Mrs Harper. I also made part of it, but now that I am Harlequin's designer and an equal partner, I'll rarely have time to do any sewing.' As fortune had it, she was standing by a small table with a scattering of cards on its surface; Caitlin took one and presented it to the woman. 'When you feel the need to replenish your wardrobe, I would be happy to assist, if you care to make an appointment.'

She smiled sweetly into the woman's astonished gape and moved away, telling herself that she must find the time soon to make a really nice blouse for Mary.

12

Alex was nowhere to be seen, and Caitlin, eager to get away from the crush and the noise and the mingled perfumes that thickened the air, went in search of him. He was sitting on a deep windowsill in the sewing room, looking down on the river below. He looked up with a faint smile.

'Had enough?' he asked.

'Yes, but it's going well.'

'With Rose Hamilton at the helm, could it fail?'

'Are you looking for somewhere else in Paisley?'

'No. We've been talking of expanding the Glasgow workshop and bringing in a manager so that I can spend more time in the shop, but I'm not sure if we will. Things are . . . happening.'

'At MacDowall and Son's?'

'In Europe. There may be a war.'

It was the first Caitlin had heard of it. 'Surely not,' she protested. 'Why would anyone want to go to war?'

'We must hope that nobody will,' he said, and turned his attention to the river again.

'Alex, is there something wrong between you and Mam?'

'No,' he said, after a hesitation so slight that it was scarcely to be noticed. But Caitlin had noticed it.

'This morning, at home, the two of you seemed
. . . ,' she searched for the right word, 'formal with
each other.'

'It's a good long while since we lived beneath the
same roof. I know that it was hard for her when I moved
to Glasgow.'

She didn't believe him. All her life she had known
of her mother's secret preference for Alex. It hadn't
bothered her or Mary, although Ewan had resented it,
but then Ewan had tended to resent a lot of things.
Watching Alex and their mother that morning, Caitlin
had been reminded of a broken china plate so skilfully
repaired that the crack could scarcely be seen with the
naked eye, although it was still there. The break she
sensed between her mother and her half-brother had
been caused by something more serious and more
recent than Alex's move to Glasgow years before.
She was trying to find some way of delving deeper
without angering him when he got to his feet and held
out a hand to her.

'Time to go back downstairs and face your guests.
They'll be wondering where you are.'

'Six definite appointments, and almost all the cards
we left out have been taken away,' Rose said gleefully two hours later. The last of the guests had
departed, and Alex had returned to Glasgow. The
others were gathered in the design office – Caitlin,
Rose and John with glasses in their hands; Kirsty,
Jean, Teenie and the three seamstresses with cups of
tea.

'It's a good start.' John drained his glass. 'Now I
must get back to the office.'

'And we've got this place tae put tae rights for the
mornin'.' Teenie got to her feet.

137

'You're not going to start cleaning now, are you?' Rose protested, and Teenie gave her a scathing look.

'The fairies arenae goin' tae creep in at night and wave their wands. I brought my apron – or have ye got a cleaner all arranged?'

Rose and John looked at each other. 'I forgot about a cleaner,' she admitted, while he asked, 'How much will it cost?'

Teenie shook her head pityingly. 'I'll away and get my apron.'

In June, Mary left school and started work in the boiling shop of Robertson's Marmalade Factory, close by Espedair Street. Each day she came home with the rich aroma of boiling fruit clinging to her clothes, and Todd claimed that just being in the same room as her when she was fresh from her work made him feel hungry.

It was her ambition to work in the office, where she could use her talent for figures. Until then she was content to stay where she was, despite the constant battle the jam workers fought with wasps drawn to the place by the smell of the fruit. Mary was proud to bring home a weekly pay packet, but she soon lost her taste for preserves.

'It must be the sight and smell of fruit all day long that does it,' she told Caitlin mournfully. 'After a few weeks you don't notice it any more, but the notion to eat the stuff seems to have left me.'

There was one consolation; Lachie, the Highland boy she had met at her first visit to a ceilidh worked at Robertson's as a van boy, and within a month he and Mary had started walking out together.

The ceilidhs had ended for the summer months, but to Rowena's delight one of the women had offered to give the child dancing lessons for a few pence a week.

Caitlin, with more work than she could handle at the fashion house, was alarmed when her mother, who still held a deep mistrust of Highlanders, showed signs of turning down the offer. For her own part, she was eager to agree to anything that would keep Rowena contented and avoid further problems at home.

'You must admit that Rowena's been more settled since she discovered dancing,' she pointed out, 'and that's what matters. Mary and I both know Flora McCall, and Rowena'll not come to any harm with her. I'll pay for the lessons as her birthday present,' she added. To her relief, Kirsty gave in.

'I don't know what it is with folk,' Caitlin said later to Mary. 'Bryce doesn't like Murdo because he doesn't understand him, but you'd have thought Mam would have been more understanding.'

Her sister shrugged. 'During the '45 rebellion there were Lowlanders who thought that Highlanders ate babies. Mebbe Mam heard about that once and it's stuck in her mind. Anyway, she still thinks Ewan'll turn up one day, and she frets in case he finds fault with the way she's raised his daughter.'

'Mebbe he'll come for the bairn's birthday. That would be the best present she could have.'

'After nearly a year without a word from him, the moon's more likely to fall from the sky. But if he does come to Paisley he should go down on his knees to thank Mam for what she's done for Rowena – and I'll be looking for him to do a bit of kneeling before me, and all,' Mary added tartly.

Ewan didn't arrive for his daughter's fifth birthday at the end of July, nor did he make any contact.

Nothing was said about his absence or his continued silence, but the rest of the family worked to make the occasion as festive as possible for Rowena. As family tradition demanded, Kirsty made a clootie dumpling, large and round and rich with fruit. A threepenny piece wrapped in greaseproof paper had been included in the mixture, and Kirsty made certain that it appeared in Rowena's slice.

Even Alex came to Paisley for the occasion, bringing with him a small hand-painted chair. Caitlin made the little girl a winter coat from the ends of cloth woven by Murdo Guthrie, while Kirsty made a cambric pinafore dress with a braid-trimmed sailor collar. Mary bought coloured hair ribbons and a pair of buttoned shoes, which Rowena promptly designated as her dancing shoes. Todd won a sparkling smile when he presented a pretty gilt frame for Ewan's photograph, which she kept beneath her pillow at all times.

Murdo had declined an invitation to attend the party. 'It'd not be right with Mr MacDowall there, and him my employer,' he told Caitlin when she tried to persuade him to change his mind.

'He'd like you to be there. You've done so well with Rowena, she'll be disappointed if you don't come.'

He was treating the yarn stretched tightly over the rollers with paste to strengthen it, using a wide, soft brush.

'Ach, I'm not one for gatherings,' he said, without looking up from his work, and she left him in peace, realising that he had made up his mind and would not be swayed.

When the meal was over, Rowena insisted on going to the weaving shop to show him her presents. 'She's going to be a beauty when she grows up,' Alex said as he and Caitlin followed her, carrying a plate of still-warm dumpling for Murdo and a mug of tea to wash it down with. 'She's got the best of Ewan and Beth's looks.' Then, as they turned into the pend, he added grimly, 'I just hope she hasn't inherited the worst of their natures.'

Murdo, who had stopped work and turned on the wooden bench, known to weavers as the saytree, to watch Rowena pirouetting around the hard earth floor, the skirt of her new dress held out to either side to show its width, jumped to his feet as soon as his employer walked in.

'Sit down, man, and eat this while it's still warm.' Alex thrust the plate into his hands. Caitlin, putting the mug on the windowsill, was certain that the Highlander would have preferred to eat and drink on his own, but Rowena ran to lean on his knee, demanding to see if there was a threepenny bit in his slice of dumpling. He had no option but to eat. Alex examined the cloth on the loom, a soft blue with a small dark green pattern running across it.

'It looks fine. You'll have it ready by next Friday?' Alex asked and, as Murdo nodded, his mouth too full of dumpling for speech, Alex sniffed at the air. 'What's that smell?'

'It's the pinks,' Rowena told him importantly, pointing at the pot of flowers on the windowsill. 'Murdo grows them 'cos all the weavers used to have them in their shops.' She began to poke her fingers into what was left of the dumpling.

'Rowena . . .' Caitlin swooped down on her. 'Will you let the man eat his food in peace?'

'I only wanted to see if Murdo's got money in his bit of dumpling too.'

The weaver scooped up the mauled remains and pushed them into his mouth, washing them down with tea.

'Not a penny,' he told the little girl, who dipped a hand into the pocket of her new dress and brought out her threepenny piece, still wrapped in its paper.

'Here – you take that one.'

'I cannae take your money!'

'It's all right. I've got other things.'

'But this is your birthday, the day folk give things to you.' He gently folded her small fingers over the coin, then reached behind the pot of pinks and brought out a tiny glass vase filled with fresh wild flowers. 'This is for you.'

Rowena put the threepenny piece back into her pocket and took the vase carefully in both hands. 'Look, Aunt Caitlin!'

It was made of cheap glass, but it had been delicately cut, and the light from the window sparkled off its facets.

'It's beautiful,' Caitlin agreed, smiling over Rowena's head at the weaver, touched by his thoughtfulness. His dark brown eyes were fixed on the little girl, his mouth curved in a faint smile.

'Where did you get the flowers?' Rowena wanted to know.

'They grow by the river and up in the braes.'

'Will you take me to see them?'

'Aye, if your grandmother allows it.'

Rowena handed the vase carefully to Caitlin then turned and stretched up on tiptoe to catch a handful of the weaver's long dark hair, tugging on it so that his face was pulled down towards hers. She brushed his cheek with her lips, and Alex laughed at his embarrassment.

'D'you not think it's strange that, of all of us, Rowena's the one who's made friends with Murdo?' Caitlin asked as she walked with Alex to the station later.

'Mebbe it's because she doesn't want anything from him.'

'D'you know anything of his past?'

'Why d'you ask that?'

'I was just wondering what happened to make him the way he is.'

'He's just a man that likes to keep himself to himself. I'm a bit like that myself – or have you never noticed?'

'I've noticed you're more contented living your own life in Glasgow than you ever were here.'

'It's not a case of being contented,' Alex said. 'Our house was always too busy for me, with Mam worrying about us all and Mary such a wee frightened skelf of a thing in those days, and Ewan full of himself, and the old man . . .'

She felt the need to defend her long-dead father. 'He wasn't so bad before the rheumatics got hold of him.'

'Mebbe not, but it was always made clear to me that Ewan was the favourite – though I suppose that was just natural, with Ewan being his own flesh and blood. Not that that made him special.' A bitter note crept into Alex's voice. 'He caused nothing but trouble and heartbreak, running away with Beth as he did and then sending his bairn back here without a word of explanation.'

'Evenin' tae ye, Caitlin, Mr Lennox,' Bryce Caldwell said just then. 'It's a fine night.'

'It's yourself, Bryce. Aye, it's a fine night, right enough. Are you on your way home?' Alex asked affably.

'Aye.' Bryce whipped his cap off, twisting it between his hands and shifting from one foot to the other, his eyes on Caitlin.

'Then you'll mebbe see my sister back home for me.'

Alex put a hand on Caitlin's elbow and began to turn her round to face the way she had come. 'My train'll be along in just a minute anyway.'

Bryce needed no urging. He said a cheerful goodbye to his employer and reached out to take Caitlin's arm.

'Just a minute,' she told him, and hurried after Alex, who was disappearing down the station steps.

'You know fine that me and Bryce aren't speaking!' she hissed at him, and he grinned up at her. 'I'm just lending a helping hand, the way you did when you left me and Rose Hamilton waiting for you in the old mill that day.'

'I was with a client!'

'So you said. Here's my train.' He continued down the steps, and Caitlin had no option but to fall into step beside Bryce, who had the sense to keep quiet until they were in Espedair Street before asking tentatively, 'How have ye been?'

'Fine.' They had reached the pend. 'Goodnight, Bryce,' she said. 'Thank you for walking back with me.' She would have ducked in below the stone arch if he hadn't put a hand on her arm. 'Caitlin . . .'

'What?' She glared at his fingers, and they fell away.

'I'm . . . I'm right vexed about what I said tae ye before.'

'I can't remember what you said.'

He swallowed audibly. 'About you an' thon High-lander.'

'What Highlander?' Caitlin asked, finding a certain pleasure in making him squirm.

'Thon Murdo Guthrie. I was wrong tae accuse ye of walkin' out with him.'

'Yes, you were.'

'It was . . . it's . . . Ach, Caitlin,' he burst out, 'I'm

that fond of ye, an' at times it makes me say daft things.'

'You're right there, Bryce Caldwell.'

'If I promise not to do it again will ye go back tae walkin' out with me?'

'I don't know about that.'

'Caitlin,' he said wretchedly, 'I miss bein' in yer company. There's just somethin' about ye that the other lassies don't have.'

'You've tried some, have you?'

He must have heard the amusement in her voice, for suddenly he was on the defensive. 'If ye must know, aye, I have! And some were well enough, but they're not you. Surely a man's got a right tae ask—'

'I will.'

'What?' asked Bryce, taken by surprise.

'I said I'll start walking out with you again – but just as friends, mind. And there's to be no more of your silly jealousy.'

'I promise!' Before she realised his intentions, he had caught her up in his arms and kissed her soundly. 'Tomorrow, eight o'clock?' he asked, beaming, and when she nodded he went racing off along the pavement, leaping to slap one hand against a lamp standard as he went.

Caitlin laughed and shook her head. He still behaved like a child at times, she thought, as she made for the back door. But there was no real malice in him.

It wasn't until much later that she realised that Alex hadn't answered her questions about Murdo.

13

As most of Caitlin's time was spent in the sewing room, she got to know the three seamstresses well. A natural hierarchy was swiftly established, with Lizzie Galloway and Iris Menzies more than content to let Grace Watson, the oldest of the three, take on the position of supervisor. It suited Caitlin, too, for it meant that she dealt mainly with Grace, a hard worker with a quick mind. The younger women were unmarried, and Grace was a widow, her husband having drunk himself into an early grave, leaving Grace with an elderly mother-in-law and three children to feed, house and clothe.

'The seven other bairns were taken from me,' she told Caitlin as a matter of fact, 'four just after they came into the world, an' three from the diphtheria.'

Caitlin thought of her own little brother, Fergus, killed in his second year. 'How could you bear to lose seven children?'

'It's the way of things. You just have to keep lookin' after them that're spared to you. I mind hearin' a minister sayin' once that God moves in mysterious ways, and I suppose He does, for when you think of it I could never have managed to care for ten. We'd have ended up in the workhouse.'

146

Local interest in Harlequin was still high, and Caitlin was kept so busy that on several occasions, to her disappointment, she had to forego the pleasure of buying materials from the Glasgow warehouse and let Rose go in her stead. Mr and Mrs Hamilton had left Paisley at the end of June to spend their usual long summer holiday in England; to her mother's annoyance, Rose had refused to leave Caitlin on her own so soon after Harlequin's launch.

In Causeyside Street, Kirsty, Jean and Teenie had their hands full getting the shop back to normal now that the others had their own premises. It had been agreed that the shop and fashion house would be run separately, though with Rose keeping the books for both premises.

Life moved on serenely, with Rowena absorbed in her dancing, Mary enjoying her new working life and her friendship with Lachie, and Todd kept busy in the workshop. When he'd read aloud from his newspaper about the assassination of an Austrian archduke and his wife in the faraway Balkans a few days before Rowena's birthday, Kirsty had tutted over the way some folk seemed unable to live with their fellow men in peace. Caitlin had paid little heed, for all her energies had been concentrated on Harlequin.

So it came as a considerable shock to them as well as to most ordinary folk when, on 4 August, Britain went to war with Germany.

Bryce Caldwell was among the first to volunteer to join the army.

'What did you do that for?' Caitlin wanted to know when he told her.

He looked hurt. 'What's wrong with wantin' tae fight for yer country?'

'But you're not a soldier, you're a cabinet-maker. What's Todd going to do while you're away?'

'He'll manage. They're sayin' that it'll no' last long. It's one way of seein' a bit of the world. I thought ye'd be proud of me.'

'I just wish you'd given the matter some thought first. There are regular soldiers in the army who know a lot more than you do about fighting.'

He preened himself. 'Are ye scared in case I get killed?'

'It's nothing to do with being scared,' she snapped at him. The declaration of war had caught her unawares; she still didn't know what it was all about, and Bryce's decision to enlist seemed to bring the whole business too close to home for her liking. 'I'm just saying that you should mebbe leave the fighting to the men that have been trained for it.'

'Well I didn't, and now I've taken the King's shillin' there's no sense in goin' on at me.'

'I suppose not. When do you go away?'

'They'll let me know, but it's bound tae be quite soon. They say it'll be sorted out by Ne'erday,' he said reassuringly. A week later, he was gone.

The declaration of war had ended the Hamiltons' holiday abruptly, to their daughter's annoyance. Rose had enjoyed her freedom and began to talk of having the old mill gatehouse renovated.

'You and I could both live there,' she told Caitlin enthusiastically. 'There's enough room, and just think how convenient it would be.'

'But we can't afford to spend a single penny on the place.'

'Not this year, that's true. But next, surely.'

'What if the war continues?'

'It won't,' Rose assured her blithely.

Recruiting posters blossomed on walls, recruitment drives were held, marching bands played in the streets and housewives hurried to stock up their larders, fearful of food shortages. Caitlin was grateful when Murdo, under pressure from Rowena, agreed to take the two of them to the Gleniffer Braes, west of Paisley, for an afternoon's walk.

Once they reached the Bonnie Wee Well they left the narrow, climbing road and took to the grass, Rowena running ahead and sometimes plunging into stretches of fern so tall that she was hidden from sight, with only an agitation among the fern tips to show where she was. The other two followed at their own pace, walking several feet apart. Caitlin had learned long since not to expect any conversation from Murdo; indeed, the silence soothed her after the thrum of sewing machines, the seamstresses' chatter and the fussing of clients in the fitting room. Up here, looking down on Paisley and picking out the abbey, the church spires and the John Neilston School's green dome like an upended porridge bowl, she felt as though she was on the roof of the world. In the distance, hazy in the sunlight, she could see Ben Lomond's peak and broad shoulders beyond the Kilpatrick Hills.

Sitting on a fallen tree, watching Murdo and Rowena's heads close together as they crouched by a stream a few feet away, dabbling in the water, she was suddenly struck by the fact that although everything about her was green – mosses, grasses, ferns and shrubs – there was a wealth of different shades. Next time, she decided, she would bring her notebook and some crayons.

Caitlin watched as Murdo produced a handkerchief and used it to carefully dry his and Rowena's hands, then he got to his feet and came to where Caitlin sat, the little girl skipping along behind him. 'Time we started back,' he said.

'Can we come back another day?' Rowena clamoured.

'If Murdo agrees,' Caitlin told her, and was pleased when he nodded.

Bryce came home on a few days' furlough in the Highland Light Infantry's tartan trews and the bonnet with its jaunty red and white cockade. When he took her into his arms and kissed her, his uniform jacket felt stiff and scratchy, and she felt shy and ill at ease, as though she was with a stranger.

'I was thinkin',' he said awkwardly when he had released her, 'that it would be a rare comfort tae me tae know that you're here.'

'Where else would I be?'

'I don't mean here in Paisley, I mean here waitin' for me. Promised tae me.'

'Promised?' Caitlin asked cautiously.

'With some sort of understandin', like. Some of the lads've got sweethearts waitin' for them an' the promise of marriage when this business is all over, an' I thought that—'

She caught his drift. 'You did, did you? Well, you can just think again, Bryce Caldwell.'

'Ach, Caitlin!'

'Did we not agree just to be friends?'

'Aye, but that was before I went tae be a soldier. A man has tae have some hope,' he said, then scooped her into his arms again, kissing her until she was almost suffocated.

'You've got plenty of hope – and plenty of cheek as well,' she said when she could speak again. 'You always have had. So just keep on hoping.'

'Will ye no' even wish me well?'

'I do wish you well, Bryce, and a safe return too. But that's as far as it goes for now.'

He heaved a gusty sigh. 'We can talk about it again when I get my next furlough,' he said.

Todd took a retired cabinet-maker on in Bryce's place, and in MacDowalls' shop and factory Alex, too, had to find other workers to replace younger men who had enlisted.

It wasn't until the first reports of British casualties, at a Belgian town called Mons, appeared in the newspapers late in August that Caitlin took in the fact that there really was a war going on. By then the household was involved in a battle of its own, for Rowena's first day as a pupil at the South School had arrived.

'I'm not going,' she announced that morning.

'You are so,' Mary told her firmly. Since the marmalade factory was near the school, she had been chosen to deliver the little girl there before going to work. 'There's folk that I know still at that school, so don't you give me a showing up!'

Rowena scowled at her and backed into the corner between the sink and the tall cupboard where the dishes were kept. Kirsty, too, glared at her daughter.

'Don't fright her, Mary,' she admonished, and Mary rolled her eyes to the ceiling. 'Rowena, hen, all the wee girls and laddies have to go to the school,' Kirsty wheedled. 'You'll learn to read and to write and to count, and you'll meet new friends.' When the child said nothing but squeezed herself further into the corner with an all-too-familiar buttoning of the features, she added placatingly, 'Just think how pleased your daddy'll be when he comes for you and finds that you can read and write.'

Caitlin and her stepfather exchanged glances across the breakfast table, while Rowena, seizing on the name, said from her niche, 'I want my daddy to take me to the school.'

'He can't take you today because he's . . . still away somewhere.'

'Then I'm not going!'

It took a lot of coaxing to get her to agree to go, and even then she dragged behind Mary, who held her firmly by the hand.

They were both subdued that evening. Rowena refused to answer any questions about her first day at school and Mary, tight lipped, ignored the little girl. Before and after her evening meal, Rowena sat outside on her dancing stone, hugging her father's photograph and staring moodily at the grass.

'I'm not taking her tomorrow,' Mary burst out as soon as the little girl had gone to bed. 'She gave me a right showing up!'

Kirsty, tired after a busy day at the shop, sighed and put aside the magazine she had brought home with her. 'I knew something had gone wrong, but she'd not say a word to me when I fetched her home. She wouldn't even look at me. What happened?'

'First of all I had to drag her all the way there, then when we reached the place she refused to go in. It took me and Miss Livingstone to carry her into the classroom, and when I left she was sitting at her desk without a word for anyone. Then,' said Mary, crimson with mortification, 'I was called out of work during the wee ones' playtime because she'd tried to run away. Everybody stared at me, and my supervisor said it wasn't to happen again. I didn't know where to put my face!'

'Did you catch her?' Todd asked from behind his newspaper.

'It seems that she ran full tilt into a policeman going down the road, then she tried to bite him when he got a hold of her. It's just fortunate for us that he's used to catching criminals, for he avoided the bite and he was carrying her back in when I arrived.' Mary squirmed, reliving the memory. 'She was nothing but trouble!'

'You should have told us sooner, Mary.'

'And let her be the centre of attention? If you ask me, that's what she wants. But I'm not taking her tomorrow, or any other day!'

'She's got to go,' Kirsty fretted. 'We'll have the law after us if she doesn't, and what'll her father think when he—'

'Don't fret yourself, hen. I'll take her tomorrow.' Todd came out from behind his newspaper. 'She'll be fine with me.'

Mary sniffed and gave him a sidelong glance. 'You think so?'

'I was much the same when I first went tae the school. I mind my father had tae give me a good leatherin' before I'd settle.'

Mary said darkly, 'Mebbe that would be a good thing for Rowena too.'

Todd's attempt to coax Rowena to settle into school life had no more success than Mary's. She tried to run away several times on the short journey to the school buildings, and in the end he was forced to carry her, mute and rigid, into the classroom.

'Puttin' her intae her wee seat was worse than tryin' tae thread a needle,' he told his family that night.

'You've never threaded a needle in your life, man!' Kirsty snapped, sick with worry.

'I've seen you often enough tryin' tae get that bit of thread through the wee hole in the needle. That's what it felt like, with the bairn stiff as a board and her knees bangin' against her desk till I was feared we'd hurt her.'

At least Rowena hadn't tried to run away during the school day, but when Todd went to fetch her, he was told by the thin-lipped teacher that she had flown at a little boy who'd jeered at her in the playground, and scratched his face. On the way home she had eluded her grandfather, racing ahead and out of his sight.

'Luckily when I got back she was where I expected tae find her – in the weavin' shop with Murdo.'

'She could have fallen under the wheels of a van or a cart,' Kirsty fretted. Mary said nothing, but her face showed clearly that she wouldn't have minded if Rowena had been mown down.

Caitlin sighed and offered to take the child to school the following day.

'You'll regret it,' Mary told her when their mother was out of the kitchen.

'I know I will, but I have to try. Mam looks worn out with the worry.'

'She'll settle eventually. Everyone has tae,' Todd predicted.

'Rowena,' said Mary, 'isn't like everyone.'

'I'm not going!' Rowena stormed as Caitlin buttoned her into her jacket.

'You'll like the school well enough once you get used to it.'

'I won't.' She refused to take her aunt's hand, marching instead along the inside of the pavement and letting the shoulder of her good jacket brush against the damp stone walls as she went. Knowing that she was watching out of the slanted corners of her eyes for a reaction, Caitlin held her tongue and

154

concentrated all her attention on getting the child into the school building, then into her classroom.

They had just reached the playground, which was swarming with children bellowing at the tops of their voices, when she realised that Rowena had disappeared like a wisp of smoke. Caitlin looked up and down the street, and even peered through the railings in the vain hope that the child had somehow slipped in through the gate unnoticed, but she wasn't to be seen among the throng in the yard. Panic-stricken, recalling Kirsty's worry about Rowena being run over, Caitlin began to retrace her steps at a run.

As she turned the corner into Espedair Street, she caught sight of a small figure scudding along the pavement ahead of her.

'Rowena, come back here!'

The child ignored her, hunching her head down and rushing across the road. Caitlin's hands flew to her mouth in horror as the small figure slipped in a puddle and almost fell in front of a small motorised van, but miraculously Rowena recovered her balance just in time and leapt onto the opposite pavement, landing in front of Murdo Guthrie on his way to the weaving shop. Pedestrians turned to see what was going on as the van screeched to a halt, its horn blaring an off-key protest.

Caitlin ran across the road to find Murdo staring down at Rowena, who had locked her arms tightly about one of his legs.

'Oh, Rowena!' She tried to gather the child into her arms and was rewarded with a backward kick that grazed her shin.

'I'm not going!' Rowena screeched into Murdo's trouser leg as the van driver jumped down from his cab.

'Ye wee monkey, ye . . . ye could have got yersel' killed! What d'ye think ye were playin' at?' He pushed Caitlin aside and tried to wrench the child round to face him. Murdo's hand clamped over his wrist.

'Leave her alone.'

'Leave her, is it?' the man spluttered, turning to appeal to the small crowd that was gathering. 'And her nearly murderin' herself under my wheels? Whose fault would it have been then, eh?' He thrust his face aggressively into the Highlander's. 'What would ye have done tae me if that had happened, eh? An' what would the polis have done?'

'Leave her be.' Murdo put his free hand protectively over the head pressed against his thigh. 'Just let her alone,' he repeated, his voice quiet but at the same time hard. 'We'll see to her.'

'I'm sorry about what she did, and I'll make sure she doesn't do it again. But nobody was hurt.' Caitlin tried to calm the situation.

'No thanks tae her, missus,' the man said. He wrenched his wrist free. 'Ach, I've got work tae dae.' He stamped back to his van, the watchers scattering to let him through. Looking after him, Caitlin saw Annie Mitchell, Beth's sister, standing with her husband and a knot of onlookers at the door of the tobacconist's shop.

'If ye've got any sense ye'll give her a right thrashin',' the van driver yelled from the open window as he drove away. 'It's the only way tae teach them right from wrong!'

The onlookers murmured their agreement, and a woman's voice said clearly, 'If folk cannae look after their bairns, they've got no right tae birth them!'

Murdo swung Rowena up into his arms and carried her into the pend. Casting an apologetic glance round at the bystanders, Caitlin saw that Annie Mitchell, arms folded tightly across her bosom, was holding forth to the people with her. No doubt, she thought as she followed Murdo, the woman was portraying Rowena as the wayward product of wayward parents – without admitting to her listeners that one of the parents was her own sister.

In the weaving shop, Murdo was seated on the saytree with Rowena standing before him. At the sight of Caitlin, she tried to move nearer to him, but he held her back gently at arm's length.

'Now, what's amiss with you?' he asked Rowena.

'I'll not go!'

Anger flashed across his face as he looked up at Caitlin accusingly. 'You're sending her away?'

'Only to the school.'

His face cleared. 'Is that what it's all about? You don't want to go to the school?'

'I won't go!' Rowena whirled round and shouted at her aunt. 'I'll not go and you can't make me!'

'That's enough, now.' There was a steely note in Murdo's voice that neither of them had heard before. As Rowena's mouth fell open, he added to Caitlin, 'You've got mud on your skirt.'

She looked down and gave a vexed exclamation at the sight of the black wet smear on the pale-grey material.

'Why don't you go into the kitchen and clean it off while me and Rowena have a wee talk?' Murdo suggested, so completely in control of the situation that she did as she was told without question.

Caitlin had sponged the skirt and was holding it out to let the heat of the fire dry it when Murdo arrived at the open door, Rowena small and subdued by his side.

'We're walking to the school now. I'd be grateful if you'd come along, for she'll be late, and no doubt her teacher would prefer an explanation from one of her family and not a stranger.'

Rowena, declining the offer of a hand, stamped ahead of them while Caitlin, keenly aware of the wet patch still marring her skirt, and Murdo followed. At the school door Murdo detained Rowena with a big hand on her shoulder and squatted, turning her to face him. 'Mind what I said now. I'll weave that much cloth . . . ,' he held his big hands out at a distance apart from each other, 'then I'll have a bite to eat and I'll practise the music you like best for when you're finished here. After that I'll weave this much cloth . . . ,' again he spread his hands out, 'then I'll walk along from Espedair Street and be waiting for you when you come out. While we walk back home you can tell me all about what you've been doing in the school. D'you understand what I'm saying to you?'

She stuck her bottom lip out but nodded reluctantly.

'That's a good lass. Now your aunt'll take you in and explain to the teacher that it's not your fault you're late.' For a moment he let his hand rest on her head, then he straightened to his full height and told Caitlin solemnly, 'You can take her in now.'

When she emerged, he was waiting by the gate.

'Your skirt looks fine now,' he said, falling into step with her. 'Has she settled all right?'

'I think so. What did you say to her?' He shrugged. 'Oh, we just had a wee bit of a crack, her and me. If your parents are willing, I'll walk with her to the school in the mornings and walk home with her as well until she's more comfortable there.'

'I don't see that happening.'

'She'll be grand,' said Murdo Guthrie easily. 'It's just that the bairn's still trying to find a place for herself.'

'We've done all we could to make her feel welcome,' Caitlin said, stung by what she saw as criticism.

'I've no doubt you have, but making the step from one life to another's a hard business for an adult, let alone a wee bairn. It's only someone who's been through it that can understand.'

'Someone like you?'

They had reached the turning into Espedair Street.

'It's all right, then, if I fetch her home?' he asked, and when she nodded he went off briskly in the direction of his weaving shop without a backward glance.

14

Although he lived in a city spilling over with opportunities for the social pleasures of every class, Alex MacDowall was a solitary man and content to be so. By day he was either in his father's large furniture emporium or in the factory where, until recently, he had spent much of his working day.

His free time was taken up with visiting his family in Paisley or working on furniture designs in his spacious tenement flat on the first floor of a building his father owned just off Paisley Road West.

A capable cook-housekeeper came in every day to clean the flat and prepare his meals, and every Friday evening he travelled by tramcar to Pollokshields to dine at his father's large house, set in the middle of a well-cared-for garden and sheltered from the road by a small shrubbery.

The house, bought originally for Angus MacDowall and his daughter, Fiona, was large for just one person, but although Angus had talked of moving to a smaller place when Fiona married and settled in Fort William, he liked his house and had gradually given up all idea of a move. Neither father nor son had mentioned the likelihood of Alex moving in when he first settled in the city; they were both fond of their privacy, and after living cheek by jowl with the rest of his family in cramped housing all his life, it suited Alex to have a place of his own. He revelled in his right to spend his free time exactly as he chose without having to consider other people's wishes.

Alex travelled to his father's house as usual on a pleasant evening in mid-September, getting off the tram a few stops earlier than usual in order to extend his walk. The trees on either side of the road had not yet begun to relinquish their leaves to autumn and through the branches sunshine dappled the broad pavements pleasantly as Alex swung in at the double gate and up the driveway, humming 'Alexander's Ragtime Band' to himself.

Angus kept a good staff around him to cater for his needs. There was a full-time gardener with an assistant, an excellent cook, a scullery maid and two upstairs maids, the older also acting as a housekeeper, and a laundry woman who came in twice a week. He had never had a valet, believing that there was something wrong with a man who was unable to dress himself unaided.

The younger of the upstairs maids opened the door. 'Good evening, Ellen. Isn't it a pleasant evening?' Alex handed over his hat and stick. 'Is Mr MacDowall in the drawing room?'

'He's not come downstairs yet, sir, but—'

'No hurry, I'll wait for him.' In the drawing room Alex, who felt quite at home in this house, went towards the small table where his father kept decanters and glasses. Angus enjoyed a glass of whisky before his evening meal.

'Good evening, Alex.'

Startled, he swung round, and at the sight of the

woman by the fireplace his heart gave a double thump before seeming to stop in his chest.

'Fiona!'

She smiled, giving him a glimpse of small white teeth. 'You're surprised to see me.'

'I . . . I'd no idea. I thought you were in Fort William.'

'I came from there today. Perhaps you will pour some sherry for me.'

He was glad of the excuse to collect his thoughts and to give his heart time to return to a regular beat, though faster than usual. To his annoyance his hands were shaking, so that the neck of the decanter rattled against the glass in his other hand.

'Let me.' Fiona appeared by his side and took the decanter and glass from him. 'I'm used to pouring drinks for George.'

Her sleeve brushed against his, and her perfume brought back memories. Alex turned away from her, towards the windows, thrusting his hands into his pockets. Ever since that terrible time when he had discovered that the girl he had fallen in love with was his half-sister, he had kept well away from this house on the few occasions when Fiona had visited their father.

'Seeing me here must be quite a shock to you,' she said, as though reading his thoughts. 'Papa couldn't warn you, for he didn't know that I was coming. I decided to make the journey at short notice.'

Her hand swam into his vision, bearing a glass. He took it, grateful to see that it held a generous measure of whisky. He took a quick, deep swallow of the liquid before turning back into the room. Fiona had seated herself on a large sofa by the fire, a long-stemmed glass in her hand; she patted the cushions by her side in invitation, but Alex chose an upright chair opposite.

'To your good health,' she said demurely, raising her glass.

'And to yours.' He took another good swallow of his drink, wishing himself anywhere but in his father's drawing room with Fiona.

A silence fell between them. Aware that she was using his inarticulate embarrassment to study him, Alex cleared his throat then asked, 'Are you staying in Glasgow for long?' To his relief, his voice was fairly normal.

'Until the end of the year at least. George – my husband – is in the Naval Reserve and has been called to service. I had no great wish to stay on in Fort William without him, so I decided to come to Glasgow instead.' She stretched out a slender, silk-clad arm to take her glass from the small table by her side, took a tiny sip from it and added, 'The social life in Glasgow is much more interesting.'

Angus MacDowall hurried in just then. 'I didn't realise you'd arrived until the girl told me, Alex.' He glanced anxiously from one to the other, and Alex jumped up to fetch his father's drink.

It was a relief when the maid announced that dinner was awaiting them in the dining room, where Angus had no option but to take his usual place at the head of the long table, which meant that his son and daughter sat to his left and right, facing each other.

There was never much conversation at Angus MacDowall's dinner table, for he enjoyed his food and liked to concentrate on it in silence. Afterwards, he and Alex usually talked about the week's work and their plans for the following week over brandy and cigars. As he toyed with his food, his appetite completely gone, Alex sneaked swift glances across the table. Fiona was still the beautiful woman he had

163

fallen helplessly in love with when he had first set eyes on her at a furniture exhibition. Beneath an overdress of dark-red chiffon, the neat-fitting embroidered bodice of her shell-pink dinner gown was cut low enough to reveal the upper slopes of her breasts. Her hair, the colour of honey in sunlight, was swept back from her face and secured behind her head with a jewelled pin, and diamond drop earrings fell almost to her shoulders.

Time seemed to have passed her by, though once when she flicked a swift glance across at Alex, catching him unawares, he saw that her gold-flecked brown eyes, though still wide and thick lashed, had lost their youthful sparkle. And on another occasion, when she was staring down at her plate, he detected a faint downward turn to the corners of her mouth.

She waited until dessert was served before saying, 'So . . . you haven't volunteered to go to war, Alex.'

Even the sound of his name on her lips reawakened memories. He glanced at his father, then as Angus remained silent, said, 'If conscription comes in, then of course I'll go willingly, but in the meantime we both felt that I was of more use to the business.'

When the plates had been cleared away, Fiona excused herself and left the table, her flared skirt, silk overlaid with chiffon and embroidered at the deep hem, swishing softly as she moved across the room.

'I'm sorry to have put you in such a difficult position, Alex,' Angus said almost as soon as the door had closed behind his daughter's slender back. 'I'd no knowledge of her arrival until she appeared on the doorstep; if I had been forewarned I'd have sent word.'

'It's of no matter, sir. Time has brought a lot of changes,' Alex said through stiff lips, and saw relief light up his father's face.

'I'm glad to hear that the sorry business is over and

done with.' He fetched a bottle of port and a box of cigars from the sideboard and put them on the table. 'Since it seems she'll be under my roof for a few months, it's as well that the two of you met tonight. I couldn't be expected to keep you apart from each other forever.'

'No.' Alex selected a cigar.

'The whole business was most unfortunate,' Angus went on, dismissing the love his son and his daughter had known for each other before discovering that they shared the same father. 'But you've both moved on considerably since those days.'

'Yes, sir.'

'Water under the bridge,' Angus said, settling back in his chair, beaming, the matter over and done with. 'I shall rather enjoy spending time with Fiona again. I've missed her.'

Since Murdo's intervention, Rowena had gone off to school every morning without further protest, though she didn't enjoy the experience. She refused to walk beside the Highlander, who waited for her every morning at the corner of the pend, but that didn't seem to bother him. He walked behind her, made sure that she went into the playground and was always waiting by the gate at the end of the day to see that she got home safely.

'He strolls along like a gentleman with the whole day to himself, looking everywhere but at Rowena, while she marches ahead like a wee terrier and never gives him as much as a glance,' Rose told Caitlin with amusement, after cycling past the two of them one morning on her way to Harlequin.

At first Rowena refused to tell any member of her family about her school day, though every afternoon on returning home she closeted herself in the weaving shop. Caitlin suspected that Murdo Guthrie was hearing about what went on in the classroom, but it was some time before Rowena began to demonstrate to the others how she could draw, form a few letters and read a word or two from her school book.

She wasn't the only one doing homework at the kitchen table, for Mary, her mind still set on office work, had enrolled in bookkeeping classes at night school in September.

'I'd have thought you'd be glad of the chance to stop studying,' Kirsty told her daughter, but Mary shook her head.

'I like learning, and I need my diplomas if I'm to be considered seriously for office work. Anyway, it'll encourage Rowena if I'm working at my books along with her.'

In October, reviving an old family tradition, Caitlin and Mary, with Murdo and Lachie in attendance, took the little girl out into the countryside to pick brambles from the hedgerows.

'I don't know why I'm doing this,' Mary protested, trailing along behind Caitlin. 'I get more than my fill of fruit at work!'

'It's not for you, it's for Rowena,' Caitlin told her, knowing full well that the attraction for Mary was Lachie's presence. 'Anyway, it's enjoyable.' She managed to untangle a long branch laden with the sweet black berries, very similar to raspberries, and stripped it into the tin can she had brought, then she straightened up as Mary, spying a branch further along, gave a yelp of triumph and ran to claim it before the others did.

When the containers were full, they found a clearing where they could sit on the short, strong grass to eat the sandwiches Mary had prepared and drink from bottles of cold tea. Then Mary and Lachie and Rowena played tig, racing after each other with screams of laughter, while Caitlin, who had brought her notebook and crayons, tried to capture something of the browns and golds and oranges of the autumn bracken, interspersed with streaks and clumps of purple heather. Murdo perched on an outcrop of rock a few feet away, staring down over the town.

After a while Caitlin closed the book and rested her chin on her cupped hands, watching the others. It was grand to see Rowena enjoying herself. She had topped off her meal with a dessert of blackberries, which had left purple stains on the lower part of her face and her hands. Shrieking with pleasure, she was trying to catch Lachie, who kept dancing out of reach just as she got to him. When he judged that the little girl was growing frustrated, he let her touch him on the arm, so that it was then her turn to dance away from his outstretched fingers.

'You'd think they were all the same age,' Caitlin said, laughing as Mary and Lachie accidentally ran into each other and landed in a heap of grass. Rowena instantly threw herself on top of them, and the three rolled down a small hill, arms and legs sticking out in all directions.

'Once an adult, always an adult. They're right to enjoy their youth for as long as they can.'

'Did you enjoy your youth, Murdo?' The question was out of her mouth before she had time to think of it. He got to his feet without answering.

'Time to turn for home,' he said, and went to untangle the mass of humanity on the ground.

Watching him, she wondered if he had been a silent little boy, old before his time. If not, some outside influence must have made him the enigma he was.

*   *   *

They had descended the hills and were back among the streets, Rowena asleep on Murdo's shoulder, Mary and Lachie whispering and giggling a few yards behind, when a voice rang out from a knot of women on the opposite pavement. 'It fair sickens me tae see strong healthy men cowerin' at home when others are away doin' their fightin' for them!'

Shocked, Caitlin whirled round and stared across the road. Far from hiding, the woman who had spoken detached herself from her friends and advanced to the edge of the pavement. 'Aye, hen, it's your man I'm talkin' about,' she called, while her friends gathered behind her. 'It's time ye carried yer own wean an' telt him tae get a uniform on his back!'

Several passers-by, alerted by the shrill voice skewering the air, turned to look for her victim. Some of them nodded, while others simply gaped, awaiting a reaction, or glanced away and tried to pretend that they had heard nothing.

'My man's gone off tae God knows where.' Another woman stepped out from the group, shaking her fist. 'An' me wi' weans tae feed an' not knowin' if he'll come back dead or maimed. Why should the likes o' you walk the streets when the likes o' him's fightin' yer battles for ye?'

Mary and Lachie hurried up, their young faces pale with shock, but Murdo, ordering, 'Pay no heed,' kept walking, looking straight ahead. It was hard to do as he said. Caitlin was afraid that the women would follow them to Espedair Street, but to her relief the catcalls and jeering faded once they had turned the corner. Even so, she found herself walking faster and looking into the faces of the people they met. There was no doubt at all that some of them, as they drew near, measured the height and breadth of Murdo with a glance and a tightening of the lips as though they, too, were wondering why he was not in uniform.

She said nothing to Kirsty or Todd about the incident, and Mary, who had gone off somewhere with Lachie instead of going into the house with the others, was also quiet when she came in.

That evening Kirsty, already making the bramble jelly, looked from one daughter to the other. 'Did you not enjoy being up the braes today? You're both awful quiet.'

'It's the smell of the jam,' Mary said at once. 'It reminds me of work.'

Later she tapped on Caitlin's bedroom door and went in to talk about the incident. 'Poor Lachie was mortified. He's only fifteen, and there's scarce a pick of flesh on his bones as it is. He'd not have the strength to carry a rifle,' she said fiercely. 'Those . . . witches had no right to frighten him the way they did!'

'It was Murdo they were shouting at, not your Lachie.' Caitlin wondered how often he had had to endure such scenes before.

'D'you think Alex is having to put up with that sort of thing in Glasgow?'

'If he is, I'm sure he's able to deal with it, and so is Murdo.'

'It was . . . I felt dirty!' Mary shook with a sudden, violent spasm, and Caitlin sat on the bed and put her arms about her sister.

'Don't you fret yourself. Remember that words can't hurt anyone.'

'That's not true,' Mary said into her shoulder. 'They can!'

15

Alex knew as soon as he let himself into the flat that there was something wrong. The square carpeted hall looked just as it always did and, as usual at that time in the late afternoon, the place was fragrant with the smell of cooking, but there was something out of place somewhere.

A glance into the kitchen showed that it was empty, which was not unusual; Mrs Harkins often left for her own home two streets away before he returned, leaving him to dish up his own meal. Frowning because he was unable to put his finger on the problem, he hung up his hat and coat, put his cane into the coat stand and opened the drawing-room door.

The room looked inviting with the curtains drawn against the chill November night. A fire burned brightly in the grate, the electric lamps at each side of the mantelpiece were lit and Fiona half sat, half lay on the sofa, a magazine open on her lap. She looked up with a warm smile.

'Alex, I was beginning to think that you'd been delayed.' She put the magazine aside and flitted across the carpet to reach up and drop a swift light kiss on his cheek before drawing him to the armchair. 'I've made up the fire and put your slippers to heat.'

'What the . . . What are you doing here?'

She was at the sideboard, pouring whisky from a decanter. 'I've come to call on my brother,' she said over her shoulder.

'I don't recall inviting you.'

'Oh dear, you sound very cross.' Fiona bustled back to him, carrying a small silver tray bearing two glasses. She put it down on the low table by his chair, then straightened to face him, her lovely face alight with amusement. 'Are you going to stand to attention all night? It will make eating your dinner difficult.'

Over her head Alex caught sight of himself in the mirror, bristling like a turkey cock. He sat down suddenly.

'That's better.' Fiona took a glass from the tray and went back to the sofa. 'Just a little whisky and a lot of water,' she explained, lifting her glass slightly as though proposing a toast, then sipping the pale gold liquid. 'I sometimes drink it at home before dinner. I've noticed that, like George, you would much prefer your whisky on its own.'

'Does Father know that you're here?'

Her long lashes swept down to cover her eyes, then came back up. 'I confess that I told him a very little white lie and said that I was dining with the Matlocks. If I'd told him the truth he would have expected to come with me, and I thought that it was time that we spent a little time together. You didn't come to dinner last Friday.'

'I had another engagement.'

'I wondered if you might be staying away because of me. Because of . . . what we once were to each other. You haven't changed into your slippers.'

'I'm comfortable as I am.'

'You don't look very comfortable. I always put

George's slippers on for him.' She put her glass down and began to rise. 'Do you want me to—?'

He shook his head, and began to unlace his shoes. 'I can manage. Where's Mrs Harkins?'

'I sent her home after she had prepared dinner for us.' She settled herself against the cushions, totally at home. 'Do you realise that I've been in Glasgow for a month at least and you haven't even invited me here for a meal?'

'There's plenty food in my father's house,' Alex said shortly. 'And I have work to do. I don't entertain.'

'Not even your young lady?'

Alex's collar felt very tight, but he daren't let her see him put a hand up to ease it. 'I have no young lady.'

'So Papa told me, but I found it hard to believe. You're a personable man, Alex, as I know from my own experience,' she added sweetly. 'Dare I wonder if it's simply that you haven't found anyone to care for as much as you cared for me?'

Looking at the slow smile that curved her mouth he realised, too late, that he had fallen into a trap she had set for him.

'It has nothing to do with—' he bit off the word us, and finished, 'anything that went before. I'm simply too busy to socialise.'

Fiona, having achieved her aim, glanced critically round the room. 'I should have realised that you have no lady visitors. This place is far too masculine and uncomfortable. Perhaps I could improve it for you.'

'I prefer my home as it is.'

'Oh dear,' she said softly. 'If you're not careful, Alex, you'll turn into a dull, pompous old man interested in nothing but keeping his nose to the grindstone. You used to be so . . . ,' again, there came that pause that said far more than words, 'interesting,' she finished, running the tip of one finger lightly round the edge of her glass.

'Life has changed for us both since then, Fiona.' He had intended the words to be sensible and down-to-earth, but to his own ears his voice sounded artificial and, as she had already said, pompous. He felt warmth surge to his face and knew by the sudden lift of her eyebrows that he had indeed reddened.

'You were so young, that first time we met at the exhibition centre. So shy.' She looked down into her drink then added, her voice dropping to a near whisper, 'So kind and gallant. Neither of us dreamt that day that you were going to do as well as you have.'

'We've both done well. You have a husband, a new home.'

Fiona suddenly drained her glass, the muscles working smoothly beneath the creamy skin of her throat as she swallowed. 'Time to eat,' she said, standing up and taking his glass from him. 'I'm very hungry.'

Today she wore a dress of pale gold, almost the colour of her hair; as she walked ahead of him the honey-coloured silk seemed to caress her back and waist and legs, and her perfume wafted back to him.

She had found a candelabra in some cupboard and set it on the table. They dined by the light of the candles, with the rest of the room in shadow. The tiny flames winked and glittered on snowy napery, glasses and cutlery, and caught flashes of light from Fiona's rings and the single crystal hung around her neck on a fine gold chain. As she manipulated her knife and fork, her discreetly varnished fingernails gleamed occasionally in the light, and now and again, when she looked up at Alex, gold flecks seemed to dance in the depths of her velvet-brown eyes.

Mrs Harkins was a superb cook and the food was,

as always, delicious, but he ate automatically, scarcely aware of flavour or texture, while Fiona, seemingly unperturbed by his silence, chattered lightly about nothing in particular, springing up every so often to change courses or to pour more ruby-red wine from the bottle on the sideboard. She was, he thought, drinking more than was good for her.

When the meal was finally over, she offered to make coffee, but Alex shook his head. 'I think it's time I took you back to Pollokshields.'

'Already?' She screwed up her face. 'But the evening's young yet.'

'I've work to do and an early start in the morning. Where did you leave your coat?' He realised that he hadn't seen it on the coat stand in the hall; if it had been there, he would have been forewarned, and the entire evening would have taken a different course.

'In your bedroom.'

Her fur coat had been arranged across his bed, the high collar opened out over the pillow and the sleeves spread to either side. Alex gathered it up and turned to find Fiona standing just inside the door.

'I thought we could have coffee and brandy and talk about the old days.'

'There's nothing to talk about.'

She raised her eyebrows. 'That's not very gallant of you, Alex. Once you would have given everything you had to spend some time alone with me.'

'We had no idea then that we were brother and sister.'

She leaned against the doorframe. 'What if we hadn't found out, Alex?' He saw a tingle of excitement come into her eyes, while her lips parted to allow the tip of her tongue to slip through and moisten them. 'I've often wondered about that. Haven't you?'

'No.'

'If we had married, d'you think we would have been happy together in our innocence?' A shudder of sheer horror ran through him at the thought, and as she recognised it, her eyes narrowed. 'Does the thought of marriage to me disgust you so much?'

'It would have been like taking Caitlin or Mary for my wife.'

'But if we hadn't known, would it have been so wrong?' Before he realised what she was about, she had switched off the light, plunging the room into darkness. Silk rustled across the carpet towards him, then the coat was twitched from his hands and Fiona's hair was against his cheek, the smell of her in his nostrils, her hands on his shoulders and her body pressing itself against his. 'In the dark,' she whispered against his throat, her lips moist and warm, 'all cats are alike.'

'For God's sake!' Alex pushed her soft body aside and heard her give a gasp, then a brief cry, as he fumbled his way towards the door. He stumbled over the discarded coat, which slipped beneath his feet and almost brought him down. He kicked free of it, then blundered painfully into a piece of furniture before his outstretched hands touched something larger. Recognising it as the corner of the big mahogany wardrobe, he felt round it to the wall, the door and, finally, the light switch.

The light was dazzling after the darkness; blinking, Alex turned and saw Fiona half sitting on his bed, rubbing her shoulder.

'You hurt me!'

'And you disgust me!'

'How dare you say that to me after the way you've ruined my life! D'you know what it was like to be sent away from my father's house then to find out that you were being made welcome in my place?'

'Fiona, I have never taken your place in our father's affections. As for sending you away, he thought it best for you to get out of Glasgow at the time, and you've made a good life for yourself in Fort William.'

'I had a better life here!' To his astonishment, she launched herself from the bed and rushed across the room to rain blows on him with clenched fists. 'I wanted to stay in Glasgow with Papa!'

Even when Alex managed to trap her wrists she kept struggling, only stopping when he shook her so hard that her head flopped on her long slim neck, strands of hair coming loose from her combs. 'For pity's sake, you've still got your father, and a husband.'

'Husband!' Fiona spat the word into his face. 'A man as dull and boring as you are!' Then her face seemed to shimmer and crumple, and she fell against him as though unable to support herself any longer, her body so limp that he had to release her wrists and put his arms around her to prevent her from sliding to the floor. 'Why did you ever come to Glasgow?' she wept. 'I hate you so much . . . I hate you!'

It was like holding a child. Her tears dampened then soaked his carefully starched shirt front, and her entire body shook as though in the grip of a fever. Alex freed one hand to stroke her hair, appalled by her utter misery. The desire she had kindled in him years before came surging back, and he recognised with shock that it was not, and perhaps never had been, a physical longing, but merely a desire to protect and shelter her.

Her sobbing finally slowed and stilled. She drew back from him, then turned without a word and left the room. The bathroom door opened and closed. Shaken, Alex picked her coat up and took it into the drawing room, where he poured whisky into two glasses, holding one out to Fiona when she finally came out of the bathroom.

'Drink it,' he urged when she shook her head. 'It'll do you good.'

She had tidied her hair, and although her eyes were red and her face pale, she looked as beautiful as ever. But her voice was still venomous when she said, 'I don't want it!'

She looked about for her coat, and when he held it out for her she slid her arms into the sleeves then pulled away from him and made for the door. Downstairs she waited in silence while he summoned a cab and followed her into it. Throughout the journey she stared out of the window, presenting the back of her head to him, and when they reached Angus MacDowall's house she got out at once and left him to pay the driver.

'I would prefer to go into the house alone,' she said coldly when he caught up with her at the gate. He watched until she had let herself into the house, then, although it had begun to rain, he sent the cab away and walked home, arriving chilled and soaked to the skin.

He drank her untouched whisky then stripped his clothes off before climbing naked into bed. Her perfume was still on the pillow and the sheets.

When Alex forced himself to go to his father's house on the following Friday evening, he found Fiona playing hostess to about a dozen people in all. She claimed him as soon as he went in and insisted on taking him from one group to another, her jewelled hand on his arm, while she introduced him to everyone as 'my dear brother'. After dinner, when the party settled down to play cards in the drawing room, he and Angus, who had clearly found it difficult to cope with so many people in his home but had done his best to be a good host, escaped to the study on the pretext of business.

'It's dull for Fiona to have nothing to do and no friends after the life she's been used to in Fort William,' the older man explained as he closed the door on a babble of voices and laughter. 'She needs to have folk about her. We must both make sure that she enjoys her stay here.'

From then on Fiona treated Alex with a cloying sweetness that stuck in his throat. She announced her intention of calling on his mother and sisters, and when she heard about Harlequin she determined to go and see the place for herself. Her father hired a motorcar for them, and after leaving Alex in Espedair Street with Todd, Fiona drove on to the old mill, where she advanced on Caitlin, hands outstretched. 'My dear girl, how grown-up you look – and how well you have done for yourself!'

Rose came into the fitting room to be introduced, bringing with her John Brodie, who had called on business. Caitlin, who had first known Fiona as Alex's sweetheart, remembered her as a sweet-natured young woman with an open interest in everyone she met. Now she was mature, confident and the openness was still there but, Caitlin thought as she watched Fiona charm John, there was a certain calculation in it, as though the brain behind the lovely brown eyes was appraising and weighing things up.

'Alex has told me all about your new venture,' she said sweetly when John had gone, 'and hearing about you both has made me feel that I've done nothing at all with my life. But all that will change, I promise you. Now, the clothes that stood me in good stead in Fort William will most certainly not do for Glasgow, so I must begin at the beginning.'

While Caitlin went upstairs to fetch some materials and to summon Grace, Rose showed the new client sketches of some of the clothes they had supplied.

'Caitlin is so talented, but then so is Alex.' Fiona paused, glancing at Rose from the corner of her eye, then asked, 'Do you know the family well?'

'Quite well.'

'Then you're no doubt aware that although Caitlin and I are not related, we share Alex as a brother?'

Rose picked up a magazine. 'Yes, I know. This draped wrapover skirt has become very popular with some of our clients. It's a style that would suit you.'

Fiona tossed a glance at the sketch. 'Yes, I rather like it. Alex and I are very close, although neither of us knew anything of the other's existence for many years. When we first met it was as complete strangers, as unrelated as you and I.'

'Indeed? This long jacket would also suit you.'

'It's very fetching,' Fiona said casually. 'Even although we were unaware of our shared blood, we took to each other instantly. There seems to be a bond between us.'

'As there is between Alex and Caitlin.'

'But they always knew each other as brother and sister and have therefore always behaved appropriately towards each other, whereas Alex and I . . .'

To Rose's great relief, Caitlin and Grace arrived, and they settled down to discussing Fiona's new clothes. She was a demanding client, and by the time she left to visit Kirsty and collect Alex for the return trip to Glasgow the three of them were exhausted.

'That one's a right madam,' Grace said flatly.

'Grace,' Rose protested, 'if you're to work with the clients, as we hope, you'll have to watch your tongue.'

'As long as I don't say it to them, where's the harm?'

'Just because they're wealthy it doesn't mean they're daft as well. They can read your thoughts in your face.'

'In that case,' said Grace, scooping up bales of cloth, 'p'raps I should come intae the fittin' room with a bag over my head.'

'She'll never do for the clients,' Rose said in despair when the woman had departed upstairs.

'She's an excellent seamstress with a good brain. And she's tired. We all are.' Caitlin looked about the room, strewn with magazines and sketches, and began to tidy it up.

'Was that woman always so demanding?'

'Not that I recall, but I only saw her once or twice when Alex brought her to Paisley. Marriage has changed her.'

'I can't understand what a man like Alex ever saw in her.'

'She was very lovely – she still is.'

Rose shrugged. 'If you like that sort of prettiness.'

'All that matters to us is that she wants us to make clothes for her,' Caitlin said firmly.

Kirsty had noticed little difference in Fiona. 'She's a woman now but still nice enough and just as interested in other folk as she ever was,' she said, but Todd disagreed with her when he came in for his evening meal.

'There's a calculatin' sort of look in her eye that I don't mind seein' there before.'

'You're havering!' his wife said, but he shook his head.

'I met her when I was a journeyman here and Alex brought her to the workshop to meet the men there. She was an open, honest sort of lass then, and poor Alex was fair cross-eyed with love for her. It was a sad business altogether.'

'And not one that any of us cares to remember,' Kirsty said tartly. 'It's over and done with long since.'

'Mebbe so, but if you ask me, it's left its mark on both of them. They're harder, but in Alex's case he's made good use of the strength he had tae find in himself. As to Mrs Chalmers, I think her sorrow turned in on itself, and that's never a good thing.'

To her annoyance, Mary had missed seeing the visitor, while Rowena had kept well out of the way, eeling from the weaving shop as Fiona and Alex entered and slipping back in there to hide after they had gone into the house for tea.

16

Far from being over by the New Year, the war seemed to be settling in. Although enemy troops had been prevented from taking Paris, they gained Belgium's main cities.

On New Year's Day, Rose, Caitlin and John Brodie attended a party held by Fiona Chalmers at her father's home. Neither Caitlin nor Rose was enthusiastic about accepting the invitation, but as John pointed out, it was a matter of business, since it gave them the opportunity to meet potential clients.

Fiona, in a rose-pink velvet and lace evening gown that Caitlin and the seamstresses had worked through several evenings to complete in time, fluttered like a butterfly among her guests, making a point of introducing Rose and Caitlin to her friends, whom she advised to visit Harlequin.

'Do you work there too, Mr Brodie?' one woman asked archly. 'I know that in Paris and London men design divine clothing for ladies.'

John turned pink with embarrassment. 'Oh no, I'm just a lawyer!'

'Now don't be so modest!' Fiona tucked one hand into the crook of his arm and told the people around them, 'Mr Brodie attends to all the tiresome financial business while Rose . . .' with her free hand she drew Rose, stiff and awkward with humiliation, to her other side, 'looks after the clients, and Caitlin makes wonderful clothes for them.'

Knowing Alex's dislike of social events, Caitlin wasn't entirely surprised to see that he tended to hover in quiet corners with his father. He and Rose had scarcely exchanged a word, but he finally came to Caitlin when she was on her own to say gloomily, 'I suppose you're having an enjoyable time.'

'Quite, although I scarcely know anyone.'

'Neither do I.'

'Never mind.' She slid her hand into his, squeezing his fingers. 'It will soon be over.'

'Did you design that frock Rose is wearing?' he asked. When she nodded, he said, 'It suits her.'

Rose's gown consisted of swathes of chiffon in varying shades of gold, bronze, deep glowing red and pale brown, falling to handkerchief points at the hem. As she moved through the crowd the skirt flowed and swirled about her long legs.

Alex's gaze followed her. 'It reminds me of autumn bonfires in the country.'

'The idea came to me when I saw the autumn colours of the bracken one day when we were blackberrying on the braes,' Caitlin told him, pleased that he had recognised something of the thought behind the design.

'Are she and Brodie seeing much of each other these days?'

'They still go to functions together, and John comes to the fashion house about once a week.'

'He's quite smitten with her.'

'Do you think so?'

'Surely you can see it for yourself. Is she taken with him, do you think?'

Caitlin remembered what John had said to her at the fashion house launch but decided to keep it to herself. For one thing, it had been said in confidence, and for another it was clear to her from the way Alex watched Rose that he himself was smitten. She had even seen Fiona Chalmers glance, narrow eyed, from him to Rose, as though she too had recognised his feelings. 'I don't know,' she said lamely.

'It must be good to feel sure of yourself and know who you are. Sometimes,' Alex suddenly said, startling himself as much as Caitlin, 'I feel as though I'm neither one thing or another. Not a Lennox or a MacDowall.'

She understood. 'Has Fiona's coming made such a difference to you?'

'Yes, it has, but not because of what went before,' he added hurriedly. 'The difference is in me. I feel as though I belong nowhere. Even my sisters are half-sisters, not related to each other yet sharing a parent with me.'

'You have Mam, and your father.'

'Do I? I feel as though I'm moving apart from them, or them from me. I wish to God, Caitlin,' he said passionately, 'that they had never set eyes on each other!'

'If you mean that, you're wishing your own life away. For my part I'm glad they met and that they loved each other, for otherwise I'd never have known you, and I'd have hated that.'

There was cynicism in the amused twist to his lips. 'You can't miss what you never had,' he pointed out. 'But you're right, there's no sense in thinking of what might have been. The thing to do is to shape what we've been given to suit ourselves.'

Then Fiona swooped down on them, insisting on introducing Caitlin to someone else, and Alex returned to his father, leaving Caitlin wondering, uneasily, what he meant.

Several of the women who had attended the New Year party found their way to Paisley over the next few months, and some of them put in orders. Caitlin wondered, since the war seemed set to continue, if the fashion house could survive, but Rose dismissed her doubts.

'The women we cater for have money, and war makes little difference to their lives. Oh, their menfolk might go off to fight, but our clients'll want to look specially nice when they come home again,' she said cynically. 'You've no idea how many young men I know who've taken advantage of this war to persuade their sweethearts to become engaged so that they have someone to fight for.'

Caitlin thought fleetingly of Bryce urging her to wear his ring.

'Or to marry them, just in case,' Rose went on.

Within a month Rose was proved right when Harlequin had to deal with no less than three hurried weddings before fiancés were sent overseas.

Tidying the fitting room after a hectic session with a tremulous young bride to be and her overexcited mother, Caitlin said, 'I don't think I could bear to marry a man who was going off to fight and mebbe to die.'

'That's not the way these lassies see it.' Grace shook out a petticoat and hung it up. 'Most of them cannae bear tae send their men away without givin' them all the comfort they can.' She sighed and stopped work to gaze at the far wall. 'I was like that mysel' when my man went tae fight the Boers. That's how I fell wi' my first, daft fool that I was. There's more than one left wi' a full stomach an' no ring on her finger down our street at this very minute. I was luckier than most, for my man came back and wed me. And I lived tae regret that an' all.'

Bryce came home in March, changed in a way that worried Caitlin.

'War's bound to mature him,' Kirsty soothed when her daughter tried to explain her thoughts. 'He went away a laddie and now he's a man.'

As Caitlin saw it, Bryce had hardened rather than matured, spending his afternoons in public houses and complaining because she was unable to be with him every evening. 'It's not as if I'm home for long,' he girned. 'If Alex had only got the mill and Todd had taken charge there—'

'And if the moon was only made of cheese we could toast it for our suppers every night,' Caitlin said, exasperated. 'Nobody can turn the clock back, Bryce. Things are as they are and we'll just have to wait to find what the future holds.'

'I want my future tae hold you. Come to think of it, I want tae hold you right now,' he said, wrapping her tightly in his arms and locking his mouth onto hers. He had drawn her round a street corner and into the deep shadow of a factory wall where even the thin pale light from the street lamps couldn't reach. At first she responded, then as he tried to back her against the brick wall she began to struggle, for even his kisses were different. Bryce had always been demanding, but now it was as though his sole intention was to pleasure himself, with no regard for her feelings at all. When he paid no attention to her struggles but only pinned her body closer to his with one arm while his other hand began to grope and knead, she fought back in earnest, finally managing to force him away.

'Now what's botherin' ye?'

'For pity's sake, man,' she said when she could speak, 'what has the army done to you?'

'What d'ye mean?'

'You're . . . different.'

'Of course I'm different! So would you be if ye'd lived in muck and filth and seen what I've seen. Come here.' He made another grab for her, then swore as she danced back, out of reach. 'You think I'm the only one that's changed? Look at you, all mealy-mouthed and "don't touch",' he jeered, his voice harsh and ugly. 'Is that any way for a woman tae behave when her man's back from the fightin'?'

'You're not my man, Bryce Caldwell!'

'Then who is?' His hand shot out and seized her wrist, the fingers digging in as he dragged her close. 'Who's been pleasurin' ye while my back was turned?'

'Nobody. I don't need to have a man in my life.'

Bryce laughed shortly, 'Of course women need men – what else are they for?' he asked. Then, breathing cheap whisky fumes into her face, he said, 'It's not thon Highlander, is it? Thon weaver?'

'It's not anyone!'

'I've heard about him, still hiding behind his loom, hopin' that the army never sends for him, takin' advantage of lassies whose men've gone to fight for them.' He was close enough now for his spittle to moisten her dry lips. 'If he's been puttin' his filthy hands on ye, he'll . . .' The words became a wet mumble as his mouth smothered hers again, his tongue probing deeper until she felt herself choking.

The need to gulp in air was great enough to give her fresh strength; recalling a crude piece of advice she had once heard Grace give to the younger seamstresses, Caitlin brought one knee up sharply between his thighs. He gave a muffled exclamation then staggered a few steps along the length of the wall before fetching up against its bricks, clutching at his groin.

'Bitch,' he choked, his back to her. 'Fuckin' wee bitch!' Then she heard the splatter of liquid on the ground as he vomited up his afternoon's drinking spree.

'Bryce . . .' She was more frightened for him than for herself now, convinced that she had done him terrible harm.

'Get away from me!' As he swung round on her the moon appeared from behind a cloud; in its light, still crouched over, eyes glaring and a thread of mucus drooling from his lips, he looked like some misshapen goblin. 'Get out of my sight before I . . .'

She fled down the road and around the corner, and kept running until she reached Espedair Street, where she stopped before the tobacconist's shop, using the window as a mirror while she tidied her hair and scrubbed tears of fear from her cheeks.

Something moved behind her reflection, and she jumped back and spun round, fearful that Bryce had followed her and come up behind her. There was nobody there, and looking back at the window she realised that Annie Mitchell was standing in the darkened shop behind the banked shelves of pipes and packets, watching her with cold eyes.

Her heart thundering, Caitlin turned away and hurried across the street, grateful when she went into the house to find that the others had gone to bed.

Kirsty had left a stone bottle in her bed; it was comfortably warm beneath her bare feet, but even so Caitlin shivered beneath the blankets for some time

before falling into a restless sleep, plagued by dreams
of Bryce chasing her through cobbled streets while
Annie Mitchell watched from darkened windows, her
eyes flat and dead.

Caitlin plucked up the courage next day to ask Grace,
under the roar of the sewing machines, whether she
might have done Bryce a serious injury.

'Ye mean ye . . . ?' Beneath the shelter of the cutting
table, where they were both working, the older woman
lifted one knee slightly. 'Ye did that tae a man?' When
Caitlin nodded, biting her lip, Grace gave a shriek of
laughter.

'What're you talkin' about?' Iris asked at once, while
Lizzie, always ready for a gossip, stilled her machine.

'Nothin' at all – get on with yer work,' Grace
snapped, and they obeyed, exchanging exasperated
glances, as she went on, low voiced. 'I never thought
ye had it in ye, hen. Ye're such a prim wee thing.'

'I had to do something. But now I wish I hadn't, for
he was in terrible pain.'

Grace's large plain face began to break up, and she
turned away hastily, a hand to her mouth and her
shoulders shaking. 'Sometimes,' she said when the
bout of laughter was over and she had turned back
to the table, 'ye have tae dae more than keep yer hand
over yer ha'penny.' She picked up the cutting shears
and began to slide them deftly through the material on
the table. 'Ye did the right thing, hen, for at times like
that we've got tae put ourselves first.'

'Mebbe I should go and see him after work to make
sure he's all right.'

'You keep away,' Grace ordered at once. 'If ye go
tae him all worried in case he's been hurt, he'll just try
tae take advantage again. He'll be fine. A nudge wi'

a knee can bring tears tae a man's eyes, but they're made of strong stuff – more's the pity. He'll be fine,' she repeated reassuringly. 'The only thing is, ye'll no' be able tae catch him unawares again. Next time he'll be ready for ye, so ye'd best watch yersel'.'

'I'll not be going out with him again.'

'Best not,' Grace said briskly. 'Not unless he's the one ye want.'

As usually happened these days, Caitlin worked late at the fashion house, walking back home through the busier streets and avoiding dark corners just in case Bryce was looking for her. She arrived home to find Murdo Guthrie in the kitchen, holding a reddened cloth to his face while Kirsty attended to a cut on his forehead and Mary fussed round the stove. Rowena was leaning on the weaver's knee, anxiously staring up into his face, and the room smelled strongly of carbolic.

'It's nothing much,' Kirsty said as soon as her daughter came in. 'It looks worse than it is. Hold still now,' she added sharply, clapping Murdo's hand back in place as he tried to remove the pad covering his nose. 'Fetch some fresh water, will you, Caitlin? Someone found him just round the corner,' she went on as Caitlin took the basin from the table and emptied the bloodied water down the sink, then refilled it with hot water from the kettle. 'They brought him here, since they knew he worked in the weaving shop. Mary, I'll need another clean rag and you can bring the vinegar bottle while you're at it.'

Caitlin cooled the basin's steaming contents with water from the tap and took it over to the table. Beneath his tumble of dark hair, Murdo's face – what she could see of it – was ashen. One eyelid was swelling and blackening, and blood still welled from the deep cut Kirsty was attending to just above his brow. Caitlin, remembering the days when Alex and Ewan used to come home from play covered in scrapes and bruises, took the bottle and clean rag from Mary and shook vinegar over the rag before applying it to the swollen eyelid.

'Not a sign of anyone, but I didnae expect them tae hang about,' Todd announced from the back door. 'How are ye, lad?' He laid aside the stout walking stick he had been carrying and came over to inspect the patient.

'I'm fine.' Murdo's voice was thick and muffled. Despite Kirsty's protestations, he sat upright, pushing the ministering hands aside and taking the bloodied cloth from his nose. At the sight of his face, Rowena began to cry. 'I'm fine,' he insisted again through swollen lips, speaking directly to her, putting one finger beneath her chin so that her face was tilted up towards his. 'See? I've still got two eyes and a nose and a mouth.'

'Mebbe so, but they've a right second-hand look to them,' Kirsty said bluntly. 'You've taken a terrible thrashin'.'

He had. His nostrils were crusted with blood. There was another cut and a livid bruise along the cheekbone below his blackening eye, and a nasty raw scrape across the opposite cheek from ear to jawline, as though that side of his face had been rubbed along rough ground. Caitlin exclaimed at the sight of him.

'Have ye still got yer teeth?' Todd asked. The weaver nodded. 'And what about yer ribs?' Murdo put a hand to his chest and nodded again.

'Then ye'll live – unless ye get smothered tae death by the womenfolk,' Todd added as Kirsty began to protest. 'Ye've done all that needed doin', lass. What he needs now's a dram.'

'A cup of tea would be better.'

'With split lips?' Todd said from the cupboard where he kept his precious bottle of whisky. 'He'll no' be able tae take hot liquid.'

He poured a generous dram for Murdo and one for himself.

Kirsty, concerned about Rowena's schooling the next day, persuaded her to go to bed.

'You'll fetch me in the morning for school?' the child asked Murdo as Mary led her to the hall door. He nodded.

'If you're not up to it, I'll take her,' Caitlin said, and he looked levelly at her with his one good eye and said, 'I'll manage.'

When Murdo had downed his drink and Kirsty had bandaged the cut on his head, which was still bleeding, he got to his feet. Caitlin noticed him wince, and Todd wanted to walk with him to his lodgings, 'just in case'. But Murdo refused the offer.

'Did you see the way he got up from the chair? I don't doubt there's a rib or mebbe two been cracked for all that he said no,' Kirsty fretted when he had gone. 'Who could have done such a thing to the poor man?'

'It was mebbe a thief,' Mary suggested, and Todd gave a derisive snort.

'It took more than one man tae dae that tae a big laddie like Guthrie. Anyway, who'd want tae steal from him? A blind man could tell that he's not got more than a penny or two in his pockets.'

Todd was right. Murdo's clothes were always clean, but they were shabby.

'Come on now,' Todd urged his womenfolk, 'it's

time we were all in bed. We've had more than enough excitement for the one night.'

For the second night in a row, Caitlin found it hard to sleep. Kirsty's 'Who could have done such a thing to the poor man?' echoed in her skull over and over again.

She thought that she knew the answer, and hoped that she was wrong.

17

After some coaxing, Rowena agreed on the following morning to let Caitlin walk with her to school, but only on the assurance, made with crossed fingers, that Murdo, who she accepted needed to rest his poor sore face, would be waiting for her as usual by the school gate in the afternoon. When they went into the pend and found him waiting there, Rowena gave a whoop of joy and ran forward to throw her arms about his legs.

His face reminded Caitlin of the colourful map of the world that had hung in her school classroom. His left eye and the cheekbone below were badly swollen and bruised, and the scrape on the right side of his face was now an angry scarlet. He had washed his face and taken the bandage from his forehead to reveal a blood-encrusted gash that still looked nasty, and as he untangled Rowena from his legs, Caitlin saw that the knuckles of both hands were scraped and bruised.

'Are you all right?'

'I'm fine.' The expected words were spoken through swollen and broken lips. 'Come on now, you'll be late for school.' He gave the child a slight push towards the pend entrance, but instead of running ahead as she usually did, she put one hand in his and they walked out onto the pavement together.

At midday Caitlin took time she could ill afford from her work and walked swiftly to the street where Bryce lived with his parents and a clutch of younger brothers and sisters. The tenements here were old, and the close smelled sour and stale. As she climbed the stairs she saw that here and there on the small-paned landing window cardboard had been wedged into the square frames. The windows must have been broken some time before, because most of the cardboard patches were soggy.

Mrs Caldwell's eyes widened then almost immediately hardened as she recognised her visitor. 'It's you,' she said flatly. 'What d'ye want?'

Once or twice when she and Bryce had been walking out together in the innocent days before the war, this woman had made Caitlin welcome when she'd visited the flat. Now it was clear from her belligerent stance and the way her body barred the entrance to the flat that she knew of the quarrel between Caitlin and her son.

'Is Bryce in?'

'Mebbe.' Although it was after noon, Mrs Caldwell's hair was still entwined in paper curlers. After a night's sleep, some of them had almost unwound themselves and clung precariously to the ends of her hair. The large floral apron that almost engulfed her skinny body was badly in need of washing, and a cigarette heavy with ash hung between two nicotine-brown fingers.

'I want to talk to him.'

'I didnae say he was in, I just said mebbe. And if he is, mebbe he doesnae want tae talk tae you. It's a fine thing,' the woman had got over the surprise of seeing Caitlin and was snatching at the chance to air her grievances, 'when a laddie that's volunteered tae fight for his king and country comes home tae find that his wee sweetheart doesnae even want tae know him!'

'Mrs Caldwell—'

'Think yersel' better than us now, dae ye, just because ye've found work in that fancy clothes shop down by the river? Well let me tell you, milady . . .'

The ash on the end of her cigarette tumbled onto the faded linoleum floor as Bryce, in a singlet and trousers with the braces dangling round his hips, shouldered her aside.

'What d'ye want?' He put both hands on the door-frame, his burly body all but hiding his small, skinny mother from view.

'Whatever it is, ye're no' bringin' her intae this house,' she quacked from beneath his arm. 'I say who comes in here, and she's no'—'

'Shut it,' Bryce said quite pleasantly, his bloodshot eyes still fixed on Caitlin. He reeked of stale drink from the night before, and he had been in a fight; she noticed that the brow above one eye was thick with congealed blood and a blue knot disfigured his jawline beneath the stubble on his unshaven chin. The big hands he rested on the doorframe were skinned at the knuckles, like Murdo Guthrie's.

'Away an' make us a cup of tea,' he commanded his mother. As she slunk away he eased his body slightly to one side. 'Come on in.'

In order to accept the invitation Caitlin would have had to squeeze past him, ducking beneath a hairy armpit. She shook her head. 'I've not got much time, Bryce. I just wanted to know why you and your friends attacked Murdo Guthrie last night.'

His eyes widened in mock surprise. 'The High-lander? Did someone give him a beating? Oh my,' he said, unable to hide a smirk.

'You know very well that he got a beating, and one he didn't deserve.' She clenched her fists tightly by her sides. 'I came here to tell you what I told you already, though it seems you didn't understand me. I've not been walking out with Murdo or with anyone else, and even if I was it's no longer any of your business. So you can just leave him alone in future.'

'I've not laid a finger on the man!'

'No? Then what happened to your face and hands?'

'My . . . ?' he looked at his hands, then stuck them into the waistband of his trousers. 'Nothin' happened,' he said swiftly, then wheedled, 'Ach, Caitlin, come on in and have a cup of tea and we'll go back tae the way we were.'

'I'm not coming in today or any other day, Bryce. I've finished with you once and for all – and you just leave innocent folk alone or I'll get my stepfather to you,' she said in a rush of words, then turned and fled down the stairs, fully expecting him to follow. Instead, he shouted 'Fuck you, you bitch!' after her and slammed the door with a crash that must have shaken the nails half out of the hinges.

One of the doors in the close creaked open as she reached the bottom of the stairs, and she caught sight of a waxen face peering from the gloom beyond the gap. Just as she gained the pavement a window somewhere above squeaked open, and a sudden avalanche of water crashed onto the pavement to her left, splashing her skirt, ankles and feet. As she whirled round, a knife bounced on the flagstones dangerously close to her shoe then clattered into the gutter. Potato peelings and several whole potatoes, some peeled and some still in their jackets, littered the wet pavement.

'Ye daft lummox!' she heard Mrs Caldwell screech

from above her head. 'That's the dinner ye're throwin' out of the windae!'

'Bitch!' Bryce's infuriated roar drowned out his mother's voice. The window slammed down, and Caitlin took to her heels and ran, her breath catching in her throat. She didn't stop until she was near enough to the river to feel safe, then she halted to put her hat straight and examine her skirt and stockings. The water splashes had dried during her headlong flight. During the rest of the walk back to Harlequin she kept breaking into giggles as she played the scene back in her mind. She longed to tell Grace all about it, but at the same time she knew that she couldn't. It would never do for Grace or anyone else to know that Harlequin's dress designer had just had a basinful of dirty water and potato peelings thrown at her.

Alex was furious when he discovered, on questioning his housekeeper, that Fiona had been in the habit of calling at his flat while he was out.

'I thought there was no harm in it since she's your sister,' the woman protested. 'She just wants to make sure that you have all you need, and she only stays for the time it takes to drink a cup of tea.'

'Even so, I would prefer it, Mrs Harkins, if nobody was allowed in while I'm absent.'

'And how am I to tell Mrs Chalmers that she's not to be allowed into her own brother's home?'

'I'll tell her myself, and I'll see to it that you're not troubled again,' Alex assured her grimly.

'Mrs Chalmers is in the dining room, sir,' the maid said when he arrived at his father's the following afternoon, assured that Angus was at the emporium. 'She's entertaining her sewing circle ladies.'

He had forgotten about the women's groups Fiona had organised to knit and sew clothing for the troops.

'How much longer will they be here, Ellen?'

'Only another five minutes, sir.'

'Then I'll wait in my father's study and you can tell Mrs Chalmers that—'

'Who is it, Mary?' Fiona called from the dining-room door. 'My goodness – Alex!' She came into the hall. 'What a pleasant surprise.'

'I've just heard that you're entertaining friends. I'll wait in the study until they've gone.'

'Not at all.' She took a firm grip on his arm. 'You must come and bid them good afternoon. They were just about to leave in any case. Ellen, we'll have more tea in the drawing room when the ladies have gone, if you please.'

The eight or nine women gathered round the dining-room table clucked and fussed like a hutful of hens when he was thrust unwillingly into their midst. 'Such a treat to speak to a young man these days,' one middle-aged woman gushed at him. 'So many of them are away now.'

'It's becoming quite impossible to arrange a decent party, let alone a dance,' complained another. 'I'm at my wits' end wondering how I'll ever manage to give Kate a decent eighteenth birthday party.'

'There's a war on, Margaret,' a white-haired woman dressed all in black boomed across the table. 'Our very lives are at stake, and the country has more to do than mess about with birthday parties!'

Margaret bridled. 'I'm quite aware that we're at war, Janet, but it seems wrong to deny Kate when both her sisters had such fine eighteenth birthday parties. If I could only be sure of exactly when her cousins expect to be home on furlough it would help. Officers have very smart uniforms . . .' Her voice trailed off as the white-haired woman gave her a scathing look, then turned to fix her eyes on Alex.

'While we work at our sewing we like to discuss the latest news, Mr MacDowall. Just before you came in, we were discussing the struggle to gain ground at Ypres. A sorry business!'

'It is indeed.'

'Have you yourself enlisted, Mr MacDowall?'

'Father needs Alex here,' Fiona said at once. 'And my dear husband, George, is already representing the family somewhere at sea.' She bit her lip and added in a lowered voice, 'I can scarcely sleep at nights for worrying about his safety.' Then, acknowledging the murmurs of sympathy with a delicate inclination of the head, she said, 'I couldn't bear it if I had to fret over Alex as well.'

The older woman tightened her lips and said nothing more, but Alex could read her thoughts as clearly as he had read the thoughts of most of the folk he had encountered over the past seven months – a fit young man like himself should be in uniform instead of lurking around at home.

The group broke up almost immediately after that, despite Fiona's protests. Alex helped to gather up sewing bags, materials, scissors and tapes, then to hunt for elusive needles, pins and reels of thread that had rolled beneath the furniture.

'So kind,' the woman who had been addressed as Margaret murmured as he handed over a long and lethal needle he had found on the seat of the chair his father normally used. 'You must come to Kate's birthday party.'

When Fiona came back from seeing them out she closed the door and leaned back against it, smiling at him. 'I thought they would never go! Shall we go into the drawing room? Our tea will be served in a moment.'

'I must get back to the store. I just came to say that I would appreciate it, Fiona, if you would stay away from my flat in future.'

'Oh dear.' Her eyes mocked him. 'I rather enjoyed talking to your housekeeper. Do you feel that I get in her way?'

'Not hers, mine. I had already noticed on more than one occasion that papers and files on my writing desk had been disturbed. I presume that that was you?'

She shrugged. 'You don't keep anything private in there, do you? Only papers to do with the store and the factory. And as Papa's daughter, I have every right to look at them.'

'Not when you're doing it behind my back.'

'Are you frightened, Alex?'

'Frightened?'

'In case I try to take the business away from you.'

'Don't be ridiculous!'

Fiona was still leaning against the door, her hands tucked behind her back. Today, in deference to the war work being carried out by the group, she wore a demure white broderie anglaise blouse and plain green skirt. The simple outfit made her look very young and innocent, but the gleam in her eyes belied the overall picture.

'I'm so glad that I've had the opportunity to meet your sister Caitlin again and to make Rose Hamilton's acquaintance. I admire Rose in particular, for she has no need to earn her living and yet there she is, doing so well. You like Rose's spirit too, don't you, Alex? I could tell by the way you looked at her at our New Year party.' She waited, then as Alex said nothing, went on,

'Some men would find her rather too bold, but not you, or John Brodie. He adores her. They would make a very suitable couple.'

'I've told Mrs Harkins that you are not to be admitted to my flat when I'm out. I trust you won't embarrass her by trying to gain entrance.'

'I wouldn't dream of it. After all, Mrs Harkins is a working woman too. This very afternoon we were talking about how this war has resulted in women taking over men's work. I'm quite sure that running a large furniture store must be easier than carrying coal or operating machinery in a factory.'

The maid tapped at the door. 'I've put the tea tray in the drawing room, Mrs Chalmers.'

'Thank you, Ellen.'

'You must drink it on your own, Fiona. I have to get back to work.' Alex swept past the two women and let himself out, slashing angrily at the shrubbery with his stick as he strode down the short driveway.

'The truth of the matter,' John Brodie told his fellow partners bluntly, 'is that Harlequin is in difficulties.'

It was mid-May. Caitlin, looking through the upper part of the nearest window at small white clouds floating in blue sky, had been fretting over a report in Todd's newspaper that the Germans had started wafting clouds of chlorine gas towards the British lines. Ever since, she had been wondering fearfully if Bryce was among those men choking and blinded by it. It was terrible to think of someone she knew suffering like that.

John's words brought her back to Paisley with a bump that made her heart lurch. 'You mean that we might have to close Harlequin down?'

'That's exactly what I mean.' He spread his hands

wide to indicate the building around and above them. 'When this place opened for business you both knew that there was very little money left. You've done well to keep it going for over a year – mainly because you've taken very little out of it, Rose.'

'The important thing is to repay Kirsty and Todd. I can afford to wait until we're bringing in more money.'

'But you shouldn't have to.' Caitlin felt guilty at taking a wage when her partner didn't, but unlike Rose she wasn't living with wealthy parents.

'Caitlin's right. All you're doing at the moment, Rose, is playing at running a fashion house.' John hastily lifted both hands, palms out, as she turned on him. 'You can bluster all you like, but you have to face the truth. If Harlequin can't support its staff, including you, while at the same time repaying investors, then it might as well close down.'

'No!'

'You knew at the beginning what you were taking on. You can't run away from it now.'

'But we've got as many orders as we can cope with.' Caitlin's mouth was dry at the prospect of failure. 'I often have to work into the evenings, and so do the women upstairs. In fact, I was about to ask if we could employ another seamstress.'

John shook his head. 'We couldn't possibly afford to meet her wages. You must understand that business consists of balancing outgoing costs against income. There must always be more coming in than there is going out. Unfortunately in your case you have to pay for your materials before you can make the garments, and you must pay your bills promptly if you want the warehouse to go on providing materials. Your clients, on the other hand, are under no such obligation to you.'

Rose began to pace the floor. 'But there must be something we can do.'

John tapped the end of his pencil on the table as he studied the rows of figures before him. 'Could you buy cheaper materials?'

'If we do that we'll lose orders,' Caitlin said at once. 'The women we cater for won't accept anything but the best.' Car tyres crunched on the gravel outside and she jumped to her feet. 'That's Miss Langmuir for her fitting. I must go.'

Rose continued her pacing when Caitlin had gone. 'John, there must be something I can do!'

She was wearing one of Caitlin's designs, a high-waisted costume with a wrapover skirt draped with such skill that, though narrow, it allowed the freedom of movement Rose needed. Caitlin had scoured Glasgow's shops to find the right material, silk patterned with varying shades of green in such a way that the suit seemed to flow around its wearer's long slim body. She looked, John thought as he watched her, as though she was walking in a forest with dappled sunlight shining on her through the trees. Then he coloured slightly, embarrassed by such poetic, unlawyerlike thoughts, and sat upright, riffling through the papers before him.

'You could let me put more money into the business.'

'No.'

'Why not? I could afford enough to help you over this patch.'

'I don't want the responsibility of using your money.'

'You keep telling me that I'm too stuffy,' John pointed out. 'I believe that I would rather enjoy taking a risk. Not that it would be, since I have every confidence in your ability. If I hadn't, I would never have agreed to you buying the mill in the first place.'

'You had little choice,' Rose told him dryly, 'since my heart was set on the place from the moment I saw it.'

'Will you accept my offer?'

She reached the window and turned, her silk jacket and skirt swirling about her body. 'I'd worry about you losing your money because of my hot-headedness,' she said, and John took a deep breath.

'If you married me it would be our money, and I could keep a closer watch on how it's spent.'

Rose stared at him for a long moment. 'That's the most unlawyerlike thing I've ever heard!'

'I mean it.'

'You can't possibly!'

'I most certainly can. Dammit it, Rose, I'm twenty-nine years of age, a bachelor in my right mind.' It was his turn to get up and start pacing, while she stood rooted to the spot. 'And I've just asked you to marry me. Why won't you take me seriously?'

'But you're . . . we're . . . friends,' Rose said feebly.

'We used to be friends, after we became business partners. Now we've – I've – moved on. I've been wanting to propose to you for weeks now . . . months.'

Rose looked about her, as though seeking help, then said, 'But the thought of us marrying is preposterous!'

'Why? Am I so unlikeable?'

'Of course not, it's me. Why should anyone want to marry me?'

'Because . . . for God's sake, woman,' John said angrily, 'don't ask such stupid questions. I want to marry you because I happen to love you. And before you say I can't love you, I can. I can do anything I want.'

'And so can I.'

'So . . . you're turning me down.'

She spread her hands out helplessly. 'John, I don't want to marry anyone.'

'I see.' He began to gather up his papers. 'I'll still lend you the money, of course.'

'I couldn't let you do that.'

John stuffed the papers willy-nilly into his briefcase and snatched up his hat and cane. 'Sometimes, Rose,' he said without looking at her, 'you infuriate me!'

18

True to her word, Fiona didn't call at Alex's flat again, but she did start visiting the store every day, working her way through one department after another, getting to know the staff and meeting some of the customers. She spent entire mornings in the offices and questioned Alex and his father at the dinner table during their Friday evening meetings. Angus was pleased with her interest.

'She never used to bother her head about the place,' he told Alex over their after-dinner brandies, 'but she's older now, of course, and no doubt marriage and learning how to run a household have given her an insight into the value of money. In any case, it keeps her occupied and takes her mind off fretting over George, so we must encourage it.'

Early in May the Cunard liner *Lusitania* had been sunk by torpedoes with great loss of civilian lives, and those few people who still clung to the notion that the war would be brief began to realise they they were mistaken.

Alex knew utter despair as he read about the drowning of innocent men, women and children. It wasn't just his own life that had fallen apart, but the entire world. Only the day before he had had to visit the confused and bewildered mother of a former employee of his furniture factory, a cheerful apprentice who had been among the first to enlist, convinced that after a few months in uniform he would be back at the workbench, a hero in the eyes of his less courageous mates. Instead he was lying in some makeshift grave in France. Alex had taken the mother a sum of money donated by those who had worked with the boy and a larger sum from himself and his father.

'Enough tae pay for a decent burial,' the woman had said when he'd spread the notes and coins before her, 'except that I don't think we're goin' tae be allowed tae bury him, for this is all they've sent me.' She'd indicated some possessions lying on a table by the window – cigarettes, matches, an open razor-blade, a notebook, some well-handled letters and, most poignant of all, it seemed to Alex, a clean, folded handkerchief.

'He was just seventeen,' she'd said, over and over again.

'Can we do anything to help you?'

She'd shaken her head. 'Not unless ye can turn the clock back . . .' Her voice had trailed away, but the red, swollen eyes raised to his face had asked why he was standing before her while her boy's lifeless body lay in another country, denied the comfort of being buried by the folk who had known and loved him.

It was a look that Alex had even begun to see when he looked into his own shaving mirror in the mornings. He could no longer believe that his father had more need of him than his country had. He finished reading about the *Lusitania*, folded his newspaper, went to the nearest recruiting office and enlisted.

He told nobody what he had done but began to spend what time he had left making sure that the factory supervisor knew enough about the business to look after it in his absence and that everything he had been dealing with in the store was in safe hands.

Early in June Fiona received word that her husband's ship had put in at Portsmouth and left hurriedly to spend some time with him before he returned to sea. The day after she left, Alex's papers arrived. He told his father first.

'Aye, well, I knew it was bound to happen sooner rather than later,' Angus said heavily, 'though I'd hoped that it would have been a while yet.'

'This war's dragging on too long, Father. There's no sense in fooling ourselves any longer that it's going to end soon. Best get over there and get on with it.'

'Aye, I suppose so.' Although they admired and trusted each other, Angus MacDowall and his son had never been close, probably because Alex had been a grown man by the time they'd found each other, and a harsh childhood and youth followed by a long, hard struggle to improve himself had leached away any emotions that Angus might once have had. There must have been some warmth there once, Alex sometimes thought, looking at his father's stern, lined face, for how else had he himself come into the world? His mother was a warm, caring woman, and the Angus she had known all those years ago must also have had warmth; Alex couldn't imagine her giving herself to a cold and unloving man.

Kirsty must have known the best of Angus MacDowall, but for Alex and Angus there were no memories of childhood and fatherhood to share and to bind them closer. All Angus's paternal love had gone to Fiona and was still hers.

It was a relief to both men when they were free to settle down to the practical side of things. Alex explained how he had left matters in the small factory and on his side of the store management.

'I'll go to Paisley tomorrow to see Todd and Murdo and my mother. Todd can run that side of the business easily enough, and I've arranged for the factory supervisor to keep in contact with him and with you.'

'Your mother'll be grieved.'

'Yes, she will.' Alex wasn't looking forward to breaking the news to her. 'But she's got Todd and Caitlin and Mary with her. She'll be fine.'

'Give her my regards when you see her. You'll have a dram . . .' Angus poured two generous tumblerfuls of malt whisky and raised his glass to his son. 'To your health, and to your safe return.'

'To the end of the war,' Alex acknowledged. They were in Angus's small study, the room he preferred to use when on his own in the house. Angus stared into the fire he always insisted on having, even in warm weather, then said after a long pause, 'It's too bad that Fiona's away. You'll not have the chance to say goodbye to her.'

'You can do that for me.'

'It's a blessing that Fiona's been taking such an interest in the business,' Angus said. 'She'll mebbe be able to help out a bit while you're away. And it'll give her something to do.'

Alex went to Paisley the following afternoon, when he was certain that the house would be empty and Todd closeted in the workshop at the end of the yard. He went straight to the weaving shop, where Murdo worked at his loom, and tested the new cloth between finger and thumb, enjoying as always the texture of strong, well-woven material. 'It's good.'

'They're coming for it tomorrow afternoon. I'd

already decided to work on tonight, so you can be sure it'll be finished in time.'

'That's not what I came about.' Alex pushed his hands into his pockets. 'I came to bid you goodbye, for I've enlisted.'

The Highlander turned to sit sideways on the saytree, facing his employer. 'I thought it would come to it.'

'I knew it must, sooner or later. I go tomorrow.'

'So soon? Have you told your mother?'

'Not yet. I'll come back tonight to see her and the others. I don't want you to say anything in the meantime.'

Murdo nodded. 'Am I to go on with the weaving?'

'Of course. Our customers have been pleased with their chair coverings, and Todd and Jock Beaton from the Glasgow factory'll let you know what's wanted. I've told my father that you'll be here for as long as you can.'

'You know that I'll certainly not be enlisting like yourself.'

'I'd not expect you to, Murdo. You stay here for as long as you like – or as long as you can.' Alex took a bottle from his pocket. 'I thought you might drink my health before I go.'

'It would be an honour, Mr MacDowall.' Murdo got up and went to a shelf at the back of the weaving shop.

'Alex,' Alex corrected him.

The weaver, returning with a tin mug in one hand and a china mug in the other, gave him a long steady look. 'As I've said before, I'm not comfortable with calling my employer by his given name. I'd as soon stay as I am.'

'You're a stubborn man, Murdo Guthrie.'

A faint smile flitted across Murdo's broad face. 'I've

been told that many a time.' He held the mugs steady while Alex poured the amber liquid into them, then offered him the china mug. Alex studied the farmyard scene painted on it with raised eyebrows.

'It's Rowena's mug,' the Highlander explained. 'She likes to keep it here for when we have a wee drink of tea.' He raised his tin cup to Alex and said something in Gaelic. 'That's a wish that the world treats you well and sends you homeward at the end of the day.'

Alex nodded and drank. 'Rowena's not getting in your way?'

'Oh no, I like to hear her talk and see her wee face about the place.'

'My mother says she's doing well now. Caitlin says it's thanks to you.'

'I'd not say that at all.'

'That Highland dancing you introduced her to seems to have settled her.'

'She's a rare wee dancer, and she loves the ceilidhs. She's doing fine at the school, too.' Murdo paused, then said carefully, 'I know that she seems difficult at times, but she's known more hardship than a bairn of her age should be expected to carry.'

Alex nodded. 'We can just hope that she has a better life to come.'

'Oh, she'll see to that.' The smile crossed Murdo's face again. 'She's got a strong will, has Rowena, and a determination that'll stand her in good stead throughout her life. It's just now, when she's wee and helpless, that she needs the strength of others.'

Alex left soon after and wandered round Paisley, revisiting old haunts. He walked along the banks of the River Cart until he had almost reached the old mill, then found a patch of shrubbery where he could watch without being seen. A car stood in the flagged forecourt, and after a while another drove in and a uniformed chauffeur helped two women out. They went into the building, then Rose Hamilton escorted another woman and a man out. They got into the car and she stood talking through the window for a few minutes. She was wearing a slim dark skirt and the long harlequin jacket Alex liked. When the car had gone, she stood for a moment, studying the outside of the building, then went back indoors.

He wandered into the town again and bought two pies, eating them while he walked back towards Carriagehill. The gates leading to the Hamiltons' long driveway were open, as always; Alex stepped inside and walked halfway to the house before stepping into the shrubbery. He leaned against a tree and waited, hearing the distant hooters of factories and mills marking the end of the working day. In the streets men and women would be hurrying along the pavements and queuing for trams and buses to take them home, but here it was peaceful, with only birdsong and an occasional rustle in the undergrowth. Time passed, but there was no sign of the bicycle Rose usually rode home from the fashion house. After a while, a motorcar turned in from the road, and Alex, recognising Mr Hamilton's car, peered through shielding branches to see if she was in it but could only make out one figure in the back seat. At last he made his way back down the drive and set out for Espedair Street.

Rowena had had a dancing lesson that day and came home impatient to show off her latest steps. After the evening meal, she coaxed Murdo from the weaving shop to play for her while she performed on her dancing stone. Shy though he was at being among them, he agreed on that particular night, and after

Todd had set chairs in the back yard for his wife and stepdaughters, the weaver came to the end of the pend, where he leaned against the wall.

Rowena seized the hem of her smock in both hands, her wrists delicately raised and fingers spread as she had been taught, and nodded at him. 'Now, Murdo.' He began to play, and she began to dance, twirling and spinning and leaping, light as thistledown and placing her feet, heel down and toe up, with practised precision.

There was no doubt that she could dance. Even Kirsty clapped enthusiastically when she had finished, and Rowena's grin almost split her small face in two.

'Another one, Murdo,' she called as the Highlander began to edge back towards the safety of his weaving shop.

'It's almost time for your bed,' Kirsty began.

'Please, just one more . . . please!'

Todd couldn't resist the pleading in Rowena's eyes and in her voice. 'It'll not hurt to let the bairn show us one more dance, Kirsty. It's a fine night tae sit out in – and ye've earned a rest, surely.'

It was a lovely evening. 'Just one more, then,' Kirsty agreed, and Rowena ran to drag Murdo back. This time, although the others watched Rowena again, Caitlin found her gaze travelling to Murdo. His waistcoat was unbuttoned, his shirt open at the collar, and his sleeves rolled up to above his elbows. His eyes were fixed on Rowena, but the lids drooped half over them, as though he was seeing other things besides the small figure dancing before him. His broad hands cupping the small mouth organ almost hid it from sight, and his fingers manipulated it deftly as he blew sweet music into it, music that she knew could change in an instant from merriment to sadness.

All too soon it came to an end and Rowena, after a final leap, drooped low on the flagstone in a graceful curtsey, accepting the flurry of applause just as Alex came through the pend and into their midst.

'A back yard concert, is it? You've got a fine night for it.'

'I'll get back to my work,' Murdo said, and was gone almost before the final word was out. Kirsty scooped Rowena into the house and her daughters followed, while Todd drew Alex down the yard and into the workshop to show him the work in progress.

Rowena was in her bed by the time the men came into the kitchen, Alex first and Todd following with an expression on his face that had Kirsty immediately demanding to know what was wrong.

'Nothing at all, Mam.'

'There is so. Todd Paget was never able to hide his thoughts.' She looked from one to the other. 'Is it the business? Has something gone wrong with it?'

'Ye'd best just tell her and get it over with, lad,' Todd advised his stepson, reaching as ever for his tobacco pouch.

'I've enlisted, Mam.'

Her face crumpled with shock. 'Oh, Alex! When d'you go? How long do we have you with us?'

'I've to report to Maryhill Barracks tomorrow.'

'Tomorrow?' Kirsty dropped into a chair, her hands to her mouth. 'So soon?'

'I've known for a week or two.'

'And you never said a word to us?' Mary asked in disbelief.

'I never said a word to anyone. I didn't want a fuss.'

'But . . . tomorrow! Oh, Alex!' Kirsty said, and burst into tears. He knelt by her side, pushing a handkerchief

215

into her hands, trying to soothe her, while Mary and Caitlin automatically set about making tea.

When it was ready, Todd announced that he had forgotten to do something in the workshop. 'Mebbe,' he said awkwardly to Mary and Caitlin, 'yer mother and Alex should have a wee minute tae themselves.'

They took the hint, carrying their cups into the front room, where Mary perched on the edge of Kirsty's good couch and Caitlin stood at the window, looking out at the folk who passed by, wondering what difference the war had made to their lives.

'How'll we manage without Alex?' Mary asked from behind her.

'It won't be for long. He'll come back soon.'

'I hope so,' Mary's voice, usually so confident, was small and wobbly. 'I know he's not been living here for a long time, but he was always here in spirit, if you know what I . . .' She began to sob, and Caitlin put her cup down on the sideboard, heedless for once about the danger of leaving a mark, and went to sit by her sister. 'How's Mam going to manage without him?' Mary sniffled damply into her shoulder. 'He was always her favourite. If anything happens to him I don't know what she'd—'

'Nothing's going to happen to him! Nothing could happen to Alex. Of course he'll come back!'

When Kirsty called them back into the kitchen her face was swollen, but her eyes were dry. 'Alex has to go back to Glasgow now. I'm walking to the station with him.'

'Me too,' Mary said quickly.

'I'll stay with Rowena, just in case she wakens,' Caitlin offered. Like the others, she desperately wanted to be with Alex until the last possible moment, but someone had to stay behind.

Her mother summoned up a grateful smile. 'I'd be happier in my mind if someone was here with her. Mary, go and fetch Todd, he'll want to come with us. I'll just go upstairs and get my good hat and coat,' she added as Mary darted into the hall for her jacket then hurried back through the kitchen and out into the yard, pushing her arms into the sleeves.

'What'll happen to Murdo with you gone?' Caitlin asked Alex.

'Nothing,' Alex said with some surprise. 'My father appreciates his worth as much as I do, so his job's safe.'

'Unless he goes into the war too.'

'He won't, unless he must. Murdo Guthrie and the army have little time for each other.'

'So you do know more about him than you've let on?'

He smiled faintly. 'Even if I do, it's still his business and not mine to go telling to folk.'

'Did he do wrong? Can you tell me that much?'

'He did nothing wrong,' Alex assured her, then spoiled things by adding, 'not in my eyes, at least.'

'What about Rose?' she remembered suddenly.

His eyelids flickered, then stilled. 'What about her?'

'Are you going away without a word to her?'

'I'm certainly not going to her house with her parents there.'

'She's not at home tonight,' Caitlin suddenly remembered. 'John called for her at the fashion house. The two of them were going to his parents' house for their evening meal, then to a meeting in the town hall.'

'In that case you'll just have to tell her tomorrow.'

'D'you want me to give her a message?'

'You could tell her that . . .' Alex began, then

stopped. 'Just say that I hope Harlequin continues to do well, for both your sakes.'

Kirsty came in, dressed in her best hat and coat, her eyes bleak but her head held high, just as Todd and Mary arrived from the workshop. There was a last-minute flurry of goodbyes before they went out.

After they had gone, the kitchen seemed small and airless. Caitlin escaped into the yard for a breath of fresh air, walking over the grass to stand on the dancing stone where, less than an hour before, Rowena had been giving an impromptu concert and everything had been fine.

She tried a few tentative steps on the flagstone, then a few more. The lilt of Murdo's mouth organ came into her head, followed by the fine, clear notes of a fiddle then the rapid, light beat of the small drum.

Caitlin started dancing in earnest to the music in her head, her feet twisting and turning, heel and toe, her skirt flaring out around her as she spun and leaped, the tears on her uplifted face shining in the twilight.

19

―――――――――

'What do you mean, Alex has gone?'

'He's volunteered for the army.'

'So he'll still be in Glasgow for a few weeks before he goes.'

'Rose, he volunteered weeks ago and didn't tell anyone. We didn't know until he came to tell us last night that he goes today.'

Rose's eyes blazed like sapphires set in white satin. She snatched her hat from its peg and jammed it onto her head, then made for the door while still struggling to get into her coat. 'There's one appointment for this morning and another for early afternoon,' she said breathlessly. 'They're in the book on my desk, but you'll need to keep a lookout for them. They hate it when nobody's on hand to open the door when they arrive.'

'Where are you going?'

'To Glasgow, of course, to see Alex before he leaves.'

Caitlin pursued her into the foyer. 'It's no use, Rose. He had to report to the barracks first thing this morning.'

Rose, one hand outstretched to open the door, rounded on her. 'Are you telling me that he left without even saying goodbye to me?'

'He did ask if you were at home, but I knew that you'd gone out with John. He left a message for you.'

'What is it?'

'He . . . He hopes that Harlequin goes well,' Caitlin said, and watched a tide of red suddenly flame into Rose's ashen cheeks.

'Is that all?'

'He had very little time. And you know Alex, he hates a fuss.'

'Oh yes, I know Alex!' Rose almost threw herself past Caitlin and back into the office, tearing the coat off as she went. 'Alex, the friend who can't even take the trouble to say goodbye!' She tossed her coat at the stand and missed.

'Rose . . .' Caitlin gathered it up, and hung it on its peg, then picked up the hat that hurtled down at her feet. 'I'm sorry. I wish I'd insisted on getting a proper message from him.'

'It's not your fault, it's his!' Rose was staring at one of the walls, her arms clamped tightly across her chest, her back to Caitlin. 'Just . . . go and see that the women are getting on with their work, will you?'

It was a very difficult morning. The client who had insisted on being seen at exactly ten o'clock failed to turn up until twenty minutes to eleven and was dissatisfied with almost every aspect of the coat that was being made for her. Rose made matters worse by treating the woman with a brittle formality that almost ended in a quarrel between the two of them, only averted when Rose left, pleading essential work waiting to be done in the office. Once she had gone, it took Caitlin and Grace all their time to smooth the client's ruffled feelings and win her approval of the work they had already done.

'I'd as soon volunteer for the French trenches as for another morning like this,' Grace said flatly when Caitlin returned to the fitting room after seeing the woman out. 'What's the matter with Miss Hamilton?'

Caitlin, too weary to prevaricate, explained briefly about Alex's hurried visit the evening before. 'Rose was out, so he didn't see her to say goodbye.'

'Is that all?'

'They were good friends.'

Grace raised an eyebrow at her. 'More than friends, if she's that upset about him going.'

Caitlin sighed. 'There was a time when I thought they might mean more to each other, but ever since Alex wanted this place and Rose bought it instead, there's been a coolness between them.'

'On the surface, mebbe, but underneath that madam's coolness there's a furnace blazing, you mark my words. D'ye think he feels the same way about her?'

'It's hard to tell with Alex.'

'And what about Mr Brodie? He's near daft with love for her.'

'You think so?'

Grace gave her a pitying look. 'I know so. Down our street the folk live so close together that you cannae sneeze without your neighbour blowin' his nose. It gets so's it's easy to read faces and voices, whatever words they might be using. Who'd have thought a plain stick like Rose Hamilton would have two nice-lookin' men daft about her?'

Caitlin snapped out of her reverie about Rose and Alex when Todd said during the evening meal, 'Young Bryce Caldwell was at the workshop this afternoon.'

She felt a sudden nervous thrill run through her. 'Did he mention me at all?'

'He was too busy braggin' about him an' his mates in the trenches. A right hero, that one.' Todd shook his head tolerantly. 'If half of what he says is right, he'll have the Germans skelpin' back tae their mams by Christmas.' He helped himself to another slice of bread. 'An' the things they get up tae when they're allowed time off would make yer hair curl.'

'What sort of things?' Mary asked at once, and her mother glared at her then at Todd.

'Never you mind, miss – and we don't want to know, Todd Paget.'

'I wasnae goin' tae tell ye. He was makin' out that he's above the rest of us now that he's in uniform and trusted with a rifle, but come the end of the war he'll be in that yard, cap in hand, lookin' for his job back.'

'And lucky if he gets it, the cheeky wee upstart,' Kirsty snapped.

'Ach, there's no harm tae him or any of them. They've got tae keep their spirits up somehow, and sometimes braggin's the only way tae keep goin'.'

'Did he go into the weaving shop?' Caitlin wanted to know.

'I made certain tae walk with him tae the road when he left, just in case. I know you think it was him that attacked Murdo thon time, lass, but I'm not so certain of it. Still, I thought it best tae make sure he was off the premises.'

Caitlin saw Bryce once during his furlough, when he passed by on the other side of the road one evening when she was walking back from the fashion house. There was a girl with him, and when Bryce saw Caitlin he gave her a long hard stare then put his arm about his companion, pulling her tightly to him and nuzzling her ear. Possibly he wanted to show her that there were other, and more malleable, fish in the sea, but all she felt was that a weight had been lifted from her shoulders and that both she and Murdo were surely safe from Bryce's attentions in the future.

John Brodie enlisted in July and left Paisley almost at once. The day before he went, he and Rose were closeted for an entire afternoon in the small office going over all the Harlequin books, which John had brought with him.

'Keep an eye on Rose for me,' he said to Caitlin when he was saying goodbye. 'And try to prevent her from doing anything that might harm the business.'

'She wouldn't do that. She's just a bit impetuous at times.'

A shadow crossed John's face. 'Unfortunately not all the time,' he said enigmatically, and left.

Rose had remained in the office; when Caitlin went in she was sitting at the desk, her head in her hands. Caitlin thought for a moment that she was weeping, but when she looked up her eyes were dry.

'Has he gone?'

'Yes.'

Rose heaved a great sigh, then asked, 'Can I eat at your house tonight? My mama will be in a terrible pet, and I don't want to face her.'

'You know you're always welcome. What have you done to annoy her this time?'

'Sent John off to fight.'

Caitlin sat down suddenly. 'You told him to enlist?'

'Of course not. I don't even want him to go.' Rose sighed again, then said, 'You might as well know. John asked me to marry him and I refused. And I think that that's why he decided to enlist rather than wait to be called.'

'And your mother knows.'

'Unfortunately he told his mama, and she immediately told mine. Apparently she had set her heart on getting me off her hands and onto John's, and she's been going on about it ever since.' Rose thumped a fist on the desk. 'I really must try to find enough money to do up that gatehouse! But the only way I can do that is to let John invest more in Harlequin, and then I'd have to agree to marry him.'

Caitlin was scandalised. 'Are those his terms?'

'No, but how can I turn down his proposal and yet take his money? Oh, Caitlin, what a mess I've got myself into. And now,' Rose thumped her fist down again, this time onto the ledgers on the desk, 'I'm left with all these dratted books to see to!'

Fiona Chalmers came to Paisley to see Todd on her father's behalf and to order a new gown from Harlequin. When the design had been agreed and the materials chosen, Rose brought tea in. As soon as she set the tray down, Fiona jumped up and took both Rose's hands in hers.

'My dear, Caitlin has told me about John.'

Rose shot an astonished glance at Caitlin, who said hurriedly, 'I told Fiona that he had enlisted.'

'And so suddenly, too. You must miss him dreadfully.'

'No more than you must miss Alex.'

Fiona gave a musical little laugh. 'There's a difference. Alex is my brother, whereas John is—'

'A friend.' Rose freed her hands. 'Do you take milk?'

'Yes, I do.' Fiona stirred her tea, sipped delicately, then beamed at them both. 'I can't tell you how grateful I am to you.'

Caitlin and Rose exchanged puzzled glances. 'Grateful?'

'Now that Alex has gone, it falls to me to help my father in his business. And I could never have found the courage to do that if I hadn't met you and seen this place.' A sweep of a gloved hand indicated the building around them. 'I told myself that if you two could become businesswomen, then I could too. And I've found that it can be very soothing to have something positive to occupy one's mind at a time of such worry. This war has been a blessing to women.'

'I doubt if women with families to raise and no man to support them would agree with you,' Rose said dryly.

'I'm talking about women like us, who have been set free to find their real potential.' She beamed from one to the other. 'Life will never be the same for us again, and that, I believe, can be nothing but a blessing.'

'The more I see of Fiona, the more I dislike her,' Rose said ten minutes later as they stood together on the steps watching Fiona leave for Espedair Street. 'She makes me itch.'

'She's a good customer.' Caitlin waved as Fiona's hand fluttered a farewell through the open car window.

'Don't you think that there's a sly look about her? She reminds me of a cat that's found all the cream and lapped up every drop.'

'You're being unfair!'

'Mebbe so.' Rose turned back into the building. 'But when I look into those wide, innocent eyes of hers, I get the feeling that she's up to something, and that whoever gets hurt, it won't be Mrs Fiona Chalmers.'

Caitlin arrived home that evening to find an air of mourning about the kitchen. Kirsty looked upset. Todd, who was usually the last to arrive home after work, was sitting at the kitchen table with a face like a thundercloud.

'Thon Fiona Chalmers was in today.'

'I know, she came to Harlequin to order a gown. Did she find fault with the workshop?'

'No, she seemed satisfied enough with that . . . for the moment at least. But she's turned Murdo Guthrie off.'

'What?'

'Told him and me that MacDowalls' can't afford their own weaver and from now on they'll be buyin' their cloth from a factory.'

'After the man stayin' up half the night to finish off the cloth he was working on so that the order'd be ready in good time,' said Kirsty, who had changed her opinion of the weaver.

'But what'll Murdo do now?' Caitlin asked.

'God knows. I cannae take him on for her father's my employer too.'

'We must write to Alex.'

'What can he do, away in England? In any case, it seems that the lassie's got Angus MacDowall's permission to do as she pleases.'

'What about Rowena?' It was the school holidays, and the little girl had spent the day at the shop with Kirsty.

'She's upstairs, putting her doll into a wee dress Teenie made for it today. She doesn't know yet, and I'm dreading the moment when she finds out.'

'I'll fetch her down and tell her in the weaving shop,' Caitlin offered.

The former storeroom in the pend was empty, the loom bare. On the shelf where Murdo's battered tin cup and Rowena's china mug normally stood side by side, the mug was on its own. Caitlin took it down and gave it to Rowena. 'We'll take it back into the kitchen, will we?'

'Where's Murdo?'

'He's finished his work and gone home.'

'Is he coming back tomorrow?' Rowena asked anxiously.

'No, pet. There's no more cloth to be woven.'

'When's he coming back then?'

Caitlin knelt down on the solid earthen floor and took the child's face between her palms. 'He's not coming back, Rowena,' she said, and watched the tip-tilted blue eyes blink rapidly several times as the little girl tried to take in the thought. Understanding dawned, and with it the realisation that for the second time in her short life Rowena had been deserted by the person she most trusted. Her face began to melt as tears filled her eyes then spilled down her cheeks. 'I want Murdo!' It was a cry from the heart.

'Rowena . . .'

'I want him,' she insisted, stamping her foot. She broke away from Caitlin and ran to the saytree, thumping at it with her fists. 'I want him here!'

When Caitlin picked her up she resisted at first, turning her fury and her small knotted fists on her aunt until finally, worn out, she collapsed against Caitlin's shoulder, sobbing over and over again, 'I want M – Murdo!'

Caitlin sank down onto the saytree, rocking the child, feeling her grief soak into her own skin, and she too cried for the loss of Murdo Guthrie, with his square, expressionless face and his hooded dark eyes beneath the tumble of hair, his kindness and his deep loneliness and his beautiful music.

*   *   *

She went in search of him the next day, sending word to Rose by a young lad willing to run a message for twopence that she would be late. Since nobody seemed to know where Murdo lived, Caitlin started with the Highland woman who was teaching Rowena to dance. From there she was directed to Mhairi's spotlessly clean single-roomed home in Orchard Street. Fortunately, the woman was home when Caitlin knocked at her door.

'Murdo? He lives in a wee lodging house down by the river, near Abercorn Street. But he'll not thank you for disturbing him. Murdo likes to keep himself to himself.'

'I must speak to him, Mhairi. He's just been turned away from his work.'

The woman shook her head. 'Is that right? Ach, poor man, he never seems to get the best of things. Aye, well, if you think you can help him I'd be glad to tell you how to find him.'

Her directions took Caitlin into a part of Paisley she had never visited before, where a warren of small factories and old tenements clung to the banks of the River Cart. Here the roads were narrow and the pavements clung to the building walls, with scarcely room for two people to pass. There was no indication as to the names of the lanes or the numbers of the closes, but just as she thought that she would never find Murdo's home, a woman passing by said inquisitively, 'Are ye lost, hen?'

'I'm trying to find a man called Murdo Guthrie.'

'Would that be the big Highlander?' The woman pointed at the next close. 'In there, and it's the door to this side of the close.'

The tenement was much older than the place where Bryce Caldwell lived with his family, and made their home seem like a palace. It was a relief to know

that Murdo lived on the ground floor and she didn't
have to attempt the stone steps leading up into darkness above.

There was no answer to her knock. She waited,
knocked again and finally had to accept the fact that
he wasn't at home. Slowly she turned away, just as
what little light shone into the close was blocked by
a tall figure. She peered at it. 'Murdo?'

'What are you doing here?'

'I came to see if you were all right.'

'I'm fine. Why wouldn't I be?' he asked abruptly,
angrily.

'Can I speak to you?'

He hesitated, and for a moment she thought that
he was going to refuse then he said reluctantly, 'If
you must.'

The room was small, its sagging ceiling so low that
Murdo had to stoop slightly when walking about. There
was a small table, two straight-backed chairs, a sagging
cupboard and, Caitlin saw when she peered into the
shadowy bed recess, a low narrow cot. There was
no fire in the small range, though even on that warm
August day the room was chilly with the damp that
came up from the creaking floorboards and probably
permeated the entire building.

'Sit down.'

She sat in one of the upright chairs, noting that it
and the rickety table were both well scrubbed. The
range had been blackleaded recently, and the curtain
at the small window was clean. Murdo stayed on his
feet, head bowed beneath the flaking plaster ceiling.
Caitlin wished that she hadn't come; she could almost
feel his pain at having to watch her in it, aware of the
poverty he had to live in.

'I'm sorry that you were turned off. We all are.'

Then, when he said nothing, she struggled on, 'Alex would never have allowed it to happen.'

'As he's not here any more it's not his concern.'

'It will be when he finds out about it. What are you going to do?'

'Look for work.' Although there was no change in his tone she sensed the dryness of the remark and flushed.

'In Paisley?'

'Wherever I can find it.' He paused, then said with patient courtesy, 'It's not your concern.'

'But it is. It concerns all of us – my mother and my stepfather and my sister.'

'You've no obligation. I'll manage.'

'And there's Rowena. Murdo,' she said on a sudden whim, 'you could live in Espedair Street, in the loom shop. There's room for a cot and chairs, and you could eat your meals with us.'

'I'll not take charity, however well meant it is.'

'It's not charity, it's what Alex would want us to do. He's bound to come home on furlough soon, and when he does he might be able to find you other work or persuade his father to take you back.'

'It's meant kindly, I know, but I'd as soon see to my own affairs.'

'But you can't go on living in this place!' she burst out, and regretted it as soon as she saw his face tighten.

'I've managed until now,' he said stiffly, and she had no option but to leave him alone in his tiny damp-smelling room with only his pride for company and comfort.

20

The key was stiff, and Rose had to use both hands and all her strength before it finally turned in the lock. 'All it needs is some oil,' she said as she pushed the door open and led the way into the gatehouse.

The place smelled stale and dusty. They groped their way along the hall and into the room on the right, where they managed to wrest the shutters from the windows. Light flooded in to reveal a fairly large square room.

'Big enough for a loom,' Rose said with satisfaction.

'There has to be a space in the floor for the treadles. That's why most loomshops have earthen floors.'

'Then we'll have some floorboards taken away. At least the loom belongs to Kirsty and not to that dreadful Chalmers woman, so we know we'll be able to move it here. Look, there's a cupboard and some shelving, and a fireplace to heat the place in the winter.'

They explored the rest of the ground floor, opening the window shutters as they went, then mounted the stairs to inspect the upper floor.

'It's waterproof, and snug enough,' Rose said at last when the two of them had gone back downstairs. 'We needn't bother with upstairs. We could put the loom in that front room, and Murdo could live in the kitchen.

There's even a range and a sink and a cold-water tap, and a privy out at the back.'

Hope tingled through Caitlin, but she pushed it away. There were too many obstacles. 'We'd have to clean the place out.'

'That wouldn't take long.'

'And furnish the kitchen.'

'He could bring furniture from the place where he lives now, and we'll buy anything else he needs from a second-hand shop or a pawnshop. We'll buy some material too so that the women can make curtains.'

'But can we afford to employ Murdo?' Caitlin voiced her greatest worry.

'We'll manage somehow. You've always wanted to have material woven to your own designs, haven't you?'

'Yes, but—'

'Now's the time to do it. If we don't move now,' Rose said, eyeing Caitlin closely, 'he might have to leave Paisley to find work.' She examined her hands. 'I'm covered with dust, and so are you. We'd better get ourselves cleaned up.'

On the way back across the courtyard she said, 'I'll go to see Murdo this afternoon to ask if he'll agree to work for us.'

'I'll do it.'

'Best leave it to me,' Rose advised. 'From what you say he's prickly about accepting anything he considers to be charity. As he scarcely knows me, I can keep things on a business footing. You care too much for the man to be properly businesslike.'

'What nonsense!'

'Is it?' Rose asked, with a gleam of amusement in her blue eyes.

*   *   *

There was little laughter in Rose's face when she returned to the fashion house that afternoon. 'You said that the place he lived in was poor,' she said when she swept into the design office to find Caitlin working there, 'but I didn't realise it was as bad as all that. I have friends who wouldn't let their dogs or their horses live in such conditions! You were absolutely right, Caitlin, we must get him out of there.'

'You spoke to him?'

'Yes.' A marble-topped washstand stood at one end of the room; Rose poured water from the flower-patterned ewer into the matching basin and reached for the scented soap, then washed her hands vigorously. 'I shall have a bath as soon as I get home. How can anyone live in such squalor?'

'Murdo keeps the place as clean as he can,' Caitlin said, on the defensive.

'Indeed he does, though I don't know how he manages it – or any of the other poor souls. It should have been pulled down years ago!'

Caitlin was almost dancing with impatience. 'What did he say?'

'He was suspicious at first – convinced that I was just being kind. But I wore him down in the end.' Rose took the towel from Caitlin and proceeded to dry her hands. 'He's agreed to work for us and live in the gatehouse.'

Despite her efforts to remain calm, Caitlin felt a huge smile of relief spread across her face.

'We don't even have to pay him all that much since he doesn't have to pay rent. He's offered to keep an eye on the place in return. So now we must set about getting the gatehouse ready and the loom moved. It pleases me,' she added with a gleeful smile, 'to know that I've managed to do something that would annoy Fiona Chalmers!'

*   *   *

Rose Hamilton wasn't one to drag her heels once she had decided on a course of action. Two scrubbing women arrived the next day to clean out the gatehouse, and a joiner of Todd's acquaintance came in two days later to make a well in the front-room flooring to accommodate the treadles of the loom.

'So much for your plans to live here,' Caitlin said when he had left and the two of them had crossed the courtyard to inspect his work. The place smelled of carbolic instead of dust and neglect, with a pleasant underlying aroma of new timber.

'Once we're really successful we'll build a loom shop and a nice wee house for Murdo in the ground between Harlequin and the river, then I'll get this place back. The floorboards can be replaced easily enough. In fact,' Rose said thoughtfully, 'I could keep that well as a sort of priest's hole to hide in when annoying people like my mama come to call. Now . . . ,' she dusted her hands together in the brisk movement Caitlin had come to know well, 'we must get the walls whitewashed here and in the kitchen, and curtains made for the windows, and move Murdo Guthrie in.'

Rowena soon learned the way to the gatehouse. The school year had started again, and with Rose's ready permission Murdo continued to meet the little girl at the pend each morning and walk with her to school before settling down at his loom. Not that she needed to be shepherded to school any more, but after the shock of almost losing him, Rowena liked to confirm that he was still in Paisley at the start of each day. After school she walked down to the gatehouse instead of going back to Espedair Street and stayed with Murdo until Caitlin took her home.

Despite Rose's insistence that it cost very little to

house and employ Murdo, Caitlin had her suspicions, fuelled by Rose's bouts of unaccustomed silence and the worried frown that was beginning to sketch fine lines between her eyebrows, that all was not well financially. Caitlin had always been content to leave that side of the business to John, and then to Rose, but a week after the weaver moved in, she insisted on being shown the books.

Even she, with her rudimentary understanding of finance, could see that matters were becoming serious.

'I'll have to put in another order for materials soon, and how are we going to pay for it?' she asked. It took time to weave cloth, which would only be used for special orders anyway. They still had to buy almost all of their materials from the Glasgow warehouses.

Rose jutted out her chin. 'I shall write to John. He told me that his offer of investment still stood.'

'And his offer of marriage? Does that still stand?'

Rose bit her lip. 'As a matter of fact, it does.'

'You said that you couldn't take one without agreeing to the other.'

'I know what I said. And don't look at me like that, Caitlin. There's a lot to be said for being Mrs John Brodie.'

'If it's what you really want.'

'What I really want,' said Rose fiercely, 'is to keep Harlequin going.'

'At any cost?'

'There's no hardship in marrying John. He's a fine upstanding man and he knows how much this place means to me. He would never try to make me sit at home and hold tea parties and talk about how difficult servants can be.'

'We're talking about marriage, Rose, not a partnership.'

'A good marriage should be a partnership, and I shall have a good marriage with John,' Rose snapped, and left the room, refusing to discuss the matter further.

Caitlin went over the figures before her again, but they refused to change. She wished that Alex was only a train journey away in Glasgow, for it would have eased her mind to be able to talk over the situation with him. He was still training in England, and his letters to his mother tended to be brief, giving little information. Kirsty clung to the hope that he would be allowed home on furlough before being sent away, but as yet there had been no word of it. Nor had he replied, as yet, to the letter Caitlin had written, telling him about what had happened to Murdo.

That night, she sat at the kitchen table when the evening meal had been cleared away and wrote to him again.

The maid's mouth fell open when she opened the door. 'Mr Alex!'

'Good afternoon, Ellen. Is Mr MacDowall at home?'

'He's out for the evening, sir, but Mrs Chalmers has some friends in for dinner. They're in the drawing room at the moment.'

'I hope there's plenty to eat, for I'm very hungry. Perhaps I could just eat in the kitchen,' Alex began to suggest.

'Oh no, sir, Mrs Chalmers wouldn't like that, sir. She'd be ever so cross if she found out you were here and she hadn't been told!' Ellen's alarmed expression added, *I don't want to have to entertain the master's son in my private kitchen.*

'You're quite right. I'd best show my face,' Alex said with considerable regret.

The drawing room buzzed with animated conversation. It died when he walked in, and the half-dozen people in residence turned to stare at the figure in the doorway. Then Fiona ran forward, both hands outstretched. 'Alex! Oh, Alex!' She threw herself into his arms, and he held her awkwardly, aware of the heady scent of her usual perfume and aware, too, of the flash of jealousy in the grey eyes of the uniformed young man she had deserted to rush to him.

'Why didn't you let us know you were coming?' She pushed herself back from him, still holding his arms.

'I'd no knowledge of it myself until yesterday.'

'Where's your uniform?'

'I went straight to my flat and changed.'

'Oh, Alex! How could you deny us a sight of you in uniform?'

'Very easily. It's not in the least comfortable, nor does it fit me very well.'

Fiona pouted at him, then said, 'Papa's out for the evening.'

'So Ellen told me.'

'Come and meet my friends.' She turned back to the group by the fire, sliding her arm into his in a way he remembered vividly, and drawing him forward to meet them, announcing proudly as she did so, 'This is my very dear half-brother, Alex MacDowall, home from the war!'

All Alex could think about as he shook hands with a clutch of men and women he had never seen before was that his stomach was in imminent danger of proclaiming its emptiness with a loud rumble.

'Fiona's brother, eh?' The young man in the uniform of a captain of the Royal Scots Fusiliers shook his hand heartily, clearly relieved that Alex wasn't a rival.

'Half-brother.'

'On furlough?'

'For four days.'

'Expect to be travelling across the water soon?' he asked. Alex nodded. 'I'm not long back from France myself. Which lot are you with?'

'The Argyll and Sutherland Highlanders. A private,' Alex added deliberately. He had begun to find a perverse pleasure in seeing officers' lips curl, as this man's were doing at that very moment, when they discovered that they were in the presence of the lower ranks.

To his great relief, Ellen announced dinner just then, and Fiona claimed Alex. 'Walk into the dining room with me,' she demanded, and the captain's cold eyes grew even colder. Alex, placed between two young women, was content at first to concentrate on his food and leave the others to chatter. When he did take time to listen, the talk was so boring that he tuned it out again.

Fiona occupied her father's seat at the head of the table, bestowing most of her attention on the Royal Scots captain to her right. The overbodice of her yellow-and-brown-striped dress led the beholder's eye from her creamy neck to a gold silk rosette at her trim waist, which was snug in a brown velvet cummerbund that matched her eyes perfectly.

After dinner the others played cards while Alex prowled the room restlessly, wishing that his father would come home. But Angus had still not returned when the guests left.

'Did Harlequin make your gown?' he asked when Fiona came back into the drawing room after seeing them off.

'How observant you are. Yes, they did.' One beringed

hand smoothed her skirt, gathered in soft folds at the knee in front, then falling to a scalloped hem that just revealed her slim ankles. 'Isn't it lovely? Your sister is very talented.'

'How is George?'

The fingers of her right hand automatically flew to the handsome diamond and sapphire engagement ring and the broad gold wedding band that George Chalmers had given her. 'Very well, as far as I know.'

'You must miss him a great deal.' Alex was on the couch at one side of the fireplace; when Fiona eyed the cushions beside him he turned slightly, stretching his legs out towards the fire and blocking any thought she might have had of sitting by his side. She took the seat opposite. 'It's fortunate that you have . . . friends like Captain Gibney to comfort you.'

She coloured. 'Martin Gibney is the brother of a dear friend of mine, nothing more!'

'Indeed. I believe that Murdo Guthrie has been dismissed.'

As he had intended, she was taken aback by the sudden change of subject. 'Who?'

'The weaver we employed in Paisley.'

'Oh, that Highland man who never had a word to say for himself? We decided that we couldn't really afford him.'

'We?'

She shrugged. 'I decided.'

'Does Father know that you turned the man off?'

Fiona smiled across the carpet at him, a small, malicious smile. 'Things have changed since you left, Alex. I know that Papa had decided to leave the house to me and the business to you, since you are his son and I'm only his daughter and he believes that women know nothing about business. But he's quite wrong;

women can deal with business just as well as men, and it's my view that Papa needs one of us on hand. So I've taken over some of the less important business matters, although, of course, I confer with him before making final decisions.'

'But he usually lets you have your own way.'

'Usually.'

'Murdo Guthrie cost MacDowall and Son very little, Fiona.'

'But probably more than it costs to simply buy in the small amount of material we need. I really don't see why you're making such a fuss over one man, Alex.'

'I'm making a fuss, as you put it, because I installed him in Paisley myself, and I introduced the use of specially woven cloth in our furniture. It was a factor that pleased many of our clients.'

'And you introduced hand-painted furniture too, but now that you're in the army that side of the business has had to go into abeyance. We must cut our cloth to suit our purse, Alex.'

'And now we have to buy the cloth first instead of having it woven,' he said dryly.

She shrugged the matter aside. 'Have you visited your mother yet?'

'I came straight to Glasgow. I'll see her tomorrow.'

Fiona's eyes narrowed. 'Then how did you know that the weaver had been dismissed?'

'Caitlin told me in a letter. Fortunately she and Rose Hamilton have offered him work and moved his loom to Harlequin.'

She shrugged, a movement that momentarily raised the upper curves of her breasts over the low-cut underbodice. 'So you've no need to worry about him,' she said. Then, with a hint of malice, she added, 'I thought you would have rushed straight to

Paisley to thank your friend Rose for rescuing your protégé.'

'I will, tomorrow.'

'Do give her my regards. She's a fascinating woman, don't you think?'

'I admire her compassion, and her sense of honour,' he said deliberately, and two angry spots of colour flared over Fiona's cheekbones.

'So, do you intend to run to Papa to complain about the high-handed way I've treated your favourite employee?'

'I haven't decided yet.'

Fiona got up and with an angry flounce walked to the window. 'Who owns that loom?' she asked after a pause.

'My mother, and my great-grandfather before her. So you can't claim it back as MacDowall property, Fiona. Such a pity.'

'Indeed.' She turned and came back to stand over him. 'But I can make life difficult for your stepfather if you keep trying to anger me,' she said, her voice suddenly venomous.

Alex leaned forward, all his pleasure at teasing her gone. 'You try that, Fiona, and you'll be very sorry!'

'My dear, what can you do about it? You'll be too far away to trouble me.'

It was perhaps as well that Angus MacDowall arrived home just then, his normally sombre face lighting up at the sight of his son.

Fiona went to bed soon after, leaving the two men to talk late into the night over a bottle of whisky.

'You'll have heard that Fiona's taken some of the burden of running the business from my shoulders during your absence?' Angus asked eventually.

'She said something about it.'

'She's surprised me in the past week, Alex. I'd never have thought that my daughter would have such a wise head on her shoulders. She's good with the staff as well as the clients. And having something to do keeps her contented, which is the main thing.'

Alex took a long drink of whisky and said nothing.

21

Alex spent the following morning at the emporium and the factory, where the supervisor seemed to have everything running smoothly. He had lunch with his father before catching the train to Paisley, where he went first to the shop. He was cheered to encounter Aggie, the old dressmaker's dummy, in her usual place on the pavement, chained to the wall so that no passing youths could whisk her away. Today she wore a high-necked pale blue blouse with frills round the neck and the three-quarter-length sleeves and a dark-grey serge skirt with a blue sash tied round her ample waistline.

Alex gave her an affectionate pat, feeling that as long as Aggie stood sentry in Causeyside Street, nothing too terrible could happen to his world.

Jean, busy behind the counter, gave such a scream when he walked in that the woman she was serving jumped a good six inches into the air and another customer browsing through the pattern books on their stand spun round and knocked the lot down.

'You near frighted the life out of me,' Jean squawked, rushing round the end of the counter. He barely had time to drop his bag to the ground before she threw her skinny arms about him. 'Where did you spring from? Does your ma know you're home?'

'I thought I'd surprise her.' He hugged her, then squatted to gather up the pattern books.

'Do me a favour, son,' the customer by the counter advised, her hand over her heaving bosom. 'Make it a gentle surprise. Ye just put ten years on me!'

Kirsty and Teenie were so busy that the thunder of their sewing machines had drowned out the commotion beyond the curtained doorway. Teenie saw him first and slammed her hand hard on her wheel to stop it. Any other woman would have taken the skin from her palm on the racing wheel or had her fingers jerked from their sockets, but Teenie, who knew what she was doing, hung on, although she was almost jerked out of her seat before the wheel stopped.

'What's amiss?' Kirsty, working with her back to Alex, peered up at her friend, letting her own machine whir to a halt more slowly. Teenie's eyes were like saucers, and when she tried to speak her mouth opened and shut like the trout Alex had once guddled for in the burns up in the braes as a youth. Speechless, she pointed, and Kirsty twisted round in her chair, then came out of it with a rush that took her straight into her son's arms.

'Alex! Oh, Alex!' She laughed and cried and hugged him and clutched at him as if trying to convince herself that he was really there. Teenie clasped her hands and twittered like a nest of birds, and Jean, who came in as soon as she had disposed of her customers, stood beaming, tears in her eyes.

'When did you get here? How long do you have? Are you staying the night?' The questions poured out of Kirsty when she finally released him from her grip.

'I came from England yesterday and stayed the night at my place in Glasgow. I've to start back to the camp tomorrow morning, but I'll sleep in Espedair Street tonight, if there's room.'

'There's always room for you, son, you know that.' She mopped her eyes with her apron then said with a half-laugh, half-sob, 'Will you look at me, crying like daft bairn. It's the surprise that's done it.'

'A woman's got the right to have a good greet when her son comes back from the wars, hen,' Jean assured her friend. 'I'll away and put the kettle on.'

Alex would rather have gone straight to Espedair Street to see Todd and find out what had been going on in his absence, but Jean and Teenie were so thrilled to see him, and so full of questions, that he stayed for a while, drinking a mug of strong tea sweetened with condensed milk and telling them about the training camp.

'What happens when you go back?' Kirsty asked anxiously.

'I don't know, Mam. They'll probably move us out now that our training's over.'

The three women looked at him with frightened eyes. 'Will you be going abroad?'

'Probably,' he said reluctantly, then, at the panic in his mother's face, he added, 'I'll be fine. It'll take more than a few enemy soldiers to best me.'

Jean reached out to clasp one of Kirsty's hands. 'He's right,' she comforted. 'Alex knows how tae look after himself.'

'Mam, Caitlin wrote to tell me what happened to Murdo Guthrie,' he said as they walked to Espedair Street, Kirsty clinging to his arm.

'She told us she had. Poor lad, it was a sad business, but there was nothing Todd could do to help him.'

'I know that.'

'We offered him a home in the loom shop, but he'd

have none of it. Rose was grand, though, having the gatehouse cleaned out so that he could work there.'

'It was good of you to let them move the loom.'

'It was the least I could do for him. I always thought Fiona MacDowall to be a nice lassie,' Kirsty said after a pause, 'but it wasn't kind, what she did to Murdo. He never did anyone any harm, and though I wasn't altogether happy about Rowena taking to the man so much at the beginning, he's been grand with her.'

They had reached the pend; when they had walked through it she gave him a push in the direction of the workshop. 'Away and give Todd a surprise,' she urged, 'then come to the house.'

She hated to be away from him for a single second of the short time he had in Paisley, but she was also glad of the chance to get indoors on her own so that she could have a good weep and get it over with in private. By the time she had finished and washed her face and patted some flour round her eyes in an attempt to disguise their redness Mary and Rowena had come home.

'Away down to the workshop and see who's there.'

Mary looked at her mother blankly, then her eyes widened. 'It's not—' She stopped abruptly, glanced at Rowena, then turning so that the child couldn't see her face, she mouthed the word, 'Ewan?'

'God save us, of course not!' Even Kirsty had given up all hope of seeing Ewan at her door.

'It's Alex?'

'Of course it is.'

'Come on, Rowena,' Mary caught the little girl's hand. 'Come and see Uncle Alex!'

By the time her family had returned from the workshop, Todd wearing a broad grin, Kirsty had the preparations for the evening meal well in hand. Mary started Rowena on her homework, then began to help her mother.

'When's Caitlin due home?' Alex asked.

'She's working on tonight,' Mary said. 'That's why I fetched Rowena from the gatehouse.'

'I think I'll just take a stroll down to the fashion house and have a word with Murdo.'

'Mind and get home in time for your dinner,' Kirsty called after him as he went out.

He stopped at the gatehouse first. Murdo Guthrie opened the door to him, beaming when he saw who the visitor was. 'Mr MacDowall, you're back home.'

'Only for a day or two, Murdo. I thought I'd look in to see your new place.'

With a certain pride, Murdo showed him the loom shop, with a stretch of cloth on the rollers bearing the pine-cone pattern made world famous by Paisley shawls the century before.

'Caitlin was always anxious for you to weave cloth for her, so she'll be pleased now that it's happening.' Alex followed the weaver into the kitchen, where something simmered in a pot on the range. 'I didn't mean to break into preparations for your evening meal.'

Murdo lifted the lid and gave the pot's contents a quick stir. 'There's enough for two if you'd care to join me.'

'I've to go back to Espedair Street for my dinner. Are you contented here, Murdo?'

The man ducked his head in a quick nod. 'I wasn't certain at first that I should accept Miss Hamilton's offer, but I want to stay in Paisley. There's nowhere else I can call home,' he added with not a trace of self-pity in his voice.

'I'm glad you did accept, for you're as good as one of the family now and we'd have worried if you had disappeared, especially Rowena.' Alex held out his hand.

'She's a good bairn,' the other man said as he clasped it. 'She keeps me in mind of what might have been.'

'I thought you'd want to forget that.'

'A man should never forget his past,' Murdo said gravely as he accompanied his former employer to the door, 'for it shapes his future.'

Caitlin, working on a sheet of paper in the design office, threw herself into his arms when he walked in. 'Alex – I'm so glad you're back!'

'Only until tomorrow, but I've said I'll stay the night in Espedair Street.' He held her at arm's length so that he could study her. 'You look bonny, and successful.'

'I've never been busier or happier. You've seen Murdo?'

'I have. It was good of you to give him work and a place to stay.'

'It was Rose who thought of it, and I'm glad she did, for I've always wanted our own woven cloth. You got my letter?'

'I did, and I'm glad you told me what Fiona was up to. Not that I can do anything about it, having to go back to England tomorrow night. But at least I know that Murdo's found a safe haven for the time being.'

She was searching his face. 'Did you mind me asking about the money?'

'What money?'

'The investment we need for Harlequin.'

He frowned down at her, puzzled. 'You never mentioned money in your letter about Murdo.'

'You didn't get my other letter, about Harlequin running short of money and Rose agreeing to marry John?'

His face went suddenly blank, as it always did when

he received a shock. 'No.' He guided her into a chair and then perched on the edge of the desk. 'You'd better tell me what you're talking about.'

As Caitlin explained about the cost of renovating the gatehouse's lower floor, the investment John had promised and the proposal of marriage that Rose had turned down, he listened without comment. When she had finished, he asked, 'And has she written to him?'

'I don't know. But I thought that if you could invest some money in Harlequin – if you were willing – it would be better than Rose agreeing to marry John. She's very fond of him,' Caitlin hastened to add, 'but I know she's putting Harlequin before her own wishes . . .' Her voice trailed away as Rose burst into the room.

'Caitlin, where's—' she began, then stopped abruptly, still clutching the door handle, as Alex jumped to his feet and turned to face her. The colour fled from her face then returned in a rosy tide. Caitlin closed the sketchbook she had been working on and reached for her jacket. 'I'd best get home. I'll see you there later, Alex.'

He nodded, his eyes on Rose. 'Tell Mam I'll be there directly.' Then, as the outer door closed behind Caitlin, he asked Rose, 'D'you happen to have any of that fine malt your father gave you?'

Rose swallowed, then said calmly, 'There's some left.'

He watched as she crossed to the corner cupboard. He could hear the neck of the bottle clattering softly against the tumbler as she poured the whisky, and as she brought the drink to him he saw that a tremor in her hand made the amber liquid tremble. It was only when he took the glass from her that he realised that his hand, too, was shaking.

'Thank you.'

She nodded, and went back to the cupboard to pour whisky into a second tumbler. 'I didn't know you were in Paisley,' she said, her back to him.

'I'm on furlough, just till tomorrow.'

'Does that mean that you're going to be sent abroad?'

'I don't know yet. Probably.'

She had only put enough drink into her own glass to moisten her lips. She swallowed it down in one draught then crossed to sit behind the desk Caitlin had been working at. 'Sit down.'

He sat on the edge of a small armchair. 'I hear that John Brodie enlisted.'

'Not long after you left.' She was wearing a dark green skirt and a high-necked pink blouse with three-quarter-length sleeves tight to just above the elbows, then spilling in a loose frill halfway down her forearms. She looked tired; there were violet shadows beneath her vivid blue eyes and strands of hair had come loose from the knot at the back of her head to fall in soft ringlets about her cheeks. To his surprise, Alex discovered that he was having to fight back the desire to tuck the curls back and smooth the weariness from her face.

'You'll be missing him,' he said instead.

'I miss his ability to deal with ledgers. I don't have that gift.'

'But you always kept the books for the shop, surely.'

'They weren't as complicated as Harlequin's, and John was always there to fall back on.'

A sudden mental picture of Rose falling back into John Brodie's welcoming, cushioning arms turned the taste of good whisky sour in Alex's mouth. 'I looked in on Murdo Guthrie on my way. He seems very comfortable.'

'I believe he's settled in well enough.'

'It was good of you to assist him when he lost his position with MacDowalls'.'

She looked at him searchingly. 'Did you know that it was going to happen?'

'I did not! It came as a shock when Caitlin wrote to tell me. It was Fiona's doing – she has my father wrapped about her little finger, and at the moment there's little I can do about it.'

'She has a gift for wrapping men about that little finger,' Rose said dryly, and he felt colour rush into his face.

'Until they find out the truth about her,' he said stiffly, and a hand flew to her mouth.

'I didn't mean . . . I forgot that you and she had . . .' She stopped, then said formally, 'I'm sorry, Alex, I shouldn't have said that.'

'It's all in the past now.' He leaned forward, elbows on knees. 'About Murdo, it must have cost you to get the old gatehouse habitable for him, not to mention his wages.'

'He takes very little, since he can live rent-free now.'

'Even so, I'd like to make a contribution.'

'There's no need.'

'I'm the man who brought Murdo to Paisley in the first place, and I feel responsible for the way my half-sister has treated him. At least let me show my appreciation for what you and Caitlin have done for him.' He took out his cheque book and moved purposefully to the desk.

'If you insist.' Rose relinquished the chair to him and moved restlessly about the room while he wrote the cheque and blotted it before handing it to her.

'I'll give you a receipt, of . . .' She broke off, staring

down at the slip of paper, then said, 'This is far too much. I . . . We can't possibly accept it!'

'Look on it as an investment, if you prefer.'

'I can't accept it,' she repeated. 'I won't.'

'You would if I was John Brodie.'

'What has John got to do with it?'

'For God's sake, Rose, we've known each other for too long to play games. You had to spend money in order to save Murdo, and it was money that Harlequin could ill afford. It makes more sense for me to replace it than John.'

Her face was white now, her eyes dazzling in their anger. 'What has Caitlin been telling you?'

'That Brodie offered to invest money into the business, – money that you need badly, – and you refused because he also asked you to marry him. She also told me that now Harlequin is in such a precarious situation you've decided to take up John's offer – both his offers.'

'That,' Rose told him icily, 'is my business. It has nothing to do with you or Caitlin.'

'If it concerns Harlequin it's Caitlin's business as much as yours, and if you're being forced to take steps you don't want to take just because of your compassion towards Murdo Guthrie, then it's my business.'

'You make marriage to John sound like a fate worse than death!'

'It could be, if you don't go into it with all your heart. Is that fair to him, or to you?'

'I adore John Brodie!' Rose stormed at him.

'Then marry the man, with my blessing,' Alex shot back at her. 'But at least get rid of your financial concerns first. Don't just sell yourself to him.'

'That's a disgusting thing to say!'

'It's a disgusting thing to do, especially to a man who cares for you as much as he does.'

She stared at him, white to the lips, then tore the cheque into shreds, tossing the pieces on the ground between them. Alex immediately returned to the chair and began writing out a second cheque, the pen biting into the paper.

'I won't take it!'

'You will.'

'Why should I accept a penny from you?'

'Because we both understand business. I know a good investment when I see one, and after all you've done for Harlequin you're not going to be daft enough to throw away the chance to stay solvent.' Once again he blotted the cheque, then he added, 'And because I care about what happens to you.'

'Care?' Rose asked scathingly. 'Is it caring to go off to join the army without a word?'

'I didn't tell anyone until just before I went.'

'You didn't tell me at all!'

'I waited for an hour in your father's shrubbery for you to come home on that bicycle of yours, but you didn't arrive because you had gone out with John.'

'You didn't write.'

'Because you didn't write to me.'

'Because you'd gone off without—'

'Rose, I've learned two things in the past few weeks apart from how to march and hold a rifle and shoot it,' Alex interrupted, suddenly tired of pretence. 'One is that when life's as uncertain as mine is right now, only the important things matter. And the other is that I love you more than I will ever love any other woman – though God alone knows why. That's why I want to help you.' He got to his feet and picked up his hat.

'Caitlin will give you the cheque in the morning, when your temper has had a chance to cool.'

'Alex . . .' She said when he had reached the door. He turned, his fingers on the handle. 'Don't go.'

He crossed to her, and reached out to her and knew the physical pleasure of smoothing her hair back and kissing the shadows from beneath her eyes. And, finally, he knew the ecstasy of kissing her lips and holding her, and knowing that at last he had found out who he really was and where he belonged.

22

The evening meal, which Kirsty had delayed until the rest of the family began to complain, was long past when Alex finally came through the back door.

'Sorry, Mam, I got on the crack with Murdo and the time just ran by before I knew it.'

'As long as you're here now. I've kept your dinner hot for you.' It had long since dried up, but he wolfed it down as though he hadn't eaten for a week, finally pushing the plate back with a satisfied sigh. 'Nobody cooks like you, Mam!'

'Away with you,' Kirsty said, delighted. Todd had fetched in bottles of beer, and some lemonade for the womenfolk, and they sat late into the night for once, talking and reminiscing but never mentioning the future. Once or twice, when Caitlin caught Alex's eye, he winked at her; there was no opportunity to get him on his own to find out what had transpired between him and Rose after she had left the fashion house, but she was certain, from the sparkle in his eyes and his ready laugh, that the two of them had finally settled their differences.

Kirsty was tearful when he left immediately after breakfast, clinging to him until he had to ease himself free of her embrace.

'I must go, Mam. My uniform's in my Glasgow flat and I have to change into it before I catch the train south.'

'You'll take care of yourself?'

'I'll take very good care,' he promised, adding, as his gaze met Caitlin's over his mother's head, 'for I've got a lot to come back to after this business is over.'

Rose was later than usual; when she finally came in it was to find Caitlin gathering up scraps of paper from the design room floor and studying them with a puzzled frown.

'This has got Alex's writing on it,' she said when her partner arrived, 'and so has this bit. Look, there's part of his name.'

'It's just some scribbles.' Rose plucked the shreds from Caitlin's fingers and tossed them hurriedly into the wastepaper basket by the desk.

'It looked to me like pieces of a cheque.'

'As a matter of fact, he did invest some money in Harlequin.' Rose produced the slip of paper from her bag and handed it over. Caitlin's eyes opened wide. 'This is enough to make him a partner!'

'He doesn't want to be, at least not yet.'

'What happened to the other one, the pieces on the floor?'

'He made a mistake while he was writing it,' Rose said airily.

'So you won't be asking John to invest money in Harlequin after all?'

'There's no need, thanks to Alex's generosity.'

'Giving money away seems to suit him,' Caitlin observed. 'He was glowing like a street lamp when he came home last night.'

'Was he?' Rose concentrated all her attention on

taking off her hat and stabbing the long pins into it before hanging it up.

'You're doing a bit of glowing yourself.' The previous evening's weariness had vanished from Rose's face and had been replaced by a sparkle in her eyes and pretty colour in her cheeks.

'It's riding my bike that does it – all that fresh air.'

'Mmmm,' Caitlin said, and left it at that, but as she went upstairs to start work she envied Rose and Alex. It must be a grand feeling, she thought, to love someone with all your heart and to be loved in return.

When the ceilidhs began again in the autumn, Rowena clamoured to be taken to them. Mary needed little urging, for it meant that she could spend time with Lachie, and Caitlin, who had begun to love the gatherings and the music, was happy to return to the Gaelic church hall.

Rowena had become something of a celebrity among the Highlanders. Her dancing lessons and the hours of practice she put in had developed her natural skill, and she often danced on her own in the midst of an admiring circle of adults and children. She was happy to do it, too. Watching her spin and twirl and step around the floor, hands tucked in at her waist or poised lightly above her head, Caitlin marvelled at the confidence that dancing had brought to the stormy rebel who had once insisted on sitting beneath the kitchen table or in a corner of the room.

Fewer people attended the ceilidhs now, since most of the young men had gone and the dancers mainly consisted of women, children and older men. One young couple who had always been among the first to take the floor was no longer to be seen; the man, Mhairi whispered to Caitlin and Mary, had been among thousands killed during the assault on Gallipoli, and his young widow had left Paisley to stay with relatives in Inverness.

'Folk she scarcely knows, but they're all the kin she has now and she couldnae stay here with the memories of Colin. Like the rest of us, they had to come south because there was work to be had here.'

Murdo and the other musicians struck up a lively tune, and Lachie immediately arrived to claim Mary as his partner.

'Did Colin and his wife come from Inverness?' Caitlin asked when her sister had been whirled onto the dance floor. Mhairi shook her white head.

'They're from the Black Isle, like me and Murdo. Have you ever seen the place, lassie? Oh, it's beautiful, just! It was because Murdo knew Colin and Peggy and me from there that he went to Glasgow when the army freed him. It was good that he found work right here in Paisley after a time, for it comforted him a little to be near folk from his own place. And now there's only me and him left.'

'Murdo Guthrie was in the army?' Caitlin asked, astonished.

'Did you not know that? I suppose there was no reason why you should, for it's not a time that he'd care to speak about, poor man.'

Mary danced by with Lachie, still too young to enlist and impatiently counting the months until his sixteenth birthday.

'If he was a soldier, why hasn't he gone back to it now we're at war?' Caitlin wanted to know, and Mhairi sucked breath in sharply through her teeth, making a hissing sound.

'After what they did to him? He'll not go until he

has to, and there isn't a soul here who blames him, not even the lads that have already gone.'

To Caitlin's annoyance, a stout middle-aged man claimed her as his partner at that point. It was a dance she knew, so her feet followed the music automatically, and her mouth smiled at her partner, but her mind was fixed on Mhairi's words. Alex must have known about Murdo's army days, but had not told her.

As soon as she could, she rejoined Mhairi, but by that time she was chatting to someone else, and Caitlin had to bide her time until after the interval before she got the old woman to herself again.

'You were telling me about Murdo—'

'I was mebbe talking out of turn, lassie, for it's his story to tell, not mine. But at the same time,' Mhairi leaned closer and peered into her face, 'mebbe you should know, for you've been kind to him, and you care for him.'

'Yes, I do,' Caitlin heard herself say, and realised with sudden shock that she was speaking the truth. 'I do,' she repeated slowly, and Mhairi nodded.

'I thought so. I hoped so, for he needs someone to care for him, though he'd never expect it, or even seek it. But that's all part of his sorrow.' She patted Caitlin's hand. 'Well now, it was when work was scarce just before the turn of the century that Murdo went off to join the army – not because he wanted to leave his home but because he'd a family to support.'

The room swayed around Caitlin, then steadied. 'Murdo had a wife?'

'Of course he did.' Mhairi gave an amused chuckle. 'D'you think a fine-looking young man like that would be single? If I'd been nearer his age, I'd have set my cap at him myself – not that Elspeth ever chased after him, for they'd had an understanding since they were wee bairns together. Murdo was a different laddie then, full of laughter and hope for what was still to come.'

Mhairi's eyes were dreamy as she looked back into the past. 'I mind the ceilidh we had when he and Elspeth were wed – it was grand! Then just nine months later the wee laddie was born, the spit of his father. They named him Dougald. Then the work got scarce, so several of the young men went into the army together, Murdo and Colin among them. They were sent to South Africa to fight against the Boers there. It was while Murdo was far away that his wee laddie got drowned playing in a burn by himself. He hadnae long since learned to run about, and he was full of mischief, just like his father.' Tears filled her pale-blue eyes at the memory. 'There was no consoling poor Elspeth; she got it lodged in her mind that the blame of it was hers, though it never was. I mind Murdo's own mother worrying about him when he was that age because he was so adventurous. Not long after the bairn went, Elspeth took a chill, and since her love for life had gone with her wee laddie, the chill went into pneumonia and she died of it.'

The music stopped, then started again, a slow sad air that suited the story Caitlin was hearing.

'Word had been sent to Murdo when the bairn was lost, and again when Elspeth followed him, but seemingly the army refused to let him come home, so he took matters into his own hands.'

'He deserted?'

'That's what they called it when they caught him. But what man wouldn't try to get home at a time like that?'

'What happened to him?'

'Oh, they put him on trial, then into an English prison for some years. By the time he came out, his mother had passed away and there was nobody left for him to go home to, so he came to join us in Paisley. And now,' said Mhairi, 'he's determined that he'll not fight for the King or any other man until he must, and who could blame him for it?'

'I wouldn't.'

'You'll not let him know that I told you, lassie, for he's a proud man and the last thing he'd want is anyone's pity.' Again, Mhairi laid a hand on Caitlin's. 'I only said because it seems to me that someone should know.'

Mary and Lachie went off together, as had become their habit, as soon as the ceilidh ended, while Murdo escorted Caitlin and Rowena back to Espedair Street. Rowena, still fired with excitement, ran on ahead, whirling out of sight at street corners then sticking her head round to see where the adults were. As sometimes happened now that he was working for Harlequin, Murdo talked about the cloth he was weaving and asked about Caitlin's plans for future designs. Tonight, her head buzzing with the story she had just been told, she found it hard to concentrate on work.

When, as always happened at some point, Rowena's energy suddenly ran out, she came back to walk between them both, holding their hands, leaning more and more heavily on them until the Highlander finally swung her up against his shoulder, where she fell asleep almost at once. Caitlin, loitering a step or two behind, watched his broad back as he strode along, trying to picture the younger man Mhairi had described to her, laughing and carefree, with a small boy's head in place of Rowena's tucked trustingly into the hollow of his neck and shoulder and a shadowy unknown woman by his side, her arm touching his.

*　　*　　*

'What was Mhairi saying to you last night?' Mary wanted to know over the breakfast table.

'Nothing in particular.'

'It didn't look like nothing. She was talking away, and your eyes were like saucers.'

'She was just telling me about something that had happened to her when she was younger,' Caitlin said firmly, and would say no more.

September brought heavy rain in France, or perhaps it was Belgium; geography had never been Alex MacDowall's strong point at school, and he had long since lost any sense of direction. To tired men one trench seemed much the same as another, and the same went for the enforced marches along country roads, through lanes deeply rutted from cart and wagon wheels, past the skeletons of trees stripped of their branches and leaves by shelling or destroyed by fire, and sometimes past worse sights than devastated countryside without hope.

Occasionally on their marches they had come on villages or solitary farmhouses long since deserted by their original occupants and pounded to ruins by heavy artillery from the Allies or the Germans. Sometimes, when a halt had been called, shelter of a sort had been found among the walls still standing.

Now, wedged into a trench hacked out from the clay, with a constant drizzle of rain descending from the low grey clouds above, Alex looked back enviously on those moments he and his comrades had spent in ruined buildings, with the stone walls and partial, sagging roofs providing some shelter from the elements and the opportunity, if sufficient timber could be found nearby, of a fire to huddle round.

Somewhere close by machine guns were chattering

nervously, accompanied by the frequent dull thump of heavy artillery. Today, the worst of the fighting was somewhere to the west of the trench where Alex stood on duty. Thankful for small mercies, he rested one shoulder against the wet clay wall and set his mind to what had become one of his favourite pastimes these days, designing and decorating furniture for the house he hoped, one day, to share with Rose.

The daydream had first come to him on the ship bringing him and his mates over from Britain, as a way of taking his mind off what was to come. It had started as a single room, but as the days dragged by and life became more confusing, frightening and fragile, the house had grown until now it was the size of his father's. If this bloody war didn't end soon, Alex thought with a grim smile, he would soon find himself mentally working on Buckingham Palace.

By the time his relief came splashing along, Alex was stiff with cold.

'Fuckin' hell,' the man said, squinting up at the lowering sky and blinking the raindrops away. 'It's not just the Almighty pissin' on us today, he's got the whole band of bloody angels at it too.' He stuffed a cigarette into his mouth and searched his pockets for a packet of Lucifers. 'Cup o' cocoa waitin' for you back there, you lucky bastard.'

Icy rainwater, yellow from the clay, had gathered almost ankle deep in the trench, splashing over Alex's puttees as he trudged back to the dugout he knew as home these days, round corners, up earthen steps, along again and down more steps. Some men had managed to gather together timber to make doors for their dugouts, others had scrounged real doors from derelict buildings, but a tarpaulin was all the privacy that Alex and the handful of men he shared with had.

The floor was wet in here too, but at least it wasn't raining. He dropped his kit into a corner, sloughed off his raincoat and rummaged among his possessions for his precious towel.

'You'd think we'd all be dead of pneumonia, living like this,' he said as he scrubbed the worst of the rain from his face, hair and neck.

'Death by pneumonia isn't allowed in the British Army, pal,' a man stretched out on one of the camp beds said laconically. 'Cocoa in the jug if you want it. I'd've made tea, but we're out of Darjeeling and the missus just wouldnae go out into the rain tae buy more. Anyway, a passin' rat asked tae borrow the lemon slices and I didnae have the heart tae refuse it.'

'Cocoa'll do me fine.' It tasted like nectar, and it was still hot enough to spread some warmth through his limbs. Alex settled down on his camp bed and unfastened his tunic, pulling a small bundle of letters from an inside pocket. He knew them off by heart but rereading them was his greatest joy. Caitlin, his mother and Rose were regular correspondents, while his father wrote once every fortnight. Angus MacDowall's letters tended to be dry single-paged missives, mainly concerning business, but Alex treasured them as much as the others, knowing that his father felt more comfortable with ledgers and invoices than letters.

Kirsty's letters, too, were fairly short, her fears for Alex and her determination not to voice them almost leaping from the pages. Caitlin, on the other hand, wrote freely and with confidence about her everyday life, the ceilidhs and the walks up the braes with Rowena and Murdo and, sometimes, Mary and Lachie, and she wrote with news of Harlequin. Now and then she included a note from Mary, mainly about her work in the jam factory.

He always kept Rose's letters till last. She wrote as she tended to speak, in short no-nonsense sentences, telling him amusing stories about Harlequin and about herself and her parents; but always, towards the end of each letter, came the section written from her heart for his eyes only. He read each letter thoroughly, word by word, then put them carefully away before lying back, hands behind his head, returning in mind if not in body to that evening in the design office when he and Rose had finally stopped sparring and faced the truth about themselves. It had been a long time in coming, but as she had said in several letters, it had been all the sweeter for the delay.

He recalled the taste of her skin and her mouth, and the sheer, unexpected femininity of her. He remembered how he had waited on the pavement by the station steps the next morning and how Rose had come careering down the street on her bicycle just as his train had been signalled, skidding to a halt and wrestling it across the pavement. He had taken it from her and carried it down the steps, propping it against the wall, then, suddenly nervous, had turned to see that she was equally hesitant.

'Did it really happen?' she had asked. 'Did we really . . . ?' And when he'd nodded she had launched herself into his arms, heedless of the folk on the platform.

'Let's not tell anyone,' she had said as he leaned his head through the open carriage window. 'Not until you come back. Just in case we change our minds.'

'We won't!'

'I know we won't,' she had said, running alongside the train as it gathered speed.

He fell asleep smiling at the memory, and almost immediately a hand shook him awake for his next spell of duty. Outside it was dark, but the rain was still there, and so were the machine guns and heavy artillery. The night above was frequently shattered by brilliant white star-shell flashes, and now and again the entire sky seemed to burst into scarlet flame as a bomb or a land mine exploded. As Alex took up his position again, there was a sudden commotion further up the trench.

'Some bloody idiot decided tae have a look tae see what was happenin',' he was told by a soldier hurrying past. 'A sniper took his face off, stupid bugger. Now they'll all start aimin' at us.'

A stretcher party went by at a run, returning some time later with their burden. A sheet had been tossed over the body. As they went by the light from a star shell showed that over the area where the man's head should have been the sheet was defiled by a great wet splash of crimson.

As the soldier had prophesied, the enemy's attention suddenly focused on their section of the trench, and for several days their eardrums rang to the constant chatter and thud of machine guns and artillery as well as the crack of rifles. They went over the top in an attempt to gain ground, running through mud and jumping over barbed wire cut by an advance party, but the heavy artillery hadn't destroyed the enemy after all, and the German lines held firm, forcing those still on their feet to retreat to their trenches.

After listening all day to the cries of the wounded who hadn't managed to get back, they had to go back out at night, falling into water-filled craters, tramping in the dark over dead men and scrabbling in the mud for wounded they could drag back to precarious safety.

It seemed to go on for ever, but at last it was their turn to be relieved and marched back behind the lines to rest for a few days in a makeshift tent village.

Crowded in with a dozen other men, Alex slept for a full twenty-four hours and awoke starving. He made himself take time to shave and to bathe in a tin hip bath, which brought back nostalgic memories of the proper bathrooms with proper baths in Espedair Street, his father's house and his own flat. Then he put on fresh clothing and walked to the mess tent, where he ate until his stomach felt as though it was about to burst. Unlike most Scots, he hadn't taken up the cigarette habit until now. Since enlisting, he had come to appreciate the comfort of tobacco. He fetched a second cup of coffee and lit a cigarette, drawing the smoke deep into his lungs.

A noisy group of Australians sat at the next table; he glanced at them, then looked again as the man facing him whipped off his distinctive wide-brimmed hat, pinned up at one side, and waved it in the air to illustrate the final line of his story. For a moment Alex stared at the familiar rugged features beneath short-cropped brown hair, then he leaped to his feet, pushing past a group of men walking between the two tables. He put his hand on the other man's shoulder, stopping him in midsentence.

'Ewan?'

Ewan Lennox turned, brows furrowed at the interruption, and blinked up at his stepbrother.

'Christ, Alex,' he said. 'A fellow can't get away from his family anywhere!'

23

'D'you know what you've put Rowena through, sending her to Paisley on her own and leaving her there without a word?'

Ewan shrugged and took a mouthful of beer. They had found a table in a corner of the big mess tent, away from the worst of the noise. 'She's all right, isn't she? I knew Mam and Dad would look after her, and I couldn't take her with me.'

'Ewan, your father died not all that long after you . . . went away.' Part of Alex wanted to throttle Ewan for all the misery he had caused, but at the same time he knew that now that he had made contact with the man he had to handle the situation fairly cautiously for fear of losing him again before he had heard his story.

Ewan took the news of his father's death calmly. 'That's too bad, but he was in a pretty poor way when I last saw him. Mam's still at the house?'

'Yes. She married Todd Paget a few years after she was widowed.'

Ewan stared, then threw back his head and roared with laughter. 'That's rich,' he gasped when he began to sober up. 'Me and Beth run off together just before she was supposed to marry Todd, then Mam marries him instead. Beth'd love that one – if I only knew where she was.'

'She's still alive, then?'

Ewan took another deep drink. 'As far as I know,' he said, then added with an ugly downward twist of the mouth, 'not that I care if the bitch is rotting in hell with her fancy man!'

'What happened?'

It took some time, and several drinks, to get the entire story out of Ewan. He and Beth had gone up north and had married when they discovered that Rowena was on the way. At first, as far as Alex could make out, things went fairly well for them.

'We ended up working for this rich man with an estate out in the country. I worked with the outdoor staff while Beth was employed in the kitchens; they gave us a cottage to live in, and they didn't mind the kid. Sometimes Rowena was in the kitchens, sometimes she was out on the moors with me. She's got guts, that kid; she should have been a boy. Then,' the downward twist marred his pleasant mouth again, 'there was a big shooting party, out on the moors every day, banging away with their guns. Not like this lot we're in among,' he added sarcastically. 'They had motorcars and picnics brought from the big house, and chairs to sit on and plenty to drink. I've often wondered how many of them ended up here, popping away at Germans instead of pheasants and grouse and having to drink from puddles instead of opening another bottle. I wish I could meet some of them; I'd show them a thing or two. If they are here they're probably wearing officers' gear, holed up in some comfortable château with manservants to look after them. Did you know that the really rich don't even know how to wipe their own arses? They need servants for everything.'

'What happened to you and Beth?' Alex asked patiently.

'What d'you think? I was one of the beaters and she was among the women bringing the nice lunches out to the moors and setting the tables, putting out the knives and forks and the glasses. And this man got his eye on Beth.' He sneered. 'He wasn't even a man, just a kid not long out of university. He hadn't even started shaving yet, which was just as well since he didn't have a chin anyway. You know the type – a youngest son, all set to be pushed into some nice job hand-picked for him.' He paused for a while, his face tight with anger, his fierce eyes fixed on patterns he was drawing with one finger in some spilled beer. 'And when the birds had all been shot out of the sky and they all got into their motorcars and went home, Beth went with him.'

'What did you do?'

Ewan looked across the table, his gaze hard. 'What else could I do but go after them? I should have said good riddance to bad rubbish and left them to it. He'd have got tired of her – or she might have got tired of him first and asked to come back to me. Who knows? But I went after them with some idea of dragging her back where she belonged with me and Rowena. Or beating the hell out of her. One or the other, it didn't matter much at the time.'

He hadn't changed all that much. The Ewan that Alex had grown up with would never have let anyone take anything away from him. 'You caught up with them?'

'I did, and the silly little fool tried to protect her. Can you imagine that?' Ewan asked with amusement. 'I was bigger and fitter and older, but he had some daft idea in his bird-sized brain that it was his place to defend her. So he got it instead of her.'

'Did you kill him?'

Ewan stubbed out his cigarette and lit another. 'No. I could have, without thinking twice about it. But the very first blow bloodied his nose, and that sent Beth screaming for the law and the army and God knows what. So I had to get out of there and go on the run. Me and Rowena.'

'You took her with you?'

'I'd no choice. Beth had left her behind – she didn't want to be lumbered with a kid. I could have just left her too and hoped that somebody would see to her, but it didn't seem fair. She's always been a decent brat, and she favoured me more than her mother anyway, so I went back to where I'd left her waiting and we went off together.' He shrugged. 'I didn't mind trailing her along. She'd spent most of her time with me anyway, in the gardens or out on the moors. Beth didn't have much time for her once she got past being like a doll to play with and began to get into mischief and ask questions and talk as if her mouth had forgotten how to stop. With me, she learned fast enough when to shut up and keep out of my way, so I didn't mind her.'

'So you went on the run with a little girl?'

'No other choice. But things got difficult. The law wouldn't let up – they're like that when folk like us have the nerve to hurt folk like them – and once or twice we nearly got caught. Rowena was slowing me down, so I found a carter to take her to Paisley and I told her I'd come for her when I could. Right after that I heard about a ship heading for Australia, and I thought that'll get me away from the lot of them once and for all. So I managed to get work aboard and off I went. I found work easily enough when we got there, and things were working out fine when this lot started up. Next thing I knew, I was back on a ship, in uniform.'

'You'd no intention of getting in touch with Mam, had you, or your daughter?'

'I might have,' Ewan said evasively, 'once I'd got on my feet.'

'You might at least have written to let us know that you were still alive. Do you have any idea what that wee girl's gone through, waiting for you to come back for her and not knowing what was going on?'

'I knew Mam'd look after her.' Ewan fumbled for another cigarette and muttered a curse when he found that the packet was empty. Alex laid his on the table.

'You'll go and see her on your next furlough?'

'Best to leave things as they are. I'll only unsettle her.'

'Go and see her, Ewan! You owe her that, at least.'

'I'm a wanted man, remember?'

'With a war going on the police'll not be likely to be looking for you that hard. Besides, you'll only be in Paisley for a day or two. I'm going to write home and tell them I've met you, and I'm going to promise Rowena that you'll see her on your next furlough.'

Ewan finally agreed, adding, 'But I can't take her back to Australia with me, for I've been living in a bunkhouse with the rest of the men. It's no place for a kid.'

'Mebbe one day, when you're more settled. She's started school now, and she's doing well from what I hear.'

As the men who had been sitting with Ewan came by on their way out of the mess tent, one laid a hand on Ewan's shoulder. 'All right, mate?'

'Just coming.' Ewan picked up his hat. 'Our rest period's over and we're heading back to our lines.'

'Where are you?' Alex fished in his tunic pocket and pulled out a notebook. When Ewan told him, he said,

'We're just a bit to the west of you. Give me your army details and your address in Australia.'

'Think I'm going on the run again?'

'You've done it before,' Alex said levelly, and Ewan shrugged and told him what he wanted to know. Alex scribbled it down, then flipped to an empty page and pushed notebook and pencil over to his stepbrother. 'Write a note to Rowena, and I'll send it with my next letter.'

'For Christ's sake . . .'

'Do it! It'll mean a lot to her.'

Ewan sighed and scribbled a few words. '"Dear Rowena, hope you're well and being good. I'm fine,"' he read aloud, then said, 'I'm not a letter writer – I don't know what else to say.'

'Write, "I miss you, and I'll come and see you on my next furlough."'

'For—'

'Just do it, Ewan!'

When Ewan had gone Alex, unable to settle, walked round the camp, stepping over guy ropes and tramping along duckboards laid down over the soft, sticky mud. He found a lane and followed it between scraggy bushes until it ended at a ruined farmhouse, its windows gone and its front door hanging drunkenly by one hinge. The farmer and his family must have left hurriedly; the remains of a doll lay in a sheltered corner of the courtyard, half of its china head missing and one glassy blue eye staring up at the sky. He picked it up, wondering what had happened to the child who had played with it, then laid it back on the ground gently, smoothing its limbs and its clothing, and walked back to camp to write to his mother to tell her that he had found Ewan.

*   *   *

When his unit returned to the lines, its numbers replenished, the bombardment was still going on.

'It's been hell on earth,' someone told Alex. 'Dave McGill's gone, and Mack Polmont . . .' The air above screamed as a heavy shell ripped through it, and they both ducked automatically. The scream cut out, then came the explosion. A great fountain of earth, mud and water shot up towards the sky before showering back onto them.

'And Robbie Ballantyne lost a shoulder,' the soldier went on, brushing mud from his tunic. 'Shrapnel. They took him off to the sick bay, but he was losing blood fast and I reckon he'll be gone by now.' He recited the casualties in a flat voice, name after name after name, ending with, 'And I've heard that a bunch of Aussies further along had an even worse time, poor bastards. Scarcely one of them left.'

Alex's captain, considered by the ranks to be a decent bloke, promised to do what he could to find out what had happened to Ewan. Alex decided not to mention the Australian casualties in his next letter home, for there was no point in alarming Kirsty with rumours.

Twenty-four hours after returning from the rest camp, he felt as though he had never been away from the trenches. His Paisley family, his father and Fiona, and even Rose, were like a dream he had once had. It was as though he had spent his entire life being deafened by guns and blinded by the flash of explosions and star shells. The rifles he and the other men fired in return felt as puny and as useless as children's toys. He had never known such exhaustion, despair or sheer bone-dissolving terror. He couldn't remember the pleasure of eating food that wasn't cold or didn't taste of mud, or the joy of walking on dry firm ground, free of rats. The wet-walled trenches were the only home he had ever known, and the only escape he could hope for lay in climbing out into the wasteland beyond and walking into a bullet. He began to like the idea of death and found himself hoping that the chaplain's pictures of heaven and the angels were wrong. All he asked of death was blessed silence and darkness, peace and rest.

The rain seemed set for the winter, or perhaps forever. When he was despatched to the captain's dugout with a message, it took him a long time to get there, stopping every now and again to haul one foot or the other from a particularly gluey patch of mud.

'Just a minute,' the captain said as he turned to go after making his delivery. 'MacDowall, isn't it?'

'Yessir.'

'Didn't you make enquiries about a cousin fighting with the Australians?'

'My stepbrother, sir.'

'Oh yes. Got a note here.' The man, probably younger than Alex, rummaged through a pile of papers on his desk then brought one out and peered at it. 'Ewan Lennox – that right?'

'Yessir.'

The man's eyes were red rimmed with exhaustion, but even so there was sympathy in them. 'I'm afraid he didn't make it. There doesn't seem to be any doubt, for he's listed here among the dead. Sorry.'

'Yessir. Thank you, sir.' Alex saluted and made for the door. As he reached it the world suddenly exploded in a blinding flash and a noise that split his head open. Then, at last, the wonderful, welcome darkness took mercy on him and came to fetch him.

24

Rowena was delirious with joy when Alex's letter arrived. Even though she was doing well with her reading, Ewan's brief scribble was beyond her, so she insisted on having it read out to her over and over again until she had learned it by heart. She took the single page with her everywhere she went and tucked it carefully beneath her pillow every night before settling down to sleep.

'She's fair worn the entire household out with her excitement,' Kirsty told Jean. 'And she's going to wear that dancing stone of hers out too, the way she thumps and birls on it all the time she's at home.'

'She's bound to be excited, hearing from her father after such a long silence.'

'Aye.' Kirsty's eyes misted over. 'It's a miracle, Ewan going away to the other end of the world then our Alex finding him in the middle of all the fighting. It'll be good to see him again.'

She and Todd agreed that there was no point in letting Mr Laidlaw and his daughter know about Alex's meeting with Ewan. The Laidlaws had made it quite clear when they rejected Rowena that they no longer considered Beth to be part of the family, and in any case, as Mary pointed out, not even Ewan knew of Beth's whereabouts.

'I doubt if they'd want to hear that she'd deserted her lawful husband and her wee daughter and run off with another man,' she said, and they agreed.

Since her husband had enlisted, Annie Mitchell had become even more sour faced and irritable with her customers. It seemed to Kirsty, when she went into the tobacconist's shop, that Annie was becoming more like her grandmother every day.

Each time the thought came to her, she vowed to herself that, whatever happened, Rowena, who after all had old Mrs Laidlaw's blood running through her veins, would not follow the same bitter, twisted road as she grew up.

Caitlin and Murdo took Rowena brambling on the braes in October and, as had happened the previous year, the little girl ate most of the sweet black berries and ended up with purple stains about her broad grin. While she ran off to explore, the adults studied the sketchbook Caitlin had brought with her, discussing the possibility of Murdo weaving some of her cloth designs. Now and again he took the pencil from her hand to sketch deftly a more workable variation of one of her ideas. It was a mellow, pleasant late-autumn day, and they were sitting comfortably side by side on a large rock; occasionally Murdo's sleeve touched Caitlin's, and once, when he bent over the book, his hair brushed her cheek. For a man, he had surprisingly soft hair, with a pleasant soapy smell to it. His soft, deep voice was pleasing to her ears and she liked the way his square, blunt-fingered hands moved swiftly, confidently, across the pages on her lap. She felt safe with this man, much safer than she had ever felt with Bryce Caldwell.

As soon as the thought came to her mind, she scoffed at it, for after all Bryce had wanted to be her sweetheart, while Murdo was just a friend. But the sensation persisted. She did feel safe with him, and at home with him. Just then, Murdo turned his head to ask something, and when she looked into his deep-brown eyes, so close to hers, her reply died on her lips and the pencil fell from her fingers. He immediately stooped to pick it up and return it. When she took it from him, their fingers made contact for a brief moment, and she felt her cheeks grow warm. He seated himself beside her again, and she answered his question, looking at the sketchbook, speaking to it, longing to look into his face again but unable to. Almost immediately afterwards she snapped the book shut and announced that it was time they started for home.

Rowena was nowhere to be found, and when Caitlin called her name there was no answer. Caitlin called a second time, then again.

'She'll be hiding somewhere,' Murdo said easily.

'She'd have answered if she'd heard me, surely. She might be anywhere – she might have fallen over an outcrop of rock and been hurt, or . . .' She could hear the panic in her own voice. What if something had happened to Rowena while her aunt, who was supposed to be looking after her, had been thinking of her own pleasures instead of the child's safety?

'Rowena?' Murdo didn't even raise his voice much. 'Behave yourself now, and stop worrying your Aunt Caitlin.'

Immediately a bush some fifteen yards away rustled, and Rowena's purple-stained face appeared at knee level. 'I'm in my wee house,' she called. 'Come and see!'

The thicket looked impenetrable, but Murdo pulled the branches aside and bent to look through the gap. When he straightened up, he was grinning. 'She's found a wee house right enough. Give me your book and see for yourself.'

Caitlin gathered up her skirts and crawled between the branches he held back for her to find that the thicket was in fact a tight ring of bushes, with a space several yards in diameter within. A young tree grew in the middle of the open area, its branches entwining with the lower bushes to form a fairly thick ceiling. The sunlight that filtered through revealed Rowena squatting on a dry floor spread with dead leaves, hands linked around her knees.

'See?' she said, delighted. 'This is my own wee house.' When Murdo crawled in she insisted that they sit down on either side of her, then took their hands in hers.

'Now you're visiting me. When my daddy comes to see me we'll live here, him and me, and nobody can visit us but the two of you.' She tucked their hands into her lap and began to play with their fingers, so that all three hands became entwined.

When they started back towards Paisley Caitlin lagged behind, as she often did, to watch Murdo and Rowena, hand in hand, stepping confidently down the tussocky hill. Murdo's jacket, well worn and neatly darned, was a little too tight for him. It clung to his broad shoulders, and when he put his free hand up to brush hair back from his face, she thought for a moment that the arm seam might split, but it didn't. She felt a sudden wave of tenderness for the man. Rose had been the first to tell her that she cared for Murdo, and she hadn't denied it. Now, watching him walk away from her, she knew that Rose had been right, and that she did care, probably far more than was good for her, for Murdo Guthrie had already chosen his woman and loved her and given her his child. Since he had lost them both, it seemed unlikely to Caitlin that he would ever want to walk that road again.

Kirsty was worried about Alex. He hadn't written for several weeks, and the silence wasn't like him. She had wondered aloud on a few occasions if someone should go to Glasgow to ask if Angus MacDowall had heard from him, but she wouldn't go herself, and Todd, Caitlin and Mary were all reluctant to make the journey since none of them knew the man well.

Rose had become quieter than usual, and somewhat withdrawn, and Caitlin suspected that it was because she hadn't heard from Alex either. Although neither of them had mentioned it, she was fairly sure that her half-brother and Rose were now corresponding. Finally, when Kirsty's concern began to reach the stage of panic, Caitlin asked Rose point-blank.

'I haven't heard from him for several weeks, and it's not like him.' Rose was too worried to prevaricate. 'D'you think something's happened to him?'

'If it had, if he'd been wounded or . . .' Caitlin couldn't bring herself to say the word, so hurried on, 'I'm sure that Mam would have been notified. If Mr MacDowall's down as Alex's next of kin, I'm sure he'd have let Mam know if he'd had word.'

'If anything's happened to him, Caitlin, I couldn't bear it,' Rose said fiercely.

'It hasn't. Alex wouldn't let anything get in the way of his future!'

Just before Kirsty had reached the stage of insisting that one of them go, Fiona paid a visit to the workshop and to Harlequin for a fitting for her new coat.

'I don't believe that Papa has received a letter from Alex for some time,' she said vaguely.

'Then he must just be busy, for the War Office would let us know if anything had . . . happened,' Caitlin said, with one eye on Rose. Fiona, too, was watching Rose closely.

'Has he not even written to you, Rose?'

'Why should he?'

'I thought that you two were such friends.'

'Men fighting the war have more to do with their time than write to every last acquaintance,' Rose said dismissively, then remembered some urgent business in the office.

'I couldn't bring myself to admit that Alex and I are exchanging letters,' she told Caitlin when Fiona had gone. 'There's something about that woman that makes me reluctant to let her into any part of my life.'

One morning in early November, Kirsty ran into the workshop waving a letter in Todd's face. 'It's Alex – he's been hurt, and Ewan's . . .' She burst into tears, and it took some time before Todd could calm her down. When he finally read the letter, he took her back into the house and made her a cup of tea. Kirsty wrinkled her nose at the first sip. 'It's terrible, and there are tea leaves floating on it. You've not let the water boil properly!'

'I'm a cabinet-maker, no' a cook.' He fetched the whisky bottle and tipped a generous dose into the cup. 'Here, this'll make it taste better.'

'Todd Paget, you're just wasting good whisky – and good tea!'

'Take a mouthful of it at least,' he insisted. 'It'll help to calm you.'

When she had recovered her composure the two of

them walked down to Harlequin to tell Caitlin and Rose that Alex had suffered severe concussion in an explosion that had killed his unit captain, only feet away from him at the time, and that Ewan was dead.

'Are you sure Alex is all right?' Rose asked, white faced.

Kirsty handed over the letter. 'See for yourself. He was expecting to return to the lines within the next day or two. He'll be there now,' she added despairingly. 'To think that he was safe in the base hospital and we didn't even know it! And poor Ewan—' She stopped short, then said firmly, 'Rowena mustn't know about her father, not after getting that letter.'

'But she's expectin' the man tae come here on his next furlough,' Todd protested. 'She'll be lookin' for him.'

'Todd, I couldn't bring myself to tell her what's happened. She's too wee to bear so much grief!'

'Mam's right,' Caitlin said. 'It would break her heart to hear that he's dead. We'll just have to keep saying that he's not been able to get away, at least until she's a bit older and more able to understand.' And so it was agreed, though they found it difficult to listen to Rowena wondering aloud if her daddy might be allowed to come to Paisley for the New Year celebrations.

John Brodie was among those who were able to get back home at the turn of the year. He visited Harlequin and expressed his satisfaction with the ledgers. 'But you'll need to do something about getting folk to pay their bills in better time.'

'It's not easy since most of them are friendly with my parents. You can't ask a man you're sitting beside at a dinner party when he's going to settle the account for the frock his wife's wearing further along the table.'

'I know. I had the same problem myself when I was seeing to your books.' John turned a page, then paused. 'This investment . . . Alex MacDowall?' He looked up at Rose. 'So that's why you didn't take up my offer.'

'Alex was . . . generous.'

'So I see.' There was hurt in his eyes, and in his voice. 'I didn't know that you were going to approach him.'

'I didn't. Caitlin told him that we were having financial problems, and he . . .' Rose faltered to a standstill, then said in a rush, 'To tell you the truth, John, I think that Alex MacDowall and I will get married when the war's over.'

His face went blank. 'I see.'

'I'm sorry.' She put a hand on his arm, but he pulled away at once.

'Sorry? I wish that you'd at least have had the decency to tell me about MacDowall before I made a fool of myself by proposing to you.'

'I didn't know, then. At least, I didn't realise—'

John got up and held a hand out to stop her. 'Save your breath, Rose, I'm not really interested,' he said coldly, and walked out, brushing past Caitlin in the foyer, without a word. She went into the office to find Rose slowly gathering up the ledgers.

'What's amiss with John?'

Rose didn't turn round. 'He found out about Alex putting money into the business.'

'But why should that make him so angry?' Caitlin asked, confused, then as her friend said nothing, 'Rose?'

Rose gave an almighty sniff and swung round to face her. 'If you must know, he also found out that Alex and I are planning to marry.'

'Oh, Rose!' Caitlin flew across the room and hugged the other girl. 'I'm so pleased for you both! I've always known that you were meant for each other, but at times I was beginning to wonder if you would ever find . . .' Realising that her friend was as stiff in her embrace as a clothes-pole, she stepped back. 'Aren't you happy about it?'

Tears glittered in Rose's eyes. 'John was so angry, Caitlin. He thinks I've deliberately deceived him, but I haven't. Alex and I didn't even know until the end of his last furlough. That's why we didn't tell anyone, but now John's found out and . . .'

Her voice broke, and again Caitlin put her arms about her. This time Rose gave in and leaned against her. 'Oh, Caitlin, why does happiness have to cause so much misery?'

'It's just the way things are.'

'The last thing I wanted to do was to hurt John. I should have found a better way of telling him.'

'He'll learn to accept it, in time.'

'But I don't have time,' Rose wept. 'We're both going to a dinner party tonight . . . it'll be dreadful!' She snuffled, then pulled away from Caitlin, sudden horror in her face. 'Mama will be there . . . you don't think he'll say anything to her, do you?'

'Of course not. John would never do anything to hurt you or your mother, no matter how upset he might be,' Caitlin reassured her.

She was right. On the following morning Rose reported that John had kept out of her way at the dinner party and had said nothing to betray her.

'But Mama smelled a rat, and I had to go through a Spanish Inquisition on the way home as to what I had done or said to annoy him.'

'At least he kept your secret.'

'And so must you, until Alex's next furlough. We'd better confess then, for I couldn't bear to go on like this.'

'Not a word will pass my lips,' Caitlin promised.

When John returned to the office that afternoon he found Rose alone. She jumped nervously to her feet, fingering the brooch pinned to her bodice, and he gave her a wan smile.

'It's all right, I'm here to apologise.' He put his hat on the desk and squared his shoulders. 'It was wrong of me to lose my temper yesterday. I realise now that that's not the answer.'

'It was all my fault. I should have written to you as soon as I knew.'

'I'm quite glad that you didn't. Better to get bad news in the comfort of my own home town than in the thick of battle. Not that your news is bad,' he hastened to add, 'At least, not for you or Alex MacDowall.'

'John, Alex and I didn't realise . . . not until his last furlough . . .'

'I should probably have guessed that this might happen. The two of you quarrelled rather too much. I take it that your parents don't know about this?'

'Nobody knows except Caitlin. John, I wish I could have said yes to you when you asked me.'

He forced a smile. 'Don't be daft. Think how much more difficult things would be for all of us if you had accepted me then realised that you really wanted him. At least I can't fault his choice in women.'

'I can, but then I always said that there was something wrong with Alex MacDowall.' Rose tried to return the smile, but failed.

'It seems to me that there's very little wrong with

285

him.' He gave her a long look, as though memorising her features, then said, 'So there's nothing left but to wish you both well.'

'I wish . . .'

'So do I, my dear, but there we are.' He went to the door, then hesitated and turned. 'Tell Alex that if he's looking for a best man at his wedding, I'm willing.'

'D'you mean that?'

'Why not? If I can't have you then he's my next best choice for you.'

Rose went to him and kissed him on the cheek. 'You're the kindest man I know, and the most honourable.'

'Oh, I'm well aware of that,' John said wryly. 'Perhaps if I'd had more fire in my belly you'd be marrying me instead of Alex MacDowall.'

Shortly after John returned to his unit, a crisis hit Harlequin when Iris, who had recently become engaged to be married, left the sewing room to work in a factory. As soon as Lizzie heard what her friend was being paid in munitions she, too, handed in her notice, and Rose and Caitlin had to advertise for two new seamstresses. They appointed two older women, one of them a skilled embroideress as well, but it took a while for the newcomers to settle into the work, which meant that Caitlin had to spend more time at a sewing machine for several months, just when the fashion house was busy.

In deciding not to let Rowena find out about her father, they had forgotten for once the thriving grapevine that carried news throughout every community. One afternoon early in December Mary fetched Rowena from her dancing class and brought her home to Espedair

Street because Murdo was busy completing a piece of cloth. The little girl spent some time practising on her dancing stone, then wandered into the kitchen, where Mary was preparing the evening meal, and asked if she could play hopscotch on the pavement.

'As long as you don't wander off. There's a bit of chalk in that drawer.'

Rowena found the chalk and and went through the pend. She was missing her usual visit to Murdo, and on that day even a game of hopscotch seemed tame and uninteresting. For devilment, knowing that Mrs Mitchell hated children to play on the pavement outside her shop, Rowena hurried across the road and began to draw on the pavement.

In no time at all the shop bell pinged and Annie Mitchell appeared on the step. 'What d'ye think you're doin'? Go and defile the pavement on your own side of the street!'

Rowena, at a safe distance, stuck out her tongue, and the woman's face crimsoned. 'Don't you dare to cheek me, ye wee bizzum! Bad seed, that's what you are, no better than your father!'

Rowena felt her own cheeks burn. Nobody insulted her daddy! 'When he comes here he's going to break your window!' she shrilled defiantly.

'I've no doubt he would if he could. He's already broken my poor father's heart, so why not his window as well? But luckily for us all he can't, now he's dead and gone.'

The words hit Rowena with such force that her eyes almost popped out of her head and her mouth fell open. Then she pulled herself together.

'He's not dead!'

'Aye, but he is – killed in the war, and good riddance tae bad rubbish!'

'He's not, he's not!' All Rowena wanted to do was to hurt the woman who was hurting her. She threw the chalk at Annie Mitchell then charged, head down. Her skull and the woman's stomach smacked together with a force that sent Annie reeling against her shop wall, the breath sucked out of her lungs. For good measure, Rowena kicked her in the shins then whirled, her head still down, and ran blindly along the pavement with no thought of making for home. Even though it was getting dark, all she wanted, at that moment, was to get away from Espedair Street and from Paisley and all the nasty folk who lived there.

Kirsty came home to find Mary and Annie Mitchell shouting at each other on her doorstep.

'For pity's sake, what's going on?'

'Well might you ask! That wee tinker of yours needs a right good thrashing!'

Kirsty's heart sank. She was tired and cold, and looking forward to a quiet evening in her warm comfortable kitchen. 'Rowena? What's she done now?'

'Playin' hopscotch right outside my door, she was, and when I told her tae get back tae her own side of the street the wee bizzum started on about gettin' her father tae break up my shop!' Annie sniffed loudly and folded her arms across her flat bosom. 'I told her he'd not get the chance, seein' that he's been killed in the war.'

'You told Rowena that her father's dead?'

'Next thing I knew she'd butted me.' Annie foamed on. 'It's a mercy I'm still on my feet!'

Kirsty turned her back on the woman and raised her voice above the whine. 'Mary, where's the bairn?'

'I don't know, Mam.' Mary was near to tears. 'She asked if she could play hopscotch, and I said she could if she stayed on this pavement. But there's no sign of her.'

'Run to the workshop and see if she's hiding there. As for you, you evil, foul-tongued witch,' Kirsty rounded on Annie, 'get off my doorstep and out of my way!' And she pushed the woman aside then went into the house and slammed the door in her face.

Rowena wasn't in the workshop or in the room that had been the weaving shop.

'She'll have run to Murdo,' Todd said, 'I'm certain of it. Don't you worry, lass, I'll just away and fetch her home.'

'She'll be making for the bushes on the braes,' Caitlin said when Todd and Murdo came looking for her.

'Up on the braes?' Todd shook his head. 'She'd not go there in the dark.'

'I think she would, for she called the place her wee house.'

'You're right,' Murdo said. 'I'll go there now.'

'I'll come with you.' She snatched up her jacket. 'Todd, let Kirsty know.'

With every corner turned, Caitlin strained through the darkening winter evening, hoping to glimpse a small figure trudging just ahead, but it was never there.

'How long ago was it that she met up with Annie Mitchell?' she asked breathlessly, half running to keep up with Murdo.

'About half an hour, as far as I can judge. If she ran, she could be quite far ahead of us.'

They reached the town's edge and struck out along country roads, leaving street lights and houses behind. They were climbing now, and Caitlin soon got a stitch in her side. She struggled on, pressing her hand tightly against her waist to hold the pain at bay. Once, stopping to catch her breath, she saw the town sketched below by street lamps and house lights. The wind sighed and murmured in the trees, and when she turned back to look at Murdo his sturdy figure was just a shadow in the night, moving away from her and leaving her on her own. She pressed her fist hard against the sharp pain and struggled after him, suddenly afraid to be alone. How much more frightening this place must be for someone the size of Rowena, she thought, as she fought her way through a clump of broom that seemed to have risen up from nowhere to entangle her.

When he stopped she almost ran into him. 'I think it was near here,' he said. 'It all looks different in the dark.' Then, with concern, he asked, 'Are you all right?'

She was almost too breathless to speak. 'I'm fine,' she started to say, then suddenly she wasn't fine at all, for the tears were pouring down her face and she could do nothing to prevent them.

'It's all right.' Murdo gathered her into his arms. 'Hush now, it's all right. We'll find her.' For a moment he held her close, stroking her hair with one hand, then he eased her back and fumbled in his pocket, bringing out a handkerchief to mop her face. He must have spread it on the bushes behind the gatehouse to dry after washing it, for it smelled of fresh air.

'Mebbe you should sit down on this bit of log and wait while I go on.'

The sharp pain of the stitch was subsiding now. 'No, I have to find her!' Caitlin insisted. He took her hand and drew her to his side without wasting time on an argument.

As he had said, the area was quite different in the

dark; they stumbled around together, changing their minds several times and trying another direction. Occasionally Murdo called Rowena's name, but the darkness around them seemed to absorb his voice like blotting paper, and there was no reply. They heard the sound of rushing water, and Caitlin felt Murdo's hand tighten painfully on her hers before he let her go.

'Stand by that tree over there and wait for me.'

'Murdo . . .'

'Do as I tell you!' he shouted at her and disappeared into the night, heading for the sound of the water. As she fumbled her way to the tree she could hear Mhairi's lilting voice telling her of how Murdo's little son had drowned in a burn.

She waited for some time before he finally came crashing back over the grass. 'There's no sign of her by the water. Come on.' The hand that caught at hers was wet; he must have been feeling his way along the bank, dreading what he might find.

She had only gone a few steps when something caught at her free hand, digging into her skin with tiny needles when she gasped and tried to pull away. 'Bramble bushes!'

Murdo released her hand again and moved past her. 'And a dry-stone dyke beyond,' he said. 'There was a dyke by the brambles we picked, wasn't there?' Then the moon slipped for a moment between the overhead clouds. 'There's the rock we sat on. This way.' He caught at her arm and pulled her after him, slipping and stumbling on the rough ground.

'And here . . . ,' his breathless voice was rough with triumph, 'are the bushes. Wait.' He stooped, then disappeared into their midst. Caitlin knelt down, praying that they had been right in their guess as to where Rowena might have taken refuge, and almost immediately Murdo's face appeared right in front of hers. 'She's here!'

Caitlin pushed through the bushes, heedless of the way they caught at her hair and her clothing, and he guided her hands until they touched a small cold face, wet with tears.

'Oh, Rowena!'

'I want my daddy!' Rowena whimpered against Caitlin's fingers.

25

Murdo wrapped Rowena in his jacket and carried her all the way home. At first she struggled against him, then she gave in and wept hopelessly. Then she slept, worn out by grief and her long, lonely trek through the dark.

Caitlin thought at times on the downhill journey that they were never going to reach home. Several times, tripping over unseen obstacles, falling, picking herself up again, she wondered if they would have been better to have stayed in Rowena's wee house until daylight, huddled together for warmth.

Finally they gained the streets, where cobbles and flagstones under their feet instead of grass and stones made the walking easier. And at last they reached Espedair Street and trudged through the pend. Kirsty, alerted by some sixth sense, threw the back door open just as Caitlin was about to lift the latch, and at last they were in the warm, gaslit kitchen.

Rowena, wakened by the sudden light and the clamour of relieved voices, woke and began to cry again for her father. Kirsty, clucking and fussing over the little girl's filthy appearance, tried to take her from Murdo, but he shook his head and said firmly but courteously, 'If you please, Mrs Paget, I think it would be as well if we just got her into her bed. If you'd show me the way?'

Flustered, she went ahead of him into the hall while Todd guided Caitlin into his chair and Mary ran to ladle soup from the pot on the cooker.

Kirsty came back into the kitchen almost at once. 'He wants to stay with her for a wee while, till she's asleep.' She looked at her family, bewildered. 'I didn't know whether it was the right thing to do, but he was so insistent, and Rowena wouldn't let go of him.'

'Ye did the right thing, pet,' Todd assured her. 'The bairn trusts him, and at a time like this he's mebbe the best person for her. You can make a fuss over Caitlin instead – and I've no doubt that Murdo'll be ready for a meal when he comes downstairs.' He eyed the bowl of broth in Caitlin's hands hungrily. 'I know I am.'

'She's sleeping now,' Murdo said when he finally came downstairs. 'I think that'll be her till the morning.'

For once it wasn't difficult to persuade him to stay to eat with them. First, despite his obvious exhaustion, he insisted on taking a lamp into the wash house so that he could clean himself up. As his clothes were splashed with mud and torn from struggling through bushes, Kirsty fetched some of Todd's clean clothing for him.

Dour man though he'd been, Kirsty's father had adored his wife and had converted an upstairs bedroom into a proper bathroom for her – one of the first to be installed in Paisley. As Caitlin bathed in warm water in the comfort of the house's four walls, she was grateful to her grandfather for his foresight. She changed out of her blouse and skirt, as muddy and torn as Murdo's shirt, into clean clothes and brushed twigs and leaves from her hair before tying it back with a ribbon. Her hands and, she saw when she looked in the bedroom mirror, her face were covered with tiny scratches from the bushes on the braes, particularly the bramble bushes.

When Murdo came back into the kitchen he, too, carried scratches and tears that stood out against his scrubbed face and neck and hands. He had washed his hair, towelling the worst of the water from it then combing it with his fingers so that it lay sleek and shining over his skull, back from his forehead for once and emphasising the strong bone structure of his face. He didn't speak much during the meal, leaving it to Caitlin to tell the others how they had found Rowena.

'How could that Annie Mitchell have done such a wicked thing?' Kirsty fumed. 'Rowena could have died up there if you'd not known where to look for her. I'm going to go over there first thing tomorrow and—'

'Ye'll do nothin' of the sort,' Todd told her firmly. 'Ye'll let the matter drop, for it'll only make things worse for Rowena if ye start a quarrel with Annie Mitchell. Anyway, the woman's not worth it.'

Caitlin glanced across at Murdo. As the warmth of the room dried his hair it had begun to curl slightly, and the lamplight, catching the soft wisps at the ends, framed his head in a soft golden halo. His hands, as he spread margarine on a slice of bread, were calm and capable; she lowered her eyes to her plate, remembering the feel of those hands on her back and on her hair in the brief moment when he had held her in the darkness of the braes. She wished that he wasn't so set on keeping his own company, for it was good to have him there, a part of her family for once.

None of them was the worse for their journey to and from the hills, but to Kirsty's distress Rowena slipped back somewhat to her earlier days, retreating into silences and occasional tantrums.

'The bairn's got tae get the shock over Ewan's death out of her system,' Todd told his wife. 'Just leave her, however hard that might be. She'll sort herself out, given time.'

He made a frame for Ewan's letter, and Rowena kept it by her bed along with her father's photograph. She spent a lot of time with Murdo, who seemed to be the only person who could soothe her.

Alex came home for a few days in March, looking older and thinner and very tired. Caitlin, knowing how desperate Rose was to see him again, invited her to the house, where she hung back a little while Alex hugged his mother and his half-sisters and Rowena.

'Hello, Rose,' he said then, almost shyly.

'Hello, Alex.'

Caitlin, looking from one to the other, longed to shout out their news, but clamped her mouth shut, knowing that they themselves would decide when the time was right. Kirsty yearned to hear about Ewan, but nothing could be said in front of Rowena, so while they ate their evening meal they talked about the shop and Harlequin, and Todd enquired after Angus MacDowall's health. As before, Alex had gone to Glasgow first.

'He's fine. How are things in the workshop?'

'Everything's grand. Mrs Chalmers seems pleased enough with what we're doin', so she's made no more changes.' Todd said nothing about the anxiety he had suffered after Murdo had been turned off, wondering if he or his journeyman and apprentice would be next to meet with Fiona Chalmers' disapproval.

While Kirsty put Rowena to bed Alex and his step-father went to the workshop.

When they returned and they had all gathered round

the table again, Kirsty finally gave free rein to her curiosity. 'How did Ewan look?'

'Just the same – a bit older, mebbe, but as jaunty as ever, despite what he'd been through. I think he liked it in Australia.'

'Did he ask about us?'

'Of course he did,' Alex lied. He wasn't about to tell them that Ewan, as before, had shown little interest in any of his family. 'He was pleased to hear that everything was going well and that Rowena was happy here and doing well at the school. He said that he'd come and fetch her once the fighting was over and he had made something of his new life.'

'Poor laddie.' Ready tears rose to Kirsty's eyes. 'Mebbe Australia would have been the making of him.'

'We'll never know now,' Todd said enigmatically.

'We won't, but I'm sure that Mam's right and it would have worked out well for him. At least we know what happened to him, thanks to my captain. Not every officer would have taken the trouble to do what he did for me.' Alex paused, staring down at his hands, then said, 'And not a minute after he told me about Ewan he was dead himself, poor man.'

'And you almost gone with him,' Kirsty said with a shiver.

'If the shell had landed in the trench a few seconds later, I'd have been blown to kingdom come,' Alex agreed, 'but it happened just as I was on my way out. The door blew right off its hinges and smacked straight into me, and I was thrown into a corner with it on top of me, sheltering me from the worst of the blast. The captain and his aide caught the full force while I escaped with a cut face and concussion. I was very lucky.'

Rose could contain herself no longer. 'That's it, then,

Alex MacDowall,' she announced. 'I'm not going to let you go back to the fighting without putting a ring on my finger first!' Then, appalled by what she had just said, she stared round the circle of astonished faces and added, her voice wobbling, 'It's time everyone knew that you're mine.'

Kirsty gave a little scream, while Mary gasped and Caitlin yelped, 'At last! I thought I was going to burst!'

Todd puffed a cloud of tobacco smoke and said, round his pipe, 'I thought somethin' was goin' on between you two.'

Alex looked as astonished as the others. 'You might have told me first instead of blurting it out like that.'

'I told them because it's just occurred to me that if you walk into any more shells I'll at least have a ring to pawn. Do you have any objections to making our engagement official?' she challenged him, her eyes very bright.

He got up, walked round the table, drew her from her chair and kissed her full on the lips. 'No objection at all,' he said. 'But I warn you, if you insist on getting that ring then find someone better while I'm away, I'll be able to sue you for breach of promise.'

Kirsty burst into tears.

Alex felt more alive than he had for months as he marched up the Hamiltons' long driveway the following morning. Once again he was going into battle, but this time it was on a more level footing than the military struggles he had been involved in for so long. This time he wasn't a nameless, unimportant part of the whole, but a man in his own right, determined to win against all the odds.

Rose, who had stayed at home instead of cycling to

Harlequin, opened the door to him, drawing him into the hall and into her arms.

'You've told them?'

'I have.' Her blue eyes danced. 'Mama took an attack of the vapours, but that's only to be expected. Papa humped and grumbled a bit, but I think he's willing to give us our blessing. He's waiting for you in his study.' She led him over to the door and straightened his tie. 'Be firm, and don't take no for an answer.'

'I don't intend to.'

Rose's father was a neatly built man, smaller than Alex but with the air of authority expected of a man who was partner in a well-established Glasgow firm. He shook Alex's hand firmly then nodded him towards a chair on the other side of the desk.

'I'll be blunt with you, young man. I've been through this same business twice before, with my two older daughters' suitors, but at least I knew them and their families. I know nothing at all about you, other than what Rose has said, and she's naturally biased.'

Alex was fully aware that Mrs Hamilton must already have given her husband a damning report on his background and his suitability as a husband for their youngest daughter. He was also certain that he had only been granted this interview because of Rose's insistence and perhaps her father's curiosity to see the applicant for himself. Attack, in this case, might well be the best form of defence, and if his judgement was correct, he had nothing to lose and everything to win.

'If I may, sir, I'll be equally blunt with you. My mother was your wife's sewing woman at one time and I only met my father a few years ago, but even so . . .' he began flatly then plunged on, as the older man's eyes widened and his jaw dropped, into a detailed description of his work as a cabinet-maker, the discovery that he had a talent for hand-painting furniture, and the results that had come from meeting his true father.

'If you're about to tell me that I have entirely the wrong background to be a fit son-in-law, I would be the first to agree with you – although I must say that I'm proud of my family and what they have all achieved. I should also point out that I only hold the rank of private in the army. But now that we've got my unsuitability out of the way I'd like to concentrate on my assets,' he said smoothly, and went on to list them, throwing false modesty to the winds and ending with, 'And as for your daughter, I love her deeply, and it's my intention, should I be spared, to make her the happiest woman in the world and to ensure that she will never want for anything for the rest of her life.'

'So . . . Your mind's quite made up, is it?'

'It is, sir.'

'Mmm. You're aware, I suppose, that my daughter is not the easiest person to live with.'

'I am, sir, but I'm determined in any case.'

'And you know as well as I do that if I withhold my consent she'll go ahead and marry you anyway?'

'Yes, sir.'

'You'd marry her in the face of our disapproval?'

'I would, Mr Hamilton, for her wishes are far more important to me than yours.'

'You put me in a very difficult situation, MacDowall.'

'I regret that, sir, but there's little either of us can do about it.'

'I suppose not. You'd best come with me to face her mother, then,' said Rose's father.

Angus MacDowall held a hurried dinner party on the following night, the night before Alex returned to his unit, to mark the engagement. Kirsty, terrified at the thought of going into Angus's home, would have stayed behind to look after Rowena, but both Alex and Rose insisted on her presence.

'If it hadn't been for you we'd never have met each other,' Rose protested, while Alex, who had already arranged with Jean Chisholm to stay with Rowena so that the rest of the family could travel to Glasgow, said firmly, 'This is the most important moment of my life, and I want both my parents to be with me.'

Once the first five minutes or so were over, Kirsty began to relax and enjoy herself. Angus treated her as he would have treated any other guest, and Fiona, as his hostess, was at her most charming. When it came down to it, Todd was more intimidated by the size of the house than his wife was.

'I can't help thinking,' he murmured when they had a moment to themselves, 'that if things had turned out differently, you might have been the mistress of this place instead of sitting in Espedair Street with me.'

In his eyes she recognised the doubts that she herself had known just after Rowena's arrival, when she had realised that if his marriage to Beth had gone ahead as planned, Todd could have been the child's father. She reached for his hand and squeezed it. 'You're wrong, I'd never have been mistress of a grand house like this. If things had been different and . . . ,' she hesitated, then used the name she had known Angus MacDowall under, 'if Sandy and I had been able to marry when Alex was on the way, he'd have stayed on as my father's apprentice and I'd still have ended up in Espedair Street.' Then she leaned over to whisper in his ear, 'But I'm glad about the way things turned out, for I'd much rather be there with you than with him.'

Mrs Hamilton, who had had to struggle to maintain a pretence of pleasure over her daughter's choice of fiancé, was considerably relieved when she saw his father's handsome, comfortable home. Her husband and Angus, both silent men, took to each other from the first and disappeared into Angus's study not long after dinner to smoke and drink brandy and talk in peace.

Rose was radiant in a long tunic patterned with intermingled blues and greens, worn over a hobble skirt in sea green. The outfit, designed as usual by Caitlin, went well with the emerald and diamond ring she and Alex had chosen together that afternoon.

'I can see that I'll be paying large amounts of money over to you when I'm married for my wife's clothes,' Alex told Caitlin.

'We don't charge much.'

'You deserve more, and you'll get it once the war's over – if it ever is over,' he added grimly.

'It will be one day.'

'I hope you're right, for all our sakes. But when the day comes Harlequin will do well for itself between your talent and Rose's determination. In fact I wouldn't be at all surprised if Fiona doesn't soon put in an order for an outfit very similar to Rose's. She's been eyeing it all evening.'

'Has it bothered you that Fiona has become so involved in your father's business?'

'Not at all,' Alex said, though she saw a muscle along his jawline suddenly tense. 'It keeps her busy and my father happy.'

Caitlin let the subject drop, but she had noticed that he tended to avoid speaking to Fiona and had seen the malicious glances the woman shot at him when she believed she was unnoticed. Once they had believed that they loved each other, but now . . .

Caitlin shivered and put the thought out of her mind. There was no point at the moment in brooding over a future that might never come for any of them.

26

In May 1916 compulsory conscription into the armed forces was brought in, and for the first time since taking up residence in the gatehouse Murdo Guthrie came to the main building. He told Rose and Caitlin that he was leaving. 'I'm sorry about the cloth still on the loom, but they've not given me time to finish it.'

'Don't you worry about that. It'll stay where it is until you can come back to complete it,' Rose told him briskly, adding, 'You will be coming back to work for us when you can, I hope?'

'If it's your wish.'

'It certainly is. And in any case you'll be returning to the gatehouse when you're on furlough.' She shook his hand heartily. 'Good luck, Murdo. We'll miss you.'

When Rose had gone upstairs to see Grace, Murdo said to Caitlin, 'I'm going to fetch Rowena from school and bring her back here for a wee while. I'll try to explain what's happening and why I have to go away.'

Caitlin swallowed to ease the sudden dryness in her mouth. 'She'll miss you very much.'

'And I'll miss her.' Fumbling in the old canvas bag he carried over his shoulder, he produced two thick exercise books. 'Could I leave these with you?'

'Of course.'

'They're letters to Rowena,' Murdo said. 'I'll write to her, of course, but just in case . . . If anything should happen to me and my letters stop coming, I thought mebbe you could post these to her, one by one. I know how much she treasures the one letter she got from her father.'

He held the books out to her, and she thrust them away, appalled. 'How can you talk about the possibility of your own death so calmly?'

'Because whether we like it or not, men are dying in their hundreds on both sides.' For once, there was an edge to his soft voice. 'Rowena's had a hard time of it, poor wee lassie, with losing her father twice over, and it'd be cruel for her to lose someone else to this war. She's got the right to feel sure of the other folk in her life, at least until she's old enough to understand the ways of the world better. And . . .' He paused, then said, 'I thought that you'd be more able to understand my thinking than anyone else.'

Caitlin held her hand out for the books. 'I'll make sure she gets these if they're needed,' she said through stiff lips.

'I'm grateful.' He hesitated before saying awkwardly, 'I'm expecting a lot of you . . .'

'If there's anything else I can do, I will.'

'Mebbe your brother's told you something of what's happened to me.'

'Alex hasn't said a word, but I did hear something from Mhairi.'

He smiled faintly. 'That old woman worries over me as if I was her own. Since you know, I wondered if you would keep this for me.' He delved into the bag again, this time bringing out a framed photograph. 'It's of Elspeth, my wife, and the bairn.'

Caitlin looked down at the formal portrait of a thin young woman, her dark hair drawn back, her large eyes anxious, although her mouth was curved in a smile. Her arms were around the child on her lap, still in the long dress some little boys wore until they were 'shortened' and put into trousers at five years of age. His long, dark curly hair stood out around a chubby face, and his eyes, also dark, were alight with the glee of being alive. It looked as though he had worked one arm free of his mother's grasp, for he brandished it triumphantly in the air, short fingers outspread as though reaching for freedom. He was so like Murdo that Caitlin caught her breath.

'I don't want to take it with me in case it gets lost or damaged, but I don't like the thought of leaving it behind on its own,' Murdo was saying earnestly. 'I'd feel better about it if I knew someone was looking after it for me.'

'I'll take good care of it,' Caitlin promised, and he nodded, then held his hand out. 'I'd best say good-bye, then.'

They shook hands formally, then as he turned to go, Caitlin asked, 'Can I . . . Would you mind if I wrote to you?'

He gave her a smile that lit up his whole face and briefly emphasised the similarity between himself and his long-dead son. 'I'd like that,' he said.

When he had gone she opened the exercise books. Every page contained a short letter that began 'Dear Rowena' and ended with 'From your friend, Murdo Guthrie'. Between, in a strong, clear hand, were a few lines about the weather and how busy Murdo was, and how everything was fine, and he hoped that Rowena was doing well at school and keeping up with her dancing practice.

Caitlin found a sheet of paper to wrap the books and the photograph in. By leaving them with her, Murdo had made her guardian of the people he held dear: Rowena and his dead wife and son. She supposed that she should feel pleased and honoured by his trust, but part of her wanted desperately to be among their number and not just the outsider appointed to look after them.

When she went to the gatehouse to collect Rowena at the end of the day, Murdo said, 'I'll walk with you to Espedair Street, if I may, and make my farewells to your mother and Todd before I go on to see Mhairi and some of the folk from the ceilidhs.' He put a hand on Rowena's head. 'We're going to write to each other while I'm away, aren't we?'

The little girl, who looked as though she had been crying, nodded, her eyes on the floor.

Murdo put on his jacket, then patted the pockets and looked around the kitchen. 'Did you see where I put my mouth organ, Rowena?'

'No.' Her voice was deep and grumpy.

'You'll want to take it with you.' Caitlin glanced around, but the place was so neat that it was easy to see that the instrument wasn't there.

'Ach well, mebbe it's as well to leave it behind, for I doubt if I'll have much time to play it and I'd not like to lose it,' Murdo said, and shepherded the two of them towards the door.

He didn't stay long at Espedair Street, and when he turned to go Rowena, sulking in a corner, suddenly ran to him and threw her arms about his legs.

'Don't leave me! Take me with you!'

He picked her up and held her tightly for a moment. 'Sweetheart, I have to go, but I'll be back. I promise you that I'll be back,' he said, then pushed her into Todd's arms and left.

Caitlin lay awake for most of the night. When she went to work in the morning, the gatehouse had an empty, deserted look.

Rowena treasured the letters she received from Murdo, guarding them jealously from the rest of the family and refusing to let anyone know what was in them. She herself wrote to him every day after school, sitting at the kitchen table with her tongue sticking out from between her teeth and her head so close to the paper that the pen sometimes got tangled in her long hair. She kept up her dancing classes and still spent a great deal of her spare time on her dancing stone in the back yard, moving to music that only she could hear.

Murdo wrote regularly to Caitlin as well, short formal letters at first, but gradually developing into longer missives revealing glimpses of his life and his thoughts. As with her letters to Alex, she wrote about Harlequin and her family and life in Paisley.

Some of the men and boys who had flocked off to war so enthusiastically in 1914 had returned to the town, all their dash and glory gone. Those able to get out and about were to be seen on the streets, some on a crutch to compensate for a missing foot or leg, others with empty sleeves pulled inside out or pinned out of the way. Some bore scars, some had been blinded; some coughed and wheezed, their lungs destroyed by chlorine gas.

In August it was Mary's turn to start worrying when Lachie finally achieved his sixteenth birthday and went off to don a uniform. As had happened with Alex and John, he was allowed a short furlough between completing his army training and being sent overseas, but to Caitlin and Rowena's bitter disappointment Murdo was packed straight off to France from his training camp.

'In view of my past record as a soldier, I think they're afraid to let me go in case I don't return,' he wrote to Caitlin. 'And instead of trusting me with a rifle they are sending me to serve with the Medical Corps. This suits me very well, as I would rather do what I can to help wounded men than add to their numbers.'

On a pleasant breezy day in early September, Caitlin set about the task of bringing the brown-paper parcels that held the family's winter clothing from the top shelves of the wardrobes and carrying them to the back yard to be unpacked and pegged on the clothesline to air.

Every spring for as long as she could remember, her mother had made a point of wrapping the winter clothes in paper with camphor in the pockets to deter moths. It was a custom that had led to many protests in the past, for it meant that in early autumn every garment had to spend several days on the clothesline to let the fresh air remove, as much as possible, the strong smell of camphor. If for some reason the clothing couldn't be sufficiently aired, such as during a wet autumn when it was impossible to hang clothes outside or a sudden early cold snap that meant that the coats and jackets had to be worn, the wearers exuded a pungent smell that caused heads to turn and noses to wrinkle. When that happened the entire family complained loudly, but Kirsty paid them no heed and refused to give up her custom. 'I'd sooner have a smell of camphor about my clothing than have holes in it,' she insisted.

When she opened the wrappings round Rowena's warm coat, which would certainly need unpicking and lengthening before it could be worn again, Caitlin dipped her hand into the pockets to remove the camphor and brought out a familiar object instead. She stared at it, then turned to Rowena, who was sitting on her dancing stone, talking earnestly to her doll in a low voice.

'What's this?'

The child tossed a casual glance in her direction, then her small face went blank and she jumped to her feet. 'It's mine.' Whipping the mouth organ from Caitlin's palm, she pushed both hands tightly behind her back.

'It's not yours, it's Murdo's mouth organ, the one he thought he'd lost just before he went away.'

'He gave it to me!'

They faced each other challengingly, then Caitlin said, 'Come in here,' and led the way into the wash house, where they were less likely to be overheard. She had half expected Rowena to take to her heels, but the child followed her, and Caitlin closed the door behind them. 'You took it without Murdo knowing, didn't you?'

'I'm looking after it!'

'Did he ask you to?' When Rowena shook her head, staring at her shoes, Caitlin went on, 'So he still thinks it's lost, and he's still wondering what happened to it.' The child said nothing, and for a moment Caitlin looked at her bent head helplessly, unable to judge how to deal with the matter. Then she said tentatively, 'You shouldn't take things that don't belong to you, Rowena.'

Rowena, chin well down, muttered something into her chest.

'What did you say?'

Rowena took a deep breath. 'He'll have to come back for it now,' she said, and suddenly it all made sense.

'You took it because you knew he'd want it back?' Caitlin asked, and when the copper head nodded she knelt down on the flagged floor and tipped Rowena's chin up so that they were eye to eye.

310

'You'll have to write to Murdo and tell him it's safe – and tell him you're sorry you took it without asking.'

'Can I keep it?'

'Until he comes for it. But put it in a better place this time,' she added when the child's face lit up. 'In a drawer, mebbe.'

'If I do that Granny'll see it.'

'We'll tell her that Murdo asked you to keep it safe for him – but you must tell him in your next letter, mind.'

When Rowena had taken her precious burden into the house Caitlin went back to the clothesline. It occurred to her, as she worked, that there was little difference between herself and Rowena. They both nurtured the superstitious hope that one day Murdo must return to claim his possessions – the mouth organ from Rowena and the framed portrait of his dead wife and child from Caitlin.

In January the members of the Gaelic ceilidh band, invited to play at a concert to raise funds for the war effort, asked Rowena to acompany them and give a dance demonstration. To her family's surprise, she agreed. Kirsty made her a ruffled white blouse and a tartan skirt and almost burst with pride at the applause the little girl received.

'I just wish her daddy could have seen her,' she said emotionally as they walked home later, Rowena skipping ahead.

'I wish Murdo could have seen me,' Rowena said sleepily to Caitlin when she was in bed.

'I'm sure he wishes it too.'

'I'll tell him all about it in tomorrow's letter,' Rowena said, and was asleep before Caitlin reached the door.

*   *   *

'We can't allow matters to go on like this!' Rose brandished a fistful of pages at Caitlin during their usual monthly business meeting. 'Look at these unpaid bills. No wonder we're finding it difficult to pay our debts.'

'Write and ask them to settle.'

'I've done that already, but most of them ignored the letters.' Rose sank into a chair on the other side of the desk. 'And several assured me that their outstanding accounts would be dealt with when they next came in to order a dress or a jacket or a skirt. Only they weren't.'

'Is there nothing else we can do?'

'Not that I can think of. Some of them have even used the war as an excuse – their husbands are in uniform and they themselves know so little about how to deal with the household finances.' Rose flapped her hands and fluttered her eyelashes and dropped into a childish voice, '"And it's such a burden, my dear, with the servants just flocking off to work in those nasty factories without so much as a thought for all we've done for them in the past. My poor little head was simply not made to deal with nasty things like cheque books and accounts and handing money over to people who need it and have earned it. Why else do you think I got married in the first place?"' Then, reverting back to her own voice, she said, 'The next time some silly little powder puff of a woman says that to me I shall point out that even society women are possessed with brains and that their only problem is that they choose not to use them.'

'Then they'll take umbrage and you'll lose most of our clients.'

'We might as well not have them, since they cost us in time and materials yet give nothing in return. I do wish that John was here!'

'D'you want me to try writing to them?' Caitlin suggested, very much against her will.

'You're our designer. You shouldn't have to do that,' Rose protested, though hope gleamed in her eyes.

'As you say, John can't do it for us any more, and you know most of these people too well socially to dun them for money. I could try it.'

Relief radiated from Rose as she scooped up the bills and handed them over. 'You are a darling!'

After the meal had been cleared away that night, Caitlin spread the invoices over the kitchen table, turned to a blank page in her sketch pad and began to note the various amounts down.

Mary, helping Rowena with her homework at the other side of the table, craned her neck inquisitively. 'What have you got there?'

'Unpaid invoices.' Caitlin completed the list and added it up laboriously, then added it again, tutting her irritation when the totals differed.

'Here, let me.' Before she had time to object Mary had spun the book round, whisked the pencil from her hand and had begun to move the point briskly from total to total, muttering under her breath. 'There.' She turned the book back to face Caitlin, who saw that Mary's total was different from her two.

'Are you certain?'

Mary, who had taken over Jean's shop books after gaining her diploma in bookkeeping at night school, eyed her sister scathingly. 'Of course I am. Look.' She deserted Rowena and came to stand behind Caitlin, the pencil deftly skimming up and down the page as she chanted numbers. 'No doubt about it,' she said, then whistled softly. 'Are you and Rose owed all that money?'

313

Caitlin nodded. Now that the total was before her in black and white, she too was horrified to discover how much was owed to the fashion house and how few people had paid their accounts promptly.

'How on earth can you keep going if people don't pay you?'

'We can't, that's why I said I'd try to collect the money.'

'But you're supposed to be designing clothes.'

'I know, but Rose has already done all she can, and there's nobody else.' Caitlin thought longingly of the shop days when all she had been expected to do was make alterations to second-hand clothing.

'I could do it.'

'You?'

'Why not? None of your clients knows me, so I can be as firm as I like.' Mary swept the invoices together. 'I'll begin by writing to them.'

'Rose has already done that.'

'I,' said Mary grandly, 'will write a different sort of letter. And if they ignore it I shall call on them after work and on Saturday afternoons.'

'You don't think she'll be too hard on the clients, do you?' Caitlin worried to Rose the next day.

'I don't know, and frankly I don't care. Somebody needs to take these women in hand, and if Mary's willing to do it then I'm behind her.'

'But if she offends them they'll go elsewhere.'

Rose raised an eyebrow at her. 'That would be their loss, for you're an excellent designer and we charge less than anyone else. And they all know that.'

Within three weeks Mary's letters, written in her clear, firm hand and signed 'Miss M. Lennox, Accounts

Department', had resulted in settlement of more than half of the delayed accounts. After she had called at their homes, dressed in her best clothes, all the others paid the money owing, apart from one extremely difficult young woman.

'And she can find some other fashion house,' Rose stated. 'She won't be missed, and when word gets out, as it will, it will teach the others a lesson for the future.'

'Can we afford to turn anyone away?'

'Caitlin, the woman was never satisfied with anything we did for her. I think we've reached the stage where firmness is advisable.'

'I would certainly prefer not to deal with Mrs Clark again if I could help it.' The woman had indeed been very difficult to please and had at times driven Caitlin and Grace almost to distraction.

'So would I. Even with the war we're doing quite well for clients, and now that we're being selective those who do stay with us will feel quite privileged. It might even bring in some new clients. Do you know that two people even apologised to me for having taken so long to settle?' Rose added gleefully. 'They'll respect us more now that we have an accounts department run by our very capable Miss M. Lennox. That's the way business works.'

She gloated again over the ledger before her. 'D'you think Miss M. Lennox would allow us to use her services again? We will, of course, be paying her commission for what she has already done for us.'

27

Mary was delighted to receive her commission and to agree to continue dealing with any clients slow to settle their debts.

'I don't know how you could face folk in their own homes and ask them for money,' Caitlin shuddered. 'I'd be too nervous.'

'Each to her own. I'm not able to design clothes, like you. To tell the truth, I enjoyed it. I was polite, but firm.'

The two of them had taken Rowena to the braes to gather brambles. Their containers filled and the picnic lunch they had brought with them eaten, the sisters were sitting on a grassy hillock while Rowena gathered an arrangement of ferns to take home to Kirsty.

Mary pulled a grass stem and began to chew it, staring thoughtfully into space. 'I shall put the money into a bank account,' she announced finally.

'A bank account?' Caitlin twisted round to gape at her sister.

'Why not? My money's as good as anyone else's. I don't see the bank turning up their noses at it.'

'But folk like us don't have bank accounts!'

'I'm not folk like us,' Mary said serenely. 'I'm me. And since I've no intention of spending the money and

I'm certainly not going to keep it in an old sock beneath my mattress, it'd be as well in a bank. I've been reading about such things, and it means that the bank will pay me for the privilege of holding my money. It's called interest. It's a good way of saving up.'

'What are you saving up for?' Caitlin asked, then sat up abruptly when her sister said, 'Mebbe for a place to live once this war's over and Lachie comes home.'

'The pair of you are thinking of getting married?'

'I doubt if he is, but I am.'

'Mary Lennox, you're only sixteen, and Lachie's just seventeen!'

'I know, but we won't be sixteen and seventeen forever.'

'You're too young to think of settling down. You might meet half a dozen other lads before you find the right one.'

'Mam was my age when Alex was born.'

'That was different.'

'Mebbe so, but sometimes you just know when you've found the right man. At my age,' Mary said earnestly, 'you think you'll live forever and there's always going to be plenty of time to do all the things you want to do. But war soon teaches you that things might not go on forever after all, so then you have to grow up faster.'

'What if Lachie doesn't come home?' Caitlin asked tentatively. There was a long silence before Mary spoke again.

'If he's killed I'll still need money to live on, and there'll mebbe even be more reason for me to provide it, since I might not find another man that I like as much as I like him. So,' she ended triumphantly, 'whatever happens, I'm bent on putting my commission in the bank.'

As Mary went to help Rowena, who had entangled her skirt in a thorny bush, Caitlin sat up and wrapped her arms about her knees. Her mother had always said that Mary was an old head on young shoulders; watching her sister's deft movements as she freed Rowena and the serenity in her face when she walked back towards Caitlin, she felt at the moment as though she, and not Mary, was the sixteen-year-old.

'In any case,' Mary picked up the conversation as though it hadn't been interrupted, 'Lachie will come home. I've set my mind on it, and if you want something badly enough you're bound to get it. Look at Rose, getting the old mill and starting up her own business.'

'Rose had money behind her.'

'Even if she hadn't she'd have found some way of earning it.'

'D'you know how to go about setting up a bank account?'

'No, but Rose will. I'll ask her to go with me the first time.'

In April of 1917 America had entered the Great War, and with the influx of its young, eager servicemen it began, in the following months, to look as though the battle might turn in the Allies' favour after all.

But the way ahead was still hard, and local newspapers throughout Britain continued to carry long lists of dead and missing servicemen. Todd always made a point of reading the names and one evening in spring, Caitlin came home to find him waiting for her, his normally cheerful face grave.

'Ye'd best see this, lass.' He thrust the *Paisley Daily Express* into her hands. Halfway down a list of names, underlined in pencil, was Bryce Caldwell's name.

Caitlin sank into a chair, staring in disbelief. It had

been hard enough to imagine the world without Ewan, let alone Bryce, with his strength and his swaggering and his utter confidence in himself.

'Are they certain?'

'They must be, or he'd not be listed as killed in action.'

'His poor mother,' Kirsty said tremulously. 'I'll go along and see her after Rowena's gone to her bed. D'you want to come with me?'

Caitlin thought of her last meeting with Bryce, and the splash of water and potato peelings on the pavement, and doubted if Mrs Caldwell would be pleased to see her. 'I'd best leave it, Mam.' She put the newspaper aside and went upstairs, in need of time to herself. All at once it seemed to her that the world had shifted slightly, and would never be quite the same again because Bryce was no longer part of it. She wished that she could have been kinder to him in the past, but at the same time she knew that that hadn't been possible. They had each had their own paths to walk.

She had slipped into the habit of opening up the gatehouse once a month to dust what little furniture Murdo possessed and making sure that everything was as he had left it. On the following day she found time to take the key down from its hook and hurry across the yard.

Seventeen months had passed since she had last seen Murdo, and now the suddenness of Bryce's death wakened within her the fear that she might never see the Highlander again. In the kitchen, she ran her fingers over the things Murdo had touched, then settled herself in his fireside chair, laying her arms carefully along the rests and leaning back against the wooden strap that had supported his head. For a few minutes she stayed

319

where she was, eyes closed, pondering over Mary's firm views on life and envying her sister's certainty over her feelings for Lachie, then she leaped to her feet as the outer door opened and Grace called her name.

'In here!' Caitlin shouted back, applying the duster vigorously to the chair. 'I'm just keeping the dust away,' she explained when Grace put her head round the door.

'Mrs Langmuir's arrived early for her fitting. I'll finish this off for you,' Grace said, whisking the duster from her hand.

In July the staff and pupils of the South School held a small concert for parents and friends to mark the end of the term. Following her success in the fund-raising concert, Rowena was invited, to Kirsty's delight, to demonstrate her dancing skills. On the night Kirsty insisted on bustling her daughters along the road a good forty-five minutes before the concert was due to start; as a result they managed to get seats in the front row, where they sat listening to mysterious thumps and footsteps on the other side of the dusty curtain, laced with the occasional squeal of juvenile excitement and sharp adult reprimand and the ripple of keys from the piano that bulged out of the curtain at the front of the stage. Behind them the hall began to fill until every seat had been taken and the walls vibrated to a buzz of excited conversation.

Rowena had been placed quite far down the pro-gramme, so they had to wait for some time while children of various ages sang songs, recited poems, fumbled their way through musical items and gave a demonstration of physical exercises. Although there was a shortage of almost everything because of the war, parents and teachers had managed, by utilising old clothes, cardboard boxes, empty tins and what coloured paper they could find, to improvise some splendid costumes.

'Poor wee soul,' Kirsty whispered as they waited for the curtain to open on Rowena's performance. 'She'll be that nervous, having to wait for so long.'

'Not Rowena,' Mary whispered back, leaning across Caitlin. 'She'll be loving every minute of it!'

'Shh!' her mother told her sharply as the curtain began to part in the middle and jerk back towards both sides. The stage was empty, but before Kirsty could begin to panic a small, familiar tartan-clad figure marched confidently in from one side, stepping up to the centre of the stage then bowing briskly. The audience applauded warmly, and Caitlin felt her mother swell with pleasure as someone behind them said in a loud whisper, 'That's the wee lassie that danced at the concert tae raise money for the soldiers. Awful good, she is.'

A skirl of music came from the wings, and white-haired Hamish from the Gaelic church strode on stage with his accordion to take his bow. When the last clap had rung out from the audience, he settled the accordion more comfortably into place over his round stomach and looked across at Rowena, who carefully placed her feet in position and lifted her thin arms above her head in a graceful pose. She gave a brisk nod of the head, then sprang into action as Hamish began to play.

The applause at the end of each of the three dances proved beyond doubt that she was the star of the show, which ended with all the children squeezed onto the stage in red, white and blue costumes, singing patriotic songs. When the curtain finally closed and the lights went up, tears were streaming down Kirsty's face.

'The wee souls,' she choked, fumbling in her bag for a handkerchief. 'The wee, innocent souls!'

She wasn't the only one in tears; the hall was filled with the sound of snuffles and the blowing of noses. When, after a moment, the curtains opened again to let the young performers flock in a colourful stream down the wooden steps to join their families, they were greeted by another hearty round of applause.

Rowena was one of the last to come onto the stage, her face flushed with excitement, her eyes searching the thronged hall for familiar faces. Waving to her, Caitlin saw the child, about to step onto the highest step, suddenly stop, staring wide eyed at the back of the hall. Then, with a piercing scream of 'Murdo!', she hurled herself down the stairs, narrowly avoiding a collision with some of the children already on their way down, and started struggling through the crowd, passing her grandmother and aunts without a glance, even when Kirsty called to her.

'What's amiss with the bairn?' she asked in astonishment, while Mary wanted to know, 'Was that Murdo's name she shouted out?'

'It couldn't be! Caitlin, what d'you think you're doing?' Kirsty squawked as her elder daughter scooped up her skirt with both hands, heedless of whoever might be looking.

'Hold me, Mary,' she said, and scrambled onto the chair she had just vacated to get a better view. Not meant for such use, it wobbled beneath her and she had to put all her faith in Mary, who gripped her with one arm while trying to hold the chair steady with her free hand. Peering above the milling, bobbing heads, Caitlin almost lost her balance altogether when she saw Todd beaming and gesticulating at her from the back of the hall. Beside him, in army uniform, Murdo Guthrie ducked down into the crowd, both arms outstretched, then straightened up and hoisted Rowena high into the air, the red paper skirt she had worn for the final number flaring out around her thin body.

Caitlin tried to jump down from the chair, but Mary's tight grip forestalled her. 'Get me down!' she commanded, and after a clumsy struggle the solid floor was beneath her feet again. 'It's Murdo, he must have been allowed home!'

'Only for two days,' he explained when the three women had finally managed to reach the outside door, where he and Todd and Rowena were waiting.

'I got the surprise of my life when he arrived at the door,' Todd chipped in, beaming. 'Then I decided that the best thing was tae fetch him along tae the school.'

'Did you see me?' Rowena, still in Murdo's arms, was clamouring into his ear. 'Did you come in time to see me?'

'I did, and you were a grand sight!'

Hamish arrived, the shabby case that held his accordion helping him to forge a way through the people who still stood in chattering groups in the small foyer. He and Murdo greeted each other warmly in Gaelic, while Kirsty began to organise her family.

'We'd best get home and out of this cold night air. It was that warm in the hall that we could all catch our deaths if we don't walk fast. Murdo, you'll follow along and eat with us?'

'Of course he will,' Todd said heartily when Murdo began to shake his head. 'We all want tae hear what ye've been doin'. Yer friend an' all,' he added, grinning at Hamish.

'Of course,' Kirsty chimed in, though Caitlin could see her eyes narrow as she tried to calculate whether or not the meal keeping hot in the oven could stretch to feeding two unexpected guests.

Hamish explained that his wife was expecting him home and would worry if he was late, but Murdo agreed to follow them back to Espedair Street in a few minutes. Rowena wanted to stay with him and clung to him when Todd tried to lead her away. When Murdo said quietly, 'No, do as you're bid, Rowena,' she stopped struggling and went quietly along the footpath.

He arrived just as Mary and Caitlin had finished setting the table and he insisted on having a wash before joining them for the meal. Murdo looked tired, Caitlin thought when he came indoors again, but even so he wasn't as reticent as he had once been. No doubt that came from being with people all the time. From what Alex had told her, soldiers had few opportunities to be on their own.

He didn't say much about his duties, other than that he and his colleagues were kept busy most of the time. He ate hungrily, leaving it to the others to do most of the talking. Rowena chattered happily about school and the ceilidhs and going to the braes with Caitlin and Mary to collect brambles for jelly.

'But I didn't eat so many this time because I'm older and more sensible,' she explained, yawning hugely.

Kirsty pounced. 'Time for bed, young lady.'

'But . . .' Rowena began, then slid a glance at Murdo from the corners of her slightly slanted eyes and changed the sentence to, 'Can Murdo come and say goodnight when I'm in bed?'

'If your grandmother allows me to. Then I must be off to my own place.'

'You could stay here,' Todd offered, but the Highlander shook his head. 'I'll be fine at the gatehouse.'

'Can I come and see you tomorrow?' Rowena asked at once.

'You can, but right now you're going to your bed.' Kirsty held out her hand. 'Come along.'

'Don't forget to come up and say goodnight, Murdo.' Rowena widened her eyes and lowered her voice dramatically. 'I have something for you.'

When they had gone, Rowena's voice receding as she mounted the stairs, Todd got to his feet. 'You'll have a glass of beer with me before you go. Sit yourself down by the fire, man.'

Murdo drank his beer, then spent five minutes upstairs with Rowena before thanking Kirsty and Todd for their hospitality and departing.

When Caitlin left for Harlequin the following morning, Rowena insisted on going with her.

'Murdo might still be in his bed,' Caitlin protested. 'He'll be tired after all his travelling to get here.'

'Then I'll stay with you until he wakes up,' the little girl told her, but when they reached the gatehouse they found Murdo, in his usual clothes, working at the loom.

'I've been thinking of this unfinished cloth all these long weeks and months,' he said when Caitlin protested that he should be enjoying his free time instead of working, 'and looking forward to sitting at the loom again.'

He ate his midday meal at Espedair Street, and afterwards he took Rowena with him while he visited his old friends. The ceilidh that night became a celebration of his homecoming, with even the oldest Highlanders coming along to welcome him home and hear about his time away from them.

'You'll have to excuse us our rudeness in speaking Gaelic,' Mhairi said to Caitlin and Mary. 'It's not the right thing to do at all when there are those among us who only know English, but there's some things that come from the heart that can only be said in our own tongue.'

'We don't mind at all. It's a beautiful language,' Caitlin assured her, but there were times, as she listened to their laughter and studied their animated faces, when she did feel left out and longed to know just what they were saying to each other.

Murdo took his usual place on the dais with the other musicians when the dancing started, but after a few dances Mhairi jostled her way to where the band stood, calling, 'Now, Murdo Guthrie, it's not seemly for you to go hiding behind that mouth organ of yours when the place is filled with women wanting to dance with you – even old bodies like me!'

'Ach, Mhairi, I've never been one for the dancing, for I'm too clumsy. Why else d'you think I learned to play this thing?' He held the instrument up, but she flapped her arms at him.

'Stop your excuses, man, and take me round the floor this minute!'

He shrugged, smiled and, after a word with Hamish, stepped down and took Mhairi's hands in his. After that he alternated playing with dancing with every woman and girl in the room. It was true what he said, he wasn't a good dancer, but nobody cared, for pleasure was all they were after.

Caitlin was his partner for the last dance, a delicate strathspey that was one of her favourites. When it was over he walked with them back to Espedair Street as he had always done. Dusk had fallen, and as they turned into the street the lamplighter was at the far end, lighting the last gas lamp. Murdo shook his head when he was invited in.

'You're all tired after the dancing. I'll get back to the gatehouse.'

'Can we go up the braes tomorrow?' Rowena wanted to know.

'We could bring some food for a picnic,' Mary chimed in eagerly.

Murdo glanced at Caitlin, who nodded. 'It would be nice,' she said.

'I'll be here at ten o'clock, then.'

'We'll be ready.' Mary seized Rowena's hand. 'Come on, it's long past your bedtime.'

The two of them scurried through the pend, but Caitlin lingered to watch Murdo walk away. As he passed beneath one of the lamps, its light haloed his hair, now much shorter than before, as befitted an army man, and edged his square shoulders in soft warm gold against the darkness. The sight triggered off a memory; for a moment she couldn't think why, then she recalled the night she and Bryce had been kissing in the pend and she had almost fallen in through the door of the weaving shop when Murdo had opened it.

The moment was so far in the past that it seemed to belong to another life. That was the night, she remembered, that Alex had come to Paisley to ask Todd if he was willing to take over the new factory he had intended to set up in the old mill.

Murdo turned the corner without looking back and disappeared from her sight. Slowly, she walked through the pend, but instead of going into the house she stepped off the path and onto Rowena's dancing stone as the memories came flooding back. Since that night Rowena had come into their lives, and Ewan and Bryce had been obliterated from the world like stains wiped from a kitchen shelf, their lives ended cruelly and suddenly in a country far from home.

She and Rose had come to own a business, Rose and Alex had at last found each other, and Murdo, a stranger that evening, had become as much a part of her life as the yarns he wove together on his loom to make cloth. She did a few steps of the strathspey they had danced together, humming the music softly, then jumped as the back door opened and Mary put her head out.

'Are you coming in or not?'

'I was just having a look at the night sky,' Caitlin apologised, and hurried into the house.

28

The four of them spent the entire day on the braes behaving, as Mary said to Caitlin later, 'like daft bairns'.

'I think it was a good thing for all of us. I've never seen Rowena enjoy herself so much.'

'You're right,' Mary admitted. 'It was grand to be able to stop fretting about what folk might think and just make fools of ourselves.'

They played childish games, ran races and even took their socks, stockings and shoes off and paddled in a fast-flowing burn so cold that it numbed their feet and legs. Even Murdo joined in, and Caitlin felt that day that she had finally caught a glimpse of the carefree young man that Mhairi had once described to her.

As usual, she had brought her sketchbook and coloured crayons with her, and eventually she settled down with them, while the others crouched by a pool below a waterfall where Murdo was supposed to be teaching Rowena how to guddle for trout. After a while Rowena and Mary began to walk along the river while Murdo came back to where Caitlin sat, using his handkerchief to dry his hand and arm, which he had plunged into the water as he demonstrated how to tickle a basking trout before deftly whipping it from a pool and onto dry land.

'Did you catch any?'

'There were none to catch, but at least Rowena knows now what to do if she ever does finds a trout.' He settled a few feet away, elbows on knees.

'I noticed last night that she had returned your mouth organ.'

'Aye. She'd already written to confess.'

'It was wrong of her to take it.'

'Mebbe, but it's understandable. The lassie had nothing to remind her of her father, other than that photograph your mother gave to her and then the letter he wrote just before his death. I should have thought to leave something of mine with her. I'll give the mouth organ back to her before I go, to keep for me.'

'Then you'll have to do without it again.'

'To tell the truth, I have another that I got when I thought that one lost. But I'll say nothing of that to Rowena.'

Caitlin suddenly remembered the portrait he had entrusted to her care. 'If I'd know you were coming back, I'd have set your family's photograph in the gatehouse.'

'No matter. I carry its image with me wherever I go,' he said shortly, then lapsed into a brooding silence. Reluctant to break into his thoughts, Caitlin went on trying to capture the different shades of the bushes and grass and wild flowers, occasionally slipping a sidelong glance at his profile. After all these months she was scarcely able to believe that he was really there, sitting close to her. But only for a short while, for tomorrow he would be gone. There was so much she wanted to ask and to say, but the day had been perfect and she didn't want to do anything to spoil it.

It was Murdo himself who finally broke the silence. 'It's knowing that places like this exist that's kept me in my right mind over the past year.'

'It's been bad, then.'

'Aye. You couldn't know unless you saw it with your own eyes what metal can do to a human being. And anyway, I'd not want you or anyone else to see what—' He bit off the final word sharply, as though slamming a door against his own thoughts, then said after pause, 'I'll tell you one thing, though, spending day after day in the presence of death makes a man realise that life's meant to be lived looking forward, not back. Even when it seems that there's not much ahead.'

'The war must end one day.'

'God willing.'

She was unable to hold her tongue any longer. 'Will you come back to Paisley when it does?'

'Where else would I go?'

'You didn't go home to the Black Isle when you last left the army.'

He shot a glance at her across his shoulder. 'I see old Mhairi's tongue's been clacking again.'

'She spoke as your friend.'

'Aye, I know she did. I didn't go back because there was nothing left for me there. In Paisley there's unfinished cloth waiting on the loom, and there's Rowena.'

Caitlin's heart had begun to rattle about beneath her ribs as though it had broken loose. She drew a deep breath to calm it, and set her sketchbook aside. 'Rowena's not the only one who wants to see you come back, Murdo, . . .' she began, then all at once Rowena herself came running up the hill, Mary behind her, calling to them to come and see a little waterfall they had found, and the moment was lost.

*   *   *

After her success in getting clients to settle their bills, Mary had taken over total responsibility for Harlequin's invoices and collections in her spare time. When she suggested that those women who objected to settling their bills within a reasonable time should be given to understand, politely but firmly, that they could no longer expect to continue as clients, Rose applauded the idea, but Caitlin was horrified.

'They'll complain to their friends and we'll lose everyone, and then where will we be?'

'Folk value a service more if they think it might be taken away from them,' Mary said implacably. 'Anyway, they'll be too embarrassed to tell anyone.'

'Mary has the right idea, Caitlin. I know these women, and most of them are terrible snobs. They'd clamour to buy a duster if they thought that there was some privilege in owning it.'

'I don't want to take the risk of losing clients.'

'Caitlin,' Rose said firmly, 'you're a better designer than you realise. Why else d'you think we've done so well for clients? They like wearing your clothes, and they'll not want to lose you. Apart from any other consideration, we're the only fashion house in Paisley. It would be different if we were in Glasgow, where the clients would have a wider choice.'

As it turned out, she was right; the understanding that if they were lax in settling their accounts they would be required to find someone else to design their clothes made most of the clients eager to settle their accounts, and Harlequin continued to thrive, so much so that a few months later Rose suggested to Caitlin that Mary should be invited to become Harlequin's bookkeeper.

'Thanks to her efficiency we're making enough to support another wage, and it means that there'll be someone else here to meet clients if we're both busy. Mary's good at dealing with people, and she can go on doing the shop accounts, since the businesses are connected anyway.'

It was agreed, and by Easter, Mary, to her delight, was well settled in the small office, while Rose moved her desk into the design office.

By the autumn of 1918 the Allies had begun to make notable advances, forcing the German troops back step by step. The enemy was being defeated at last, but by that time another enemy was on the loose in the form of a virulent influenza epidemic that swept through the Western front, killing hundreds of troops on both sides, then stepping effortlessly across the Channel to invade Britain. The Espedair Street household was fortunate, for it passed them by, but it claimed a number of Paisley folk, including old Mr Laidlaw in his flat above the tobacconist's shop and Mhairi, the kindly Highland woman Caitlin had come to regard as one of her dearest friends. Caitlin found it hard to find the right words to tell Murdo of the woman's death.

Shortly after she wrote to him with the news, the influenza claimed another victim; having come unscathed through the entire war including the Battle of Jutland, George Chalmers, Fiona's husband, fell ill on the ship bringing him home and died in an English hospital.

In November church bells pealed, firecrackers were let off and the people of Paisley and every other town, city and village in the country flocked onto the streets to celebrate the end of a long and bitter war, the war to end all wars.

'No more having to order yards of black to make

mourning clothes!' Rose exulted as she and Mary and Caitlin struggled through the crowds to reach the Cross. 'Just you wait and see – we're going to be rushed off our feet making clients look stylish now that their menfolk are coming back home! But first,' she stopped and caught Caitlin by both hands, swinging her round so that they were face to face, 'comes my wedding dress, for after all the waiting I've done I'm determined to marry that brother of yours as soon as he sets foot in Scotland!'

Her predictions were correct. Within two weeks they were inundated with orders, and Rose had to bring in another sewing machine and appoint another seamstress to operate it.

Alex came home in January, and he and Rose set the date for their wedding for February. Mrs Hamilton would have much preferred to have had the time to organise a big wedding, but Rose refused to wait.

'Now she's in a terrible pet about the whole thing because she says that all her friends will think we're having to hurry the marriage along in order to make room for a christening,' she told Caitlin and Grace as they worked on her gown, adding, 'I hadn't realised how boring fittings were. How can women go through this for pleasure?'

'For some of them, it's their main pleasure. We won't be much longer,' said Caitlin. With Rose's approval, she had designed an ivory satin gown in the tunic style that suited her friend so well, overlaid with Chantilly lace falling in folds from the plain square neckline to end in handkerchief points just above the ankles. A broad satin sash encircled Rose's hips, and the lace veil, also falling to points, was to be held in place by a tiara of orange blossom.

'Mind you, if Mama had got her way and we'd to

wait for several months, there may well have been a christening to follow.'

'Rose!'

'Don't be such a prude, Caitlin. Alex and I have known each other for years and yet we've scarcely had half a dozen hours together since we became engaged. Is it any wonder that I, for one, feel completely frustrated?'

'It's only human nature,' Grace agreed placidly. 'Separation does that to folk.'

'Mama should just be grateful that Alex is willing to take me off her hands at all now that I'm over thirty. I'm sure my papa is. This war's going to result in hundreds of elderly marriages. You'll have to hurry up, Caitlin, if you don't want to find yourself on the shelf.'

Caitlin rearranged the lacy folds then stepped back to study the effect. 'I'm happy enough as I am.'

'No you're not. You're longing for Murdo Guthrie to come back.'

'Rose!'

'No point in denying it, my dear. Is it, Grace?'

'Not to us,' agreed Grace, who was kneeling behind Rose and pinning up her hem. 'But don't let us fret you, hen, we've neither of us said a word to anyone else.'

'Not even to Alex, though it's been hard to keep my mouth shut. My skin's beginning to itch – can't we stop for today?' Rose appealed.

When the fitting was over and she was getting dressed again, Rose waited until Grace had left the room before saying, 'There's another reason why I want to marry Alex as soon as possible. Oh, this dratted skirt!' She peered over her shoulder, trying to match the fastenings. 'Now that she's widowed, Fiona has decided to stay on in Glasgow with her father.'

'Turn round.' Caitlin slotted hooks into eyes with precision. 'What does that mean for Alex?'

'That's just what he's wondering. At the moment she's in mourning, but she's been getting more and more involved in her father's business during Alex's absence, and he has a suspicion that she intends to continue along that path.'

'But Mr MacDowall took Alex in as his heir. He'd not turn his back on his own son after all Alex has done for the business.'

'Of course not, but when he first approached Alex, Angus MacDowall's intention was to leave the house to Fiona and the business to Alex, with the money divided between them. In those days Fiona had no interest in the business and he wanted it to go to someone of his own flesh and blood who would continue to run it after he was gone. In any case, Fiona married soon afterwards and settled in Fort William. If it hadn't been for the war she might have stayed there and things would have remained as they were. But Fiona's changed a great deal since then, and there's no knowing what way the wind will blow. As I see it, the sooner I'm Alex's wife and able to support him in whatever he may have to face, the better.'

She smoothed her hair before the mirror then turned to smile at Caitlin. 'It's a good thing that Mary's with Harlequin now,' she said. 'It means that if need be I can spend more time in Glasgow.'

The light of battle gleamed in her eyes, and Caitlin saw a familiar bounce in her step as she left the room. There was nothing Rose relished more than a challenge, and clearly she sensed one in the air. At least, Caitlin thought, watching her friend's straight back as she left the room, Rose and Alex were on the same side this time.

* * *

Despite what Mrs Hamilton referred to disapprovingly as the speed of her daughter's nuptials, the church was almost filled with well-wishers when Rose and Alex married. John Brodie was best man, while Caitlin and the daughter of one of Mrs Hamilton's closest friends were the bride's attendants in dresses of dark-blue lace over ivory satin, with flowers in their hair.

The weather was cold and the sky grey and lowering, but when Rose stepped from the car that had brought her to the church she was so radiant in her happiness that she seemed to light up the day. She could scarcely contain her impatience as she waited in the porch for Caitlin to arrange her veil and for her father to smooth his hair and straighten his jacket. When the organist, after a dramatic pause, broke into 'Here Comes the Bride', she seized her father's arm and almost whisked him up the aisle, though at least she remembered to match her step to his instead of striding out. In the grey stone church, Alex's red hair glowed like a beacon, drawing his bride straight to him. Following Rose along the aisle, Caitlin kept her gaze fixed on her half-brother and was rewarded by the expression in his eyes when he turned and saw Rose approaching in her wedding finery. When she reached him he took both her hands in his and gave her such an adoring look that his mother and his future mother-in-law, in the front pews, both started weeping.

'Possibly for different reasons,' Alex told Caitlin at the reception in the Hamilton's house. 'Mam was always soft-hearted, but I have a suspicion that Rose's mama might have been sobbing because it was me standing beside her daughter and not John.'

'I don't think it'll be long before she starts singing your praises.'

'I don't care whether she does or not.' Alex, restless

when he and Rose were apart, turned to search the crowded drawing room for a glimpse of her. 'All I care about is making sure that Rose never regrets her choice.'

Kirsty had dreaded having to attend the reception in the very house where she had once worked as a sewing woman, but once the elaborate meal laid out in the huge dining room was over she began to feel more comfortable. Mr Hamilton had gone out of his way to make Todd and herself welcome, and his wife, while a little stiff, had been courteous. Now that Alex and Rose were safely wed, and clearly delighted to be so, Kirsty's nerves began to subside. She even slipped out of the drawing room when everyone was occupied and went along to have a look at the small room, little more than a cupboard, where she had once worked and where she and Rose had first met.

It hadn't changed at all, nor did it hold any memories for her, happy or sad. It was simply a room that belonged in the past. Recrossing the hall, she sat down on a straight-backed chair for a moment, unwilling to face the crowd in the drawing room. Her new, stylish shoes were cutting into her ankles, and she tried to ease them away with one finger, then jumped as Angus MacDowall said from above her bent head, 'Mrs . . . er . . . Kirsty, are you all right?'

Embarrassed, Kirsty wrenched her finger out of her shoe, which, tight though it had been, promptly popped off her foot and clattered onto the parquet flooring. 'I'm fine.' She looked up at him, her face burning with embarrassment.

'Allow me.' He went down on one knee and slipped the shoe back on as easily as picking up a dropped glove, then glanced up at her. 'Would you like a glass of sherry?'

'To tell the truth, I'd prefer a nice cup of tea.'

'Why not? Wait here.' He went unhurriedly into the dining room, while Kirsty, flustered, wondered how a woman should behave towards a stranger who also happened to be the father of her first-born. She cast an imploring glance at the drawing room door, hoping that Todd, Caitlin or Mary might come through it and save her, but it remained closed, and she felt that it would be rude to scurry back into the room and let Angus return to an empty chair.

'Here you are.' He was back, followed by a capped and aproned maid holding a small tray set with tea things and a glass of some pale amber liquid. Angus set a small table close by Kirsty's chair then positioned another chair for himself while the maid poured tea into the single cup.

'Will that suit, madam?'

It was far weaker than Kirsty liked, but she nodded.

'Have lemon instead of milk,' Angus advised, taking the glass from the tray and seating himself beside her. 'You'll find it refreshing.'

She didn't care for the idea at all, but she didn't like to argue. To her surprise, she found when she sipped at the cup that he was quite right. 'How's your daughter?' she asked tentatively when the maid had gone. A shadow passed over his face.

'Grieving, and there's so little I can do to help her.'

'There's not much anyone can do. You'll have to let her take her own time.'

'So I'm told. But at least Alex is happy. You've got a fine lad there, Kate.' He used the name that only he had called her when they were both in their teens, and when she allowed herself to look at him she saw that his expression held more than a hint of the orphaned boy she had once known and loved.

'We both have a fine lad there, Sandy.'

'The way things turned out, it's you that had all the worry of raising him.'

'Mebbe so, but you've not done so badly by him yourself.'

He leaned over and touched her cup lightly with his glass. 'To both of us, Kate, and to our boy and his new wife,' he said.

When he finally rose to return to the drawing room, he almost bumped into Mary in the doorway. She beamed at him, as she had beamed at everyone, friend and stranger, since receiving word the day before that Lachie was on his way back to Paisley.

'There you are, Mam.' She settled herself in the chair Angus MacDowall had vacated and reached over to the tray for a biscuit. 'What were you and Mr MacDowall talking about?'

Kirsty smiled at her daughter, thinking that the path that had started with Alex's conception had just completed its full circle.

'Just about old times,' she said.

29

It was April before Murdo Guthrie returned to Paisley.

On the day before he was due to arrive Caitlin, Kirsty and Mary gave the gatehouse's ground-floor rooms a thorough spring-cleaning and stocked the kitchen cupboard with food, then Kirsty, admitting freely that her nose was bothering her, insisted on a tour of the upper floor.

'I know I've seen through the place before, when Alex was thinking of buying the old mill and he wanted us to live here, but to tell the truth I was in such a state that day that I can't mind what the place was like.'

Caitlin, too, got a chance to have a proper look at the place, and was surprised by the size of the rooms which, despite their thick coating of dust, were elegant and airy.

'It's a shame that such a bonny place isn't being put to its proper use,' Kirsty said when they arrived back in the entrance hall. 'You'd have thought Rose and Alex would have wanted to bide here instead of renting that flat out along the Glasgow road.'

'The flat's handy for Alex's work in Glasgow and Rose's work here, and if they'd taken this place over we'd have had to find a new weaving shop and somewhere else for Murdo to live.' Caitlin opened the front door while Mary gathered up the bag containing their dusters and scrubbing brushes.

'I suppose you're right.' Kirsty cast a final glance round before following her daughters into the yard. 'But mebbe one day it'll become a home again. A bonny place like this deserves to be lived in properly.'

That evening Caitlin walked back to the gatehouse. She set paper and sticks in the kitchen grate, made certain that the coal scuttle was full, then took the framed portrait Murdo had entrusted to her care from her bag and sat on Murdo's fireside chair, studying the photograph as she had studied it so often in the two years it had been in her possession. His small son beamed back at her, while the child's mother still stared from the frame with anxious eyes.

Having heard from Mhairi how some Highlanders possessed second sight, Caitlin wondered if Elspeth had had it and if she had known, or guessed, that her happiness was not to last.

After a while she set the portrait on the dresser and went home.

Murdo's letter had simply said that he would be travelling by train from Glasgow and expected to arrive in Paisley before midday. Caitlin, suddenly anxious and apprehensive about seeing him again, would have gone to work as usual, but Rose would have none of it.

'The man's been away for two years. Surely someone should be there to welcome him back.'

'It doesn't have to be me. Perhaps Mam or Mary.'

'He didn't leave his most precious possession with Kirsty or your sister,' said Rose, who knew about the photograph and the letters in the exercise book. 'And he didn't write to them either. Of course you must go. You want to, don't you?'

'Yes . . . no . . . I don't know, Rose. He might not want me to be there, and anyway I won't know what to say to him.'

'"Welcome home" would be nice after what he's been through. You're going to Gilmour Street Station to meet him, and no arguments.'

'Would you come with me?'

Rose sighed, then said, 'If it's the only way to get you to go, I will – but it's not me he'll want to see, it's you.'

'You don't know that.'

'I think I do. Mary can be left in charge while we're away. I don't know how we managed before she came to Harlequin.'

Mary had certainly settled smoothly into her duties. Adult and sophisticated in discreet, smart outfits supplied by the fashion house, she had swiftly acquired the art of greeting each client with just the right mixture of respect and friendliness for that particular individual and of making sure that their every need was catered to. John Brodie, who was once again supervising the bookkeeping, was impressed by her efficiency, and she got on well with Grace and the other sewing women. For her part, she said that she was quite pleased to be free of the smell of jams and marmalades.

Rowena, determined to meet Murdo's train, refused point-blank to go to school that morning, so a welcoming party of three waited on the platform for him. He wasn't on the first train to arrive.

As the guard's van disappeared from view, Rowena surveyed the empty platform stretching out before them. 'You don't think he's changed his mind and gone to live somewhere else?' she asked anxiously.

'Of course not,' Rose told her briskly, while Caitlin

assured the little girl, 'He'll come on the next train,' though she herself was beginning to worry.

Rowena's well-shaped brows, so like her mother's, drew together above her neat little nose. 'Perhaps he's arrived at Canal Street Station and he thinks we don't care because we're not there to meet him.'

'He said he'd be coming in at Gilmour Street. We'd best wait here.'

They waited while the minutes ticked by and the platform began to fill again with people preparing to board the next train from Glasgow and travel on it to Ardrossan. It seemed to Caitlin that hours dragged by before the signals finally rattled then collapsed into a new position, though when she glanced at the platform clock she saw that less than thirty minutes had passed since the last train.

When the engine finally appeared from round a bend it seemed to take a long time to puff into the station and grind to a halt. Caitlin and Rowena, hand tightly clutching hand, studied the windows that flashed by.

'Did you see him? Did you see Murdo?'

Caitlin shook her head, and Rowena danced with impatience. There seemed to be a lot of folk disembarking at Paisley and a considerable number of travellers anxious to board. Rowena would have darted up the platform, but Caitlin kept a grip on her fingers, worried in case the child got tangled in the throng and swept onto the train by accident. They stayed where they were, jostled by people hurrying to the entrance and by late-comers running to catch the train. Doors had begun to slam shut along its length when Rose, taller than Caitlin and standing on tiptoe, her neck stretched to its full extent, said, 'There he is!'

'Where?' Rowena wrenched her hand from Caitlin's and scrambled up onto a nearby bench.

'Right up at the top. He's been in a carriage just behind the engine.'

'I see him! Murdo!' Rowena leaped from the bench, landing on her feet with a thud that must have sent a shock wave up through her entire body, and began to run, heedless of her aunt's call and narrowly avoiding a collision with a woman making her way down the platform.

Now that almost all the travellers had either boarded the train or gained the exit, Caitlin could see Murdo's tall figure at the far end of the platform. He was carrying a suitcase in one hand and a kitbag in the other, and as Rowena hurtled towards him he put them both down and opened his arms wide. Although she was now nine years of age, more than halfway to adulthood and almost up to Caitlin's shoulder, she launched herself from the platform when she was yards away and flew through the air into his embrace. As she landed he took an involuntary step back, then steadied himself and spun her round, her long black-stockinged legs flying out behind her.

'Her dad just back from the wars, is he?' The woman Rowena had almost bowled over reached Caitlin and Rose and paused, turning to look at the reunion.

'He isn't—' Caitlin began, then as Rose's elbow dug into her ribs she amended it to, 'Yes.'

'God bless the wee soul – and God bless you too, my dear.' The woman put a hand on her arm. 'It's grand to see a family reunited after all we've been through.'

'Isn't it?' Rose agreed warmly.

Murdo had put Rowena down; she caught his hand and tried to tug him towards the exit, but he resisted. The stretch of platform between himself and Caitlin made it difficult for her to make out his expression in detail, but she sensed that he was hesitating, just as uncertain and apprehensive as she was herself.

'Go on – go to him,' Rose urged. 'He's waiting for you to make the first move.'

'What if he isn't. What if he's wishing Rowena had come to meet him on her own?' Now that the moment had come Caitlin's throat muscles were so stiff that she could scarcely get the words out. Her heart thundered in her ears and she felt as though she was about to burst into tears, though whether of joy or fear she didn't know.

'For goodness' sake, d'you want the four of us to stand here for the rest of our lives?' Rose asked impatiently. 'Someone has to make the first move. The poor man needs to know how you feel about him. Show him!'

Caitlin took a tentative step forward, then another and another, until she was walking then running along the platform. Her skirt caught about her legs, and she knew that her hat was coming adrift and her hair loosening from its pins, but now that she had made her decision she no longer cared.

Murdo freed his hand from Rowena's and began to move forward, his hands reaching out to her. Close enough now to see the smile spreading over his face, she knew that everything was going to be all right for the two of them, today and tomorrow and for always.